THIS SIDE OF BONKERS

This Side of Bonkers

by

Laura J. Cutler

TURNSTONE PRESS

Turnstone Press
Artspace Building
607-100 Arthur Street
Winnipeg, MB
R3B 1H3 Canada
www.TurnstonePress.com

Turnstone Press gratefully acknowledges the assistance of The Canada Council for the Arts, the Manitoba Arts Council, the Government of Canada through the Book Publishing Industry Development Program and the Government of Manitoba through the Department of Culture, Heritage and Tourism, Arts Branch, for our publishing activities.

Cover design: Doowah Design
Interior design: Sharon Caseburg
Printed and bound in Canada by Friesens for Turnstone Press.

Library and Archives Canada Cataloguing in Publication

Cutler, Laura, 1966-
  This side of bonkers / Laura J. Cutler.

ISBN 0-88801-312-4

  I. Title.

PS8555.U8464T55 2005   C813'.6   C2005-904041-6

To all of us whose behaviour has been labelled crazy, when inside we know it's just a temporary reaction to life.

To Jamie, who lives with yours truly and has somehow managed not to go bonkers.

CONTENTS

THIS SIDE OF BONKERS

Waiting Up

I am lying in bed and Dread is stretched out on top of me. It presses down on my eyeballs, fills the valley of my belly, penetrates the gully between my thighs. If I turn this way or that, Dread is quick to redrape itself over me, to fill orifices and pin down limbs.

Take me now.

But that is not Dread's job.

It has been seven hours.

Finally, I gather the strength to reach for the lamp. I yank on the chain and the shock of harsh light diffuses Dread, alleviates it just enough for me to escape from under. I yank my clothes back on and dash frenetically around the murky rooms, straightening this, wiping the spotless surface of that, all so I can't be caught by Dread again.

Doesn't she know how out of my mind I go?

She knows. But does she care?

Once, in desperation, I telephone Mississauga, her father. I call his cell phone number, which he has repeatedly told me is for emergencies only. Calling him, period, is to be only in crisis.

I am in crisis. So's she, she just won't see it. And he, *the father*, goddamn should be as well.

There is a party going on in the background when he picks up.

"Saul. It's Judith. Melissa's gone. Again."

There is a pause, the music and merriment fade ever so slightly. He has moved around a corner. "Say again, Judith? Is it serious this time?"

"What do you mean, *this* time. Every time she walks out the door these days, it's serious. I always think it's the last time I'll see her."

I can picture him, his Tanqueray martini with a half spritz of vermouth in one hand, a du Maurier in the other, the slim phone tucked under his chin. Or did he say he quit? Smoking. He'll never give up drinking.

"Christ, Jude, she's seventeen. We've been through this. Let it go."

"You don't understand. The crowd, the attitude she bleeds out—"

". . . the piercings and the different boyfriends."

So, he was listening during my last call.

"Our daughter needs help, Saul. We all need help."

"So you've said. You've obviously called for my opinion—"

No, your support.

"—so it's my opinion she either needs a slap on the ass or for you to mellow out and stop treating her like a child. I suspect the latter's more in order."

Anger pounces on me, pulls the short greying tendrils of hair around my face, tweaks my nipples, makes sharp stabs up and down my back.

"Thanks for nothing, Saul."

I am at the pool, swimming laps. On bad days, every stroke threatens to draw me under and sometimes, that is my hope. Give me the peace, twenty-four hours—shit! one hour—that I can find by lying still on the bottom tiles, all air expelled to keep me down.

On good days, I am able to match my stroke to one of my many mantras. For the Australian crawl, it is: Let It Go (breathe); Let It Go (breathe).

For the breaststroke: It'll be (frog kick) O-K. It'll be (frog kick) o-k.

Melissa comes in early one night. I swear to be casual when I hear the click of the front lock.

"You're nice and early, honey." *A mistake? Am I starting something?*

"Yeah. Party was a drag."

Unsolicited information. A rare treasure.

"Bummer," I commiserate and see her smirk turn almost to a small grin, but say nothing. But something is wrong. I see it in her face when she sits on the opposite end of the couch and picks up the remote control. "Are you okay? Have you been crying?"

She jerks her head back and snarls. Says nothing. But I cannot leave well enough alone. That, apparently, is my problem. "Are you sure? You look upset."

"I'm fine, Mom. Can we just watch the show and not get into anything?"

Caution binds my words and my hands from trying to reach her.

Suddenly, Melissa mutes the TV and swivels her lanky frame around to face me. Her eyes are brimming with tears. "Mom, what's wrong with me?"

Thankfully, Caution is still embracing me. What does she mean? Physically? Emotionally? Behaviourally? Damn. Wait, Caution whispers softly. Just wait.

"Why can't I keep a boyfriend? All I want is a real boyfriend. What's wrong with me?"

Caution gives me a last squeeze and nudges me forward.

"Baby, nothing's wrong with you. You're smart and beautiful and funny. You just haven't met the right boy yet."

She groans and rolls her eyes. "Oh, I knew you'd say that." She stands in a huff, picks up her purse and disappears down the hallway. Shortly, I hear the sound of her bedroom telephone extension being picked up.

Caution shrugs and flounces off as well.

In the morning, there is a huge blowout about wasting my forty-dollar-a-jar wrinkle cream on her baby-perfect skin. (I tell Caution to take a hike upon this discovery.)

My girlfriend Jayne, a United Church minister, says Mel needs to find her personal concept of spirituality.

"I'd settle for a sense of common sense and courtesy," I concede.

She nods. She knows what I mean. "You too, chickie. You seem to be suffering in that department."

"Can't make church when I've been up half the night waiting for her to come home." To break the maudlin atmosphere that's threatening to ruin our lunch, I add, for levity, "Your sermons are good, babe, but I'd need a good fire and brimstone Baptist service to keep me focused these days."

"Kiss my grits," she replies and steals my last teriyaki prawn.

At the pool one day, a particularly bad day because I have just been informed by the grade eleven counselor that Melissa has not been in school for two weeks, I surface from shimmying along its tiled bottom and cling, gasping, to the water gutter.

Two large and masculine feet step in front of my eyes. Then I'm treated to a yellow Speedo'd crotch view when the legs to which the feet are attached drop into a squat. I tilt my head back. A relatively handsome man is smiling down at me.

"I see you here a lot," he opens. "You've a great stroke. It pays off by giving you a hey of a bod."

I do not have a great stroke. I have a stroke that gets me from the shallow end to the deep end and back again a few dozen times. I suck in the bod compliment, true or not. I wonder if there's snot streaming out my nose, and wipe self-consciously with the back of my hand.

"I'm Ray," he says pleasantly. "Would you like to go for coffee sometime? A drink maybe?"

"Thanks, Ray, I'm flattered, but alas no. I'd be too distracted with thoughts about my daughter's spiral into hell to be good company, but how do you feel about lesbian United Church reverends?" I push off and make it a record fifty-three laps.

"The matter of the school taking two bloody weeks to notify me of your truancy is a whole other ball game, which I will take up with Principal Peters. But your protracted absence, my God, Melissa, what are you thinking?"

"I'm failing everything anyway."

"Because you skip so much and are too busy socializing to do your homework," I accuse.

She scoffs. "No. Because I just hate it and I don't get it, any of it, and I could study all fucking night and not pass a test."

"Hey!" I warn. "Mouth."

She picks up her black nail polish from the counter and slides off the kitchen stool.

"We'll get you help, then. Get you tested first, for the right kind of help. You're not stupid, honey, you just don't apply yourself."

"Save your money. I'm not taking no test to get an answer I already know. One answer I know." She starts down the hall. "Besides, I have a job, so I'm dropping out anyway."

Les is a friend, a romantic companion for the odd dinner out, and a few times, he's been an adequate lover. We're at the Ramada lounge, close to my house.

"She's running you, Judy. Ground the bejesus out of her. Take away her privileges."

I suck out the pimento from my olive. Not Tanqueray, bar brand vodka. Les is buying and he's not really that well off. "I have grounded her, Les, 'til I'm blue in the face. She walks out the door without a word of where she's going and I end up being the one punished. We're the same weight, give or take, so I can't physically restrain her."

"Then you need to kick her out. Do the Tough Love thing from the '80s. Or whenever."

The tie Les wears every rendezvous is really hideous. An easy and cheap Christmas present for me to pick up, I note. "I can't, Les. What happens if I kick her out and she ends up on the street? What then? What if she gets into drugs? Hooking?" I am on my third martini and acknowledge the loudness of my voice, but don't care. "She could end up dead, and I'd carry that guilt. No, I'd kill myself."

He places a meaty hand on mine to quiet me. "You're killing yourself now—with worry." I snort. "You need a full-time man in your life, Judith," he tacks on hopefully.

"You're stoned out of your mind! What the hell is wrong with you? Who were you with?"

"I'm going to bed."

"Don't walk away from me. Melissa! Don't. Your eyeballs are the size of oranges. Tell me what you're on."

"Let go of me. You're hurting my arm. It's only a little pot."

"Only a little pot? Do you know what that can lead to? A little pot?"

"Yeah. Crystal meth, coke, heroine, theft, prostitution, criminal charges, halfway houses and death. Leave me alone. You don't understand."

At Jayne's fortieth birthday party in the church basement we sing, "For she's a jolly good Reverend."

Joyce Butterworth bustles over to me with her Dixie cup of unadulterated punch. "We're praying for you, Judith."

"Thank you." *I'll not ask why. I'll not go there.* "Why, why will you pray, Joyce?"

"Chuck and I heard you're having a tough time with Missy."

"A tough time, yes."

"We had a rough spell with Scott, when he was sixteen. He cut out church, sports, took to wearing black all the time. Two years. Have faith, Judith, this too, shall pass."

"Thanks for the kind words, Joyce. What's Scott up to these days?"

Please God, turn this Kool-Aid into wine.

"Fourth year, Simon Fraser U. Archeology, though that won't be the end of it. There's no actual jobs to be had with a single B. Arch degree."

I sip. Still far too fruity to be wine.

Joyce leans into me, a co-conspirator of sorts. "Dr. Aslin helped us immensely, Judith. He's in the book."

"I'm saying, either you go to school, or you pay rent."

"How much rent?" She is not wearing makeup, her hair is ponytailed and I want to put her under a glass cover to preserve this look forever.

I am ready for this. Jayne and Les have been consulted. "I think two hundred dollars a month is fair."

She breaks through the glass, comes out raging. "Two hundred? It's a minimum wage job, Mom. I only make, like five-something a month."

"That's the kind of job people with no high school diploma get," I advise smugly. "Besides, just try to live anywhere, anywhere, for less than six hundred, and that's without food."

"I'll think about it."

Therapist Number One says, "Hello, Melissa. Judith. Take any seat you want."

I sit across from the thousand-dollar aquarium. What plastic scuba diver, what gold-plated shipwreck, did my $150.00 buy?

"Melissa, I understand you're having some problems communicating with Mum. Can you tell me about them?"

"Screw this. This is fucked, cause you're only going to take her side anyway."

She is up, she is gone.

"Would you like to stay and chat, Judith? After all, there's fifty-six minutes remaining."

I have removed the batteries from the remote control. I know she will not think to check, or get up and use the manual buttons. Plus, I have unplugged the phones, so the distractions are minimal.

"Mel, we can't go on like this. You've got to play by the rules, the very liberal rules of my house, or you've . . ." Intimidation bulges out my eyeballs. "Or you've got to make other arrangements."

"You're kicking me out?"

"It's your choice."

"Fine. I'll go tonight."

Suddenly, Panic whooshes in. It pulls me up by the roots of my hair and spins me around like a circus act. Then it punches me, repeatedly, in the stomach and taunts, "Sucker, sucker. Now you've done it."

"Where will you go?" Panic asks.

"Wherever. Christine's, Doug's, Laticia's."

"Doug's?" Panic echoes. "Who's Doug?"

"No one you know. And just a friend, don't have a conniption."

"We can work this out. Why don't I go make dinner, we'll talk, make a game plan. Here's a pen. We can work this out, if we both want to."

"Nah. I'm gonna go grab some stuff. I'll go to Christine's and call you tomorrow. Satisfied?"

I swoosh Panic quickly away. *Not now, Panic.*

It'll be (imaginary frog kick) O-K.

She's made angel food cake. Better yet, she's home.

"Hi, Mom."

"Hi, Missy. It's really great to see you. I've been worried."

Her flawless brows knit, but she smooths them. "I'm sure. I'm really sorry. Really, really. Please Mommy, it's awful at Christine's, please let me come home."

Hope kisses the tip of my nose.

"Of course, the door has always been open. You'll follow the rules? Go back to school?"

Too much.

"You're gonna start with the rules and we haven't even been together for two seconds?

"Wait! Okay. I'm sorry. We'll talk about them later. The cake smells delicious. I bought whole wheat pasta for you, just in case. Let's whip up dinner together, have a girls' night."

"Well, that sounds great, the pasta, but I'm meeting friends at seven. I have to jump in the shower."

"Friends? You just got home after being gone two days? Stay. Talk to me." I hold up two fingers in a Guide salute. "Nothing heavy, I promise."

She groans, but oscillates. "Fine. I'll be on the phone, canceling. Call me for dinner?"

"Okay, honey."

The receptionist at the Y pool says, "Mrs. Dalgliesh, your card has expired."

"Really? You're sure? Well, just a minute. Let me get out my bank card. Just a moment." Extracting the plastic card from its little slot in my wallet proves impossible, my fingers feel as thick and unyielding as the neck of a wine bottle "Oh, dear."

"Mrs. Dalgliesh? Are you okay?"

"Of course. Just a moment now, I've got it." My purse splats onto the floor and I burst into tears. My face is wetter than while I swim. "Oh, dear. Oh, damn."

"Why don't you just go in, Mrs. Dalgliesh. We'll renew your membership next time."

"Okay. I'm very sorry to trouble you. My daughter, she . . ."

"I'm buzzing you in now, Mrs. Dalgliesh."

As I navigate my lane, I think about my grandmother's wedding ring, twenty-one dollars left by the door for the paperboy and the new blow-dryer. Gone. Vanished.

"Four days!" explodes Saul in my ear. "She's been gone four days, and you're just choosing to let me know now?"

"Ach, four hours, four days, I didn't know your cut-off point."

"You're drunk."

"And you're not?" I retort. Anger is tweaking and pinching, but Sarcasm wins out. It massages and licks my ears with false sensuality.

"How could you let this happen? Do I have to fly to Vancouver and straighten this out? I'm flying to Vancouver to straighten this out."

"Now, Saul, that'd be two times in one year and you wouldn't want that, would you?"

I hear him drag on his goddamn du Maurier. "Jesus H. Christ, Judith, she's only seventeen years old!"

Maliciousness has bumped out Sarcasm. Maliciousness bites me hard on the neck and deep throats my mouth. "Seventeen, yes. Wasn't that Lydia's age, your little chippie, give or take?"

"I can't talk to you like this. Call me when she shows up. On the cell."

"I thought you were coming to straighten things out?" Petulance tugs at my lower lip.

"Well, what good would that do? Am I to search Vancouver for her myself? Just call me the second she shows up."

Dr. Schwartz says, "Melissa. Judith. Take a seat anywhere you like. Melissa, your mom tells me you're acting up a little lately and have a drug problem to boot. Is this true?"

"I didn't say that exactly," I burst out.

"I'm outta here," Mel says.

Lisa Town, Master's in Social Work, says, "Now, Judith, aren't you just trying to overcompensate for not being able to keep your husband?"

"I want a refund," I demand.

Shar Crystal, Holistic Healer and Certified Reflexologist, says, "Judy, I peg you right away as metallic and Missy, you're pulpy, so no wonder this relationship isn't working."

"Oh, man," we both sigh.

"Talk to me, Melissa! Please, baby! Tell me what's going on in that head of yours. That heart. Please. You're here, you're not, you're in and out."

"You don't want me here anyway. You kicked me out."

"That was months ago. And I do want you here. I love you. I love you, Melissa."

"I love you, too."

"Then why are you doing this to our family?"

"Family? We're not a family. We're two people living together who fight all the time."

"Oh, baby, don't say that."

"Moth-er, pul-ease. Don't make me puke."

"Melissa!"

"Well, you're so phony."

"I have nothing but genuine love and concern and pride for you!"

"Really? Why did you tell Joyce what's-her-face I was 'coming along and would be back in school in no time'?"

I gulp. "It was none of her business. Besides, a mother can dream, can't she? What would you prefer, that I tell her what a selfish, angry, ungrateful little bitch you are!"

"Fuck you!"

The slap stings my hand more than her cheek. I tell myself. I hope. No, I want her to feel it to the core. I don't know what I want.

"Melissa, has something happened? Were you raped? Assaulted? Are you addicted to something? What has happened to turn you into this person I know you can't be happy with? What?"

"I'm just whacked, Mom. Lock me up, if you've had enough. Otherwise, just let me live my life."

"I have to stop asking why. 'Why' kills me. 'Why' makes me murderous and suicidal. I have to accept that I don't know why. I have to accept that I can only control myself."

Les is yanking on his trousers after an aborted attempt at a little physical comfort. Once again, I have driven us down a road he is tired of and the mood was squashed. I'm tired of it too, but it's my road.

Martyrdom pulls down my cheeks, droops my eyelids. With great effort, I peel it off.

"I'm so sorry, Les. You've been so good to put up with me. I know I've had a one-track mind. I apologize. For taking advantage of your patience and stability."

"No need to apologize." He stops to smooth his hair in the dresser mirror. "She's a great kid—well, she was, up to a couple of years ago, and you're a good mother. What you've taught her will kick back in soon."

"Mom, this is Judd."

Judd is forty years old and groping my daughter right in front of me. Okay, he's thirty. "Hello, Judd. How old are you?"

"Mom!"

"Twenty-seven."

"Twenty-seven," I echo. "And what do you do, Judd?"

"This and that. Computers, mostly."

Computers. The catch-all job of the twenty-first century.

"What are you kids up to tonight?"

"A movie, I guess. Whatever Mel wants."

Sex. Drugs. Whatever.

"Is that it, Mom?"

"Please phone if you'll be late."

"Well *duh*, I'll be late. I'll just stay at Judd's tonight, so you don't have to worry."

Not have to worry. Irony goes *boing!* Like an old wind-up toy.

"Don't you work tomorrow morning?" She shuffles her feet and looks over my shoulder. "I asked, 'Don't you work in the morning?'"

Finally, she says, "No. I quit, like, weeks ago. Can we talk about it later? We're gonna miss the start of the movie."

Jayne takes the last piece of bread and sops up some shimmering sauce from my escargot pod. I almost smile, thinking about living in a nice warm pod. "She's almost an adult."

"Pffft. She's a child in a woman's body."

"To you, perhaps she always will be."

I sip my wine. "What did I do wrong?"

"That's the three-hundredth time you've asked me. Nothing. You loved, you gave, you disciplined. Sometimes it's just chemistry."

Compassion jabs me in the ribs. "By the way, are you still seeing the woman from the bank? She was cute. Kind of."

"And you've asked me *that*, about fifty times."

"So, no?"

"No. Too butch."

"True. I thought she might help me manhandle Mel into one of those wilderness camps for wayward souls. Hey! That's my escargot."

Ever sagacious, Jayne says, "Girl, you've got to find your own wayward soul first, or you'll never find peace again."

So I do. Over the next weeks, I search for Soul. I've no idea where to look, so I race around the city, I race around my mind. I think I find it in yoga because Azima tips me out the door like a bowl of wobbly Jell-o. I think I find it within Anita's toasty massage room with its flickering scented candles and her exquisitely painful caresses.

I look for Soul, my soul, with Jason, who sports arms the size of my thighs and screams at me to pick up my pace, to do another set, to up my reps. I drift in and out of dozens of houses of worship and look for my missing bit in case it's hiding behind the pews, under the prayer mats, among the wooden school chairs in the makeshift New Age Center.

At some point of my quest, Soul quietly returns and settles back into me. It has grown while absent and fills me like never before.

"I'm moving in with Judd."

"Remember when we went to Disneyland? With your father. That was a nice time. I think you were six or seven."

"Mother, did you hear me? I said, 'I'm moving in with Judd.'"

"I heard. Frankly, I think it's for the best. I was going to suggest it."

"As if."

"I was. You're there all the time anyway. You're eighteen years old now, maybe we can build a new kind of relationship."

"Wow. I didn't think you'd be so cool about it."

"Melissa Jayne, I'm not cool about it. I am out of my mind frantic and worried and angry and resentful and terrified, just like I always have been. I'm your mother. It's what we feel. But, I am plumb out of ideas, and energy, to show you that I act out of love."

"Too much Oprah, Mom."

I will not play. I summon Grace and Dignity. They swirl around me gently. "I would like to see his apartment when you're ready to have me over. For my peace of mind, so I can visualize you there." Grace is diluted by the cold front Melissa projects, so I continue with Dignity alone. "Be sure to leave your key."

"My key? I have to give you my key? I'll still have stuff here. I'll need to get more of my stuff than I can take in one trip."

"Then call me to arrange a mutually convenient time. Like Jayne does, like Les. Like anyone else who doesn't live here does."

Grace and Dignity are both but wisps of dissipating mist.

"I can't believe you won't let your own daughter have a key."

"Yes, my own daughter. I love you, my own daughter. I always will."

At this moment, for this moment, pure, unconditional mother-love pours over me, fills me from the inside, flushes out everything else. It solidifies within me, and keeps me from crumbling.

TRUTH, COUNTER-TRUTH

Sometimes I look at my little sister and think, man, what I wouldn't give. I mean, she's got the Cape Cod house, husband and kid thing going and though I roll my eyes a lot at her domestic bliss, I don't always mean it. I had the common-law husband and kid thing too, but in a low-rent townhouse and it was never the same. Now "the system" has my girls and Jimmy's aunt has the baby, last I heard.

Don't get me wrong, Cindy, my sister, has her own problems, but her problems are self-induced. Like, she's still a hundred pounds soaking wet and still lives on microwaved popcorn and egg whites. Six egg whites, I think she said. Six times seventeen calories each.

My problems just fall in my lap and it's totally unfair.

Take Jimmy.

I have to back up a little—freakin' deacon, back up a lot considering I turned thirty-four last month—to just after high school. Yeah, past the Best Dressed Award and the Best Girl Butt Award. The Butt Award was by secret poll.

I did okay in school, thanks to a little studying and a little cheating and one romp with the chemistry teacher during

19

which he singed his sleeve on a Bunsen burner some dork had left on.

After high school, I don't know what happened. I couldn't decide what to do and my parents were the "get a job and pay rent, or go back to school" type. I tried cosmetology college for four months, okay two months, but I already knew all the crap they were teaching, so what was the point? I cashed in my tuition and went to Puerto Vallarta for two weeks. Hash and tequila city, two weeks. Beauty School, my ass.

I met Jimmy right after that. I was all tanned-up from Mexico, nice and bony, my hair sun-streaked. I was twenty, Jimmy was twenty-four and we moved in together after a few weeks. My mom had a conniption, but she came around because what else could she do?

Jimmy was super nice at the beginning and I thought I loved him. Even when he got mad, because I'd blown his share of the party money, or had my nails touched up with grocery money, he never hit me. I thought that was just pretty f'ing fantastic.

I looked good in those days. Real good, and tons of men besides Jimmy were after my ass, but I stayed pretty loyal. I finagled jobs here and there. The Roxy Love Shack was the funniest. You wouldn't believe the pervs that'd come in there, looking for rubber sheets and dolls, multi-pack dildos. Too funny. Sometimes my parents' friends would come in and be shocked to see me. You can be sure my mother stuck to her "grocery clerking" story about me. Anyway, then the middle-agers had to make up some story about borrowing the Yellow Pages, or needing a gag gift for a fiftieth birthday.

I landed the exotic dancing job after barging into a club in search of Jimmy. Me and Carla were looking to hit a classy place downtown because the trash gyrating around the fringe pubs were too much and Jimmy was holding the cash and credit cards.

So I walk into Peeler's, squinting into the black, prepared to score some cash and get out real quick, but something about the place kind of appealed to me, so I stretched out the visit. Like I said, I was dressed to kill. I remember leaning over Jimmy wearing my micro-mini skirt and then kind of starting this lap-dance thing. We were both trying to keep straight faces, given that we were already a couple. The men around Jimmy were enjoying the impromptu show.

After a couple of minutes, the manager came over and told me to get the hell down because that's why he hired the other chicks.

"Why don't you hire her then?" said Jimmy.

"Jimmy!"

"Seriously, Sherilyn, you're definitely as hot as them. Marty, look at her for Christ's sake."

Marty did look, looked hard, and at first I was freaked out, but then I thought, what the hell, it'd be better than running into my godparents at the Roxy Love Shack. I started doing a little undulating and twirling and ended up by swinging my leg up and resting my stiletto-clad foot on Marty's shoulder, right gracefully. Like a Rockette.

"How old are you?" growled Marty, but with a little gleam in his eyes and I knew I was in.

"Nineteen," I said quickly. Of age, but just. He'd like that.

Marty grunted and I don't know whether he believed me younger or older but he said, "Stay for the shows. Familiarize yourself. Come Saturday afternoon for amateur hour and we'll take it from there. And stay off them customers until I say," he warned and stomped away. I ditched Carla, who's way too dumpy and pimply to be an exotic dancer, and spent the night flitting around Peeler's like I owned the place.

For the next couple of weeks, Jimmy was like a proud dad— as far as I'd freakin' know what that was—meeting me after shows and swooshing away lecherous old farts. Swooshing away a couple of slick businessmen too who I thought it'd be good to talk to, but you can't have it all ways, I guess. The money was awesome, but it was a job that cost a lot too. Like, I had to get one of the other girls' mom to revamp a few of my existing outfits with Velcro, plus buy a tanning pass again and acrylic nails, so you know, it added up. Marty bought his girls a couple of rounds before their show, but if you wanted to stay and socialize after, it was your tip money.

"And," Marty was quick to point out, "if they end up socializing you, twenty per cent is mine."

I didn't just get off the lobster boat, and obviously I knew what he meant, but I wouldn't be going that direction. Give me a break, I thought.

That was a good scene for a couple of months. I laid low with my parents, but Saintly Sister Cindy noticed how flush with the bucks I was.

"You're getting that much from Avon?" she said, incredulous like. "I find that hard to believe."

I shuffled around the Avon catalogues I kept on the table for good measure.

"Yes. I'm a great seller. And I'm younger than the doddery old hags who usually sell."

"Sherilyn," Cindy said, scraping non-existent butter off her lettuce sandwich. "I think you're lying."

"Play the Truth Game, then, smartass."

The Truth Game. Tried and true. We used to play it as kids, when one of us wanted to know something. The deal was, you had to be prepared to answer any question back. Truth, then counter-truth.

She rolled her eyes. "That's kid stuff."

I pushed away my own sandwich, ham and cheese with shitloads of ketchup. She made me feel guilty for being hungry.

"Okay. Where are you really getting the money?"

"I am really getting the money exotic dancing." I smirked. I had to. Daring her to freak.

"Stripping? Where? Peeler's?"

"Peeler's." I felt like getting cocky and chatty now. "I make five hundred a week, cash, for, like, three hours a night." I saw her lips twitch in distaste, so I had to get my dig in. "If you weren't so damn skinny, if you had any tits left, you could go for it too."

She scrunched her face up and pushed the air sandwich away. "Yeah. Thanks but no thanks. Doug would really love that."

Doug's her husband. Married two weeks after high school grad, if you can believe it. Bully for her.

She stood up. "Well, I gotta go. I'm going to the gym."

"Whoa! You know the rules. I get my Truth question."

She tensed, like she might know what I would ask, which was nothing I didn't think everybody else hadn't, but she was bound by code to actually answer me.

"You making yourself puke?"

Her eyes flashed. "No! Gross!"

"Cin, it's the truth game. You making yourself puke?"

She shrugged. A yes, obviously.

"What's that like?"

"That's two questions. I have to go."

My little sister scooted out of me and Jimmy's apartment, leaving me with eight hours to kill 'til showtime. I went and stuck my fingers, then a toothbrush, down my throat, to puke the half a sandwich, but nothing happened. Fuck that. If I wanna lose a couple of pounds, I'll stick to a week of prescription speed, from the Good Doctor that helps out the dancers with everything from abortions to acne. Way easier, that.

Had to go on a dancing hiatus when I got pregnant *wham!* and *wham!* Two kids in two years. Jimmy ran around clucking and crowing like the scrawny, obnoxious rooster he is, but he was also pissed that I screwed up the dancing gig. Can't have it both ways, baby. I was pretty excited in most ways because I wasn't going to be at work all the time like my mom was and even though Jimmy had grabbed my wrist during a couple of fights and pulled my hair a few times, I knew he wasn't a child abuser. I downgraded to the odd toke and drinking Kahlua and milk, and my girls turned out fine, so I don't know what the big deal is. My mother swears she never touched a thing, during Cindy and me, and look how screwed we turned out, right?

The girls, Jasmine and Saffron—cool names, huh?—were fun to dress up and stuff, especially when I finally returned to dancing and could afford them matching pink dresses. But they were a shit-load more work than I had imagined. Jimmy did squat, looking-after-them-wise, and we fought a lot about that, but my mom and Cindy were good about taking them. And Carla. And Jimmy's little brother, Rich. Rich was seventeen then and looked like a young Lou Diamond Phillips. Sometimes, when I'd be showing him diaper stuff, or bottles, we'd brush against each other and the electricity was unreal. I'd think about his hard, lithe teen body, and compare it to Jimmy's. At twenty-eight, Jimmy was getting paunchy. Too much sitting around as a guard for a used-car lot.

I, of course, was looking hot again. I had to, a lot of freaking sixteen-year-olds were trying to get Marty to hire them, and I could tell he was really considering it. So I'd take Jas and Saffy to the tanning salon and they'd sit outside the booth because the UV rays wouldn't have been good for them and I'd yell at them to knock on the door and say hi every few minutes, so I'd know they were still there. At the nail place, they went into one of the empty massage rooms and looked at hair mags, or sometimes one of the cosmetologists would babysit. I only had to put them to bed on the couch in the dancers' lounge a dozen times or so. Once, only once, I smacked Saffy so hard it left a mark. Scared the shit out of myself. Little brat got into my baggie of weed and shook it all over the floor.

Whenever I couldn't stand any more phone message from my mother, I went for Sunday dinner at my parents. They only lived five kilometres away in a '70s-style bungalow, but it may as well have been five hundred.

"Sherilyn, the children seemed all hyped up when you came in. Have they had a lot of sugar today?"

"Hyped up? Ma, they're barely two and three. They're hyped on life. Relax."

"Well, they were climbing all over your father and he doesn't like that."

"Really? He used to pay me and Cindy to climb all over him. A buck. I remember."

"What?"

"Nothing. I'll go check on them."

I went into the den and Jas and Saffy were glued to the TV, to the *Little Mermaid* video I'd brought especially. My father was hunkered down in the same chocolate brown recliner he'd had forever. Jimmy was stretched out on one end of the couch and Doug, Mr. Stability, was on the other, but perched like a dripping teabag on the rim of a cup. Slouchy, but precarious.

"Hey. Everything okay here?"

Grunts all around.

Then Jimmy said to my sister who was tucked in beside Doug —I guess he said it for my benefit—"So, Cindy. When're you going to start popping them out?"

Apparently he hadn't noticed Egg White Queen, Stick-Insect Woman, Period-Free Princess for the past few years.

Cindy looked at Doug and he elbowed Jimmy's feet. "None of your friggin' business. The world's got enough unwanted kids as it is."

"Like what's that supposed to mean?" I interjected. I knew. People always know when they ask that question. Everyone knows it's just a dare to the person to repeat their opinion.

"Come on, Sherilyn, you're telling me you think you made a contribution to the world by having kids? That getting pregnant made you happy? It fulfilled you as a woman and person and all that Oprah shit? You'd rather be out turning tricks than baking cookies, so why the hell d'you have them?"

I punched Doug out before Jimmy even registered what my sanctimonious, shithead brother-in-law had said.

The girls started crying when they saw Doug's bloody nose. Cindy, her eyes full of tears too, scooped them up and hustled them upstairs. Great. They'd gone from hyped to hysterical. My dad started hollering at everybody and Jimmy told him to shut the F up, so we got told to leave. Nice, eh? Did I start it? See what I mean about unfair crap dropping in my lap?

It took Cindy three weeks to clean up the mess her stupid husband made. Since I sure as shit wasn't going to apologize to anybody, she eventually got Doug to grovel sufficiently to Jimmy, so the two of them could unite against my father. Between them, they convinced him I was only dancing, not hooking, though in his eyes, the margin was slight. My mother hovered on the fringe of the various kiss-and-make-up sessions, baking her damn head off. Doug never did apologize to me directly.

"Truth," Cindy said, about a month later while we waited together in a prissy lilac room at my salon. I'd bought her acrylic nails for her birthday because I was sick of looking at her serrated stumps. Our nail technician, Juan, had stepped out to do a colour consult with somebody.

"Hmm."

"Are you, you know, doing it with men, for money?"

I looked over at her and laughed. "You'd waste a truth question on that? You're nuts. The answer, really, is no. I make plenty of money dancing."

She nodded glumly, started caressing her jutting collarbone with the hand Juan hadn't started. I knew what I wanted to ask. I'd wanted to ask it for a long time. If Cindy agreed with me, it would explain a whole lot.

"Counter-truth. Did Dad ever molest you?"

She gasped, arched and strained in her chair. "Sherilyn Michelle! Jesus! How could you ask that? No, not how. *Why* would you ever ask that? That's disgusting." Her eyes were huge sockets of flashing green in her peaked face. "You're not suggesting ..."

I held up my hands, already completed with long, burgundy tips. "Hey, relax. I was just asking. You're anorexic, I'm not exactly Miss America, don't we fit the books?" For some reason, I couldn't look at her. "Sometimes, I think I remember stuff."

"What stuff?" my horrified little waif of a sister eeked out.

"Touching, fondling." I paused, trying to remember. Really. "Intercourse."

Cindy just, like, folded into herself.

"What else would explain how we are? Are you sure you don't remember? We'd be in it together." Cindy was quaking and went from her usual pasty white to a florid pink, but I pressed on. "You suit yourself. Live in denial if you want. You've got about five more pounds of denial before you keel over, but I know shit happened." I clicked my nails together to check their dryness. Still tacky. "I'm thinking of getting hypnotized, to really see what's what."

"Don't, Sheri. Please don't. You're just imagining stuff, from books and TV. And you're still mad at Daddy and Doug for that Sunday dinner thing. Don't make stuff up. Please, Sheri." Always the do-gooder, she suggested in her whispery voice, "You could come with me to Dr. Lowe. She's really nice. She really listens and gives me good ideas to, you know, be myself and stuff. You could come."

I groaned dramatically. "Thanks, but I'll pass. Your shit is your shit. I don't need a shrink, just the truth. I'm okay, except Jimmy is pissing me off and I need to figure out what I'll do after dancing."

We sat in silence until Juan returned. Cindy dithered and twitched and basically burned off more calories than she consumed that whole week while I wondered if Carla still had her coke contact.

Life started going really downhill when I started sleeping with Rich, Jimmy's brother.

The bastard Jimmy hadn't been home for three days, for starters. I was going off of my rocker, handling the kids alone. Carla was doing a few months in detox, the bitch, and Cindy and Mom had some pact going about teaching me about responsibility and refused to babysit anymore. I traded a blow job with Rich for four hours of peace from the monkeys. No real big deal. I mean, the kid was nineteen and had no staying power. I used my free time to go to the hypnotist.

It was different than I thought it would be. There was no dangling pendant, only music and her voice talking me down, talking about golden fields and stuff. Then, being under wasn't what I thought either. I could hear myself answer her questions, could scratch my nose if I wanted, but I did feel really relaxed. I remember thinking, well, this sucks. I wanted to get woken up and have her just tell me everything I'd said, you know?

She asked about early memories and I'm kind of panicking, thinking, what am I going to say? I'm in here to confirm sexual abuse from Dad and I thought that would just kind of float up. I told her about the beatings, which weren't really all that bad, or often, but I couldn't explain about the molesting.

"Sherilyn," she said softly, "I sense a panic, and that's not conducive to recall. I'm going to stop asking questions, and relax you again. Remember, you don't have to work through everything, even anything at all, today."

And still, I couldn't get out what I wanted to.

I paid her the sixty bucks and left. If all else failed, I could just tell Carla's story, because I figure it's not the details that matter, it's the act.

Jimmy finally showed up back home and said he'd lost his job. Rich offered to move in with us as a boarder, so we'd have extra money. "After all," he said, "What's family for?" He said that with a really goony look on his face that I wanted to slap off. Jimmy was still too drunk to notice.

Since Jimmy had no job, you'd think he'd be home all the time to do the father and the husband thing. He wasn't. He was out drowning his sorrows somewhere and that place wasn't even Peelers. On the other hand, Rich was home. Rich was home all the time and more than willing to fill both positions. Finally, Jimmy called from Toronto and said he'd found a job and had no intentions of sending money since I was making so freakin' much.

I screamed until he hung up on me and I *69'd him and screamed until he hung up again and took the phone off the hook. Bastard.

Rich was mad that I was mad. He said he'd take care of us, and that I should forget about Jimmy. You're just a kid, I said, and he lost it completely. But Rich didn't hit like his big bro, or even pull hair. He dragged me upstairs and pounded the shit out of me. Pounded the shit into me, if you know what I mean.

Then he took me again, the regular way, which was just as bad because I didn't have any foam and I haven't been on the pill since high school because taking it puts ten pounds on me and I couldn't afford being a pudge with my career and all.

The day I looked in the mirror and decided I couldn't dance anymore, I went into Peeler's early to tell Marty, but he told me.

"After this one, Sherilyn, get your tubes tied or something, for God's sake.

"I'm only twenty-seven, Marty. Anything could happen. They're not knotting me up. I'll just have to be more careful. I'll be dancing again in seven months, tops."

He was behind the bar, polishing beer glasses. He reached across and took my hands. "Well, Sherilyn, it's only fair to tell you now, that I won't be taking you back after this one."

"What?" I yanked my hands away. "What the hell are you telling me Marty? I'm fired? People come in, just to see me, Marty. Me. You don't want to fire me. Is this because I told you I'm twenty-seven, because if it is . . ."

"In part it's because you're twenty-seven. Part because you've lost your edge. Mostly it's because, Christ, Sherilyn, you're a mother. Act like one. Go get a good man and bake cookies for your kids."

"Fuck you!" I yelled and smashed one of his precious shiny beer steins on the floor. "Fuck you, Marty."

"You can cocktail waitress here for another month," he offered, shaking his head sadly. "To give yourself time to think about things. But no dancing."

I walked out, fuming and cursing him so I wouldn't feel the panic and fear. I walked twenty-three blocks to another strip club and took a job topless waitressing. The clientele there was super scuzzy, bad tippers and lickety-split, I was sleeping with patrons for fifty bucks a pop until I was six months gone and grossed everybody out myself included.

I kicked Rich out when he held a knife to my swollen belly, to our baby, offering an early C-section.

It was humiliating to go to my parents and ask for money. Freakin' humiliating. My dad said no right away, without even listening to my plan to pay him back.

"Well, I guess I'll just have to sue you," I threatened, sounding way bolder than I felt.

"What the hell for? I should be suing you for having to put up with all your shenanigans over the years."

"You know."

"What the hell are you on about?"

"You know."

He shook his head and looked at me, real disgusted.

"Sherilyn," said my mother from her peripheral position at the kitchen sink, "don't talk so foolish. You can't sue your father. Take some cookies for the girls and call Auntie Sue like I suggested before and see if she'll take you on at the dry cleaners."

I ignored her. Dry cleaners? For seven bucks an hour? As if.

I stood right in Dad's face. My heart was pounding. The baby was kicking and elbowing.

"I'll sue you for the abuse."

"What the hell . . . ? What goddamn abuse?" His face didn't go red, or white, like I wanted him to. In fact, he looked, like, totally and honestly confused. This threw me off.

Fuck.

"The molesting," I spluttered.

His jaw dropped. My mother dropped the container of cookies.

"You get out of this house, this instant, Sherilyn. And don't ever come back. You're a lying, sneaking, loser-daughter, and I won't stand for it no more."

"Admit it, Dad. Be a man. Admit you screwed me when I was a kid. I remember and I'll say it in court."

"Get out of my house!"

"Admit it! What kind of parent would hurt his own kid like that? Huh? Huh?" I was into it now. I could feel all the details, hear the sounds. What was I? Five? No. Four. I'd have to thank Carla, if she ever talked to me again.

He raised his arm and curled his hand into a fist. I braced myself. It'd be nothing I hadn't taken before. But he didn't do it. Surprise, surprise. He stared at me for like, ten long seconds, then slowly lowered his arm.

"You know you're lying. Your mother knows you're lying. Just get out and don't come back."

Mom slipped me a cheque for five hundred bucks as I yanked on my boots in her pristine little mud room, feeling totally numbed out. The next week, I went on single-mother welfare.

When the baby came, a boy, he looked real weird from the start. Pushed in face and googly eyes. Down's syndrome, the doctor said. I remember I'd blown off the appointment for the test. Not possible to tell the full extent yet, the doctor said.

I couldn't even name him. What was I going to go with? Richie Jr.? Little Jimmy? George, after my father? I told the nurses I hadn't decided, but they kept pestering me. Cindy came in one day with some blue snugglies she'd made herself and offered to keep the girls a few extra days, since this disease-thing with the baby was so unexpected. But I didn't want her pity and I told her to drop them off the next day, like was planned. She didn't press me. I would have given in, for sure, if she had.

I wish she had, then things would have turned out differently.

Back home, the girls took to the baby real well, but they were too young to help with anything and their cooing over him drove me nuts after a while.

"Jasmine, put him down. Jesus, he doesn't need you touching him all the time. No wonder he screams all the time, seeing you come at him covered in Popsicle."

"He stops crying when I take him," she said defiantly, her four-year-old chin jutting out.

"Whatever," I said, lying down on the couch, so tired. So incredibly tired. My twat was throbbing and my gut was like a water balloon. "Pass me the medicine box, Saffy. I need some medicine."

She handed me the old jewelry box I kept my stash in. It was almost empty. I took two uppers to give me some energy, but they did nothing. I took a couple more and still nothing.

I remember the baby crying.

I remember *The Simpsons* was on TV.

I remember the baby crying and swallowing a couple of Richie's leftovers.

I don't remember nothing else.

From my file, I was told the neighbour called the cops. The commotion and all. They busted in when I was shaking the shit out of the baby.

I want to remember, but I can't.

Five years. I got five years. And I lost my girls. Crap, I don't know if I even want them back. I'm not cut out for it.

Chateau de Burnaby, as we call it, isn't so bad. It's minimum security and a lot of goodies get in, if you suck up to the right people. Cindy came a couple of times. The last time, she was pregnant eight months but only looking like she just swallowed a grapefruit whole. Her cookies are just cookies, but we like them anyway.

"Truth?" asked Cindy, about six months ago. Her latest or last visit, I don't know.

I didn't answer. Stupid game.

"The Dad-thing," she pressed. "You know. Did it really happen to you?"

I didn't answer, didn't even shrug. Stupid freakin' game. Nothing from my parents. Like, no shit, eh?

At least I don't have any problems anymore, like Jimmy's lazy ass, or the girls screaming for stuff. I still say life's unfair to people like me, but at least I don't really have any big problems right now. You know, biggie problems.

THE IMPLOSION

I moved a lot of mountains to create my cocoon. I thought. I
quit my job as a Welfare Act policy writer for the provincial
government. I prostrated myself for a cabin: friends' of
friends' of friends'. I kissed good-bye, literally and figura-
tively, a husband of twelve years. Okay, technically, he'd
been gone for a month already, but it sealed things, to
announce that I was leaving the city for an indeterminate
length of time.

And yet, I am sitting now on an ancient sun chair, the kind
with the scratchy interwoven plastic strips, drinking Hochtaler
wine from a metallic blue tumbler and thinking about the falli-
bility of life, cocoons or not.

Carl, my wannabe, encicingly endowed lover—so he says—
called at one-thirty to firm up plans to visit me. In my cocoon. I
hemmed and hawed. I didn't want my papery cover pierced; I
didn't know how to ask that it not be. I said things like, "I might
not stay for the weekend, after all." I said, "I might relocate to
Tofino. I'm not happy with the cabin." This latter excuse is an
utter lie. The cabin is stocked and cozy. It has exactly the right
number of conveniences, without being anything remotely like

modern. Or convenient. I need basics in my life at this juncture: water, wine, maudlin silence.

After I manipulated a fresh twenty-four hours of solitude—until he calls and begins his assault campaign again tomorrow—he gasped and said, "Good God, I must tell you. Have you had the news on?"

"No. There's a bulky old ghetto blaster on top of the fridge, but, no." I felt my face scrunching up—at the thought of intrusive radio waves or too much September sun, I didn't know which.

"Prepare yourself," he cautioned. I was sitting on the front stoop of the cabin, watching dogfish leap and belly flop in the strait. In fifteen minutes, the afternoon sun would kiss my sandaled toes, wrinkly knees, belly, pale nipples, shoulders, my lugubrious face. If I hadn't moved an inch, this is what nature would have bestowed on me, natural golden kisses.

"The US has been attacked by terrorists," he continued gravely. "Big time. The World Trade Center towers, in New York. Hijacked planes flew into them."

"You're kidding," I responded automatically, my grasp of what he was saying having seriously prodded, but not yet burst my cocoon.

"It's huge," he assured. "And the Pentagon, same idea. A fourth plane seems to have been deliberately crashed in Philadelphia. Pittsburgh. Pennsylvania. A 'p' place. You need to turn on the news. Do you have a TV there?"

"No," I answered honestly. "A radio."

"You need to tune in. It's a global catastrophe."

"Who, who is responsible?" I pressed, though I really wished he hadn't told me anything at all. My silky balloon lay around me in deflated folds.

"They don't know yet. Terrorists. They're just calling them The Terrorists." He continued on—he has an acute mind for numbers, distances, velocities and the like—and was rattling off flight numbers, capacities and altitudes like another man might hockey stats.

When we hung up, I cheated, and leaned to the right so the afternoon sun licked my face much earlier than I deserved.

The Terrorists. Them. Us. US of A. Tiny me.

That was one, one-thirty. Did I say that?

Now it's three. I am in the chair, the chair that will make gouges on the back of my legs that are more pronounced than cellulite. It doesn't matter; there is no mirror here to stand before to judge me. Actually, I have been sauntering around naked all day, trying to get comfortable with what is me.

The telephone rings again. It is old-fashioned and rings shrill and long. My heart skips a beat whenever it *brrrrrrrings*. It is someone from Nanaimo, looking to deliver curtains to a Hornby Island B&B. Next island over, I say, still quaking from the ring.

Wrong target.

I've found myself scrambling to the phone, positioned just inside the door, though I don't know why. There is no answering machine to kick in. I am not playing hooky from work so there's no need to answer in a strangulated, flu-induced voice. I am here of my own volition. And verition.

Anyway, my own choice and my own truth.

I doze and stare all afternoon. At five o'clock, it rings again.

Goddamn it. Can I not answer?

After the eleventh ring, I snatch up the receiver and bark, "Hello."

"Hel-loo-hoo. I called to wish you Happy Anniversary." My aunt, Sara, calling from Red Deer. She frequently adds syllables to innocuous words. She's also one of the three people I'd given the number to in a moment of lucidity or stupidity. That, and she had called me just as I was packing and demanded a contact number. Her pause is long, but only because I haven't responded. "So, Happy Anniversary. Were you down at the beach?"

Some of my lies rear up, surge like waves ready to break.

I had managed not to tell anyone that David, my husband, had moved in with his cousin. Especially not Sara, my only living relative, who would be personally wounded. She, after all, had introduced us a few lifetimes ago. Who am I kidding? She'd handle it. It's me, too scared to tell anyone that I drove David away. It's my fault.

No, the story is, I am simply here to paint the final pieces for a show in November, to finish painting the series of woman and her breakdown. The eighth, the last, is the woman in her own womb. Full circle. I don't plan to attend the Richards Street opening.

"Thanks. Thank you muchly," I answer with false heartiness, gripping the clunky receiver tightly. "And yes, I have taken the easel to the beach."

"What's Dave up to tonight? Has he phoned yet?"

I glance at the clock, though I know the approximate time. Such specifics were not to be necessary on this trip. "He'll call after six," I assure.

Assure whom?

"After six. Of course. We've got that ..."

"Alberta/BC daytime deal," I finish.

"Yes. Twenty-three dollars. There's a cap on the minutes, but we never reach it."

"That's good," I say, gazing at the choppy, glistening water and thinking about how busy George Bush will be, about collecting oysters, what the guy at the store will wonder if I buy more wine today.

"Have you had the news on?" she gushes. A Cuisinart, perhaps a blender, is whirring in her background like a helicopter.

"No," I fudge my knowledge for no one knows about Carl. I do not ask, "Why?"

"The United States has been attacked by terrorists! The World Trade Center, the towers ..."

"... in New York," I append.

"... in New York," she echoes. "They've been bombed, well, airplanes deliberately ran into them and then the buildings imploded and there's something in the White House and something with a *P*. P-p-p-p ..." she struggles.

"Pittsburgh?" I offer.

"Pittsburgh!" she finishes triumphantly. She hasn't heard me.

I am silent. Still astonished, but in a faker way. "Holy cow," I finally say.

I don't want to know this, dammit!

"Who's claiming responsibility?" It has been, after all, several hours since Carl's initial report. A lot can happen in a few hours.

"Eastern somethings," she says simply. "Maybe Afghanistan. The Palestinians. They're still just saying, 'the terrorists.' It's like Pearl Harbor."

"But it's not," I counter instinctively. "Right? I mean, you guys knew who bombed Pearl Harbor right off, right? And it was in the middle of a bona fide war."

I am getting myself all knotted up. I have to hang up. I silently curse her, and Carl, for destroying my four-day bubble with this knowledge. It is discombobulating because I know it's bigger than watercolour premieres, cousins, seductively curved dicks and inside-out wombs.

"Listen, I have to hit the outhouse," I say feebly. "Thanks for the good wishes."

"Okay!" she says cheerily. "I hope you create your Ren-war!"

I know who she means and shake off the harsh pronunciation of my mentor.

"Yes. Thanks, Auntie Sara. Okay, bye for now. Call any time." I hang up and nudge my paint supplies under a bunk bed with my toe. Out of sight, and all that. It only works for the tangible.

My Renoir. That was the ruse, perhaps even a potential side bonus to this solo sojourn, but not its basis. Right now, I don't even want to look at the thumbnail sketches of number eight, Imploded Woman.

What is intended to be the self-portrait

I pour a second, generous Hochtaler and squat on the front lawn.

Tens of thousands of people will be dead: agnostics, atheists, Jews, Christians, Muslims. Hindus. Buddhists. People who were possibly something spiritual at some time, but have long forgotten how they expressed it.

Now what?

The shadows are lengthening before my eyes. Why does the sun seem to set so fast? Faster than it moves across the sky all day, I mean. Like it's saying, I'm going for it now. I'm finished with you people.

Going, going, gone.

Smash.

Inside, a little before nine, I am in the rocking chair, a nubbly crocheted quilt wrapped around me. I had oysters for dinner, steamed in the microwave. I almost couldn't eat them, felt sorry for them that I was forcing them out of themselves. When I pierced them with my fork, their plump bodies collapsed and the salt water within them gushed freely. Much freer than blood.

I hear the wail of an air raid siren from the base across the water in Comox and tense up—almost panic—except I don't have enough energy to take my feelings that far. What now? Then I remember, the cabin owner cautioned me that it goes off all the time, a training thing.

The phone again. Unpluggable.

"It's David," he says. Like I wouldn't know the voice.

"Hmmm."

"I didn't know if it was appropriate to phone and say Happy Anniversary or not." He pauses, waiting for my confirmation, but I have no idea either. "So, I decided I would. I hope that's okay. I'm not disturbing you?"

I am disturbed all right. My soul is disturbed, is being beaten around my body like a clamshell in a winter storm.

"Not at all. I was . . ." I am about to saying painting, or at least reading, but I am tired of pretense, for once. "I was just sitting."

"Well, I cheers'd us with a beer."

"Really? What did you cheers? The last month or the first twelve years?"

I have thrown him off course. He clears his throat. "All of it, in a way. I guess I was saluting the good times, in general."

"Ah," I say, suddenly unable to control my inexplicable irritation. "So, the first year and a half?"

He sighs. I click my tongue. This is better than lethargy, no?

"Listen! Have you had the news on?"

This again. This global disaster. "Yes. Sara phoned."

"My God! It's unreal. New York is covered in dust. It looks like snow. The looks on people's faces are just unreal."

"Has anyone claimed responsibility?" I ask again. Assigning blame has always been very important to me.

"Nah. Probably Afghanistan. All in the name of Allah."

I don't like this umbrella reasoning. "No, not Allah."

"That's what the guy would have been yelling before he crashed the plane into the tower. *In the name of Allah.*"

"Yes, but he was just a peon, right? He was brainwashed to do it in the name of religion, but that's not what it's about, is it? It's about money and power. The top guys that orchestrated this, they did it for power. They're like, those, mas . . . no, megalomaniacs." In the background, I hear Peter Jennings. "Turn up the tube."

"Jesus," he says, after we both listen for a moment. "It's World Peace Day. Goddamn assholes, starting a world war on World Peace Day."

"Well, that clarifies why today."

Total precision and planning. Unlike me, unlike my life schedule that ebbs like the tides. I thought I had finally got it right, that I'd customized my death with as much care as I create palettes. Now my plans are smeared, a child's finger painting. Why didn't I do it the first day? Why not yesterday? Will I do it at all?

I want escape, but not in that way anymore.

What now?

"Well, anyway ..." I venture.

"Yes. Okay. Enjoy your time. Well, not enjoy. You know. Work hard."

"Uhuh." Strange, how awkwardness and easy comfort can co-exist.

"Lissa? You're okay, right? Doing, feeling, okay?"

What to say? Yes I am, David. A benevolent hand has reached into me and stirred the sandy bed of my plan, made its waters too murky to proceed. Or no, I'm not okay. I cannot pin down my soul. Come for me now? Say good-bye forever?

"I'm okay, David. Thanks."

"Okay. Call me when you get back to the city. We'll get together and ..."

"... figure things out."

"Yes."

I will have things figured out, long before that.

I hang up and wrap myself in the quilt again. It's almost dark. The light is grainy, like being underwater. I take out the orange tablets that Dr. Stanton prescribed. The ones I said I'd die before taking. He'd said, "You might very well. It's pills and voluntary counselling or the hospital, where everything you can imagine is mandatory. Take your pick. Take two a day, with food. No alcohol, it's counteractive. Make an appointment for when you get back."

I swallow them with the last of the wine. Baby steps to serenity.

I think about the peons, the hijackers who sacrificed themselves. In the name of Allah.

For what cause would I give myself?

Only myself. I have only ever thought about killing myself, to escape myself.

Selfish, wretched bitch, a voice says. You want to pin down your soul, you reach inside and find it, grasp it. Do whatever it takes to never let it go. The voice resonates in stereo from the shores, the boughs, down the flue of the chimney.

I want to learn if the sun rises as quickly as it sets.

DRAGONS

I watch Jake chain-smoke and wonder if he composes his music with lots of one-hand bits, or whether he just lets the butt hang from his mouth and the ashes sprinkle over the ivories like a gentle first snow. The fingers of his left hand are old-man yellow, the colour of the sun behind a watery grey cloud.

We're out back of Six North. The mental ward.

I couldn't believe it when his mother came up to me last night after the final set at Lancashire's. I pretty much recognized her right away, but it was strange to be approached in a two-bit jazz bar by the mother of someone you went to school with.

"Mrs. Polley. Wow. Nice to see you." I handed my pianist, Grant, his half of the tips from the brandy snifter and waved him off.

"Please, Char, I think you're old enough to call me Dini now. How are you, dear? How does it feel to be back in your old home town?"

"Singing for the madding crowds?" I added. "It's okay. I haven't seen anyone I know and we pull out for Whistler tomorrow morning. And the old home town?" I shrugged. "Sage feels the same and completely different, if that makes any sense.

43

Listen, how's Jake? It's been almost thirteen years since I spoke to him."

She took a moment to gaze around the room at the milling patrons, the servers trying to start their clean-up. "Up and down. Down right now. He's back in the hospital."

"Oh," I said. Very politely, like I was hearing news of a distant cousin's divorce.

"You should visit him in the morning. He'd love to see you."

The techies went and upped the house lights at that very moment, baring my dubious face to Mrs ... to Dini. "I can? Really. Well, okay. I will. He's my oldest friend. Yeah sure, I'll make the time."

She gave me a dry kiss on the cheek and a weary smile. "Take care. Good luck with the singing career and say hello to your mother."

I nod, don't have the heart to tell her my mother died of cancer three years ago. Does it matter, since I'm probably never going to run into her again?

I chug two Scotches from the bar and come *this* freakin' close to ordering a pizza or two, but haul my self to bed, just in the nick of time.

The next morning, I have to beg the nurse to let me into Six North outside of visiting hours with a big song and dance about visiting from Vancouver.

"He's being choosy about who he sees," she cautioned.

What could I say to that? *He'll see me, Ratched.*

"Jake to reception," she finally chirps into the P.A. system. "Jake to the front."

Jacob Polley did a quick double take when he saw me, then swaggered up and gave me a huge hug. He wore track pants, a gargantuan kangaroo sweatshirt and heavy black sneakers. His wire frame glasses looked the same as the ones he wore in high school, but probably weren't. His hair was dusted with grey as if he'd waltzed too close to a spray can.

"Fantastic to see you. Who told you I was here?"

"Your mom. I got a gig in town and she came up to me after. Since when does your mom hang out in second-rate jazz bars on Thursday nights?"

He double-shrugged, like he was getting into a coat. "The old man split a couple of years ago. I guess Lanc's hosts the only over-fifty crowd in town." He rocked back and forth and glanced around quickly. "Listen, I was just outside, having a smoke . . ."

"No problem. Let's go." He started back down the hall. "When did you take up smoking?"

"I've developed a few bad habits," he said dryly.

Me too, Jake.

Now outside, within the blocked-in little grassy area that houses a picnic table, three ash urns and a garbage can, we make small talk.

"So this nightclub thing, only jazz or what?"

I smile. In high school, we'd sworn off anything but Joan Jett and Neil Young.

"Yeah, mostly Cole Porter, Ella. Bad, huh? But it's where the jobs are."

He checks me over, up and down, with complete candour. "You got skinny."

I feel myself blush, but it's out of guilt, not modesty or pride.

"Scarsdale? Pritikin? ww?"

I give him a shove on the shoulder. "None of the above. You don't want to know."

Jesus, the guy can't stand still. If he isn't rocking back on his heels, he's bobbing his head and shoulders to some internal beat.

"What about you? What d'you get up to when you're not here?"

He jumps up on the picnic table and begins playing air guitar. "I have an apartment. I play music. Write music. It's not a bad life."

The door to the ward opens and a young patient sidles out.

"Jakey!" she croons. "Gotta smoke for me?" He has one out and ready for her when she gets to us. "Who's your friend?"

The woman is about twenty, wearing tight jeans and a red pullover. She has incredibly bad acne and a scraggy ponytail.

"This is Char, a friend from high school. Char, this is Alicia. Alicia and I cross paths once or twice a year, eh, Alicia?" They both laugh at this reference to their respective, chronic hospital stints.

Alicia plops down on the picnic table. She is much calmer than Jake. Maybe she's on different medication, or at a different state of recovery. Maybe she's not even schizophrenic. Besides, Jake was always a hyper person, always had to take a spin around the piano between songs, always in trouble for breaking rank in the choir rows. They share some quips about the staff and so-and-so the new guy as I stand awkwardly, wishing I smoked too. Or had a beer.

Or a Chinese buffet.

Jake and I have been friends since grade one. He was the only boy I ever invited to my elementary birthday parties, which he soldiered through screaming, giggling girls. In seventh grade, we were co-conspirators in organizing enough kids to bounce on the wooden teeter-totter until it split in two and we all tumbled off. Then ran like stink. In high school, we swore we'd move to Chicago or New York and make the world take note of the talent from little ol' Sage.

We were never boyfriend and girlfriend. Never kissed. Maybe we hugged after the grad ceremonies.

I'm feeling uncomfortable and thinking maybe I should go, when Jake takes a slim jackknife from his left sock. I gasp. Alicia and he find this very funny.

"Yeah, you wouldn't think they'd give jackknives to Six North, but they're standard issue with the personalized bedpans and electric shock equipment." I thought Alicia would pee her pants at this. "No, just kidding. It's a game we play. Whoever holds the knife, between the eight or so of us in on it, has to mark the picnic table without being caught, then they pass it on to someone else." He sits at the table and begins gouging the underside of the second plank.

I figure, who am I to judge what passes the time in Six North?

Alicia moves automatically to shield Jake from the sight line of the door. "Not that they come out here," she explains to me. "They've got their own little ciggy-station at the other end of the wing."

Jake yanks me down beside him. "Here," he says, passing me the blade under the table, "join the club. Mark anywhere. We're up to covering the whole thing one of these days."

The action feels naughty yet seductive, like the teeter-totter thing. With some shame and a little giddiness, I jab at a spot until I figure my mark has been made.

"Good," Jake says, when I'd closed the blade and held it in my palm. "Now you're one of us."

I smile weakly. Good to know.

"Now pass it to 'licia."

Alicia reaches for it and I see her cuticles are bloodied and ripped back, to the first knuckle in some cases. She sees me looking and fixes me with a stare. "I'll do mine later. I want to carry the blade around for awhile. See ya, Jake and Jake's old friend."

She saunters back inside. Jake is still sitting, but jiggling his legs.

"She's . . . I mean, is she like you?" *Delicate, smelicate.*

"A schizo? Yeah, and then some. I should probably report her for having a knife, but then it'll be confiscated and we'll have to wait until somebody gets discharged and smuggles one back in to score another one."

I have no response for this so I ask about his brothers.

"Scott's in Arizona with a wife and a couple of kids. He likes it down there. Don't see him much. Dale, who the fuck knows."

"But Dale and you were close. What happened?"

He stops moving, freezes, and looks me right in the eye. "He's a little pissed off because I tried to kill him."

Christ Almighty, I'm not sure I can take many more mind-blowers like this. I'm not used to being speechless.

"You know the movie, *As Good as It Gets*? Nicholson? Yeah, well, that was as bad as it got." He grins. "So far."

"I remember you said something about dragons, the time we met up, after you knew, but before you had to drop out of university. Do you still see dragons?" What the hell, he can only call for security and have me blasted off his visitor list.

"Hell, no. No dragons here where I'm not chock full of drugs. Well, honestly, sometimes even the mega-doses of sanity don't work."

We sit in silence for a moment. I feel the picnic table vibrating.

Jake says nonchalantly, "We never kissed, huh? Did we ever kiss? I remember your mom gave us money to go to Mickey D's that time, but nothing happened, right?"

I groan. "I remember that hot date, what were we, thirteen? A lot of conjecture and hormones, but no, no kissing."

"Too bad," he says mildly, deftly lighting another cig. "I like thinking about the past, the good things. Days in here, and even in my apartment, are pretty damn similar. They're not bad, but there's not a whole lot of new shit to add to the pot, you know?"

I nod, then steal a glance at his profile. He used to be a pretty innocent kid. Always short for his age, cute in a Casey of Mr. Dressup kind of way. He looks tough now, strained and shadowy.

I lean into him, stick my face two inches away from his. His eyes are open and darting around, but he holds his head still.

I kiss him. First lightly, with closed lips. Then more forcefully, parting his lips with my tongue before delving deep into his mouth. His tongue is lifeless, but hot and coated with smoke, his teeth grainy with nicotine and plaque.

I dig deeper and deeper, trying to find the Jake I knew.

Suddenly, he knocks me away, hard, and I end up ass over teakettle on the wet grass.

"What the fuck was that?" he yells and I sense faces scrambling to the bank of windows behind me.

I don't know.

"The kiss we never had," I splutter.

"Fuck that! That was a mercy kiss! You think I don't get any? That the poor fucking schizo doesn't get any and it's your job to give me a little taste of being the single, partying, professional musician I got gypped out of being? Is that what you think?" Jake is so agitated, he's almost dancing a jig. "Fuck you!"

I rise awkwardly and and back away. "I'm sorry. I just thought it would be nice. To kiss you. That's all."

"I could take you into the back broom closet right now and screw the shit out of you, you know. Don't think I couldn't."

I hold up my hands in retreat. "I've no doubt. I'm sorry, Jake. I don't know why I did that."

He starts sobbing, collapses on the bench. "I don't know why I stopped you."

I move cautiously toward him, touch his shoulder. He keeps his head in his hands. I glance to the windows. Amazing, there's no one watching after all. Perhaps similar theatrical performances are staged daily, plus Wednesday and Sunday matinees.

"I better go, bud."

"It was supposed to be us," he moans. "We were supposed to be the duo." He snorts the snot back in his nose and wipes his face with the sleeve of the kangaroo shirt.

At the exit door that he tells me is the most direct to the parking lot, I hug him. "Love you, Jake."

"Hey, I love you too." He says this super cheerily. Blasé, actually.

"And you'll always be my friend, no matter what."

He smirks at this. "Yeah? Good. Thanks for coming by." He is gone in a flash, swallowed up by the corridors, like the meds they all take. Probably wants a smoke.

In my car, I sit and shake. I told Grant we'd leave around noon, so I have about two hours. I start down Main Street till I see a Subway shop. I buy an extra-large root beer, three foot-long specials and sit in the car, and shove them in like I'm an electric pencil sharpener. Grant will be in the room, so I'll have to go to a gas station to puke. Don't I hate that.

No dragons here.

ALL THE THINGS

One would think Rhonda Elizabeth Bethune would have bruised and scarred shins from bumping into all the things: the boxes of dishes, the exercise machines, the trunks of spare towels and linens, the racks of lampshades and the metal shelving units of unassembled shelving units, the two grown children's lives of public school, represented by Plasticine art projects, balsa wood solar systems and unreturned library books. Or that her head would sport goose eggs galore, the results of all the things tumbling off shelves, out of cupboards, from the rafters and strung-up positions here, there, and everywhere.

It didn't. Her head was smooth under the sausage-roll curls and her legs were the best bit about her. They were still shapely and sported no thick blue veins, despite her sixty-three years. She attributed this to elevating them, her legs, for several hours a day. The result was a very rotund rest of Rhonda E. Bethune, but varicose vein-free legs.

Her older daughter, the one who still lived at home, sometimes cheekily said, "Ma, your butt's the only thing that gives that chair the will to carry on." Rhonda would play-smack her and say, "Now, Julie-Smulie, that's no way to talk to your

51

mother. Can you switch on *Murder She Wrote*? It's almost seven. There's a good lass."

The good lass, at thirty-five, would reply, "Are you off your rocker? I'm watching *Extreme Makeover*."

Throughout exchanges like this, whether the ingredients for turkey loaf sandwiches or the need for toilet paper from the Shoppers were of issue, Cecil John Bethune sat impassively by his wife, waiting for the silence to resume.

It never did.

"It's getting hot," Rhonda said every May fifteenth. "It'll soon be time."

That was Cecil's cue.

On June first, Rhonda would ease into the ancient La-Z-Boy chair with the maroon, fake fur throw rug because she didn't like the feel of vinyl, and say, "It's real hot, Cecil. Where'd you hide my winter?"

That was Cecil's cue to plug in the two electric fans and, in July and August only—he put his foot down about that—the two portable air-con units that stood at the ready beside the three space heaters.

"I can't stand the heat. You know I can't stand the heat. We just have to finish The Yankee House this year. My childhood house was always too hot. I can't stand the heat."

"Yes, we'll try to finish The Yankee House this year, Rhonda," Cecil said, before moving off to don a sweater and move his rocker a few feet away from the blasting units.

The Yankee House was a foundation and shell of a structure, but would be a showpiece someday, as Rhonda saw it. Nightly, in her dreams. True, it accidentally had no doors in and out— easily rectified by taking a Skilsaw to the plywood—and true, the preliminaries for an indoor pool existed in a place where no pool man lived for five hundred kilometres. Miles. US of A-style miles. Still, it was going to be the end-all, be-all house.

It would always be cool, with plenty of space for all the things.

"We need the room," Rhonda explained to quizzing or disbelieving persons when they asked why the Bethunes planned to move 1300 kilometres north to Alaska and even apply for American citizenship, instead of buying a condominium in a Comox Valley retirement village, the present hot spot for retirees. "It's because I can't stand the heat here and we need the room." To her credit, Rhonda was never impatient in her explanations, outlining her plans and at what stage the house was, treating each inquiry as if it were her first.

In the meantime, while collecting all the things needed for The Yankee House, Cecil went to push papers for the City of Coquitlam from Monday to Friday. Rhonda picked away at the crossword from *The Vancouver Sun* everyday and the payroll for the dressmaker, salon and pet grooming business down the road every second day. Julie delivered FedEx packages and always came home extremely tired and irritable because of the stress. She was consequently permitted to eat dinner first and alone while watching *Dharma and Greg* reruns from one of the TVs in the den.

Every Saturday and Sunday morning, seasonally, Rhonda ventured out to the Coquitlam flea markets and garage sales, to see if there was anything she could find at a good price for The Yankee House. To her credit, if she decided The Yankee House needed something, a Ride-On Mower, for instance, she checked out the weekend bargain outlets and front yard garage sales before finally visiting Wal-Mart and purchasing the newest model with the family MasterCard. This process showed Cecil what a responsible spender she was. Cecil might remind her that the lot was pure rock and needed no mowing, or the dining table for twelve was inappropriate because twelve people would never visit them 1300 kilometres north. Usually he did not.

Sometimes her younger son came to visit from Calgary with his wife and two children. This was nice because she liked cooking mounds of scrambled eggs for breakfast, constructing three toppling bologna sandwiches per person at lunch and serving nightly dinners fit for Thanksgiving.

"You've got too much stuff," Donald said every visit. "I can barely find the goddamn toilet. What are you gonna do with all this stuff?"

"Don't think I wouldn't still wash your mouth out for that foul language. Don't think it for a moment. It's for The Yankee House. You know The Yankee House is very big and next year, maybe the year after, if your father ever retires, we'll need it. It's very, very big, The Yankee House. We've a lot of space to fill."

This June visit from Donald and his petite wife, Patricia, was because their youngest, Lance, had an appointment with a Vancouver hearing specialist. The original plan was to stay at Patricia's sister's downtown apartment, but when Donald slipped up and revealed the plan, Rhonda's accusations and hoo-haw made it necessary to revamp the plans.

"Why do you tell her when we're going to the Lower Mainland?" Patricia had asked when Donald glumly hung up the phone, two days before they left Calgary. "Why can't we just slide in and out, for once? Stay in the city, instead of out in the boonies?"

Donald grimaced. "It just came out that we had to go down. By accident, I swear. I don't know how it came out."

"Well, don't leave me alone in that house and all those things. The junk. Seriously, it gives me the creeps. They could open a museum for the '50s onwards. It's too much. I feel the boys will crawl places and never be found again."

Three days later, Donald, his breastbone pressing against the table because the back of his chair was abutting a second-hand IKEA wardrobe, sighed and tucked into his mother's roast beef. Across the table, Patricia stirred her dinner around, passing bits of beef and spoonfuls of canned peas to the children, ages two and three. Sam was perched atop five old phonebooks and Lance was plunked in Julie's old high chair. Donald's was still around too, in the basement, but penned in by cardboard wardrobes of winter clothes and two stationary bicycles.

After the children were in bed, the adults sat in the den

watching baseball. There were chairs galore to sit in, a loveseat, a papason, the vinyl La-Z-Boy, several folding chairs behind the TV, two camp chairs and a beanbag the boys adored. The electric fans were angled at Rhonda's chair. It wasn't really all that hot anyway.

Because she'd eaten right after work, Julie was deep into a bag of Doritos when they joined her.

"Are those from The Yankee House goodie storage, Julie? They better not be. You know I hate it when you deplete the supply. We won't be able to get Doritos when we move to The Yankee House."

"They're not, Ma. Chill out."

But they were, Patricia knew. She'd seen Julie open the wall unit that held The Yankee House Foodstuffs (the felt penned sign taped outside declared it so) and pull out the bag from between case lots of instant and canned soup, Heinz ketchup, Sunlight detergent, rolls of industrial-sized paper towel and packages of gummi bears. She'd said nothing. Then again, Patricia usually said little once they crossed the Port Mann Bridge.

After the baseball game, Julie stood up and farted, grinning like a twelve-year-old. "Aaaah. I needed that."

"Jesus, Jules," said Donald, shaking his head. "You'd think you were a guy. Or with a bunch of guys, anyway."

"Perfectly natural thing. Right, Ma? Well, I'm off to bed. Big day tomorrow." She dropped the empty chip bag into Rhonda's lap and sashayed out of the den.

"Well," sighed Rhonda, patting the cellophane bag flat and folding it into a neat square. She paused and then quipped, "Well, a well is a very deep subject." No one even grunted. "It's just so hot. Donald, is that fan on high? That one, there? It's not doing a lick of cooling."

"Yes, Ma," assured Donald, without leaning over to check the dial. Rhonda didn't notice as she fanned herself with a *Martha Stewart Living* magazine.

Just when Patricia thought she would have to scream into the thick silence, Donald asked, "So, what about the house? What's the next stage?" He asked because he knew it was expected.

Rhonda slapped the magazine down on her lap and wriggled with excitement. "We'll be going up in a few weeks, as soon as your father can arrange time off. It's difficult, because there's no one to fill his position. We're going up to paint the eaves."

"The eaves?" repeated Donald dubiously.

"Yes! Forest green. To blend with the scenery. The house is so big, we'll need to blend it in, so it doesn't look ostentatious."

"There's no one to notice for forty miles on either side," muttered Cecil. "Not a soul."

"Yes, forty miles," assured Rhonda. "Complete, complete privacy. It will be wonderful."

"With no windows, of course there's complete privacy," Cecil said under his breath, to Patricia. She was shocked. He never said more than hello and good-bye to her.

"What, Cecil, what?" asked Rhonda. "You're full of comments tonight. It's the heat. This heat is making you ornery. I can't stand this heat." Cecil huddled into his chair, Donald wiped his forehead with the back of his shirtsleeve and Patricia idly fanned herself with the *TV Guide*, more for something to do than feeling warm.

The next morning, with Julie gone to deliver FedEx packages, Cecil to push papers for the City of Coquitlam, Donald to Shoppers for toilet paper and Rhonda doing the crossword, Patricia felt at loose ends. Strange, she thought. Usually I feel so tightly wound. She extracted several flattened cardboard boxes from the stack at the back door, reboxed them and showed the boys how to play fort.

"Mind they don't ruin those," said Rhonda, coming into the kitchen. "I need them to move all the things to The Yankee House.

Patricia allowed herself a glance at the three-metre stack of boxes. "No, Rhonda, we're being very careful."

"I hope so. When you go into the city this aft, for the appointment, can you do your mum a favour?"

Patricia winced. "Of course."

"There's a paint sale, at The Home Depot. Could you pick up some Forest Green, say, ten gallons? It's on sale and I'm just not going to have the time to get out there today. I've the books to do, then lunches and dinners to prepare for all you people."

"We'll be gone before lunch," Patricia reminded, trying to sound helpful. "And, we could just bring home pizza or something, for dinner. How about that?"

"Cecil won't eat pizza. He likes a nice meat and potatoes dinner. So does Julie and, for that matter, Donald. If he tells you any differently, he's trying to save a marital row."

"He loves pizza," Patricia said stiffly, yanking Sam away from upsetting a precarious stack of warped shoeboxes labeled *Spare light bulbs.*

"Well, what would I know?" huffed Rhonda. "I'm only his mother."

Patricia opened, then closed, her mouth. She was ready and waiting in the driveway with the children when Donald returned with the car.

When they returned from the city appointment, Lance was sleepy from a series of drops he had been given and Sam was cranky from the long car ride. Knowing she would pay for it later, Patricia put them both to bed. It was too late for afternoon naps, they'd be up all night, but she wanted peace and quiet. And some glugs of the secret vodka they'd brought, given that alcohol was banned in the Bethune house.

"You put the little ones to bed?" said Rhonda when Patricia went into the kitchen for a glass and some kind of mix for the vodka. "They'll be up all night."

"Yes, Rhonda. It's for the best right now."

"Well, I only raised Julie, Donald and my four little sisters, what would I know?"

Patricia poured orange juice into a large tumbler. "Donald and I will share this," she explained, noting Rhonda's raised eyebrows. "What do you mean, you raised your sisters?" This was new. Rhonda had previously given glowing descriptions of her childhood in Medicine Hat. There was a sickly but doting mother, a Little House on the Prairie camaraderie steeped in poverty.

"My mother was not a strong woman. Not like me at all. Children were too much for her to cope with."

"Oh. What about your father? Didn't he help?"

"I better go make sure Donald is unloading that paint in the right place. I've a special spot for it in the garage."

She was on her way out, about to shimmy past the boxes of dishes, the exercise machines, the trunks of spare towels and linens, the racks of lampshades and the metal shelving units of unassembled shelving units, when Cecil entered from the side door.

"You're home early," Rhonda accused. A yellowed *Redbook* magazine slipped off the shelf above and bonked her in the head. Rhonda automatically batted it away like a northern horsefly.

Cecil slapped a paper bag, the size and shape of a bottle, down on the kitchen table.

"What's that?" said Rhonda, pointing at the package. "I hope it's not what I think it is, because I forbid alcohol in this house, you know that."

Donald came in the side door and Patricia discreetly signaled him to be quiet. She herself tried to blend in with all the things.

"It is, Rhonda. It is what you think. I've honoured your wishes for forty-five years, but yes," he said glumly, drawing the bottle out of the bag with a flourish, "yes, it's a bottle. It's a bottle of Jack Daniels and I am having one, maybe two or three or four. Right now, in this, my house."

"I forbid it."

Cecil took out a crystal glass from the second cabinet around the corner and filled it with ice from the dispenser in the first fridge. He uncapped the bottle and poured enough Scotch in the glass to float the ice cubes, silently toasted the three shocked faces and meandered out of the kitchen. Shortly after, the television blared with the BCTV six o'clock news.

"And stay out there," bellowed Rhonda, her normally pink face now a pasty white. "And stay out there," she repeated, more quietly.

Rhonda punctured the plastic binding of a case lot of creamed corn and began opening can after can. She'd opened seven before Donald gently took the gadget from her.

"There won't be enough," Rhonda warbled.

Donald led her into the living room, to her chair with the burgundy fake fur because his mother didn't like the feel of the vinyl. He muted the television and faced his parents. Patricia sipped the orange juice, too intrigued to make a side trip to the suitcase.

"Pops? What's the deal? Are you sure you want to do this?"

"I'm sure."

"But all those years on the wagon," began Donald.

"On the wagon?"

"I don't remember you ever drinking. Don't blow it now, Pops."

Suddenly, without any warning, Cecil guffawed. "Donald, I'm no alcoholic. You've not seen me drink because your mother forbids it. I take a drink with the bowling team, I had a few at your wedding, albeit in the goddamn bathroom because your mother barely let me out of her sight. My God, son, I'm not an alcoholic! I just don't usually drink at home outta respect for your mother."

"Ma?" Donald choked out. "Ma, is Pops an alkie? Tell me the truth, Ma."

Rhonda, now with two bright spots of pink on her white face, was brushing the burgundy fake fur La-Z-Boy covering this way and that with such intensity, Patricia thought the chair might begin to purr.

"Your father's not an alcoholic," Rhonda said primly. Yet miserably.

The electric fans were aimed full-on at Rhonda. Donald, squatted beside his mother, was half in their range. Patricia felt a periodic fluttering of air across her knees.

The fans whirred three rotations.

"My mother, my mother was the drunk."

Patricia gasped. Donald had been told his maternal grand-mother died of tuberculosis. Cecil grunted and Donald plopped onto the couch in exasperation.

"For God's sake, Ma. Why's that been such a secret? My God, all this time of me being an adult you never saw fit to tell me alcoholism runs in the family?"

"It doesn't run in the family," snapped Rhonda. "It was just Mother. She was only like that because Daddy was in the military and we had to keep traipsing all over."

Patricia reached out to angle one of the fans in her direction, suddenly feeling the full weight of the hot, sticky air.

"Your father kept you moving because your mother kept embarrassing him and your family in every little cockamamie place he got posted."

"Cecil!"

"God's truth," said Cecil to Patricia. "Our fathers were in two or three postings together. That's how I first met Rhonda. We were fourteen, fifteen."

"Why are you hurting me like this, Cecil? You know you're lying. My mother was a sick woman, a diseased, sick woman. She couldn't help being sick."

"You got that right," said Cecil and got up to refill his glass.

"Ma, there's no shame in it for you," assured Donald, touching Rhonda's shoulder. "No shame for you. For us."

Cecil returned to the threshold of the living room, his replenished glass in hand, and leaned against the door jamb. Julie reappeared from her basement bedroom. "What's for dinner, Ma? I've had a hard day and I'm about starving." Only then did her eyes meet each face. "Whah? Whah's going on?"

"Grandma Fulton was an alcoholic," announced Donald.

"Oh, that," scoffed Julie. "Jeez, tell me some'un I don't know. Pa told me that a long time ago. Tol' me not to bring no bottles home cause it'd upset Ma. Thought it was the least I could do, me living here and all."

For free, thought Patricia.

"I can't believe you didn't tell me," said Donald petulantly. It was unclear from whom he'd expected solidarity.

His father looked at him. "No need, was there? You went off to university when you were seventeen and then moved all the way to Calgary. There was no need."

"All right, everyone!" said Rhonda. "That's enough. I'm going back into the kitchen to finish dinner and I'll not be having this topic rehashed behind my back 'til the cows come home."

"Wait!" said Donald, eyeing Cecil. "There's more. Pa, what's going on? Why'd you bring home JD today?"

Rhonda whirled around. "Yes, Cecil. Why today?"

Cecil emptied his glass. "There is no Yankee House."

"What? Don't be ridiculous. I've been there half a dozen times. I directed those nincompoops who poured the cement. You're drunk, talking off your mind."

Cecil shook his head. "I'm telling you, there's no land. The land doesn't belong to us. The whole deed is false."

"Jeez Louise," breathed Julie.

"It's on Indian land, Native land. Sacred Indian ground. The band council ruled it wasn't to have been sold by the shyster that sold it in the first place. I found out for certain today."

"Well, that's the most ridiculous thing I've ever heard. We'll take them all to court. We'll buy another northern property. We'll have our Yankee House, Cecil Bethune. We'll have our Yankee House or die trying."

Cecil continued shaking his head. "There's no money for The Yankee House. No money to sue the band over this fiasco, or to build the next one. There's no money, Rhonda!" His face was florid, his normally innocuous body a formidable presence in the room.

The middle fan cackled and sparked, emitted an acrid odour and became silent. The miniature light show drew only quick glances from the others but Patricia, alarmed, jumped back and bumped into an oak armoire.

"Mind the armoire, dear."

Rhonda's face oscillated between pink and green. Fanning herself with an old *Macleans*, she assured Cecil, "Well, not right at this second, there's no money. You'll just have to work another year or two, that's all. Patricia, we won't be able to come to Calgary for Christmas. We'll be saving money for Yankee House Two." She sounded triumphant.

"Goddamnit, woman," shouted Cecil, pushing out of his chair and winging his glass around. They all flinched as its contents splattered about. Patricia felt a drop of watery Scotch splat onto her cheek. "Rhonda Elizabeth Fulton Bethune, there will be no Yankee House Two!"

"You're not being sensible!" Rhonda admonished, then waggled her finger in Donald's face. "See, see what the drink does, see? Your father is not being sensible, full of the drink. It's liquid insanity, it is," she implored to Julie, then Patricia, who could not meet Rhonda's pink, rabbity eyes.

"I am not insane," roared Cecil. "I just don't want to move to the God-forsaken northern USA and be classified as a goddamn immigrant like I'm from some third-world country and where I won't have Wednesday night bowling and you'll be ordering a century's worth of toilet paper from the bloody-Jesus Internet! I am not moving north and I am not working for another few years! I'm seventy-one years old, woman!"

"But we have all the things, almost, for the Yankee House. We were almost ready to go," spluttered Rhonda, her face the colour of old dough. "So if you need to work for another year ..."

"Rhonda, goddamnit, I retired today."

They all stared, mouths held in little Os. The second fan made a buzzing sound, like a bee held down, then whirred itself out of motion.

"It was retire, or be fired, alright? Allow a man his own little retirement party in peace, will you!" He stalked into the kitchen. They heard the clunk of the labouring ice machine, a dull thudding of toppling boxes and the shattering of glass. The stack of light bulbs. The door to the garage was opened and slammed.

No one moved. A muscle. An eyelid. The surviving cooling appliance churned away, but the air was thickening like gravy. The dense atmosphere reminded Patricia of the goop oozing from Lance's ear.

Into these shock waves, Julie said, "Them bastards at FedEx fired me today, Ma." She collapsed at Rhonda's feet and began sobbing. Rhonda patted her daughter's head distractedly.

"You fool."

The third fan made a popping sound and ground to a halt.

"Well, I guess you all can eat them Doritos I was saving."

Patricia felt a tugging at her cheeks, her lips. She began laughing uncontrollably, a wheezing, gasping, hysterical laughing that would not be controlled by Donald's frown, Julie's wails or Rhonda's forlorn stare. She teetered out of the room, one hand over her mouth, the other supporting herself as she lurched down the hall, grasping at the boxes of dishes, the exercise machines, the trunks of spare towels and linens, the racks of lampshades and metal shelving units of unassembled shelving units.

"It's her way when she's upset," explained Donald limply.

"All I wanted was my own space," said Rhonda in a dulled voice. "My own space, shared by no one. A place where no one could find me, to ask for cups of tea with shots of brandy. A place with no little sibling whiners I was to love like a mother, with their snotty noses and dirty arses. And my own things, my own things, that no one could sneak away and sell for a bottle, or a pair of new shoes, or a piece of meat for Sunday dinner. That's all. Is that too much to ask for, Donny?"

"No, Ma. Not at all."

"I just wanted my own space, a little peace and quiet. And all the things that go with it."

HEALING

I am returning to the summer cottage of my childhood. No one in my family has been there for some twenty-two years because my father sold it when I was fifteen, when we moved from the coast to Edmonton. Tracking the owners down and arranging accommodations based on my bout of nostalgia and melancholy took more effort than I have put into anything else for many months.

I stand now, Jennifer Lee Ferguson, on the starboard side of the small ferry that takes me to a place of anticipated innocence and joy. The same wind whips my loopy, mahogany-coloured hair into my face, stings my eyes and makes them tear.

The September sun is brilliant, too brilliant, and I am cautious to wish on any of the shooting stars created by its rays striking the cresting waves. We near the end of the crossing and I am so lost in my thoughts, a burly crewman touches my arm and asks me to return to my vehicle.

Sook licks my ear when I settle back into the driver's seat. I reach back and scratch under his chin. "Not much longer now, boy," I assure. He is a hulking black presence in the back seat and resents having to share it with the cooler of food that would not fit in the trunk.

I ease off the ferry, ready to wave at the crew, but no one makes eye contact. Didn't they used to be friendlier? Greet by name? Of course, I am not an islander now, perhaps that is the difference.

The road up-island feels the same—ancient, cracked and pot-holed asphalt—but certainly it has been resurfaced in the life-time I have been gone. The many lifetimes.

I slow as I pass the General Store, which looks unchanged. Ah ha! There is now competition for the fat old codger who runs it, half a kilometre down the road. He had horrid BO, but his wife used to let me choose a gob stopper for free, every visit.

The mare is gone from the corner property, the lot before I make my first turn onto gravel. Just as well, such a beast's close proximity to the old cabin would be torturous for Sook. He whines from the back seat, like he knows he's been gypped. I've made the left, now the right, slowly now, the driveway was always tricky to find amidst the trees and bushes.

No, not now. The opening is wide and clearly marked and this unreasonably offends me. I am mollified that little has been done to reconstruct the actual driveway. Its roots and deep ruts remain.

Halfway down, flanked heavily by firs and maple trees on each side, I stop and open the back door. Sook prepares to leap, then throws me a dubious glance. "It's not a trick," I tell him. "Get out and run." Sook is a city dog. He chooses daily between four scrawny trees and two bushes at the dog park. The only interesting smells come from the rotation of elderly men who sit on the benches. Soon he is racing down the drive ahead of the car, zigzagging with delirium.

I pull the car into the old spot under the towering oak tree, then remember to breathe. I've been doing that a lot lately, for-getting to breathe, until the lack of oxygen forces me to gasp in a mouthful of sustenance.

The outside looks basically the same, white with forest green trim. I pick my way across the uneven ground and warn myself not to expect the same of the inside. My mother's crocheted afghans will not be there, nor will the old-fashioned chamber pot that held fruit on the kitchen table. I finger, for the hundredth time, the key sent by post in my pocket.

To healing, I intone.

The lock clicks and I push the door open. Sook rushes past me, on the off chance there is something more interesting inside than the plethora of canine treats outside. He races around the cabin twice before whizzing by me, still poised in the doorway, to continue his frenzied exploration outside. Stepping in, I note the air is still sweet. The new owners, the Grishams, only packed up for the summer two weeks ago and the air has not yet staled and dampened.

I am not suffused with peace. Where is the peace I envisioned, filling me like a tide pool, upon stepping across the threshold of my former sanctuary? But neither am I debilitated with pain, so I continue forward. It will be all right, I say to myself. Remember to breathe.

The cottage is one big room with bunks and a stone hearth at one end and the kitchen at the other. There has always been electricity, but the microwave in the corner and small freezer under the north window are new. I look with trepidation, but see no television. It is stripped of character, a nameless, modern cottage, and I feel pangs I swore I wouldn't. It used to be part of the routine for my mother to threaten to break the fishing rods in two that were left on the wooden kitchen table, and there were always open books on each pillow and half-finished projects of crafts, model boats or sewing on every wobbly side table.

It is positively sterile in this place. It is unnerving.

Paul, my partner of ten years, was supportive of my proposed pilgrimage, though skeptical of its magical healing qualities. He even offered, once and quickly, to come, but we both knew I'd decline. He looked quite sorrowful when I drove away, down the Sage City road. Poor Paul. Are men's feelings chronically forgotten more quickly after loss? It's difficult to know whether they prefer it that way, or resent the masculine stereotype of nonchalance placed on them.

I take my time unpacking the car. There's not much. I told the Grishams I would stay a week. When it comes time to unroll my sleeping bag, drawn from an ancient trunk in my suburban garage, I recoil at the sight of a sac of spider eggs, neatly tucked into its outer folds. My first instinct is to crush the soft ball of life in toilet paper, to howl about it bursting open with life as I sleep. I reconsider and instead, rip a piece of cardboard from my box of dry goods and carefully scrape the bubble onto it. I carry it outside, nestle it at the base of a tree stump and cover it with leaves and grass. I instruct a curious Sook to go pick on something his own size.

No, that would be a small deer, a disastrous idea. They used to shoot dogs that chased deer and no doubt still do. He is already off on a new scent. Oh, to have the free conscience to move so easily forward.

When I have methodically unpacked, as is my custom, examined the outhouse, the tool shed and water well, I join Sook on the beach. Long sleeves and pants are necessary to lessen the effects of the autumn breeze, but the sun is warm on my face. I remember the hours I spent on this rocky beach, not sandy at all. The treasures under the rocks were always more captivating and rewarding than the perpetual sandcastles other beaches offered. I try to get Sook interested in the scurrying crabs as I turn driftwood and sandstone for him, but he doesn't catch on.

The tide is coming in. I hope for low tides, so I can collect oysters—exorbitantly priced in the interior—for all seven dinners if I wish. This trip is about choice, after all.

That evening, after I crank open a can of tomato soup—the damn tide continued to rise because no one has found a way to control the moon yet—and remind myself there are six more nights, I make myself chai and watch the sunset from a deck chair. Such chairs are made infinitely more comfortable these days. Sook has exhausted himself for the moment and plunks down beside me. "Pace yourself," I tell him. "Pace yourself."

The west is at one moment pink and golden, the next blood red, swirled with ominous clouds. I scurry inside because the intensity of it makes me uncomfortable. Sook lopes in behind me and is promptly asleep in front of the stone hearth. I know he's asleep because he shudders and yips as he dreams of squirrels and steak bones. I pray his nocturnal visions are not nightmares. Like mine.

I examine the outside of the sleeping bag again, scrutinize the inside. The bag is so old, it is lined with images of Holly Hobbie. I don't remember it being mine, but her popularity fits my generation. I search the smiley doll faces for surprises, living or not, find none. Perhaps there is life between the layers of bulky stuffing I can't see, but I climb in and hope for the best. It's a teeny bit damp but oddly comforting and smells of wild tea roses and popcorn. I decide it must be my imagination.

In the morning, I awake with a start to the cawing of crows and gulls. Nature's alarm clock. We spend the day puttering about the cottage, the beach. I have forgotten pepper and we set out on the rusty ten-speed I find in the tool shed. I am huffing and puffing at the top of the drive, disgusted with myself. The next bit is downhill, but it is ludicrous to feel relief. The incline will be waiting for my return.

I reassess and bump back down the drive, misread the treachery of a root and end up sailing over the handlebars into the brambles. This circus act delights Sook, who dances around me barking gleefully before tearing off after something my ungraceful landing has disturbed.

"Thanks, bud," I call after him, tears filling my eyes. Both palms are scraped raw and I feel a warm trickle down my cheek. Still, nothing too serious. Bounce back, I instruct before I can stop myself.

Bounce back.

There were great discussions—I both overheard and participated in them—about the appropriate amount of time one should take to bounce back after a miscarriage. Actually, that was the second most popular topic. The first was the repetitive barrage of well-wishers who said, "It was obviously for the best."

Obviously.

What else could it possibly be for?

I extract my shaking body from the branches and thorns, leave the wretched, skinny-tired bike where it is and limp back to the cabin. Fortunately, though the Grishams have stripped the cupboards and beds of any comforts and personality, they have left a healthy supply of bandages in the medicine chest. There are about fourteen different kinds and sizes, several suitable for my outward wounds. None are big enough to encase my whole body.

When I have calmed myself, we drive into the townsite, and out of a weird loyalty, I buy pepper at the original General Store, for practically the same price as oysters on the mainland. The same man is behind the counter, there's no mistaking his scowl, but he is a third of his former self in size and formidable demeanor. Maybe it's just me. I don't introduce myself as Jenny Ferguson, daughter of Ted and Sheena. I relish my anonymity.

At the craft store, I buy a set of ceramic eggcups, glazed in a matte taupe and black, to match the rest of my kitchen accessories. They are as cool and smooth to the touch as an egg itself. Sook gets two organic dog biscuits from the overgrown hippie proprietor and half a sandwich he finds while I'm reading the community bulletin board.

I consider jotting down the number of the island shaman, who advertises physical, sexual and spiritual healing on neon pink paper, but resist. I have to find a way to heal myself. This is my quest.

Bounce back.

When we return, the tide is still not conducive to oyster gathering: ebbing, is the term I remember. In the middle of a change of cycle. The twenty-eighth day, so to speak.

I go to bed too early and lie tossing and turning. Eventually, I give up and immerse myself in a pocket novel, its pages yellowed, found on the bottom shelf of the bookcase. There are two Trixie Beldons and three of the Little House set inscribed within as mine. I wonder if they'll notice if I steal them back.

By four, I crawl back into bed. Sook is disgusted with me when I blindly scoop out a bowl of food for him at six-thirty and stomp back to my bunk. But his bladder is better than mine, and it is me who must journey to the loo at eight.

In the outhouse, hanging on a nail, is an actual Sears and Roebuck catalogue. A laminated sign in felt-pen above it reads, "Just joking, please feel free to use TP" I unhook it, angle it out the open door to get sufficient light by which to read. Someone has not heeded the TP suggestion, or was desperate, because the catalogue starts on page thirty-two.

The last of the baby stuff.

I make myself look at it, tell myself it's good for me. Bassinets are a mere fifteen dollars. A giant teddy bear, only nine. These things are ten times the price now.

I debate if this torture is what's necessary to heal.

Finally, I can't stand it and I rip out the remaining four pages of baby goods, lift my right butt cheek and drop them down the irrevocable hole. I am immediately overcome with guilt at the irreverent and selfish impulse.

After a comfort food lunch of canned ravioli and two apples plucked from the trees just over the property line, I concede I need to shake myself out of my funk. With determination, I haul the bicycle out of the bushes but am pleased the front tire wobbles too dangerously. So we jump in the car and go cruising like teenagers. I let Sook sit in the front seat and we ride with our heads out the windows, feeling decadent to ride without seat belts. The fastest I go is forty. The fastest it's possible to go on the bumpy side roads, is forty.

We circle around the island, the AM station of schmaltzy hits of the '70s blaring. But it's a small island, only nine kilometres end to end, and we soon run out of dead-end roads to back out of.

It's on the way back that it happens.

We're cruising along the paved, main drag, not far from my first turn-off. There's a van coming from the opposite direction. There is a doe grazing on my side of the road, and I tap the brake. You never know what deer will do.

The van is barreling along, as best I can tell. I flash my lights to signal it to slow down.

We vehicles are 100 metres apart, the doe is still at the side of the road, when the tiniest of fawns leaps out from the opposite side.

There's a squeal and a thud. Or vice versa. I slam on the brakes too, put on my four-way flashers yet know I can't get out of the car. I look at the general picture, ensure my focus is fuzzy on the spasmodic fawn. The driver is out of the car, at the front bumper. Then he's back at the back door, yelling in German and shoving in kids that are squeezing out of the opening. They manage to wriggle past him and run to the front and then there's a cacophony of screams and screeches.

I can smell the blood and guts, tinny and heady.

Sook is going crazy, smelling that. He spins around in his seat, crosses over and stands on my thighs, scrambles into the back in case the view is better. I roll up the front windows before he gets the idea that he can slip through like some kind of moray eel.

The doe is frenetically prancing in a figure-eight pattern, still on her side of the road, torn between approaching her baby and getting close to the van and its gaggle of howling humans. When another car approaches, slows and stops adjacent to the van, she makes an anguished bawling sound and leaps into the woods.

I didn't know deer made sound, but it is eerily familiar. Perhaps all mothers are capable of the same sound.

The second driver gets out and he has the look of a local. Good, locals deal with these things all the time, I needn't leave my car after all. The guy pulls out a cell phone and assists the father in strong-arming the four or five kids back into the van.

There is no 911 emergency number for the doe.

I turn off my four-ways and put the car into gear, creep away. Am I a coward? I don't care.

This can't be healing.

I thud down the cabin driveway far too quickly, rake the undercarriage. I am sweating but as soon as I step out of the car, the breeze licks it off me. The tide is out. Far. I collect half a dozen barnacled oysters and tell Sook how wonderful they will taste, steamed and liberally sprinkled with garlic and pepper.

At six, I lay my Pacific jewels in a plastic pan of water, now grateful for the Grishams' modern addition of a microwave. I hit the setting for popcorn and wait, mesmerized by the rotating plate. Like daisies opening under the morning sun, they open, hissing and spitting in protest of this unexpected end to their life.

I doctor them up and sit on the stoop, the pan balanced on my lap. Two days in the waiting. Not so long, really, to wait.

I don't know if the damn things are good or bad, for I taste nothing. I only feel the silky, meaty flesh between my teeth. I eat mechanically, all six, before being overcome with nausea and throwing up beside the blackberry bushes to the east.

I stumble into bed. The gripping cramps are familiar, less painful than before because I know this time nothing but my own gut is suffering. The Holly Hobbie sleeping bag is too short and I curl up in a ball so it covers me. Sook nuzzles the flaps every so often even though I keep telling him to go away.

Is this healing?

At three in the morning, I awake to rain. The cramps are gone. I pee just outside the door and so does Sook. He joins me on the narrow bunk and it's awkward, but comforting.

It's still pouring at nine-thirty and I am glad for the excuse to stay inside and mope. Sook will not leave my side, trotting after me on my jaunts for water, the outhouse and wood for the fire.

I eat sugary porridge and drink hot milk. When the pocketbook novel is finished, I explore the rolling drawers under the bunks.

There are a few starched tea towels, a pair of swim trunks, two wool sweaters. I reach for the third drawer and have a flash to the past.

"No. No, it wouldn't still be there." Sook cocks his head and waits.

I wrestle the drawer out and off its castors. There, outside the back, by threads of ancient, crispy Scotch tape, is a letter I wrote to myself at fifteen and ferreted away to be read the next summer. But there was no next summer; the sale of the cottage took place that January. With only vague recollections of its contents, I unfold the faded page and brace myself for adolescent angst.

> *Dear Me,*
>
> *Well, you survived the summer without Bobby Thiesson after all. Who was that mere child who threw the hissy fit back in June when the whole summer without him loomed before her? Not me!!!!!!!!!*
>
> *Bobby will still be zitty and gangly, whereas I, I have read The Thornbirds, made a hundred and eight bucks picking beans for the farm lady that I will spend on the coolest of cool back-to-school clothes and oh, yeah! I finally, finally got my period. Thank God, I was beginning to feel like a freak of nature. I mean, I'm going to get in the Guinness book of world records someday, but not for being the only woman to never get It. (Remember, ya dope, at the beginning of the summer when you told Lise you wanted Bobby T. to be the father of your children? GROSS ME OUT !!!!!) Cheryl and Dan (a.k.a. mother and father) have promised to seriously consider letting me move into the basement guest room when we get home, so I am desperately trying to not piss them off.*

*Anyhoooo, I gotta go catch the last rays. I'll think
of a good hiding place for this letter while I'm at it.
Be strong and brave, you womanly beauty, you!
(Gawd, I'm such a dork! I'll think this is soooooo
childish when I read it next year. Oh, well, it'll be a
new tradition, writing myself each summer. The only
one I'll tell is my own daughter, some day.) Chow,
Bella!*

I blow away a tear that plops onto the paper. Another. Then I am sobbing and have to put the letter aside for fear of soaking it.

There will be no daughter. Ever. No son.

Things were too messy, this fourth time.

I curl up on the nearest bunk and cry, bleat and bawl for what seems like hours. I cry, the millionth time, for the pained look on Paul's face, my mother's, for every person who laid a hand on my shoulder and said, "It's obviously for the best."

I cry for the seven months that were hers.

Ours.

I cry for myself. A first.

The doctor said it would help me to heal if I chose a name. I didn't believe him.

But I know who she was—is—from the moment of conception to the moment they laid a warm but lifeless body on my stomach to say good-bye.

"Kathryn," I say softly. "Oh, Kathryn."

It is dusk when I finally rise up, flick on lights and lamps until the cottage is as bright as possible. I check my face in the mirror on the medicine cabinet. My skin is splotchy, my eyes puffy. But they have lost the hard glitter they had for four months, my first defense against further hurt.

Sometime in the middle of the night, it comes to me how I will spend the next day. I hold on to the idea, part dream, part real and awake with determination.

I will hike around the island.

It will be a pilgrimage of sorts. I know the island measures eighteen kilometres in circumference. I have no idea if this feat is possible to complete in one day or not, given the uncertain terrain, but I decide to be fearless and try.

Sook watches me pack granola bars, cheese sandwiches, fruit and two bottles of water into the daypack.

"I don't think so, bud. It's too far for you."

He looks at me as if to say, "Who actually travels (albeit in frenzied or laconic circles) twice that far every day already?"

So we head off. The tide is up, but on its way out.

It is nine-thirty.

We hike along. I remind Sook to pace himself, but he doesn't listen. I sing to myself. I sing to Kathryn. I sing to the brilliant blue sky.

We stop for lunch by a brook that spills onto the beach. Sook laps thirstily and I guzzle from my second bottle. I have no concept of how far I've come, but I know I have passed the point of turning back, and this is all I need to know in order to carry on.

We pass people digging clams, collecting shells, strolling along—doing what normal vacationers do. I want to shout, "I am walking the island, the full circle," but I refrain.

This is a private healing.

It is just after four when I round the last bend and see the old cottage, nestled on the bank like the sac of spider eggs. Moments before, I was ready to collapse, now I am energized and injected with a serenity I have never before felt.

"Come on, Sook," I sing out, renewing my pace. He senses my energy and frolics beside me. I walk the last half-kilometre with a surreal lightness in my legs, and in my soul.

At the cottage, I draw water from the well for both of us, and know at last, gratefully, that healing has begun.

THE OFF GIRL

People have called me "off" as long as I can remember.

"That one," they used to say in the Cooper's grocery store, or in the Simpson Sears, "she's off." They'd look at me and click their tongues, kinda shake their heads sorrowfully, or the worst, pull their kids in close. My mom'd be great when that happened, march me past them, spieling Shakespeare or some Alfred Einstein stuff, who she said were the world's smartest men (Shakespeare for the humanities, Einstein for the sciences). I can't say I understood what she said, but I'd nod and try to look keen. I could never see their faces, the people's faces, because we'd be past them by that time and my mom said not to turn around because that would be lowering myself to their level. She told me they look all embarrassed. Once I stole a glance back and decided they looked awed. I said, "The awful are awe-filled," and she bought me a malted in the Woodward's when we went to their bargain centre.

Course, it's a different crowd now and something called political correctness is all the rage, so people are more careful. I'm no politician, but sometimes I still hear them say, "She touched." But now that there's the show, *Touched by an Angel*, I don't mind that one so much.

She's a retard. I don't like that one, then or now. Specially when adults say it to their kids.

My mom explained I'm off because I had a fever when I was six. Before that, I was in the morning Kindergarten, in the basement of the United Church and smart as a whippet. She said. After the fever—107 degrees for days on end—that's when I went off. Now the left side of me is all squashy and the right side's as rigid as a board. The brain bits go back and forth.

I should write a few words about my pop, I guess. I only can write a few words, because I don't really remember him from being a kid. He left us and went with a secretary from his company, the Sage Machinery Company, when I was eight. I asked my mom every so often if he left cause I went off and she says, "No, he was always off, in his own way." So, that's all I can say about him for now, except he sends sweaters for me at Christmas and cassette tapes on my birthday and two hundred dollars all the other months.

I think I am off, I really do, but not so far off. My mom said that's perfect, that a person only gets in trouble when they think they're totally on. I went to the special school across the Skookum River for a while, to learn my reading and writing and domestic science (this is not the same kind of science Alfred E. learned), but after that was accomplished, my mom hauled me on out of there because some of the kids peed themselves, or cut themselves whenever they had a sharp thing. One kid burned his parents in their beds and that was enough for my mom.

I would never do that, burn my mom. I would do anything for Mom. Would have.

I worked Tuesdays and Thursdays, giving out shoes at the bowling alley and yard stuff for Mrs. Milosovech down my street, River Road Saturday mornings. She was about 101 years old and there was always something in her yard that needed sweeping, moving, digging, weeding or hosing down. I was slow, but careful. That was my cash money that I could spend any way I wanted. Usually, I'd buy nail polish, McDonald's and secret tampons. The tampons were because my mom didn't think it was right that an unmarried girl wear anything but the pad, but I seen the commercials and I'm only off, not stupid. No one's going to marry an off girl anyway.

The bowling alley money came in a cheque and got put in the Toronto Dominion Bank on Victoria Street, for safekeeping.

I don't remember when all this healing business started. I'm thirty-seven now, and it was ages and ages ago. I guess I was twenty-one or so. And we didn't know, right away, all of what I could do.

The first time was when the Jehovah's Witnesses came to the door. My mom always said, "No thank you, we already have a faith in this house, but thank you." Super polite like that. Anyway, this time was in November and early storming like crazy. They always go in twos, the JWs, but this time it was three because the lady had a toddler all bundled up.

The toddler was spewing and fussing, I could hear and see from the living room window. The lady was trying to get my mom to take a pamphlet and the man, her partner, was all shivery from the cold because he only had a suit jacket on. Right away, I thought he was nutso. People call me off, but I always dress proper for the Sage weather, to be sure.

Anyway, my mom felt sorry for them and said they should step inside and collect themselves. I remember thinking that it was like she'd become the converter, getting them to promise to call it a day.

They said they were parked all the way down the end of River Street, by the Gingerbread House with the half a paddle-wheeler in the front yard, so she gave the man one of my dad's jackets that'd hung in the closet for thirteen years. Then she asked if they would like some tea. They said, well, maybe, a quick cup. I don't know, to this day, whether they were desperate for tea or a conversion, but that's how it went.

If they saw that I was off, they didn't say anything. Sometimes religious people are nicer to me, sometimes not. The toddler was really squawking away and the lady looked all agitated, perched on the edge of our teal brocade couch as she was, jiggling and cooing to the baby like no tomorrow. I said, "Can I hold it?" thinking they'd say something foolish because everyone else does when I ask them in the Cooper's grocery or the Simpson Sears if I can hold their little one. But she said, "Sure, it's a he and his name is Ruben. Ma'am, perhaps I could use your facilities in the meantime?" Of course my mom motioned to our bathroom and the lady passed him to me. I was in the blue velvet chair.

The JW lady bustled off and I just held the little one, who was thrashing and squawking, and I was looking at its tiny nose and ears and fingers and stuff. I remember thinking, it's not right that something so small should have to do that much squawking and I leaned over and kissed its forehead.

Well, right then, it stopped wriggling and squawking and started cooing and gurgling. By the time his mommy came back from the bathroom, Ruben was laughing and nearly kicking off his tiny rubber boots in joy.

"What happened here?" said the lady to the man, pointing at Ruben.

The man shrugged and held up his hands. "I don't know, Beth Anne. One minute he was red-faced and bawling, then next he was acting like he just found out he's one of the 144,000 going to heaven. It just happened."

So Beth Anne took him from me, felt his forehead and poked around him. "Well, I'll be. His colour's normal and he's happier than a clam in salt water. Praise Jehovah," she breathed.

"Praise Jehovah," I repeated and my mom gently reminded me that is not what I call my God.

"Well, praise be to someone," I said, and leaned back in the blue velvet chair.

They left without their tea, even though my mom had even put out Peek Frean cookies. My mom said the Witnesses have a lot of funny ways, so I figured a biblical aversion to Peek Freans was one of them.

That was really the first time, though we didn't pay much attention to my part in it.

The second time was on the street, nearer to Christmas. I remember it was a Saturday because I'd shoveled Mrs. Milosovech's driveway that morning. We were out buying a new string of green and red lights for the garage and also, I was looking to secretly price out a new, real fancy nightie for my mom.

Anyway, we was trudging along the main downtown street. I don't know why we hadn't just gone to the Kmart near our house—somebody must've had a sale on downtown. We came across this real bedraggled woman and her daughter. The woman had her hand out for spare change and the little girl, maybe four or five, was huddled into her mom to keep warm, hacking and spewing all the while into her mom's belly.

I don't know why I did, but I stopped and knelt down beside the little one and studied her face real hard. She studied me back, but she was lucky she didn't have to look at a green snotty nose, like I did. I don't know why I did, but I leaned in and kissed her forehead.

She stopped wheezing and coughing and her nose stopped running green snot, just like that. I remember thinking that was one less person spreading flu germs. Then I reached in my pocket and pulled out my seventeen dollars for my mom's real fancy nightie and gave it to the street mom.

She about fell over on both counts, that her daughter'd stopped convulsing with cough and that I'd given her seventeen dollars.

My mom and I walked off, arm in arm, humming "Silent Night" together in harmony, because we were both real good that way.

"That was your Christmas present money," I advised her when we'd done the song and was well away from the street mom.

She squeezed my arm in hers and said, "That's okay. You just gave me my present, right there on Victoria Street." I decided right then and there to ask Mrs. Milosovech for an advance payment of snow shoveling, so I could at least buy my mom a box of Laura Secord's.

After that, somehow word kind of got out that kids with the flu, I kissed and healed. I think it was the woman from the church who started spreading it. I'd just up and kissed her baby in the middle of its christening service, frankly because it was wailing away and agitating me. She told me after, that that baby'd been colicky for its entire six months, responding to nothing short of exhaustion. The mother woman looked exhausted herself. Anyway, I think it was her who told everybody, because next thing you know, there's another woman and her husband on our doorstep with a thrashing, feverish little guy.

I took the boy in my arms, he was big, maybe eight or nine years old, but this was March and I was strong from a winter of snow shoveling. His eyes met mine, kinda pleading like the street girl, and I up and kissed his forehead too.

He ran down the driveway of his own accord and that's when it really started.

"You're blessed," said my mom.

"Blessed?" I said, disbelieving. "They're coming all the time now, interrupting our dinner and our television programmes. That's not blessed, that'd be the opposite of blessed. What's the opposite of blessed, Mom?"

"You're blessed," she repeated. "Thank God and don't abuse your gift."

Things were busy, kids coming fast and furious that spring and summer. I think it was August, because I'd just come back from picking blackberries around the river bend, when Bobby Samuels rang the front bell.

He stood there with a baby in his arms, but the baby weren't hollering like all the others. His baby was real still and a bluey-grey colour, like a November sky.

"Bobby Samuels," I said, looking from him, to the bluey-grey baby, to the scrawny little thing behind him, a girl maybe seventeen years old.

"You gotta help us," said Bobby Samuels. "I heard you have a magic touch with sick babies. This is Josh and he's got emphysema, real bad." He didn't introduce the scrawny girl behind him. "I tooked him from the hospital, and brought him to you. To heal."

Even my grammar's better than Bobby Samuel's, to be sure.

"Bobby Samuels," I said, "you remember a few years back? You recall when we two first met?"

Now Bobby turned red, looked like he was the one with the fever. "Yes. But we were both young then. I was only fooling."

It'd happened when I was 'bout fifteen. Bobby Samuels sidled up to me during a church picnic, even though he was Catholic and discouraged from participating in our Protestant picnic.

"Off Girl. Leanne. C'mere," he'd said.

He tried to feel me up, my boobies, right there behind the big cement buildings of bathrooms. I told him to bug off.

With a curse about wasting good liquor on a retard, he gave me some drink from his plastic thermos and told me dirty stories about humping while the contents of the thermos took effect.

After about fifteen minutes, he looked at me and said, "Okay now?"

I did nod. I can't say Bobby Samuels was taking advantage the second time but when he took a handful of boobie under my Sean Cassidy T-shirt I didn't like it, so I shoved him backwards and threw up on his Adidas runners.

That's my history with Bobby Samuels and then there he is six years later, shoving the sickly result of more boobie grabbing my way.

"Who are you?" I asked the girl, who was still all hunched up behind him, shuffling her feet back and forth, hands jammed in her pockets.

"Krista," she said, miserably. "That's our Baby Josh. Can you help him?"

"You teach your Baby Josh more manners than his father

has," I instructed and took the limp little thing from Bobby Samuels' arms. I found his eyes with mine, kissed his bluey-grey forehead and watched him turn a nice pinky-peach shade, right before my eyes.

"Jesus!" whispered Bobby Samuels, taking back the helpless little mite. "Jesus!"

"Yes, and don't you forget it," I harped before slamming the door, thinking again of the way he'd tricked me. Not the little one's fault though, nor the scrawny girl's, which's why I done what I done.

Then the reporters started chasing me because the word really got out. I remember one day, picking Mrs. Milosovech's apples, so say, October, and one reporter wouldn't leave me alone.

"They're calling you The Off Healer, Leanne. What do you have to say about that?"

I was halfway up a tree, on a rickety ladder that weighed a ton and was no fun to drag from the shed to the apple trees. "I'm no healer," I said. "I'm just an off girl that's blessed."

"ABC News, from America, is coming up to talk with you, Leanne. What do you think of that?"

I could see Mrs. Milosovech looking at us from her front bay window, and not looking happy at my productivity level for her two dollars per hour. "Mister," I said, real polite, because I remember my mom always says, rudeness will not be tolerated. "Mister, I got to pick Mrs. Milosovech's apples right now. That's my paying job. Healing the kids is my blessed job, but it doesn't put anything in my pocket. So, what I'm politely trying to say, Mister Vancouver City TV Man, is you bug off."

"But Leanne ..."

I threw an apple at him, hard as I could. In a different kind of miracle altogether, it hit him on the breastbone and he actually kinda buckled over.

"Ouch! You nut-case! Whaddya do that for?"

Anyway, it got him and his Acadian off Mrs. Milosovech's driveway and I could pick in peace again.

Now, I'd had precious few fights with my mom over the years. If we did squabble, it was over silly stuff, like desserts and chores. I'm off and everything, but when we fought about charging people for my services, I knew it was bigger than anything before.

"Just five dollars," I said, following her into the basement, where she was about to iron. "Five dollars a healing isn't much. For a healed baby." I had visions of a big fur hat and muff, like the Russian ladies wear and new carpeting for the living room, because my mom said Pop picked out the old stuff when he was drunk.

"You were not blessed to charge money like the Bill Lynch Circus," she said, plugging in the iron and snapping out the first tea towel. "Does your heart tell you that's why you were blessed?"

I thought about this. "No. Not my heart, but my Toronto Dominion bank account and my empty pockets do."

"Leanne, you are an adult. You are but a bit off, and perfectly capable of making your own life decisions. You do what feels right, five dollars, five hundred dollars. I'm doing the ironing and you have to take the cans to the road."

I did take the cans to the road, because it was Tuesday, and that's what I did Tuesday.

Five hundred dollars a healing? Whew. I started calculating and the numbers got so many zeros, I had to stop.

The next people came at six o'clock in the morning.

"Five hundred dollars," I said, only glancing at the shaky tot, covered in scabs and pus and barely able to stand on his own.

"Five hundred?" said the father. "We came all the way from Winnipeg. We heard about you from Knowlton Nash. He said you were free, did your healing from the goodness of your heart."

I was sucking on a piece of toast, all buttery the way I like it. "Five hundred's the new price. I can't be giving away my powers and expect to live, can I?"

The Winnipeg mother and father looked at each other. "Twenty-four," she offered, digging through her vinyl purse. "How about twenty-four dollars and thirty cents."

I'd sat down with the calculator the night before and all I could see was denominations of five hundred.

"Nope. Blessings from the Off Girl cost five hundred smackeroos." I shut the door in time to hear my second round of toast pop up.

"Who was that?" asked my mom, stepping into the kitchen as I smeared my third toast with chunky peanut butter. "Folks looking for help?"

I took three big bites before I answered. "Nope. Reporters. I told them bye-bye, Miss Canadian Pie."

I remember she looked at me odd, like I was a big old Cooper's grocery bag of lies, but she only poured tea and took it silently back to bed. I left most of the fourth piece of toast. Peanut butter can get stuck in your throat like that, make you feel like you can't swallow.

But the Winnipeg people came back. That night. Nine o'clock.

"Here," said the man and thrust a big stack of bills at me. "We sold the car, so we can pay you. Please, Healer-Girl, help my son."

I was half into a program, but pleased to see the five hundred dollars, so I pulled the boy close, found his eyes, then kissed his forehead. The lesions just kinda sucked back in his skin, the yellow colour turned pinky-peach. I felt good, I admit that. I'd not done lesions before.

"Thank you, thank you," gushed the Winnipeg couple again. "We'll never forget you."

"It was worth selling the car," said the woman. "I told you it would be."

I squinted out the drive. Yes, the Escort from the morning visit was nowhere in sight. "You sold your car?"

"A car's worth a child, there's no question," said the father.

I looked at the wad of bills in my hand, and back down the empty drive. "Okay, you proved yourselves," I grumbled. I gave him back his money, shut the door fast and stomped downstairs.

My mom was just scuttling back to her TV chair after listening from the bottom of the stairs. "You did the right thing," she confirmed.

I *grrr*d like a lion, but I guess I felt good.

Adults and old people were brought to me too, but I couldn't do nothing for them. Sometimes the whole people accompanying the sick people got very angry and my mom would have to send them on their way because I'd just keep trying and trying for hours, 'til I almost fainted. Sometimes the sick people would be well enough to yell at me, beg for more kisses. I'd kiss and I'd kiss, but their eyes just never met mine in the same way as a child's. I think that was the difference. The ones who came with silly old birthmarks and yellowed teeth from smoking, well, they were easy to turn away.

They came from all over the rich world. Japan babies, Arabian babies, European little ones as well. They arrived at all hours, begging their children be healed by the Off Girl. Sometimes they waited 'til morning, camped out in the garage, sometimes they pounded on the door until one of us answered it. Half asleep, I'd find its eyes, concentrate, kiss and stumble back to bed. I had to quit the bowling alley and Mrs. Milosovech's because chances were, I'd have been up all night and would dole out the wrong-sized shoe, or fall asleep leaning against the rake.

What changed was, my mom got sick. It was right after eight Hindu women sat in their saris in the garage, waiting for the healing of the first son. I healed a daughter too, while I was at it, but they weren't as excited about that. Anyway, if that first JW baby came in late November, and the Winnipeg couple came the following November, it must have been in the spring that my mom caught her cold.

"Mom, go back to bed," I said, peering between the curtains. "There's only a few this morning."

So she took her tea and went. I remember it felt very strange, because at twenty-two, I'd never given the instructions in the house.

A few days later, she was still feeling bad. A few weeks later, in fact. The doctor had no answers, neither had I, but then, I'd already proven adults were out of my league.

The doctor said, "Rest up," when it was flu-like. He gave her stomach pills when the cramping got too bad. He took her into the hospital for tests when she couldn't eat for five days. All the while, the mothers and fathers filled the driveway and I looked and concentrated and kissed, between taxi rides to the hospital.

Finally, the doctor pronounced cancer and what's worse, said my mom was going fast. He said she must've been in pain long before she let on.

I sat and sat at her hospital bed, looking and concentrating and kissing, but it didn't do any good.

My mom.

A man who said he was my pop from Toronto came one day and asked, "Is it true?"

"Yup," I said. "She's dying fast."

"No," he said, "I mean, is the gobblygook true about you being a healer?"

I looked at him, at my mom, at the floor and I lied for the first time in my life. "No. I'm just an Off Girl, no more, no less. You know that. It's why you left."

He shunted around the square little hospital room like a box-car. "I didn't know what to do."

I nodded. "That's okay. My mom did."

After my pop left, I tried one more time to save my mom. I tried until I fell off the stool and smacked my head on the tiled floor. When I came to, I went to the children's ward, to see if I could do any good there, but I couldn't.

All the blessedness was out of me, quick as it came.

My mom died at home, a few months later. I got my job back

at the bowling alley, only it's Mondays and Wednesdays now. Mrs. Milosovech sold her house and moved to Florida and the young couple with the baby girl who bought her house? They don't need any yard help. A good friend from church sold our house and now I live with a couple of other Offs in a sprawling white house, the other side of town.

Every so often, I think I see a desperate mother or father arrive on our doorstep with a writhing child in their arms, looking for The Off Girl. I've drilled the others to deny my existence, as I do myself. Besides, it's all pretty fuzzy in my memory now anyway.

I understand that it was just a temporary thing, to make me feel off-special, not off-off.

SMALL SPACES

Sue climbed out of the car after maneuvering down the long driveway from the gravel road and surveyed the landscape before her. This was definitely the place Tom had described. She clipped back her sleek pageboy and sucked in fresh, cool air.

There was the outhouse to the left, the split tree ahead, the clearing with the view of the lake and Mount Baker keeping watch from dead centre. And the weather-beaten sign proclaiming NO HUNTING in faded orange neon paint. There was the woodpile, apparently undisturbed. Tom said there'd be nothing more here, in the way of people or conveniences.

Primitive.

Wait. It wasn't the primitiveness that was off-putting. It was the openness. The broad sky, the water that dropped off into the horizon.

Too much breathing space.

Not the climate-controlled, sealed office building,

She pursed her lips and considered getting back in the car and returning to the city. Desperation and some exhaustion held her feet in place. Better to be alone than scavenged by packs of colleagues, perhaps the police by now.

Sue unpacked the borrowed—the procured? the seconded?—Topaz. A fucking sanctimonious colleague had slashed the tires of her Camaro.

She started with the tent.

"Goddamnit!" she exclaimed when the tent listed to the left, then collapsed. For the fourth time. Gone were her romantic, nostalgic or plain old protective feelings about cocooning in a tent.

Sue turned her back on the heap, as if to punish it, and concentrated on setting the fire. Fortunately, Tom had supplied a bottle of lighter gel and the fire responded to her urban hand gleefully. Next, Sue drew out a bottle of wine from the cooler, ignoring the flaccid tent behind her.

She searched the cooler, the knapsack, the tote and tent bag for a corkscrew.

"Goddamn middle of nowhere," she swore aloud again, only briefly considering if there was a soul within earshot. "Why didn't I run to the nearest Sheraton?" She gouged at the cork with a manicured nail.

Run?

Sue Anne Crest had never started something and not finished it 110 per cent in her life.

Yessir! Boots polished, Sir. Kit ironed, Sir. Cock sucked, Sir.

The sunlight was waning and she turned again to the tent. It was an easy matter, was it not, of fitting poles and holes together? Surely easy for someone who masterminded the wooing of BarMac Industries into the folds of CalTech Enterprises.

Among other, now infamous feats.

The bushes rustled and Sue jerked her head up.

Relax, Little Soldier.

Moments later, a rotund rabbit bounded across the opening to the lake.

The lake. A serene, glinting silver-blue in the last rays of sun. But frigid, Sue knew. Cold enough to take a swimmer into the depths of hypothermia in less than ten minutes, Tom had advised. She shuddered, stoked the fire, lit the gas lamp and faced the tent again. She manipulated it to stay up this time, though it still listed terribly to one side, like an entire pole might be missing.

The next rustle in the bushes was definitely not a rabbit. She waited apprehensively for the glow of deer eyes. Tom had assured her there were no bears.

He'd sworn it, the ass.

It wasn't a deer or a bear. It carried a flashlight. And gun. And uniform.

You sleep in those clothes, Little Soldier?

"Evening, ma'am."

Sue froze. My God, she thought, they haven't progressed far enough with the investigation to warrant sending someone into the bush already, have they? Tom was supposed to buy her time. If they wanted to start tracking her, he was supposed to guarantee them she'd be back Sunday night, to make a full statement.

"Officer."

"Out here alone, ma'am?" He visually took in her camp, pausing on the lopsided tent and wine bottle.

"Well, I'd been prepared to tell anyone else my husband was just out gathering firewood, but since it's the Mounties inquiring, I'll agree that yes, I'm alone." She stood straighter.

Shoulders back. Chest out.

"It's good that I know. You're aware there're several detention centres in the vicinity?"

She tried to read his face in the false propane light. "Yes. Miles back. Closer to Chilliwack."

"Yeah, but the runaway juvies hitch out, or jump on the back of a pick up, steal a three-wheeler from a cabin until it runs out of gas. They can travel."

"Your point, officer?" She knew that her left eyebrow was slightly arched, that her mouth was arranged in a smug Mona Lisa smile. It withered staff and family alike.

He looked confused that she would rush him and she was secretly pleased.

Good, it was a welcome end to the day, to know she could still disconcert.

"My point, ma'am, is that two of the detainees in one of the medium security youth centres took off earlier this afternoon. One was caught because he fell and broke his wrist while crossing the Vedder River. The other one's still out."

"And I should be fearful?"

He shrugged thick shoulders within his straining shirt. "Nah, he's just a punk kid. In for B&ES. It's my guess he's back in the city by now, chugging beer with his buddies. Just my duty to inform you." He scanned her site again. "You're sure you wanna stay here, by yourself? It's none of my business, but ..."

She cut him off. "You're right. Not to be rude, but I am a grown woman and if I want to spend a few days with nature, that's my prerogative."

The officer snorted. "Sure is, 'til I gotta come pick up the pieces." He pulled out his notebook and pen from his breast pocket. "I'll just get your particulars before heading off. Name and address?"

"Sue Crest, like the toothpaste. 1288 Alberni Street, Vancouver." Let him find the suite number. She told him the phone number and her date of birth without being asked. "And the particulars on this escapee? Shouldn't I know what to look out for, just in case?"

"By all means. His name's Jackson Philbin, he's seventeen with long, dirty blond hair and fifty-seven kilos, soaking wet, stretched out over 175 centimetres." She started to convert in her head but he added, "Ah, an old-school girl, like myself. Five-nine or so and 120 punds. He left in the requisite sneakers, jeans and gray detention centre sweatshirt."

"Okay then, thanks for the heads up."

"Listen, Ms. Crest, you really want to stay here? There's a

decent motel just down the way, I could get you a good rate. The owner's a fishing friend."

"Thank you, but we're bordering on a very trite movie of the week here."

He shook his head, exasperated, and lumbered back down the path, now in total darkness. In a few minutes, she heard a car start on the main road, followed by a sharp, single bleep of his siren to signal his retreat.

She sank onto the cooler and held her head in her hands.

Buck up, Little Soldier.

She sprang up at that thought and began searching the cooler for the pastrami sandwich grabbed on the run from the café in the lobby of the office tower. The inside of the cooler was musty and stained. She flicked out a dead beetle, long trapped.

Sue eyed the wine, cursed the lack of the correct tool, then cracked and guzzled a can of Diet Coke, poked at the fire and tossed Tom's sleeping bag and pad into the tent, resigned to its wonkiness.

Tom. A useful friend. A wannabe lover, yes, but a friend nonetheless. He'd do anything for her—and she knew it— including pack his car with his camping gear while she systematically deleted all damning correspondence from her home computer. He'd also stocked the cooler with ice, water, white bread and two Tupperware containers of some bachelor concoction she surmised was loaded with salt, fat and carbs. And apologized to the point of insipidness that he'd only progressed as far as constructing the outhouse on his lakefront acre. He had, however, assured her there was plenty of chopped wood under a tarp, provided it hadn't been stolen. For his efforts, she'd kissed him long on the lips and hinted at dinner when everything had settled down.

At eight-thirty, fed up with her own sober company, Sue extinguished the gas light. It burned loud and raw anyway and the moths were irritating, the way they beat around it, dying to get in, closer to the light. She left the fire burning high and crawled into the tent, cursing the spot she'd chosen, obviously on the hardest bit of land on the lot. Some cocoon.

Stupid city cow.

She cringed. Her father's voice. *You're a stupid cow, Darlene. Pumping out brats—girl brats—the only thing ya good for? Anything else, Darlene?*

For the first few years, she'd curl up under the coffee table, believing herself invisible. When she grew too big, it was the closet. Until four hours ago, it was deep within the protective walls of a large corporation.

"Oof. Shit."

Sue forced herself to peer out the crack in the zipper flap. In the flickering light, she saw the outline of a male sitting on the ground, fiddling with his shoe, perhaps tying his shoelace. He wore dark clothes and had cropped hair. The juvie escapee? No. Somebody's son who'd outgrown family camping.

He finished fiddling, stood up and glanced around. Yes, he looked like some kid who'd sneaked out of his parents' tent and was looking for trouble. Sue's heart jumped when he stared at the tent, seemingly right through the nylon and into her eyes. She bit her lip.

After an excruciating few moments, he reached for the wine bottle resting beside the cooler and examined its corked state. She watched him scan for an opener and almost laughed. She felt sorry for him that she wasn't sixteen and horny, ready to flatten the wobbly tent for good cause.

"There's no opener," she barked out in her deepest and gruffest voice. "Why do you think we haven't drunk it already?"

Even in the shadows, she could see the shocked look on his face that a voice had addressed him from the tent. He slammed the bottle down, then picked it back up and ran into the woods.

She considered which fear was worse: bolts of stabbing fear for her life that crescendoed and ebbed, or the protracted dread of the last few days as the long-murmured rumours rumbled into truths, and the truths into scandal.

She patted through the knapsack beside her until curling her fingers around a paring knife and restoked the fire, then lay back again.

Two hours later—midnight or so—she heard the bleep of a siren followed by the clomp of the officer's boots down the path.

"Excuse me, ma'am? It's Constable Smits. From earlier this evening? Can you come out? We need to talk."

She groaned and pulled herself upright. Now what? At least she didn't have to dress, having worn her clothes to bed for fear of being cold, of her own nakedness in all this space.

"Officer," she greeted, smoothed her hair and relit the propane lamp. The harsh light tinted their faces, making them blue and haggard looking.

"Listen, Miss, uh, Crest, that young fella is still around here."

"And I can help you set a trap, to catch him?" she sassed.

"On the contrary, I want you to pack up and get in your car and drive back to the city immediately."

"What? It's the middle of the night! I'm not going anywhere."

"Ma'am, I'm four hours past my shift, I'm tired and hungry, so forgive me, but there was an altercation in another cabin up the road and the boy's now running around with a hunting rifle. Wrap your stubborn city mind around that and amscray the hell out of here before you're the centre attraction of some stand-off. Or do you want to be front page news?" He shone his flashlight in her eyes and she winced.

"Okay, okay. That's all you had to say. Christ, I'm going."

"Fine. Thank you. I'll be back as soon as I can to make sure you're out safely. Got a lotta cabins and sites to check."

"Aren't they sending more men, people, more officers to help?"

"They're working on it. The area will be swarming with people shortly." He paused to zip up his patrol jacket. "Immediately, huh, Miss Crest?"

Sue frowned to cover the anxiousness she felt pulling at her face. "Of course."

You scared, Little Soldier? Huh? Answer me.

He retreated up the path and Sue stood for a few moments, drinking in the silence.

"Well, the Sheraton it is," she confirmed to the embers of the fire. She dragged the cooler over to the car and heaved it into the back seat. The tote bag, knapsack and stray bits she didn't want to take the time to repack followed.

She moved toward the tent, intending to pull the poles and pegs, wad up the fabric and leave, when the gas light spluttered out.

Shaking the tank, tightening the connections, batting the lamp and finally swearing at the whole contraption and Tom's negligence did nothing to bring it to life. Out of propane, was out of propane.

Sue chastised herself for not parking closer. She stumbled into the near-blackness, towards the glint of the car. She jabbed at the lock, and then the ignition. Headlights would suffice to light the area, and then she would be gone.

Again and again, the Topaz engine strained to turn over, never quite making it. Her anxiety mounted and she pumped the gas pedal and pressed herself against the steering wheel in surrender to the vehicle.

"Come on, car! This is just too ridiculous. Fuck-ing-start, already."

Sue climbed out of the car and stood in the clearing, making a slow spin while squinting into the darkness around her. Not a light. Not a single light, close or distant, to use as a marker to go to for help. She attempted to navigate the path twice and fell twice. The second time, she impaled her hand on a pointy rock or stick and felt the sticky pulse of blood when she drew her hands together.

"Think," she commanded herself. "Think. What's logical?" Sue leaned against the car and tried to still her raging mind. "Calm down. It doesn't mean he's coming here. There are tons of other cabins that would make more sense to go to. Calm down!"

Trapped in a wide-open space. A childhood nightmare.

She considered starting the fire again. The pile of wood and kindling was next to the pit. Would that serve as a beacon to young, desperate Jackson?

She would lock herself in the car, wait for Officer Smits, or his buddies, to arrive back.

For a brief moment, the clouds parted and the clearing was awash in moonlight. She could just make out the shortcut to the main road and more germane, the outhouse. She stepped inside and relieved herself. Its rough walls, where spiders and mice and birds made their home, were not comforting. She emerged and the moonlight had waned once again.

Passing the hood of the car, she saw him standing at the opposite rear bumper, as still as a deer.

Sue backed away from him with controlled panic. Like she would a forest predator.

"Don't move," he instructed. "You know I've got a gun." To emphasize this, he tapped something hard against the side of the car.

"A gun?" she echoed, trying to sound naive, to buy time.

"Don't play stupid, lady. I been here since the cop came and told you."

"Oh." She felt her knees wobble and reached out to steady herself on the hood of the car. "What do you want?"

"Gimme the keys."

"It doesn't work. You heard me try to get it going."

"Give me the damn keys, lady. You just flooded the engine. It'll be okay now. Toss 'em over, then back away ten steps."

Sue did as he demanded, taking giant steps so she was almost back at the fire pit. At least she had the darkness on her side. If the car didn't start and take him away, could she get deep enough into the bushes before he fired a wild shot?

Moonlight poured over the clearing once again and she

watched him move to the front of the car, the rifle clenched under his left armpit, his hand on the trigger. With his right hand, he opened the driver's side door and leaned in, carefully keeping the gun on her. The engine refused to start and Sue's heart sank.

"What kind of piece of shit is this?" he said, clambering out of the car and slamming the door. "Huh? What a piece of shit."

"It's borrowed shit," she answered dryly. "My own car, my Camaro, would have peeled you out of here." Would have got me out of here, she amended.

"Fuck," he spat out. "I gotta think."

"Well, think fast. The Mounties and their sharpshooters and their attack dogs will be back soon." She stole a glance over her shoulder, wondering again about making a run for it.

He caught her checking and told her to come closer again. "Where I can see you better."

Sue studied Jackson from six feet while he alternately glowered at her and scanned his surroundings when the moon allowed.

She saw now that his hair wasn't trimmed into any shape after all, but hacked off in great chunks.

"That must have been a sacrifice," she commented.

"Huh?"

"Your hair. I heard you had long hair."

He ran his right hand over his head and grunted. "Yeah, yeah. Shut up while I think."

"You didn't think before you started all of this, why start now?" Sue blurted out.

"F-off, lady, or I'll blow you to smithereens."

Her stomach lurched but she countered, "No you won't, not if you're smart because that will confirm to them you're still in the area and give them a direction to send the dogs."

He frowned at this logic and cursed under his breath.

"Besides, smithereens? My grandfather used that expression. Why don't you just get out of here? I'll sit tight until morning, and by that time, you'll have made it to the highway and hitched the hell away from here."

"Who're you? Director of Escapes?" he sneered.

You gotta smart mouth, Darlene. Maybe you'd do less yapping if you had no teeth.

"Look, I don't wanna hurt you. I mean, I'm not gonna rape you or nothing. I just wanna get back to the city."

"That makes two of us," she said. "Listen, can I sit down? My legs quiver like Jell-O every time I look at that gun."

Jackson motioned to a stump next to the fire. "Yeah, okay. Get that fire going again."

He studied Sue as she crumpled paper and made a teepee of the kindling, then in one motion, Jackson whipped off his red sweatshirt and tossed it to her. "Here."

She held it in her lap and considered turning down his offer. She had jackets in the car, but maybe a trip to the car would be more strategic at a later time. She pulled it over her head. "Thanks." Jackson was still wearing the grey, prison-issued sweater.

She placed a few bigger pieces across the top of the pile and dripped goopy lighter fluid over the lot.

Too bad it wasn't aerosol, she thought, I'd spray it in his eyes.

The fire was blazing in moments.

"Now tie your shoes together."

"What?"

"You heard me. Tie your shoes together. The laces. I don't need you running off when I ain't finished with you."

"I'm not going anywhere," she assured him, but he thrust the gun toward her and she bent over to tie the laces loosely.

"You should feel what metal cuffs feel like," he advised.

For the first time in hours, her thoughts returned to the trouble in the city from which she'd run. If all didn't go according to plan ... "I might be finding out," she mumbled.

"Whassat?"

After a few moments she said, "Hey, where's my wine?"

He grinned at her. Surprising. "That was funny when you called out there wasn't no corkscrew. Almost pissed my pants in shock, but it was funny." He reached down the side of his baggy cargo pants and withdrew the bottle from a deep side pocket. "You gotta knife? I can get this out with just a knife."

The paring knife lay in the bare tent. She considered whether he would pass out from drinking a bottle of wine, or become even more foolhardy and violent. If she could just get his guard down long enough to get the upper hand. Plus, wouldn't wine make him pee? He couldn't hold the gun and piss at the same time. Would he go in the bushes, or could she lock him in the outhouse? "There's one in the tent," she informed him. "Right by the opening."

He moved to the flap of the tent and patted around inside. "You set up a shitty tent," he commented.

"Indeed. That's what happens when you take a city girl out of the city."

He produced the small knife, squatted down and attempted to manage the bottle, knife and gun.

"Here's your country-girl lesson. Put the knife straight in, three-quarters."

She peeled off the cover and inserted the tip into the cork, pushing and rocking the blade down.

"You're weak," he snapped, irritated it took her so long.

Toughen up, Little Soldier.

"I'd gladly swap positions if you want," she retorted, irritated that a selfish, unbalanced, delinquent seventeen-year-old should be dictating anything to her.

"Ha ha."

When the blade was embedded, he told her to hold the bottle while he worked at extracting the stopper with his right hand.

The nose of the gun was inches away from her stomach. She secured the bottle between her thighs and both hands and gripped while he began to coax out the cork.

She thought about how she could hit him over the back of the head, but they were so close together, he would no doubt grab her before she had raised the bottle for a mighty swing. Worse, sudden action on her part could set off the gun.

It was too awkward with him pulling and her holding. "It's not working."

"Let's just pound it in," she said. She reached forward to the fire pit and chose one of the smaller rocks that formed its border. Jackson tensed like a cat and tightened his grip on the gun. She ignored him and began methodically hammering the blade. The cork descended until her last pound freed it. She wriggled out the knife, placed it on the stump and held up the open bottle victoriously. The cork bobbed around inside. "Cheers," she said, and took a swig before handing it to Jackson.

He took a long drink and handed it back, but she shook her head. "Fill your boots."

He shrugged and glugged again while she watched.

"Why're you out here, anyhow?" he asked between gulps. "Never heard of some lady out in the middle of nowhere by herself."

"One of those seemed-like-a-good-idea-at-the-time things. I'm sure you've had plenty of those yourself."

Jackson scoffed.

"Oh, come on. This break from the detention centre must have seemed a lot smarter when you were planning it with your buddy than it does now."

"It's still a good idea. I just have to wait until it's a little lighter, so I can get outta here."

"And some of the burglaries you pulled? The ones you got caught for? They seemed worth the risk at the time, right?"

"Whatever."

They sat in silence.

"What does your family have to say about this? Going to jail, I mean."

"Don't play social worker," he warned.

"Wouldn't dream of it. Just curious."

"You expecting to hear how my old lady's an alcoholic and

my dad beats the snot outta me? That I'm reacting to feelings of abandonment and shit like that? I've been in all the little beige shrink rooms there is."

Under different circumstances, his bravado would have been a challenge. Amusing even. "I have no idea why you choose to rip people off instead of getting a job at McDonald's and working for things like the rest of the world." She thought he made a childish face at her, but the moonlight distorted things so.

The moonlight. Stars in 3D. Depths she'd never imagined. Goddamn country skies.

Anyway, he *was* a child, so perhaps that entitled him to childish faces. She'd cut too close.

"My father is a professor of economics at UBC and my mother works for a hotshot lawyer. The old man only hit me once, when I told my mother to fuck off. My mother's a goddamn saint who might have wine with Christmas dinner." His shift in body position told her he was challenging her, daring her next assumption. "Just like yours."

She was shocked. Never assume. "You're not rebelling against a horrific childhood. What then?"

"Why? I don't know why. Ya think a hundred people haven't asked me that already every time they get me in one of those little beige rooms with the rah-rah posters? It just happens."

Little beige rooms. Sounded safe and claustrophobic at the same time.

"You 'just happen' to find yourself rifling through someone's house, taking the stuff they worked hard for, to pawn for a few bucks? Oh, please."

"Screw you. It ain't like that."

"Tell me, then. How is it?"

"I told you not to play shrink."

"Social worker. You said don't play social worker."

"Screw yourself."

"Nice variation." She sighed. "Listen, Jackson. We both know nothing's going to happen here. Once it's light out, you can bugger off if the cops don't come first and I'll go on with my life. Maybe we'll pass on Robson Street one day. I'll buy you a glass of wine. You're not going to shoot me, you said so yourself and I'm not going to try to escape, I'm too out of shape to pull anything off. Let's cut the bull and pretend we're normal people." Sue pressed the light on her watch. "It will be a long night. It's only two-fifteen."

"I gotta piss," he said. "Don't go anywhere." He rose, lurched, and she noticed the wine was three-quarters gone. Just don't get him riled up, she cautioned herself. Her comebacks and sarcasm always popped out at the wrong time.

Darlene, you're asking for it. Get those kids outta my face.

Sue turned her head as he stepped out of the light. She heard the stream hit the ground for what seemed a long time and finally, the zipping of his pants. He laid the gun beside him on the ground when he joined her around the fire.

"So why'd you come here?" he asked, grasping the bottle and tilting it straight up.

"Needed to get away."

"From what? The downtown condo and the hoity-toity cocktail parties at the office?"

"Now who's playing social worker slash shrink?"

"Funny. You're good with the comebacks, I'll give you that. What do you do?"

"Commercials. Advertising."

"That explains your smartassed mouth."

"Indeed," she agreed. "But my smartassed mouth has got me a lot further than yours."

"Touché," he agreed before finishing the wine and she was surprised he'd allowed her the comment. "You write any commercials I mighta seen?"

She thought about the bigger accounts she had worked on. "I guess. The cell phone company series with the little kids talking to each other? That was mine. And the Dairyworld billboards, with the mice and the pigs?"

"I seen the one with the pigs. Was okay."

"Magnanimous of you to say."

Dogs barked in the distance. They both tensed. Sue sucked on her bottom lip and Jackson picked up the gun. The barking died off but each stayed tight.

Suddenly she was irritated. "What the hell are you going to do, Jackson? Who do you think you are, Jesse James? You think some loser connection you have is sending a helicopter to whisk you away to Brazil? You're nothing but a punk kid, a spoiled brat with parents who'll spend their whole lives wondering what they did wrong, while you rot in jail with not an ounce of remorse in your body. Seemed like a good idea at the time? Well, now's the time to make a better plan. Make a good idea now, Jackson. Now, or you won't get the chance to decide when you need to piss ever again." Her heart was beating wildly against her ribs, her body jerking with spasms of terror. And not over Jackson.

He stared at her, his mouth open. She stared back.

"I didn't do it."

"What?"

"The last break. I didn't do it. My buddy did, but he's nineteen and woulda gone to the adult pen. Cops were interviewing me about it, like always, and he asked me to take the rap."

"You're nuts. You went to prison for some shmuck? What were you thinking?" She was astounded at his stupidity.

"Hey, I only got three months. He woulda got a year. It's called loyalty, lady."

"It's called loyalty? You think he'd ever do the same for you? My God, you are bloody certifiable."

"Oh he'll do the same for me. It's code. You don't name your partner in this biz. Guy with the least to lose, takes the rap. Code."

She brought her hands to her face and rubbed her eyes. The strain of the last hours and the lateness of the night were taking their toll. She checked her watch. Four-ten.

Had Tom followed code?

"You've got a lot to lose too," she said softly. "Your parents are going to give up on you someday, believe you me. Even your mom."

"Whadda you know?"

"I just do. People give up on people when they keep going their selfish ways." She felt physical pain over the loss of Mark for the first time in months. Mark, who said, "Get yourself out of this mess, or I'm out of here." The lure of the money was too strong and she watched him pack his stuff while files downloaded to manipulate. No man was going to tell her that her ideas, her life, her own self, were stupid ever again.

The barking dogs began again, closer. Sue watched Jackson's face flip from irritated to scared.

"Make up your mind." She tried humour. "I'd let you hide out in the tent, but the dogs will rip it to shreds before they went for you and it's borrowed gear."

Silence.

Answer me, Little Soldier. Where's your mother?

"Jackson!"

"What the fuck do you care what happens to me?"

Why indeed.

"I have no idea," she said wryly. "Listen, it's code, right? The bad guys stick by each other? Take off now and I'll stall them. On my word. I can yell and scream at people and hold up production for ten minutes. It's my specialty when I want my way."

He hesitated, glancing from the sound of the dogs, to her, to the dark woods behind him.

With a nod, he was off to places with no boundaries, abandoning the shotgun at Sue's feet. She picked it up gingerly, placed it back down. She wasn't that kind of bad guy.

Sue stoked the fire and psyched herself into a state of frenzy for the cops' arrival. Jackson'd be caught no matter what. His was a small world. She'd turn herself in. People would analyze and surmise, put it all down to greed.

Her mother would read about it in the newspaper and maybe

have a pang of remorse for walking out. Maybe. In the name of old, protective love. Mothers have codes, too.

The colonel'd be pissed he didn't see any of the cash.

Junkyard Girl

My childhood house is no longer standing. It was bought for the tremendous value of its riverfront property some years ago. I was told the physiotherapist and his lawyer-wife then demolished what represented the best and worst of my life—including every single one of the willow trees—and built an imposing pink stucco structure fit for Los Angeles. It hurts my eyes to look at it, even if only through my imagination.

It was originally a small bungalow of two bedrooms, a modest kitchen and open living area, clunky bathroom, and a dank and forbidding basement. Over the years my father added this room and that shed, this covered workshop and that chicken coop until it was a motley mess of colours and geometric shapes that tolerant neighbours called The Gingerbread House and those more aesthetically oriented, The Eyesore. The grass was patchy: silky in some places, spiky or non-existent in others, and the sprawling back porch that overlooked the water listed to one side despite my father's best efforts to level it every spring. Even on the hottest of arid summer days, the house was shaded and cooled by those dozen or so ancient willow trees that fed off Skookum River, which was in essence my backyard. On dark and rainy days, little girls like me were ten or eleven years old before they truly understood that the knocking and whispering heard during a storm was the protective branches in the wind and not their mother's undead ghost.

Memories of my mother are hazy and there are precious few photographs to support or embellish them. I think of her when I smell bleach, because she was a ferocious housekeeper. Obsessive-compulsive, it would be called now but in the early '70s, people would have called her a perfect homemaker—if they had ever seen *inside* our house, looked past the eccentric collection of seating, storage and decor.

My mother played make-believe better than anyone I knew so my father built us a tickle trunk, exactly like Mr. Dressup's, and it held as many grown-up sizes as it did children's. Originally, it was painted blue until one day we were cutting through the Woodward's electronics department at the right time and I learned via my first contact with colour television that the magical box was actually orange. I woke up to find a ripe California orange tickle trunk the very next week. I also attribute my love of books to her, she who never dared settle me into bed for a story without donning the appropriate hat, wig or swatch of fabric to enhance, as she said, the *ambience*.

Her obsessiveness and imagination are what did my mother in when I was almost eight. The day she doused herself in lawnmower gas while wearing the Rapunzel dress and set herself afire was the last time I saw her. My father told me she died in an institution somewhere outside Vancouver when I was fifteen.

In the years before my father informed me of her death-by-natural-causes, I secretly harboured thoughts of her return while reading books far too racy or sophisticated for me, like *The Thorn Birds* and various Harold Robbins, all while tucked or sprawled under those stately willow trees.

My father, Bolodenka Varvarinski: Russian immigrant and dreamer extraordinaire. When I was about six and he started saying the growing pile of miscellaneous junk in our front yard was to be a paddlewheeler, I thought he meant like *The Love Boat* and looked forward to Julie and Gopher and Isaac (I didn't like Captain Stubbing or Doc) staying at our house on their days off. Then I read Mark Twain when I was a little older and watched a documentary on the Nile on our black and white TV, so I had a better understanding of what was being created, piece by piece and scrap by scrap, for all the world to see.

I loved my father because he talked to me like an adult usually and never complained if I microwaved Chef Boyardee three nights in a row, or celebrated Pancake Tuesday several times a month for all the years we fended for ourselves. I loved him because he only raised his bushy brow when he observed me trying to read Sylvia Plath at twelve and let me mix summer and winter clothes to my heart's content.

"Gabbi," my father would say every night at dinner, "what did my school taxes pay for today?"

When I was in lower-primary, I would recite times tables, or spell pneumonia or tell him the capital of the province was Victoria. In grade six, I oscillated between telling him something that I had learned from one of my contraband books—a foreign swear word or how to mix a perfect martini—and giving him chosen insights into my real world.

"Today I learned Spencer Dodd is an idiot."

"Really?" said my father, chewing the last of his canned spaghetti. "Was it a worthwhile lesson, or should I demand a refund from Mr. Trudeau?"

Depending on which side of the fence my pre-adolescent hormones were sitting, I would either laugh and clink homogenized milk glasses with him, or start slamming our Corningware plates into the sink in a fit of righteous indignation.

He was also my greatest source of embarrassment so what I did not tell my father was that the kids at school avoided me unless the teacher forced us into pairs and that when I said I was going over to a friend's house after school, I was either wandering around Kmart or had secretly doubled back to the house, climbed in my bedroom window and sat in the closet reading by flashlight.

I couldn't tell him because I didn't know where my geekiness ended and his started. What was my own doing and what was genetic, I often pondered. If the "A" list (Sylvia, Shayla and Winnie) wasn't chasing me around the schoolyard to tie my shoelaces around the monkey bars and rub their leftover tuna sandwiches all over me, the boys were following me home as far as the train tracks asking what my father was building now, a spaceship or a barn to house me?

Consequently, I didn't know if I wanted the paddlewheeler to take form at a more rapid pace so everyone in the district—or at least my school—would believe me that my father was indeed building a boat to start a luxury cruise company up and down the Skookum River, or if I wanted to wake up one morning and find it had been swallowed into the ground like Gilligan into quicksand.

There was one girl next door who avidly sat and watched my father do his tinkering or, barring that option, came tapping at my bedroom window several times a week. Piggy Paula. In the pubescent hierarchy of nerds and weirdos, I liked to think I was at least above someone. Paula Fisher was a year younger than me, weighed 147 pounds and wasn't even reading Beverly Cleary yet, let alone Judy Blume. If she didn't outgrow the waistband of her Big Blue jeans by the time they became too short or stained too badly with food, her mother sewed ruffles around the bottom, once in purple gingham. Sometimes I opened the window and talked to her, depending on what snack she had squished against the pane to buy my attention, but more often than not, I held my book in front of my face or feigned sleep and tried to convince myself that I wasn't nearly as bad as the Tuna Fish Trio.

I was easy enough for Piggy Paula to find, given that we were too poor to whisk me off to afternoon ballet classes, Girl Guides or piano lessons. Income was limited to what my father earned from the various repair projects and a small government pension because he crushed his left foot while working the docks in Vancouver when he first arrived, long before I was born. The subsequent wacky gait, the fact that he was more than twenty-five years older than my peers' fathers and his ferocious-looking beard, often with bits of sawdust, pollen or tobacco woven in, added to his wild-man reputation. Someone once called social services on him, on us—based on nothing but our appearances, I suspect—and we had to endure an hour of two fresh-faced BSW graduates poking around the house. They left satisfied when they saw the kitchen cupboards were full (albeit with more canned food than the prime minister's nuclear bunker might hold), that my elementary school report cards were straight Os for Outstanding and repeatedly heard my father's gentle answers to their probing questions.

Part of me wanted them to scoop me up lickety-split, provided I would be placed in a very rich home with servants and a library as big as the public facility downtown, but my readings on orphans and foster children did not support the likelihood of this scenario so I stayed on my best behaviour during their visit and told no tales of woe.

My only potential foul-up was when the lady social worker said, "Gabriella, can we call you Gabbi, like your father does? Gabbi, how do you *feel* about living here with your father and your mother so far away in the special hospital?" Having no ready answer for that, I dropped the teacup as a diversion and my father was further able to endear himself to them with a rare and gentle laugh and a tousle of my hair. "I prefer mugs anyway," he explained to the one with the clipboard, who duly took down this vital information. Somewhere, deep inside the storage facilities of the district social services division, this vital nugget of information about my father still exists in standard Bic pen on yellowed paper.

He didn't come right out and tell them that the construction work was usually done on an under-the-table basis, or at least on the barter system. It wasn't until his funeral, when condolence card after condolence card arrived, that I came to understand how admired his fine millwork, masonry and welding was by everyone who knew of his work. That reputation, however, depended on him always having some length of second-hand carpet, or warped wood, or cast-iron stakes on hand to save the day and largely were what contributed to the eyesore quality of the house on River Road.

Keeping up the necessary inventory of bits and pieces meant weekly trips to the dumps of Sage, Savona, Cache Creek and Salmon Arm. A really big deal was to drive the battered blue, gas-guzzling pickup to somewhere exotic like Kelowna or Vernon to load it up with another man's junk. My personal best find was an abandoned cardboard box of paperbacks marked twenty-five cents each—leftovers from a garage or white-elephant sale. Nearly every week represented my father's best, his takes ranging from the couch in our living room to an outboard motor he fixed and then used to tote us up and down the river after the spring thaw in search of good logs.

The easiness of our forced partnership began to shift the summer I spent musing about who to go to for more real-life information about this upcoming menstruation thing and how the growing monstrosity of a boat would affect the coming year's social status. In particular, we crossed an invisible line of mutual tolerance one day in the late summer going into grade seven, when the Tuna Fish Trio made an inaugural trek across the highway and adjacent train tracks on their shiny ten-speeds. I suppose it was to gain ammunition for the upcoming year, our last in elementary school where they would be the definitive ruling class.

"Hey, Gabbi," oozed Shayla, unequivocal leader, as she coasted up to me lying on a blanket under one of the front yard trees. She had been cultivating her Barbie doll qualities for years, which seemed to make her immune to the need for braces, glasses and pimple medications, any of the standard remedies to assist burgeoning adolescence. Her foresight about puberty also exempted her from that awkward stage of breast development, as she had been graced, overnight it seemed, with two perfectly round and suitable mounds of femaleness, whereas the rest of us struggled for months and even years with ridiculous-looking bumps that resembled the quivering, investigating noses of nervous rodents. Her counterparts, Sylvia and Winnie, while still formidable, were but faded mimeographs.

Sylvia and Winnie took positions on the other points of the square blanket. I looked at them dubiously, hoping I appeared tough and not daring to hope they were here to make amends or chat socially.

"Whacha doing, Junkyard Girl?"

"Reading, Tuna Fish Breath." I could afford to be a little bold because my father was just in the chicken coop, fixing the mesh, though I would be loath to have to call him into public view to save me.

"So funny I forgot to laugh," snipped Winnie.

"Your bra strap is showing, Winnifred Gaye," I said neutrally, but knowing this was one of the more devastating fashion *don't*s of any twelve-year-old girl.

Winnie flushed and adjusted the beige strap under her tank top. "Well, you'd be one to look, Dyke Girl," she finally spluttered out, too slow to make full impact, and even Shayla and Sylvia smirked at her delayed rebuttal.

"So what do you want, anyway? I'm busy."

Number Two Girl and Number Three Girl looked at Shayla. Apparently they hadn't planned much further than deciding to ride over and check me out.

"We just came to make sure you were still alive so we could get ready for school," drawled Shayla, even though she was pure Sage suburb and not one teeny bit cattle-ranchy. With her bouncy long blonde curls, I suspected she idolized Charlene Tilton from Dallas.

"You want some cherry pop?" I asked amiably, an idea forming in my head.

That took them off guard, but was appealing, I knew, because Sylvia was always complaining that her mom never let her have pop. The three of them were given constant detentions for running off school property to the vending machines of the adjacent Rolling Sage Motel. They looked at each other again, gave slight nods and dismounted from the shiny ten-speeds. *Thwap, thwap, thwap* went their three gleaming kickstands. The fact that Sylvia's bike proceeded to rebel and fall over buoyed me along.

I fervently hoped my father was not going to choose that minute of that day to decide to ride to Shoppers Drug Mart on my fourth-hand bicycle with the third-hand banana seat and banana handlebars. They simply weren't cool any more and his knees came up to his ears when he rode.

"Stay here," I directed, envisioning the state of the house, given that my father tended to layer the living room with materials for some component of the paddlewheeler to work on while he watched *Front Page Challenge* or if it was a Saturday, *Hockey Night in Canada,* during which he muttered at the players in Russian.

Alone in the kitchen, I poured four cherry pops in the only four unchipped McDonald's glasses, considered adding cookies, but decided I didn't want to waste anything else on the likes of them. To the Hamburgler, Mayor McCheese and the second Ronald, I added liberal doses of the Tabasco sauce that my father liked on his Sage Lake trout.

The Tuna Fish Trio snatched their drinks off the tray I carried outside. My unadulterated glass wobbled apart from theirs, close to my chest.

Shayla and Winnie took pretty much simultaneous gulps and Sylvia didn't clue in to their distress until she, too, had glugged a few mouthfuls. I took a dainty sip from my glass and adopted what I hoped was an innocent expression, my back pushed up against the mighty trunk.

Even then, I was very clear on that fact of life that dictates actions have consequences, that choices produce both gains and losses. Part of the maturation process, I was coming to understand, is choosing the long-term benefit over the quick fix. On that breezeless and scorching August day when the chance at acceptance dangled before me like a willow branch, I was never more aware of the sacrifice I was making for this instantaneous rush of one-upmanship.

The Tuna Fish Trio began spluttering, wheezing and spitting on my blanket. They aimed for me, but I had foreseen this reaction and scooted out of the way just in time for the first pinkish gob to hit the scratchy green wool.

"You little bitch!" screamed Shayla as soon as she could. "What poison did you put in here?" Her swear caught us all by surprise, not having quite reached that pinnacle of language.

"Aaaaaah, we've been poisoned by Junkyard Girl! Bleeeeech!" Winnie was dancing around so vigorously, her bra strap was straining across the small-pox inoculation scar we all sported on our arms.

I chugged my drink down and shrugged my shoulders like I didn't know what their problem was. "It's only a little Tabasco," I scoffed. "I love it with Tabasco and so," I paused, desperate for somewhere, *anywhere*, exotic, "does everybody in New York."

"Get ready to die, Turd Girl!" yelled Shayla, lunging at me.

Four shrieking young girls drew my father's attention sufficiently to bring him out of the chicken coop at quite a pace.

"What's going on here?" he boomed, waving his hammer in the air and striding towards us in overalls and a long-sleeved shirt, despite the dry heat.

I was in the middle of having my hair pulled by Winnie and countered by pinching and twisting Shayla's left nipple as hard as I could, as I had seen the grade seven boys do to their favourite girls.

My father's strong arms swatted us all apart and we stood glaring and panting from the short exertion. Winnie stood holding a sizeable tuft of my shoulder-length locks while Sylvia, somehow, had been doused with the remains of somebody's lethal cherry pop and was frantically pulling at her wet T-shirt.

"I asked, what is going on here?" demanded my father, bewildered. A barroom brawl of Sage cowboys or Russian peasants he could handle, four pre-teens on his lawn, certainly not.

Sylvia started to explain but Shayla shut her up. "Nothing. Just a misunderstanding. We thought we'd give your daughter a chance to be normal, even thought she lives in The Eyesore and has a mother in the nuthouse, but she seems incapable. So we'll be going now. C'mon girls."

Now, I was mortified. My throat was stinging so badly it felt like it had been sprinkled with astringent on a pimple I had gouged raw. My eyes threatened to float out of their sockets and into the river.

The Tuna Fish Trio clambered onto their shiny ten-speeds and rode away, the tire-spokes glinting in the sun, shouting mild obscenities and dire warnings that I should prepare for a most tortured grade seven and beyond. Their words hovered in the air along with sour wafts from the chicken coop and sweet nose-ticklings from the newly mown grass, even after they were long out of sight.

"Gabbi, were those girls your friends?"

I shook my head, not able to speak.

"Do you need to tell me anything?"

Again I shook my head: he had already been made privy to everything I didn't want him to know.

He stood studying me for a long time before making a quiet snapping sound with his mouth and moving back to the chicken coop.

He never asked me to go to the dumps with him after that, often leaving before I got up on a Saturday morning, thus breaking our long-standing routine. And I never offered to accompany him again. He also, I don't know where, scrounged up sixty dollars for back-to-school clothes. I spent thirty at the Sally Ann and saved the rest in my mother's Lake Louise jewelry box. I couldn't explain to him that I truly didn't want to be cool in the way he thought, or by The Trio's strict definition either.

I didn't know what I wanted.

I did want to be in their group, within what I perceived as a normal part of the human curve, but I also wanted to be lauded for still being me and knew I could never trade my books or my usually comforting solitude for the twenty-three available flavours of Lip Smackers or a stupid *Seventeen* subscription. To accept me on such terms would have been harder for the Tuna Fish Trio to stomach than my cherry pop concoction and as likely to happen as the sleeping hunks of fibreglass and sheet metal in our front yard had of ever becoming a paddlewheeler.

RESPONSES

Abigail—she preferred to be called Abe, insisted on it, actually—jammed the plug into the block heater extension for the Hyundai. She cursed Gina for dropping it in the snow, at her girlfriend's obliviousness to taking care with things, as usual. It was the same thing as leaving the burned crusts on the baking sheets, or not tucking in the bedsheets. Abe wished Gina would stop being so domestic, if she couldn't do it with more consistency and thought.

To further darken her mood, Abe found the back door ajar and Gina's keys dangling from the lock. Nice. Really brilliant, what with those mangy little shits who'd moved in next door. She considered, briefly, that she was overreacting to Gina's quirks she had been well acquainted with for three years. After all, it *had* been a horrific day at the wheat processing company. Rumours of takeover and layoffs were circulating faster than a combine. Faster than Gina's Mixmaster.

"Gina," she called, yanking out the keys before stepping into the mudroom and slamming the door. "Gina! You left your keys in the door again, and left the door open. It's minus twenty out there. You trying to heat Regina?"

Wheel of Fortune was blaring in the living room. Bloody Vanna. Prissy little twit. Abe smirked despite her foul mood. Wouldn't she like to show Letter Girl a thing or two.

Gina bounced into the kitchen while Abe was still struggling with her boots.

"Hi baby! How are you?"

As usual, Gina's round pink face softened Abe's judgement. "You left your keys in the lock and the plug buried in the snow," she said, more neutrally than she felt and didn't even bother commenting on the open door.

"Really? Oops. I had arms of groceries." She moved forward to kiss Abe hello, but Abe turned to the sink and began running the cold water. Gina's arms encircled her from behind, Gina's breath was hot against her neck. "We're having steak. I marinated it all day. You'll barbeque?"

The glass of water was overflowing. Wasteful. Abe turned off the tap and drank the tumbler's contents as if it were a mere shot of tequila.

Gina's full breasts pushing into her shoulder blades, her flicking tongue, motivated Abe to turn around and receive the traditional after-work caresses.

She would have to make a decision soon.

Gina slid over the Tupperware container of meat and tilted sixteen ounces of burgundy flesh at Abe before reaching for the butcher knife and sawing the flank in two. "Can you make mine a little rarer than usual? Like you have yours."

After dinner—which Gina had gamely tried to eat, until Abe snatched up her steak and put it back on the grill—they settled on the couch with the preliminaries of *A Beautiful Life* fast-forwarding across the TV. Abe asked, "How'd the job hunt go today? Did you follow up with the law office?" If Gina could only find stimulating work, it would take her focus off Abe, relieve the claustrophobic fall out of her aimless days.

"Uh. No. I forgot."

"You forgot yesterday. Timely follow-up after submitting a resumé is critical."

"I know," retorted Gina in her baby voice. "I just couldn't do it, phone them and bug them."

Abe winced. "You're not bugging them. You should feel like you're doing them a favour, offering your services."

Gina squiggled into the crook of Abe's right arm and said, "I know, but I'm not like you."

Of course, there was no correct response to that.

"How about you? Any more news on the takeover?"

Abe winced. "Just unsubstantiated stuff. I'm safe enough. I'm upper-management, after all," she added smugly. Sometimes, she liked to remind Gina of this. Unstated reference to Gina's history of minimum wage retail positions hovered between them.

That night, buried beneath Gina's great-grandmother's eider-down quilt, with Gina gurgling and snoring beside her, Abe lay awake, staring into the shadows.

It was time to say good-bye to Gina, she knew that. She'd known for months now, been in that position of slow strangulation, where her insides were squished out of every orifice until there was an empty shell of a person standing amidst a pile of guts and blood and soul.

It wasn't like that in the beginning, not at all. Abe had adored Gina's naïveté, her domesticity. She had gained strength from Gina's weaknesses—the flitting from job to job, her horror of being alone overnight in the house, her flagrant disregard for all judgements against her sexuality. Touched by this earnestness, Abe had been delighted to open her home and heart to the little bird that kept crashing into windows.

It's time, Abe.

The next-door brats came crashing through their back gate, cursing and carousing. They stayed outside, rapping on garbage bin lids and getting into raucous scuffles. Nothing new. Abe avoided them and it wasn't until she heard the distinctive sound of destruction, the splintering of wood that she got up to investigate.

From her back deck, she saw one of them, the biggest one, sprawled across the flattened flimsy wooden slats that separated their lives. Abe advanced into the icy night wearing only the sweatpants and white cotton singlet she wore to bed on winter nights. She was acutely aware of the instant goosebumps up and down her arms, the protrusion of hardening nipples.

"Jesus Christ, you guys! You, are you all right? Is he all right?"

There were five of them, the three brothers and two friends. The big one hauled himself up and stood, unsteady. They formed a motley tableau under the harsh porch lights.

"Yeah. Just foolin' around."

"Well that's great, but it's three o'clock in the morning, so can you fool around inside?"

There were mumblings of general assent. A cigarette was lit, a jacket zipped up. Abe waited defiantly, wanting them to shuffle inside before she did, fighting the impulse to stand with her arms strapped across her chest. What did she care what they thought, anyway?

"Hey," shot out one of the friends. His face was the oldest, but he was not bigger than a wiry twelve-year-old. "Are those hitch hiking thumbs in your shirt, or are you just happy to see me?"

Abe crossed her arms and took a step back, out of the pool of light. Then she cursed herself.

"Give it up, Frankie, she ain't your type, if you know what I mean." The middle brother.

"All chicks are my type, Maloney."

"She's a dyke, Frankie. Not even your famous dick is gonna satisfy a dyke."

Frankie looked from the middle brother to Abe. "No kidding? A dyke? You a fucking dyke? Shoulda known, with that haircut."

Abe knew anything she said would start a pissing contest, knew it from countless experiences. No one ever went away enlightened from a dialogue or screaming match, only further outraged or embarrassed, or in her case, both. She forced herself to look straight at Frankie, and then the big brother. "Fix my fence by five tomorrow, or I'll be over to talk to your mother."

Wooooooooooooooo, they chorused in mock fear.

"Just fix the fence, guys." Abe returned inside and stood in the kitchen massaging her nipples until they warmed and receded. Like it mattered now.

She returned to bed and bumped the alarm clock back half an hour to allow time to talk to Gina. She calculated five hours of sleep if she drifted off immediately.

In the murky morning light, exhaustion—to her favour—prevented her from elaborate words and sentimental delivery as she explained to Gina the relationship was not working for her anymore.

"You know I love you, but I think I want to be alone for awhile. To see other people."

"Those are opposite things," said Gina, her strawberry-blonde curls as flattened as the fence. An imprint of the pillowcase piping ran across her right cheek.

"You know what I mean. I think we should take a break."

"You think?" Gina's eyes were filling with tears. Abe forced herself to look at her, as she had at Frankie.

"I want to break up. I'll always love you, but it's not the same anymore. I want different things than you." The left arm she had propped herself up with was beginning to throb.

"What do you want me to do differently? Maybe we're just in a rut. Maybe we should take the trip we talked about. Get naked and tanned in Antigua."

Abe pushed herself up. Pain pulsed from her left shoulder to wrist. She shook it off.

"No, Gina. I'm sorry to spring it on you like this. I've been thinking it for a long time. It's what I'm usually thinking when you ask me ..."

"'... what are you thinking?'" Gina was being braver than Abe thought she'd be. Only a few tears had spilled out so far.

"We'll talk about it when I get home tonight." She slid out of bed and moved to the closet. Her back to Gina, Abe added, "I mean, it's not like I'm kicking you out or anything. I'm not a bitch, just a dyke." Gina said nothing. "You're supposed to laugh."

"Right."

Abe let herself in the back door after work cursing the broken fence and debating whether or not to go next door. Gina was in the kitchen.

"What? No *Wheel of Fortune?*" she teased, cautious at this first post break-up communication. "And why are you wearing a toque indoors?"

Gina faced Abe squarely. "A surprise."

Gina's normally makeup-free eyes were slashed with black kohl. Abe said nothing as Gina reached up and pulled off the red and white Petro-Can hat.

She'd cut her hair. Had it cut. Less than a pixie cut, barely more than a crew. Abe stared at the razored sides, the masculine tufts at the crown of her head. Only then did the cargo pants and button-down shirt register.

"What the hell is this?"

Gina flinched.

"What are you trying to prove?" she pressed, appalled by Gina playing dress-up.

"Just trying to shake things up a bit," said Gina brightly.

"I don't want things shaken up, Gina."

I want them disintegrated.

"I did it for us."

"You shouldn't have," Abe soothed. "This isn't about looks. Or roles."

When she arrived home the next evening, Abe expected to see signs of Gina's imminent move. Boxes. Piles. Lists.

Instead Gina greeted her naked, straddling a kitchen chair backwards.

"Gina," began Abe, dreading the next moments.

Gina stood, swung a leg over the back of the chair provocatively. "Shut the fuck up and do what I tell you." The kohl eyeliner was painted on even thicker. Gina reached into the closest drawer and drew out a length of leather cord.

"Gina, don't do this."

"I said shut the fuck up!" she screamed. Abe recoiled. Where was gentle Gina, with the playful curls and soft, pendulous breasts?

"Get undressed."

Abe did not move to slide out of her coat, suit jacket, white shirt, sturdy beige Wonderbra.

"Get undressed!" The voice was shrill and desperate, a child at the start of a tantrum for candy.

Abe peeled off the layers, placing each piece on the counter within her reach. The house was warm. Scatterbrained Gina had thought to crank up the heat. Abe stepped out of her briefs and Gina advanced, holding the cord like a skipping rope. She flung it over Abe's head and jolted her forward, then upstairs to the bedroom where Abe allowed herself to be tied to the head and foot board with Gina's endless supply of silk scarves.

She was surprised, then guilt-ridden, to acknowledge the thudding in her heart had changed from apprehension to anticipation.

Candles flickered from various surfaces, casting them in a seductive, eerie light. Above her, Gina's face was set in a hard expression.

Starting at Abe's toes, Gina sucked and nibbled and bit into the flesh, sometimes hard enough to make Abe cry out. Who was this lover? The Gina she knew kissed and nuzzled. Abe felt her excitement grow despite her wariness.

She was harshly instructed to close her eyes. She complied, now anxious, impatient even, to quell the quivering of her inner thighs, the throbbing between her legs.

Her eyes flew open at the first drop of hot wax on her belly. Gina was straddling her, a long tapered candle in each hand. It hurt, it burned, but Abe felt a bolt of electricity shoot through her body. She bucked her hips in response.

More drops to the belly. Then nipples. She started to speak and the unknown lover smacked her solidly across the jaw. Almost as good as the drops of wax. Gina tipped the candles into the crevices between Abe's dark, bristly mound and her legs. Had she writhed with such pleasure ever before?

Finally, finally, Gina demanded her own satisfaction, then rewarded Abe for duly playing her docile role.

"Holy fuck, Gina," Abe breathed when she sensed Gina's dominating persona had ebbed enough for her to speak. "Incredible. My God, just incredible."

Gina leaned into her and gave her a Gina-kiss, soft, supple and somewhat tentative. "My pleasure," she murmured.

"*Our* pleasure," quipped Abe, nestling deeper under the quilt. Her stomach burbled from hunger and they both laughed.

In the morning, a Saturday, Gina was gone when Abe awoke. She threw back the covers and examined the small red welts that dotted her body and reveled in Gina's transformation. Then the guilt and shame washed over her. She shouldn't have played. She was mean and stupid to have played. One night of erotica changed nothing.

She was in the kitchen pouring coffee when Gina returned, carrying several bags of groceries. Her spiky hair still shocked Abe, but at least the kohl had been scrubbed off.

"Hi." It was inadequate, but Abe's mind was racing ahead to choose words to explain she still intended Gina to move out. To start today, in fact.

"Hi, baby." Gina's eyes were luminescent, her voice strong. *She thinks she's fixed it.*

"I went to the open air market and we are going to have the most deluxe, scrumptious, decadent dinner you could ever imagine."

Abe's throat constricted. She took a gulp of coffee before speaking. "Really? Wow. After your efforts last night—by the way, thanks again—and the energy it'll take to start sorting stuff, I really don't expect a gourmet dinner."

There. Your ball.

"Sorting?" Gina's pitch was high.

"Well, yes. Sorting. I don't suppose you've found an apartment or anything, but I'll be around today to help. If you want me to help."

The bags thudded on the tile. A pear rolled out, stopping near Abe's left foot. "Help? You're going to help me move out? Isn't that goddamn grand of you. Help the jilted lover pack her sorry cardboard boxes of trinkets."

"Okay, okay. I get it. I'll go out. It was just an offer."

Gina began slamming items into the fridge and cupboards. Abe topped up her coffee and waited.

Harness the electricity in the air right now and heat Regina for the winter.

When the bags were empty, Gina crumpled them and shoved them into the garbage bin under the sink. Abe refrained from reminding her to recycle them.

"I thought," Gina said, leaning against the counter. "No, I guess I didn't think. Not enough. I thought ... didn't think ... we were ... I thought last night, my haircut, I thought we were back to normal."

Abe fought the impulse to move to embrace Gina. She wore denim overalls and a pink turtleneck. Except for the shorn hair, she looked so young and fresh, Abe couldn't keep looking at her.

"I don't want things to be normal," Abe finally said. "That's kind of my point."

"Well, then, I can be ..."

Abe held up her hand. "And I don't want you to change who you are, either. Normal is not a bad thing, I just don't want it right now."

"I'll wait."

"No. You won't. I don't want you to because ..." Why was she doing this? Now that her feelings were out, they seemed premature. Plain old wrong. Maybe she should have just taken them to Hawaii, like last year. "I don't know what I want."

Gina focused on shortening the straps of her overalls and whispered, "Are you already seeing someone else?"

Abe glugged the remaining half a cup of coffee. It was bitter and cold. Her stomach lurched. It was as if someone had added vinegar and ice cubes when she wasn't looking.

"Abe? Please. Be honest. Are you seeing someone else?"

Abe thought about the new IT manager and the pleasant gripping in her gut every time she saw the tall brunette. There had been one comfortable and chatty coffee and a grazing of hands in the elevator. Nothing had come of it.

"No. Honest to God. It's not about falling in love with someone else."

They stood stock-still, avoiding acknowledging the other's furtive glances. Gina shuddered. Not unlike the sound she made at sexual pleasure, Abe noted. Finally, she said, "I bought lobster. Nova Scotian lobster."

Abe noticed her largest pot had been extracted from deep in the cupboard beside the stove. "Lobster? What the hell price did . . . ," she stopped. Gina had no money, no cash. Since Gina left her last job as a clerk in Reitmans, Abe had been allotting her a hundred dollars a week for groceries for the two of them. She never questioned where the extra went. Gina deserved some privacy—even if Abe had been the one to chop up her credit and bank cards after paying off Gina's Reitmans staff bill, two months after she'd quit. But Abe knew where Gina's last twenty had gone, for gas the previous day when Abe's VISA had de-magnetized. She'd noted Gina's scalped wallet when the bill was handed over.

"Where did you get money to buy lobster?"

Gina ran the hot water. She held her hands under the flow and Abe could see the steam start to rise.

"Gina?"

No answer. Gina's eyes were squeezed shut, her head thrown back. Her hands had turned bright, bright pink, like two neon beacons. Abe yanked Gina's hands away from the spigot, cranked off the hot water tap and ran the cold. When the flow had chilled again, she thrust Gina's hands under.

"What the hell are you doing? Jesus H. Christ!"

"I don't know," whispered Gina, her eyes sloshing, blue pools. "I don't know."

"You've scalded the shit out of your hands. Look at them!" She withdrew them from the spigot and Abe felt heat still pulsing from them. Gina said nothing.

She pulled a packet of peas and one of french fries from the freezer and sandwiched Gina's hands between them before asking again, "Gina, where did you get the money to buy lobsters?"

Gina shrugged. She looked awkward, perched on a kitchen chair, her hands cocooned in lumpy plastic bags. "I sold my Discman to Mouse. She's back from Europe. Ditched Marti in Budapest. Is that in Germany?"

"Your Discman? You love that thing, why would you ever . . . ?" Abe gave up.

These were days of no correct responses.

On Sunday morning, Abe made several calls from her car to friends, soliciting couches or rollaway cots for Gina. Finally, Marti—the one mousy Mouse had heroically dumped in Hungary—and her new love Dacia, said no problem. We understand what it's like, they commiserated coolly. To be thrown out by fickle partners, went unsaid. For as long as poor Gina needs, blah, blah, blah, they said. Marti'd take anyone in for a buck, rumour had it. Regardless, Abe brought home cardboard boxes from Safeway and silently placed two beside their bedroom closet, a small one in the bathroom and two in the spare bedroom, an office-cum-junk room. She found Gina on the couch, wrapped in a red afghan and watching inane children's cartoons. After explaining, again, her feelings and yearning to separate, Abe guided a comatose-like Gina into their bed and underneath her great-grandmother's eiderdown quilt. Part of her wanted to make intense love. But she knew it would feel bad, like taking advantage of a helpless child.

Abe collected sufficient bedding from the office-cum-junk room and settled down on the couch. That was seven. She fell asleep at three.

She was reluctant to go to work on Monday and almost called in sick. What would she find when she came home? An empty house? A house stripped of Gina? Perhaps nothing different at all. For that matter, what scenario did she really want, anyway? She remembered nothing about the drive home, only plugging in the car, pushing open the gate and approaching the house with trepidation.

Everything was dark. It could mean Gina was gone, it could mean she was still curled up in bed.

There were no keys in the lock, no dinner aromas emanating from the kitchen into the back mud room. Ah. Several pairs of Gina's shoes. Abe hung up her Danier jacket besides Gina's heavy wool overcoat. Its hood and matching gloves hung limply. The mud room was deceptively warmer than the outside because the air was still. Frozen air.

She was bowled over by the gust of hot, dry air that lapped over her when she opened the kitchen door. Gina! Left the heat cranked to twenty-five degrees, no doubt. Or, had it been her?

Abe rolled her eyes and moved briskly, snapping on lights and lamps on her way through the house. Soon, the house was ablaze with light. At the closed bathroom door, she paused. The bathroom door was never closed. Gina and Abe were as familiar with each other's ablutions and bodily functions as a mother and child. She knocked.

"Gina? I'm coming in." The knob was locked. Unheard of. Even during parties.

"Gina? For fuck's sake, answer me!"

The lock was chintzy, disengaged with one pseudo Judo kick. *Gina.*

"Gina!"

The pink-tinged water undulated in time to Gina's swishing hands. She had shaved off her pubic hair with apparent abandon and the botched job resulted in the tinted water.

Gina smiled up at Abe.

"Hi, baby. I've had a great and busy day."

Abe snatched up the Lady Bic that lay on the rim of the bathtub, the Philips shaver from the shampoo caddy and the new cellophane packets of blades under the sink. She left the bathroom without speaking.

When Gina finally emerged, Abe pushed her down on the couch. "What the hell are you trying to pull? This quasi-psycho routine is pissing me off. Do I have to yell, 'Get the fuck out' for you to hear me?" Gina arranged her hands in a dainty position on her lap. They were still discoloured from the scalding and contrasted with the white bathrobe.

"Gina, please! I don't want it ugly. Why are you making it ugly? I'm trying to make this easy for you, for us, and you're cracking up on me. But that's not going to stop it happening." Abe massaged her temples, pushing harder and harder until she thought her fingers would meet. "It's over, Gina. We're over."

"I understand," assured Gina solemnly and clicked the TV on. Flabbergasted, Abe left Gina and went into the kitchen.

She opened the fridge and was visually assaulted by a tropical salad of papaya, mango, kiwi, pomegranate and rambutans. Abe stared at the large glass bowl of succulent fruit, both mesmerized and sickened. Strange, how Gina had paid for her decadence this time was less intriguing than where she'd found such delectables in Regina's frigid February.

Abe leaned in and used her hand to stir around the rainbow of juicy chunks in big, circular motions. It reminded her of a kaleidoscope and calmed her.

She called in sick the following morning, and spent the day in a scouring and polishing frenzy. Gina left the house before nine, while Abe was investigating unmarked boxes in the basement. She stayed out all day and it was unnerving.

At five-forty, exactly when Abe usually walked in the back door, Gina appeared. She wore a cobalt business suit, delicate makeup and a soft blonde wig, its falseness imperceptible. She approached Abe (who was on her knees scouring the tub), her shiny black pumps miraculously devoid of sand, salt, snow and other muck, clicked on the tiles. She wore quality, sheer nylons. Ten $100 bills were sprinkled over Abe's baseball-capped head.

"Back rent," Gina announced and click-click-clicked her way out, then down the hall.

Abe gathered the bills, fingering and arranging them in awe. Now what?

"And the money would be from . . . where?" she later asked Gina, who was tucking into a takeout feast of an Indian *thali* in front of *Jeopardy*.

"Friends. Friends who owed me."

That was an infuriating response. Abe grabbed the remote, used it to turn off the TV and sent the plastic gizmo skittering across the laminate floor into the kitchen.

"Friends? What friends? Where have these indebted friends been for the past eight months to, say, three years?"

Gina ignored her, stood up and retrieved her briefcase from the kitchen. She opened it on the table and shuffled and signed papers in a way that was most familiar to Abe.

"Gina! What the hell is going on?"

Gina snapped the case shut, shimmied out of her suit skirt, matching jacket, control top nylons, and crisp white blouse. She gathered her clothing and sashayed out of the living room in her sateen thong, without answering.

"Gina!" shouted Abe up the stairs. "Gina, I asked you a question."

Back to the couch for a restless night.

The plant called the next morning as Abe was sopping up coffee from the counter, cupboards and floor. She'd filled the machine, turned it on but, distracted, neglected to replace the pot under the drip.

"Ms. Logan? I am sorry to advise you over the telephone, and so early in the morning, but you missed yesterday when the official announcement was made. I hereby advise you of your immediate layoff from Western Wheat due to the hostile take-over of Baho Industries. I'm sure you heard the rumours. You need to come in within the next seventy-two hours, collect your personal items and receive information about your very gener-ous severance package. Be prepared to wait, as the new Human Resources is processing you and 128 of your staff and col-leagues." The telephone clicked. It may as well have been a recorded message. Perhaps it was. One poor messenger wouldn't want to deal with the profane responses to follow.

Abe hung up the phone and looked down at herself, half dressed. She wore only one knee-high and her navy trousers hung baggy, yet to be zipped and belted, about her waist. She hadn't even decided on a shirt. It seemed an impossible decision.

Gina entered the kitchen in her old whirlwind fashion but instead of her usual baggy jeans or sweatpants, she wore a tai-lored black shift dress and pearls. Abe's grandmother's pearls actually, worn only once by Abe, at the old woman's funeral.

"You look like you're about to throw up," commented Gina, deftly pouring coffee into a carry-mug. The wig had not yet been plopped on, yet she looked slick and chic.

Abe stared at her. Gina never, not once in three years, had got out of bed before, or even simultaneous to, Abe. In order to keep standing, to not crumple, Abe gripped the counter and imagined her legs as steel rods. "Why are you dressed? Where are you going?"

Gina was slipping into a smart-looking leather car coat. She looked at Abe slyly. "Got a job. Didn't I mention it? Executive secretary to some old codger who wants a pretty girl to sit at the desk in his study. Fifty grand." She kissed Abe on the cheek.

Abe felt weak, as floppy as an overcooked noodle. She leaned against the counter. She'd sworn to give Gina an ultimatum to get out by the weekend.

"Bye. Have a good day," chirped Gina.

Abe pushed off the counter and watched Gina head for the bus stop, reeling from the fact that her ardent and attentive lover—never mind that: her domestic better half—had not even asked why she, the breadwinner, *the leader*, wasn't ready for work.

All morning, Abe oscillated between a drug-like stupor and rage, screaming her plans to sue, to maim, to seek vengeance one moment and collapsing on the couch with the shakes the next. She cracked her first beer at eight-forty-five. By noon, she'd gouged the coffee table, cracked the bathroom mirror and fractured Gina's porcelain ballerina collection onto the hardwood floor.

The shattering of the white-skinned, anorexic-looking figurines shocked Abe into lucidity. She attempted to gather the bigger chunks, though they'd shot into all four corners of the living room, and then swept the shards into a pile with her forearms. They got nicked and began to bleed. Somehow, it was soothing to register the pain and gaze at the pulsing wounds. She forced herself into the shower and watched the pink-tinged water swirl around her feet.

Like her first period when she'd showered for two hours. Thank God no one was home to question or chastise. Useless function, that monthly bleeding. A crimping of her uterus, a thudding of her heart upon seeing an infant? It didn't ever happen. Gina, however, cooed and clucked whenever she saw a baby. They'd discussed adoption, in vitro maybe, a couple of times during their second year together. Not since.

She stood in the long line to collect her record of employment and severance package with dozens of others. She noted her superiors and subordinates. Some were happy, like the flaming fag in accounting. He was annoying, the way he was going on about travelling with his latest, Chad. An older, Native—First

Nations? what was the right term now?—woman from payroll, who, ironically, had always said to call her Boo, was crying.

"I got five kids," she whispered to Abe. "Five under ten years old. You think thirty-thousand-a-year jobs are easy for an uneducated Indian woman to get? Huh?"

"Don't look at me, Boo," snapped Abe. "I'm fucked too."

"You're management," Boo accused. "You make more. You got no kids, you got a chance to save. You can get married, somebody'd take you."

Under different circumstance, Abe might have laughed, might have made a sarcastic comment, or, though less likely, a calm clarification. Today, she glared at Boo until the payroll assistant moved forward to lament with her predecessor in line.

At home again, Abe polished off Gina's Häagen-Dazs and three-quarters of a box of crackers produced by her ex-company. It was a coincidence that *Wheel of Fortune* had just started when Gina returned.

She was flushed with excitement, exuberant even, ignoring the "kiss first; talk, pee, eat later" rule she herself had mandated early in their common-law relationship.

"Mr. Quigley is so easy to take care of," Gina gushed, peeling off her layers of chic as she spoke.

In her mind, Abe heard herself tell Gina to get out, but she heard nothing with her ears. The message was scrolling across her field of vision, like a theatre marquee, but when she opened her mouth to make the demand, no sound came out. Her entire face felt shot up with Botox. As frozen as the plains.

"And, the best part? Oh my God, I nearly died! He's taking me, as his caregiver, when he goes to St. Lucia next month. Can you believe it? The five-star staff will do most of the work, I figure. I intend to lie on the beach, drink 151-proof rum, and broil."

Abe found her voice. "Going straight, are we?" It was a low blow. She couldn't help it.

Gina kept her expression neutral, warm even, but said in an icy voice, "Why would you care?"

Abe shrugged, struggling to reverse the balance of power. She sniped, "You know, we lifetime members don't like to lose any of the membership. Already lost Anne Heche for this decade."

There. Better. She'd climbed on the teeter-totter, at least.

"Abe, what is it you want?" Was that boredom in Gina's voice?

Feeling desparate, Abe tried to read Gina. "What do I want?" she repeated, to buy time.

What do I want?

"I want you to stop this fucking little Super Woman charade and get back to normal."

"You stole my normal." Gina unhooked her peach satin bra and threw it on top of her suit. "Besides, you're the Super Woman, the never-forget-to-debit-the-written-account, the never-runs-her-nylons, woman." She paused, a slow, sarcastic smile rolled across her face. "Ms. never-without-an-orgasm, Super Woman. I'm taking a shower."

Abe bubbled with contrasting emotions. She wanted to throw the saucy bitch out the front door into a snowbank. She lusted to push the curvaceous lover onto the cold linoleum and pound the sexual crap out of her for hours. She wanted Gina to crack her head open from a fall in the tub and beg for mercy.

With shower sounds and Gina's inarticulate humming in the background, Abe tried to focus. She realized Gina was going nowhere unless by brute or legal force. Did she care? Did she want to be alone now? Could she? She shivered, remembered the Calgary chinooks of her youth, the warm wind that swooped in to penetrate the frozen block of air by which she was to sustain herself, and then was sucked away with no notice.

Abe retrieved a chunk of porcelain ballerina from the pile in the living room, to use as evidence of her desperation, at the same time wondering how to explain her assault on Gina's property. She entered the bathroom and began organizing the strewn towels, sweeping the various bath paraphernalia into

Gina's cosmetic sack, all the while gripping the half-head of shellacked grace and dignity.

She squeezed so hard, its ragged edges punctured the tender skin of her palm. She held her grip. Feeling like she was part of a silent film, Abe watched the rivers of blood flow through each finger crevice, down her wrist.

She drew back the shower curtain and stepped into the tub, willing herself not to yelp at its extreme temperature. Gina was a misty vision within the steam. How could Gina stand the heat?

Gina opened her eyes to acknowledge her presence. She noticed the blood and embraced Abe. She cooed and murmured.

The reversal was complete.

What do I want?

Clearly, there was no obvious response.

FURNACE CREEK

Leizal is offended that the desiccated ground of Trona grows only the carcasses of tractors, cars, refrigerators and washtubs. As many as a more fertile land might germinate stalwart firs and lush fronds. She recognizes her reaction as irrational, but doesn't care. The landscape is more than a little disconcerting.

Jerod is driving at a moderate speed. He wears light brown khakis and a beige, long-sleeved cotton shirt. Depending on how he moves his arms, she is sometimes privy to the white bandages that peek out from the cuffs, far more subtly than the silent beasts of iron by which they are corralled.

"I don't really like it here," she announces, her unspoken peeves of the trip piling up before her, big as the Oregon sand dunes. She is wary of not upsetting Jerod's delicate balance. "It's kind of creepy," she tries again, still cautious, when he doesn't respond. "It's like all these old things were brought here to die."

Jerod begins driving faster. The air-con is blasting, but that is not why his pallid cheeks take on the rosy hue of a rising desert sun. Leizal forces herself to sit back, to concentrate on the scenery. Trona, thank God, is behind them now. The flat, gritty ground and sagebrush are a bare distraction and becoming monotonous already, only two hours in. She is disconcerted by the wizened and crispy bushes. They remind her of the facial stubble of an old, old man.

But Jerod, Jerod is metamorphosing. Leizal has seen it before and cannot (will not!) interfere: look what happened last time. Predictably, a few miles further, he asks her to take the wheel, takes out his supplies which she'd insisted he pack, and begins sketching with an intensity she hasn't seen for months. The highway is arrow-straight, conducive to wedging the large, spiral-bound book of creative blankness between the dashboard and his belt buckle.

Leizal is grateful to the desert gods to witness this burst of artistry. This burst of what she has been reminding Jerod is quintessentially him, *is what he is*, for months. Still, it doesn't change her feelings.

"We need gas," she announces, interrupting his mad sketching a few miles after she has taken the wheel. "Why didn't you stop in Trona? Shit. I hate being anywhere near empty." She ups the level of accusation in her voice. "You know I hate that." She doesn't want Jerod to peak too soon after all, though Leizal knows nothing she says or does will alter his course of behaviour.

"It'll be okay," he mumbles, raising his eyes from the pad and squinting into the brown bubble of nothingness they are driving through.

It'll be okay.

How many times has she cooed that to him?

The needle drops into the red zone.

There are other passing cars, Leizal reassures herself. It isn't as if, should the custom-coloured burnt crimson Topaz splutter to a stop, there will be no one and they will be stranded in this God-forsaken dust bowl.

She turns off the air-con, to save gas. Running it sucks gas. Somewhere, she read that.

"It's too hot," whines Jerod, even before the air has stagnated. "The nibs are too soft to draw already."

"Incorporate that into the style," Leizal snaps, gripping the steering wheel, like that will encourage the car to continue the necessary forty miles to Panamint Springs, to the tiny little gas pump symbol on the tourist map. The silly cartoon map lies open on the consul between them, in the process of wilting and crisping like everything else in a hundred-mile radius. It acts as a fine buffer between lovers.

But there is no fuel at Panamint Springs. There is a restaurant to fuel the body and then—*How fitting*, thinks Leizal—an RV waste dump, but no gasoline. The lone waitress, her skin as cracked as the earth, directs Leizal deeper into the desert, to Stovepipe Wells. Leizal wants her to be apologetic for the lying symbol on the map, but the woman is not. Is she the only one to ever feel guilt?

On fumes alone, the car makes it to Stovepipe Wells. Jerod is out of the car, skittering around like a beetle, before the wheels have completely stopped rotating. Leizal watches him, feels amputated from his world. He insists on taking the wheel once he has paid the man a record two dollars and thirty cents a gallon and dragged the parched squeegee across all six windows.

His fuel is her poison.

Sometime after Stovepipe Wells, when they begin the climb that will spill them into the second, perhaps more deathly valley, Leizal reads a sign that instructs, "Turn off air conditioning, next ten miles."

She doesn't understand why at first, but Jerod, nearing jubilance, is quick to explain. "It makes the engine work too hard. It'll burn out the motor." Sure, *now* he doesn't care, doesn't care about things that suck out the life out of the engine. It is she now, who yearns for controlled and cool air, a hotter commodity than water.

Jerod drives with his left pinkie while he pats around the back seat for the salt and vinegar potato chips. He drives maniacally, again too fast, over the yellow line, onto the shoulder. He too, will burn out, but it's more difficult than the car to pinpoint when. Hours. Days. Many years ago, he once went for months, painting twenty hours a day. After the gallery show, which earned them rent money for two years, he crashed. Since then, his ups and downs were impossible to predict, impossible to gauge. Jerod's a helpless pain in the ass. At last she realized she couldn't save him from his demons.

Because of this, nine days ago, Leizal said good bye.

Jerod's internal needle shot into the red zone and he slit both wrists, upper arms really. And he slashed up and down, not across. Like any serious kamikaze would do.

Dr. Eau put him on two hundred milligrams of Zoloft, Leizal assured Jerod it was her mistake, she wasn't going anywhere.

But she wants to. Jerod's extremes are killing her. Jerod knows this, but can do nothing about it.

One can't fight nature.

Furnace Creek, Death Valley, State of California, US of A, Northern Hemisphere, Big Bad World. Furnace Creek is a hub. Tourists, released from the recycled air within their vehicles, are pushed here to the soda stand, there to the trinket shop. Their every move is the whim of the raspy wind. Tumbleweed has more power over its destiny.

Jerod pulls the car into the parking lot of the Information Center, a bulky building that rises out of the desert ground, an ugly, man-made dune. At Reedsport, on the Oregon coast, they had climbed the sand dunes, the definitive physics exercise in the meaning of two steps forward and one step back.

Though they both get out of the car, dutifully locking in their portable lives, Leizal doesn't want to go in, doesn't want to know this place, its secrets, as presented on glossy brochures or in any other manner. Its stark reality is overwhelming enough.

"Okay," shrugs Jerod. "You have your set of car keys, in case you want something from the cooler?"

"Jesus, how long are you going to be? Am I supposed to set up the barbecue or something?" More grains are added to her sand dune of peeves.

"Just checking, Lissy."

She tightens at the private and rare endearment, opens her mouth to reply, but the cavity is filled with hot, dry air, and she cannot articulate anything.

"Be good." He trots off, across the parking lot, past RVs and convertibles and rusty pickup trucks and formidable sedans. Leizal watches him fling open the Center's large glass doors and disappear inside. She tries perching on the hood of the Topaz, but the metal sears her ass like a slab of steak through her thin cotton shorts and she is left circling the lot, waiting, waiting like a vulture, for something to give up.

After fifteen minutes she returns to the car, rummages through the toiletries bag for Tylenol. Surely man can rise above nature in this case, and dilute the pounding in her frontal lobe.

In the side pocket of the red plastic case, made supple by the heat, she finds Jerod's prescription, still full. Chock full.

"Stupid bastard," she says aloud and tosses the bottle onto the driver's seat where he is sure to see it. Her chastising words hover in the syrupy car air.

She guzzles the last of the water and four grainy white tablets.

Leizal tries sitting at the picnic table in the shade, but her armpits, the back of her bent knees, her crotch, squeeze out the remaining drops of moisture her body has been hoarding. So she stretches out on top of the scratchy planks, opening every crevice to the assiduous wind. She has not been sleeping at night. Leizal lies awake, for hours and hours, in each Motel 6 bed, or family-run inn, or hovel presided over by the obese and florid man in the undershirt, whose wife shouts registration instructions from their adjacent living room with the same lethargy she shouts answers at Pat Sajak.

When the hand of God cups over the valley and stops the wind—stops it dead for a good five seconds—Leizal opens her eyes, props herself up.

She checks her watch. Fifty more minutes have passed.

Fifty? *Fifty?*

Then, the father of a sparkling family of four ties a large, black Labrador to the leg of the picnic table. We'll be right back, he says, but she doesn't know whom he's addressing, her or the panting hulk. They leave a plastic ice-cream container of water. Leizal covets it, even after the dog has taken a garrulous slurp.

She sits up, shunts down to the edge of the table and gives the dog a pat. His lolling tongue, the colour of bubble gum, is incongruent with the brown bubble in which they are both captive. Squatting beside him, she wets three fingers in the water and after much sniffing and evaluating, he licks them. By that time, the wind has already sucked off the moisture, but she has successfully ingratiated herself.

Leizal scratches her initials in the dirt with her index finger while the dog watches. She scratches D-O-G into the skin of her dry inner thigh and he watches this too. She offers him a closer look, spells it out loud for him, in fact. He leans in and licks off the letters with his precious spit. Might be erotic, downright pornographic, if not for the fucking, pulsing heat and wind.

When she draws G-O-D, they both just stare.

Because, don't erase God. Just don't.

The family rolls back from the Information Center. The mother and father titter about lunch, the son and daughter argue about the can of soda they share. The dog is unhooked and dragged away, back to the blue camper van.

Leizal goes into the Center, through the big glass doors.

Inside, the air is cold and damp. She sucks in deep breaths and imagines the mud that must be forming within her.

No Jerod. The bathroom, perhaps. What, he has liquid to spare?

She scans the newspaper, produced by Death Valley National Park. *Uhuh.* Average temperatures. *Uhuh.* How to avoid the rodent hantavirus. Uhuh. Do's and Don'ts of the desert. *Duh.* When she reads the story about the European man who was dead after only five hours alone, deep within the brown bubble,

Leizal drops the paper as if it burst into spontaneous combustion.

"Excuse me. I seem to have lost someone. A man, this tall, in beige?"

Nothing.

She asks another official, further down the information counter. "With glasses? Long sleeves? This tall."

"Try her," says the guide, motioning to a corner chair. "She might have seen him."

The Tobisha Shoshone woman, swathed in black, tells Leizal that she comes to the Information Center every day for the air conditioning. She explains that she inhales all the cold air and blows it over her tribe at night. That is her job. It's the only way the tribe has survived Furnace Creek for over two hundred years.

"Good for you," Leizal croons, but impatiently. "It's just that, have you seen the man I described? He came in, maybe two hours ago?"

"Yes."

"Yes? Yes, what?" Leizal urges, her voice conveying more force than she intends. Even, perhaps, than she feels.

"He come in. Then he go." The woman closes her eyes and inhales the man-made air. Leizal is licked by her exhalation. Like flames.

"He go where?" she insists, grabbing at the sleeve of the garb, but nothing is there. She is squeezing fabric and air. The old crank has pulled her arms inside the body of the garment.

"He go there," says the woman, motioning with her head to the brown expanse, visible through the back windows.

"Outside? There's nothing there."

"No. Nothing."

Then Leizal is screaming and shaking the woman, but it's like shaking out a tablecloth. Like trying to grab fistfuls of sand. But she, Leizal, is solid, easy for uncountable pairs of hands to grip and pin down.

"He's not well!" is the last thing she shrieks before descending into near comatose silence and stillness.

When the loud-speaker announcements calling for Jerod bring no response, troops of locals fan out from the two restaurants, the three crap souvenir stores, the gas station where one gallon costs two dollars seventy. After that, Leizal hears the approach of a chopper, hears the drone of its labouring engine circle and dip, abate and rise. Sounds less predictable than the chafing wind.

The ground searchers find the white wrap, crusted with blood nine days old, tangled in the stubby bushes and then Jerod, not far off. Three-quarters of a mile from the Center. Leizal hears this, and thinks about drowning in a saucer of water. But the sheriff reports it wasn't dehydration, not Nature's fault at all.

She envisions his fresh blood fertilizing the ground, announces to the hovering brittle masks that she must pee. A lie. It has not been necessary to urinate, to surrender precious liquid, all day.

Instead, she returns to the car, uses the keys Jerod insisted she produce for inspection, and drives away.

At the sand dunes before Stovepipe Wells, Leizal sees the aqua-coloured camper van, a bright cyst on the brown earth. Four figures are staggering across the plain.

She stops the Topaz, in the middle of the lane, keeps the van as barrier between her and them. The family has locked the doors against desert marauders, but left the windows open for the dog. She reaches in, unlocks the driver's door.

The black hulk comes to the front, greets her. Licks her dry fingers with its sandpaper tongue.

Leizal retracts, peers around the van. The family is now four dots on a distant dune.

She will call the dog Trona, though it all began far before that.

SPILLS

"Oh, at least pretend," Julie instructed Alan as they dashed through the rain, from the car to Susie's apartment entrance. "It's your mother we're pacifying. She's the one who wants us to hook up with her friend's daughter."

Alan's response was a snort. He carried the two litres of Grower's peach cider and Julie carried the plastic container of barbequed chicken wings. Strange, as she was bound to drink more than half of the cider and pick at only a few chicken wings. The sinew and jelly-bits disconcerted her. They'd not mention how Alan, upon transferring them into the Tupperware, slid three-quarters of the offering into the sink. What could be more sanitary than a sink, they rationalized as the greasy arms were scooped into their plastic pen.

"Pretend," she pressed, "for God's sake, that you've got some kind of bohemian streak. Nobody Susie would invite is going to want to converse with a tax auditor and a Tabi rep. And turn off your cell phone. We'll look pretentious."

"Everyone has cell phones these days. Homeless guys have cell phones." He looked disgusted as he scanned the bank of apartment entry codes.

They were buzzed in and made their way across the spacious lobby, across supposedly indestructible carpet, though it was stained and shredded. The elevator was ancient, the shunting, lumbering kind that Julie especially feared. She concentrated on the ascending numbers.

They found apartment 1704 after a false start in the wrong direction from the elevator. Susie answered the door promptly and waved them in, her *Eggcetera!* apron splattered with unidentifiable pink smears. She was obviously a hostess in crisis. From the foyer, where they toed off their shoes, Julie scanned the backs of the four other dinner guests, crowded together on the balcony, lurching over to view something below. She forced herself to toss down her purse instead of clutching it in front of her for protection. Perhaps she should have dug out the string bag, bought on their Jamaican honeymoon.

Susie, with her frizzy, ash-blonde hair, crinkled beige blouse and cotton vest of tan swirls, contrasted sharply with her stark and vibrant paintings, several of which hung on each wall. For the millionth time, Julie wondered if she'd dressed right. At home, the black jeans and black chiffon blouse had seemed appropriate, even *avant-garde*. Now, here, with no chance to turn back and change, she felt half urban cowgirl and half funereal.

Susie exchanged Julie's proffered chicken wings for two plastic tumblers and shouted toward the balcony, "Yo-hoo! It's the rest of the company. I lost the bet. Heinz wasn't the last to arrive after all. I said, 'Yo! You guys, the Rasmussens are here.' Leave the poor puking homeless bastard alone. It could very well be you." To Julie and Alan she added, "It *has* been one or two of them. Introduce yourselves, will you?" She dismissed Julie and Alan with a nonchalant flip of the wrist before scooting back into the kitchen.

The Rasmussens? The *Rasmussens?* Julie winced. How suburban. Still, choices were choices. She and Alan were already so far in the hole with Susie's friends—all theatre and artsy types according to Susie during their inaugural Starbucks meeting, two weeks previous—that it would be amazing if anyone even talked to them.

Be positive and inquisitive, Julie instructed herself and set her mouth in what she hoped was a left-wing, intelligent but mischievous smile.

The bodies reluctantly filed back inside, giving half-nods as they tossed out names and repositioned themselves on the eclectic furniture.

Dan, Gus, Heinz, Mare, Julie repeated to herself, then created the physical associations like the memory course had instructed. Dan the Man, looks cocky, with his long black hair that he shimmies like a shampoo commercial. What was with the shock of grey, white really, that ran from the crown to the ragged tips? Then, Gus the Bus, chubby and wearing a black and yellow sweater. He was sweating despite the coolness of the air. Beads, *marbles*, or sweat oozed out his forehead. Heinz Ketchup, easy, with his tight cap of a red crewcut. And Mare, like a full-grown colt, dramatic in her flowing turquoise caftan and toe rings.

The conversation topic was birthplaces.

"In the back of a truck between Medicine Hat and Calgary," offered Dan, who chose to lean against the faux fireplace. Swish, flick, went the hair. His hand rested on Mare's shoulder, who squatted on a wooden box, like she was about to take off. The yards of teal fabric flowed out around her. It was hard to say if the placement of Dan's hand was romantic. Julie sensed these people had the casual body contact of a litter of kittens.

Alan scoffed at Dan's announcement. Julie tucked her chin down and said, "Really?" The others looked on, nonchalant.

"How about you, Gus?" asked Heinz. The man was a giant, observed Julie. Huge. "You born around '45?" His tinkly laugh did not match the thick, sprawling body.

"Yes," said Gus, sawing around the collar of his sweater with an index finger. "And I'm sure you mean *1845*." He spoke in monotones and no one laughed, unsure if he was being dry, or offended. He had twenty years on the rest of them, Julie concurred. Gauche to bring attention to it.

"There, you see? Birthplace *is* related to the subsequent life journey. Gus is straightlaced, a puckered ass, so to speak, relative to his wartime Betty Crocker birth."

Julie winced and flicked her eyes from wall to wall, absorbing Susie's vibrant, sprawling pieces. Her appalling pieces. She stared at the stylized painting of a bleeding Virgin Mary, the gushing throat of some queen, an orally hemorrhaging Oprah. They sold for hundreds of dollars.

"And, Dan's still a drifter, because he was born on the run."

"On the go."

"Whatever."

"No. Not on the run, as in, 'on the lam.' My mother wasn't AWOL or anything, for God's sake."

Heinz laughed again, irritatingly off-key.

"I don't remember *where* I was born," contributed Mare, her stringy blonde ringlets looking like they hadn't been combed in days. Maybe she was prepping for dreadlocks, thought Julie, fighting the urge to tug through the fuzzy mass, then arrange the curls with a rat-tailed comb, the way she was once made to wear her hair.

"Of course you don't remember," Dan interrupted. "Nobody remembers *per se*, we only remember being told where." It was clear he was irritated by the topic now. Did his fingers tense as they cupped her shoulder?

"No, Danny," insisted Mare. "I remember *being* born. The screaming and blood, the gushing out. The first *suckle*. I just don't remember *where* it was," Mare assured in her ridiculous Shakespearean way. When she stood and stuck out her arms for emphasis, Julie thought she resembled an elaborate box kite. Then, to Julie and Alan, who were perched on the papason chair, Mare added, "You two *must* be hospital babies. *Straight*-forward deliveries." She leaned forward, into Alan's face, challenging. Dan's hand dropped from Mare's shoulder.

Julie and Alan glanced at each other before Alan moved his arm from Julie's knee. "I guess so," he shrugged. "It's never come up and I definitely don't remember it. Historical discussions in my family only start at the college years. You know, spilled milk, acne, all the weird stuff isn't part of the dinner repartee."

Julie winced at his white-bread answer but Mare nodded and rubbed her bare, ringed foot against Alan's sloppy, SuperStore sport sock. "*Trust* me. I know where you're coming from."

Julie saw this and was part worried, part fascinated by the overt contact of this new acquaintance, this exotic, sky-swathed stranger. What must it be like, to attract such attention? On purpose. She picked up Alan's half-filled tumbler of cider and guzzled it. Fuel for whose flight into fancy?

Into the subsequent silence, Gus patted his face with an old-fashioned handkerchief and said with quiet scathing, "How is it then, Birth Man, that you reconcile my pre-war, 'puckered ass' persona and my Ph.D. in eighteenth-century sexual fetishes and paraphernalia?"

Heinz's face reddened to blend with his hair, which accented the whites of his eyes and made him look quite monster-like.

"What do you do?" interjected Julie, trying to be polite. "Heinz, I mean." Lordy, she thought, I certainly don't want any more details of Gus' job.

"I'm an artist. Well, an artist with potential, so I'm told. Haven't painted in two years. I can't get out the images, not the way they're in my head, anyway. They just won't come out right now. I've been living off savings, and now Visa. Next, I'll have to apply for a MasterCard."

"Better not do Amex. You've got to pay that one off right away," cautioned Alan. Only Julie seemed to recognize his sarcasm.

"No, no. I'm boycotting Amex. I used to work for a company they took over."

"And Mary? Mare, I mean," Julie ventured.

Mare shrugged. "You know, this and that. I once babysat a leading actor with a coke problem, made sure he showed up for his scenes straight, *sans* nosebleed. Personally, I thought he acted better all doped-up, but the director paid me mega-bucks to shadow him." Another languid shrug, followed by a slow, circular rubbing of Dan's stomach.

Before further words or actions could be exchanged, Susie emerged from the kitchen, her face flushed a bright and sweaty pink—again, in sharp contrast to all the beige—from concocting dinner. "Okay, you people, grab a seat. Anywhere." She eased herself into the chair at the head of the table.

"Carrot up your butt?" asked Heinz, amiably.

Susie scowled at him. "Yeast infection."

Julie blanched.

Dan blinked. "Yeah, you women and the stuff that comes out of your bodies. Nothin' leaves my body that doesn't give me extreme pleasure." The men, including Alan, gave little cheers.

Mortified, Julie pressed Mare further forward when the breathy colt moved to take the seat next to Alan. It was a most uncharacteristic gesture for Julie, but she did it on instinct, on auto pilot: like a mother would swoop in to divert a child from danger. She ended up sitting between Mare and Alan, positioning her legs like a fence, lest there be any more foot groping. Julie rationalized she was protecting Alan's suburban innocence from the brash Mare. Still, Alan would reject further advances. It might be nice to watch, a point for Team Mortgage and SuperStore. Just in case, she anchored Alan's left foot with her right. To extend his right, to meet with Mare, would be convoluted. He would have to squirm and it would look like he was having severe cramps, or at least about to fart. Julie had cured him of all such public displays in their first year of marriage.

They sat, expectant, having passed around the paper towel roll, adjusted cutlery and finished beers and glasses of wine. Now perhaps, thought Julie, the discussions she had envisioned would start. She had, after all, spent three hours poring over applicable Internet sites.

Now, however, she drew a blank.

"So, have you known each other long?" inquired Julie, anxious to stir the air that suspended daggers between Gus and Heinz and droplets of saliva between Mare and Alan. It was one of the icebreaker questions learned in a four-week course called Odd One Out. That was after the memory course, and she'd been the best in the class.

"Mare and I have known each other our whole lives," Dan offered. "Mare went to yoga with Susie a couple of years ago. Gus and Suse taught night school ..."

"You taught an eighteenth-century sexual fetishes class?" interrupted Alan, sounding gleeful. Julie suppressed a whimper. Alan would know she wouldn't want to discuss such a topic. He was tipsy enough to spill some sex secret of their own. Well, make one up then.

Gus smirked. "Actually, that particular class was only model airplane building. Terribly hard to angle in sex toys, but I tried."

Enough with the sweaty sex talk. Desperate, Julie blurted out, "You know, speaking of toys, there's a new Tickle Me Elmo doll coming out this Christmas. With new words." The cider was behind her on the sideboard, just out of graceful reach.

Five expectant faces cocked in her direction. It was Alan, the rotter, who said, "Yeah? What's it saying this time?"

"No, no, no. It only giggled last time," shouted Susie from the kitchen.

"I giggle too," said Mare coyly.

"Death to bin Laden!" crowed Heinz, his accompanying laugh like that of a mutilated Elmo.

Julie nudged Alan and jerked her head toward the cider. He was closer, but made a bigger spectacle of himself than had Julie made the stretch herself. She glared at him as he poured her two inches and himself a full glass. Too full, and he had to slurp out the first mouthful. She'd only had a glass and a half. Alan wore a dopey smile. He's tight, she thought. Tight as a tick, whatever that meant.

Finally, Susie emerged from the kitchen carrying a small, steaming tureen. She ladled half-portions of corn chowder into three blue ceramic bowls, two plastic Pokemon mugs and two pink Tupperware-ish containers, which Julie remembered being part of a gas station giveaway.

Thank God the chowder's good, thought Julie. Hot. Thick. The corn niblets snapped between her teeth. Spongy white bread was passed around, Gus' contribution, Julie suspected, as she watched him slather four slices in no-name margarine, then swab out the dregs of soup from his cup. She gave up guessing who brought what when the canned bean salad appeared. What kind of cheap, processed-food dinner parties did these people have, anyway? Then Alan's chicken wings were presented with their triple-coating of Kraft barbeque sauce. Dan did not take any, Gus ate his with his knife and fork.

Mare performed elaborate fellatio on each ulna and radius bone.

Or whatever fucking arm bones chickens had.

Dan offered red wine from a keg to Julie, who declined. Alan guzzled his remaining cider and thrust out his glass, though he'd never said yes to the stuff before. He'd only taken a few mouthfuls when Mare's flowing sleeve, reaching for another wing, tipped over the melamine glass. They all scrambled to avoid the dark pool that ebbed toward the edge of the Formica table, though Julie felt some drizzle onto her thigh. At least my jeans are black, she thought. No one will see.

"Oops," giggled Mare. No apology, Julie noted.

"Not to worry," assured Susie, whipping off her apron to absorb the spill. "That's what's good about not using a tablecloth."

After dinner, they returned to the living room. Alan, in his jeans and denim shirt—its CMA logo embroidered on the left breast pocket—claimed the whole papason, forcing Julie to squeeze in between Gus and Dan on the couch. Feeling cross, she studied Alan's bemused expression. He seemed in no hurry to flee, though Julie began checking her watch with rude regularity and calculating the minimum time possible between dinner and door. It just wasn't like she thought. Nobody was discussing arts council grants, or the Fringe Festival. In fact, Dan hauled out an old copy of *Georgia Straight* and was chiding Heinz because he'd never read the Savage Love column. Dan and Mare were experts and quoted copious whines and their acerbic answers from past issues.

"What is it, some kind of wacko foreplay for you two?" growled Heinz. "You two lie in bed and read sordid crap—entirely made up, I might add—to each other." Mare and Dan began laughing and made a mock show of seductive necking.

"Remember when the guy wrote about his farting fetish?" Dan gasped, extricating himself from Mare's gangly arms and legs.

"You people and your Savage Love addiction," admonished Susie from the galley kitchen before Mare could reply.

"Really!" Dan assured. "Total turn-on for the guy." Mare's tongue deeply probed his ear. "Jesus, Mare, enough!" He pushed her away. Brusque.

Chastised, Mare twirled around a few times and trilled, "So, who's up for a little pre-dessert?"

Dan narrowed his eyes at her and yanked her back to a sitting position on the arm of the couch. "No, Mare. Shut up."

She slapped his face playfully. "You shut up. It's a *party* for God's sake. Stop trying to be my father." She galloped across the room and asked over her shoulder, "Any takers? My treat."

Julie exchanged a wide-eyed glance with Alan.

"Alan," Mare cooed. "Al-laaaan. Care to join me? It is fucking-A fantastic Ecstasy. I guarantee it."

"Jesus, Mare. This is not the time. Besides, you said no more."

She tousled Dan's hair but her eyes were steely. "No. *You* said no more, darling. We'll let the hostess decide. Suse?" she called into the kitchen. "You don't mind, do you?"

"Whatever," came the reply from the kitchen over the rush of water. "Just make sure you take everything with you."

"Alan? Come and get it with me?" She held out her hand, wiggling her fingers.

He started to rise out of the papason. "Alan!" hissed Julie. "Ecstasy, Alan. Drugs? No offense, Mare, but, we'll pass. Both of us." Alan eased back into his chair.

"Heinz? Gus? Going once, going twice . . ."

"I'm too old for that shit," said Gus.

"I'm in," said Heinz at the same time.

". . . gone!" sang Mare.

Dan slouched deep into the couch, put his head back in resignation. Julie sat teetering on its edge, rigid. She had to pee, desperately, but felt as brittle as a twig.

"Mare, I am so warning you," Dan said, but it was half-hearted.

"C'mon, Heinz. We'll go in the bedroom, where these uptight prigs won't be offended." She floated toward the closed door off the living room and Heinz trotted after her, a sheepish look on his face.

"I can't believe you," hissed Julie to Alan. "Like you'd even consider it!"

"Frankly, my dear, I did consider it," he retorted, then burped.

"Kids, kids, kids, relax," placated Gus.

Ignoring him, Alan drawled in a tone Julie interpreted as patronizing, "Calm down. I just wanted to see how to take it, what it looks like. Give me some credit, will you?"

"I think we should go."

"Don't go," said Dan, his head still back and his eyes now closed. "Don't go because she's a flake. Please. I'll feel bad."

"Alan, I want to go."

Alan hauled himself out of the bowl-like chair and settled in—tightly—beside her on the couch. Gus heaved himself out to make more room. "Just relax," the alien-Alan cooed. "Half an hour more. I'm having an interesting time."

She stared at him, unbelieving, but he avoided her look. To think she'd begged him to come, to appease Susie's and Alan's mothers, neighbours in Sarnia, who'd set things up: a blind date of sorts. If she'd only known they were all less *artistes* and more unemployed—or sporadically employed—drifters. Druggie drifters.

Just as Mare and Heinz gushed out of the bedroom, Susie returned to the living room with a tray of empty jam jars and a large glass bowl of shimmying red Jell-O blobs. She set down the tray on the upturned milk crate that served as a coffee table. "Voila! Dessert. It didn't set totally. Sorry."

Julie turned away. It looked like a bowl of blood clots.

"Here's the deal," Susie continued merrily. "You have to eat it with chopsticks. Fun, huh? I'll be the timer and I'll give one of my bookmarks to the winner."

There were groans of protest. Julie hoped the proffered bookmark was not a reduction of the bleeding women painting on the far wall. Not that she'd win. Or even try to. How juvenile was this?

Mare and Heinz had returned. Julie studied them. Normal looking enough. Mare was giving Heinz a neck massage. Alan was dishing out portions. It figured. Food *and* a competition? Alan would be in his glory.

Susie handed out sets of generic wooden chopsticks, the kind from Chinese takeouts. Julie examined hers dubiously. Who'd sucked on them and had they been soaked in boiling water, or just run under a lukewarm tap?

Dan pushed his Jell-O and allocated utensils back. "Sorry. There's gelatin in Jell-O. No can do. I'll ref if you want."

Susie winced. "Oops. Sorry, Dan. I forgot. Can you do Rice Crispy squares?"

"S'alright," he answered, sounding deflated. "Seriously, I'll referee. Give me the timer. Okay, you carnivorous gluttons, prepare to stab and ingest the marrow of . . ." Susie made a face at him. "Fine then. Take up your chopsticks. On your mark, get set . . . Go!"

Susie dived into the race, adept with chopsticks. Mare began stabbing hers and Dan called a foul on her. Gus retrieved a fork from the kitchen and Heinz wore his three attempts on his shirt, like glass buttons. Trying to be a good sport, Julie managed to slurp in four cubes before losing the fifth to the floor.

Mare had taken to picking hers up with her long fingers and dropping them down her throat like raw oysters. She sashayed over to Alan, hitched up her caftan with one hand and climbed onto his lap. Julie hadn't even decided what to say, when Mare began hand feeding him, her fingers—*Ten little prostitutes,* thought Julie—pausing around Alan's open, laughing mouth. Except for his laughing, he looked like he was trapped under a big, silky parachute.

At first, Julie was paralyzed with shock. She hadn't witnessed such a scene since Alan rented *9½ Weeks.* When Mare ripped open Alan's denim shirt and began nuzzling his hairy chest, Julie snapped to it and pushed her bowl and chopsticks onto Gus. "Hey! Hey, what the hell are you doing? Get off my husband! Jesus Christ, get the hell off, this second." She pulled at Mare's arm, but Mare was solidly placed and much heavier than Julie. "Alan! Dan! Dan, do something!"

"For fuck's sake, I knew something like this would happen." Dan pushed out of his seat and pulled Mare off Alan, plunking her on the floor like a book bag.

"Ouch," she whined. "You guys are no fun."

"Fun?" shouted Julie. "Fun? You think lap-dancing on my husband is fun?"

"It's the drugs, Julie," Dan explained. He looked tired. "It's the Ecstasy. Makes you more verbal, more physically affection-ate. I wouldn't be surprised if she had some before we came over too, knowing her. She's a goddamn junkie."

"You should lighten up, Miss Priss," instructed Mare as she struggled to stand up without standing on the yards of material in which she was draped. Once upright, she wagged a finger in Dan's face. "And you shouldn't spill the family secrets."

Julie wanted to strike her, a desire she had never before come close to experiencing, but Mare moved off and draped herself around Susie, looking as wishy-washy as a dish rag against the beige wall. Susie indulged Mare's murmured apologies and a long lip kiss.

Julie's whole mouth quivered and then, to her horror, salivated. She swallowed and willed the sweet and tangy liquid to become bile, but her inner cheeks would only secrete the same, pleasurable juices she experienced before delving into a decadent chocolate dessert. She swallowed again, panicked. Was there no end to tonight's betrayals?

"We're going. Now. I'm going, anyway. You," she hissed at Alan, feeling mortified and discombobulated—like the real Julie was floating somewhere above the drooling Julie—"*you* do what the hell you want." Frantic now, she looked around for her purse.

"I'll get your container," offered Susie, meek now. She pushed off Mare and scuttled into her kitchen.

Heinz and Mare were necking.

Julie gasped and then stared at Dan. "You just stand there? And watch? What kind of freak boyfriend are you? All of you! You're freaks." She shouted toward the kitchen. "Susie, tell your mother to stay out of your future social life, as I will tell Alan's." She dared to glance again at Heinz and Mare. She stood in front of him now, vertical spooning so to speak, his arms wrapped and crossed around her as he cupped her breasts. "Oh my God! Freaks! Drug-heads. My God, Dan, you're just as bad, if you just stand by and let . . ."

"She doesn't mean anything. She's a great girl when she's not high." He looked into Julie's eyes, pleading.

Susie returned to the living room. "I've run out of dish soap, so sorry, it's not washed."

"I'd *so* like to fuck you right now, Heinz."

Julie broke out of Dan's penetrating stare and spied the strap of her shoulder bag, snaking out from under an easel. She pushed past Dan and Gus and snatched the container Susie held before her like a ceremonial funeral flag. She plucked up her purse and slammed her feet into her shoes and did not look back for Alan.

She was standing at the elevator, jabbing the down arrow to no avail, when she heard Susie's door open and shut. Alan appeared beside her, but did not touch or speak. He knew better.

In the elevator, he turned his cell back on and cleared his throat several times, in preparation to speak, but no words came out. Julie stared straight ahead, wishing the cab would descend faster, that it would magically plummet her straight home.

She reached for the door release and his hand covered hers.

"I don't know what I was thinking," he quavered. "It just, kind of, spilled out. A weird wanting to be irresponsible." He shook his head, as if even disbelieving himself.

"I didn't know you had it in you," she whispered, hearing the horror and shock in her voice.

Outside, it was still raining: huge blobs that spilled from the sky and broke open on her head like water balloons. Alan pulled her back under the building's awning to indicate he would get the car. Julie stood and fumed while he trotted down the block, knowing she'd have to take the wheel for the long drive out to Port Moody.

It had been years since she'd cried. Infuriated, she fought the sensation. Nothing sad happened. Stupid things, infuriating things, but nothing to cry about. So Alan got drunk and had been kissed by a woman on Ecstasy.

But she began to cry anyway. Salty tears ran down her face and she stepped out from the awning to mix them with the raindrops, not wanting Alan to see.

The rain was cool and calming and she lifted her head skyward.

She was almost directly below Susie's apartment. The patio doors must be open, she could hear laughter, shouts for Gus to bring out his sex toys, Mare's pleas for Susie and Dan to go take a hit. Julie heard them like they were only a few storeys up and had a fleeting thought about the physics of sound bubbles, silent pockets. There was some phenomenon.

She recognized the distinctive approach of her and Alan's clunky Jeep, tilted back her head and blinked to squeeze out the tears and raindrops. She heard the Jeep's bleating horn, sharp but distant.

But had Alan kissed back?

She thought it was an illusion, a derivative from the glass and a half of cider, the tension, the reflection of lights and rain.

A blur of turquoise from above, it grew bigger and bigger, dropping from the misty skies like a lost shooting star, a kite without wind. There was no time to turn away, not even to think to close her eyes.

It crashed through the neon yellow awning and hit the cement with the force of a boulder. Lovely turquoise kite, now smashed, splattered with contrasting red. As bold as Susie's paintings. Only now could Julie turn away.

She sank to her knees on the sidewalk—ah! *now* the bile— and then began to vomit. Alan ran to her, knelt beside her and cuddled her. Above them, people were screaming. She felt him grope under his jacket for his cell phone. It rang as he pulled it out.

"Yes?" he said impatiently. "Hi, Mom. We'll call you back. We've got an emergency here." He jammed the phone back in his pocket. "My mom," he announced needlessly. "Calling to ask about Susie's dinner party."

THE ESSENCE OF MISS CHOWDHURY

I am standing in the Sears bargain basement in Kitchener, a million mental miles from Sage, the BC town in which I grew up. I am looking around for a sales rep to confirm that the seconds sheets I plucked from a jumble bin are queen size.

This is when I see her.

Oh. My. God.

I can see just her profile, but I know it's her. The licorice-whip braid is gone, her hair now shoulder-length. She wears stiff denims and a dull green sweatshirt. Where are the vibrant yards of soft cottons and silks that floated around her like rainbows?

Oh, Miss Chowdhury, Miss Chowdhury.

I bury my ring finger, wedding band, in the sheets. I don't know why.

She pivots and we're face to face. I yelp at her hideous disfigurement, like I am the one who has been stripped of my humanness.

The first time I saw Miss Chowdhury, the September day she glided into English Lit. 11, something deep in the pit of my stomach sprouted. A warm, yeasty ball of fascination that doubled in size each class I saw her, until I was a vessel that could no longer contain it.

She was the first Indian woman with whom I'd ever had close contact, and I thought she was delectable. Her skin was as brown and smooth as a fresh nutmeg, her black braid as thick as my forearm, and it twitched like a Bengal tiger's tail. She was covered neck to toe in a long-sleeved, crimson tunic with baggy matching pants, and a long chiffon scarf—crimson with bronze swirls—was draped around her shoulders.

Her curves were undetectable, yet she exuded delicacy and sensuality.

"Good morning, class. Welcome to English Literature. I am Miss Chowdhury."

There were murmured good mornings and a few snickers.

She regarded us with patience, unperturbed by our adolescent bravado.

"This will be a difficult class, I can assure you now. If you do not like reading and critical analysis, you'd best excuse yourself and head down to Mr. Piva in the woodshop."

That elicited more genuine smiles and titters.

"Now, before we start, I shall go out on a limb or, as my grandmother was fond of saying, 'I shall let the elephant step over me,' and declare an open question period. I am well aware I am probably your first teacher of such a different ethnicity and culture. Please, ask your questions now so we can get on with the business at hand: the study of the greatest and most influential writers in English history. If you please." She extended her hands out to us, palms up. The bangles on her wrists tinkled.

No one's hand shot up. Not often were we given *carte blanche* to ask questions of a personal nature to teachers. I summoned the courage and waggled my fingers somewhere around my ears for attention.

"Um. Hi. My name is Gillian. I was wondering what you call your, um, outfit?"

She adjusted the cascades of chiffon before answering. "It's called a *salwaar* suit, or a Punjabi suit. Punjab is a region in north India."

"So, is that where you're from?" asked Randy, a studious slip of a boy with a cauliflower complexion.

"No. I am from Delhi. The capital," she added.

"Do you eat meat?" Susan Piper asked. The class guffawed. As the city's biggest butcher, her father had donated hot dogs and hamburgers to many a school fete.

"Yes, but not beef for I am Hindu. We of the Hindu faith do not eat beef, due to our respect for the cow." She waited for the whispered comments to finish. "Anything else? No? Fine. Let's begin. We're starting with the King James Bible's version of Adam and Eve and Eve's betrayal in the Garden of Eden. Page six in your textbooks, everyone."

I went home that night and commenced my quest to acquire Miss Chowdhury's personal attentions.

Two or three classes later, I was ready to invade the East.

Before class, I sidled up to her desk and requested my name be changed on the attendance sheet from Gillian to Roop. I'd found the name in a book of short stories by Rudyard Kipling.

"Roop?" Miss Chowdhury repeated, dubious.

"Yes. Roop. R-O-O-P. Roop. It's a Hindu name, isn't it?"

She was in a pale blue *salwaar* suit that day, with white embroidery on its cuffs and borders. She studied me. "Yes. R-O-O-P. I know the name. I'm wondering why."

"Kipling," I breezed out.

"I see." She wrote my new name—in pencil, mind—in the margin beside Jefferson, Gillian. Girl with the mother as flaky as dried chilies.

I continued my studies into India and Hinduism with a fervour that surpassed watching *The Hardy Boys*, spending time with my two closest friends and musing about my mother's return.

A few more weeks into the semester, during a class before lunch, I jolted out of my Taj Mahal daydream to acknowledge I was being called upon.

"*Ji ha?*" I answered, looking up eagerly at Miss Chowdhury. The class snickered.

"Gillian—Roop—Gillian, remember this is an English literature class," Miss Chowdhury cautioned.

"Yeah, not Paki 101," whispered Brad Green from the desk behind me. I stamped on his encroaching size-twelve sneaker like it was a cockroach.

"Are you two quite done? Yes? Which of you wishes to elaborate what the albatross represents?"

I felt my face flush to the colour of tandoori paste and shook my head.

Chi chi chi, I self-chastised.

When the bell went to start lunch hour, Miss Chowdhury beckoned me to her desk, where she presided so regally from her castored chair. I approached with no sense of trepidation, certain I was about to be applauded for my bilingual efforts. Of course she would not want our new camaraderie blatantly showcased.

Instead, Miss Chowdhury demanded, "Gillian, what is going on, if you please?" Her expression was unreadable, but for her lips, which were pursed into extra plumpness.

My throat constricted and burned like I'd rubbed it raw with chilies.

"Well, I ..."

"I will not tolerate these attempts to undermine my authority in the classroom, nor will I ignore their obvious racist undertones."

I gasped.

"If it continues, to any degree, I will bring in the principal and your parents. Is that perfectly clear?"

I swallowed air, trying to clear my throat.

"Miss Chowdhury, I am not making fun of you. I'm not racist. I ..." My desire to gain her affection suddenly seemed ludicrous, humiliating even. But why should I be ashamed to admire?

"*Kripaya*, Miss Chowdhury, you've misunderstood. There's been a terrible misunderstanding."

She raised a sculpted eyebrow expectantly.

I squeaked out, "It's just that, well, I want to be like you."

Some roughhousing idiots in the hall slammed against the classroom door, and we both startled.

"Pardon me?"

I took a deep breath. "I want to be like you. I mean, I want to be East Indian."

Miss Chowdhury leaned forward, a barely perceptible flinch, blinking. Her lashes were so long and thick, I imagined I could feel them stir the air as would a cool breeze.

"Gillian, I don't know what to say. Truly, I am speechless. If my deceased relatives were the type to be buried, they would be turning in their graves." Needing confirmation, she repeated, "You say you would like to be Indian?"

I nodded, stood as still as a tamarind tree.

She considered this. "That's odd. No other Caucasians with whom I am acquainted—and perhaps many of my countrymen —want to be Indian."

Her face was endearing, like Mary in the Nativity scene.

"But why?" I asked, sincerely amazed. "You are so gentle and exotic. And serene. And beautiful. So are all the pictures I have seen of India," I added. Announcing her beauty dangled too uncomfortably in the air.

She smiled her soft, encouraging smile. "You would not think so, if you were stuck in the middle of a Delhi traffic jam, and were witness to a policeman beating a rickshaw driver senseless for no apparent reason. Then, when you alight from your taxi, having decided it is faster to walk after all, you must take care to not step in steaming cow dung and avoid the pleading gaze of a deformed beggar, made deliberately so by his own mother to make him more pathetic and thus, lucrative." She looked rueful until she shook her head and brought herself back from her homeland.

"So, what shall be done about this?" she inquired. Her words were brisk, but not angry.

"Excuse me?"

"What shall we do about this fascination of yours with my country?"

With you, Miss Chowdhury. With you.

I squirmed, not knowing what answer was expected, certain I would have to bury my desires.

She examined me once again. "You see, Roop, assimilation into Sage, despite it being the grand new decade, is bewildering at best for me, degrading at worst. Please, put yourself in my shoes. I am an unmarried Indian woman in a community with an almost non-existent Indian population. Imagine the scrutiny I am under from all parties."

The school board. Her family. Me.

"How did you come to be here?" I dared asked, afraid she would soon snap out of her intimate tones.

"My father arranged for me to be taken in by my auntie. I cannot shame them . . ."

"I would never . . ." I interjected.

She held up a delicate hand, its fingers long and graceful, the moons of her nails as white as taro pulp. "I realize, now at least, that you would not intentionally bring inappropriate attention to me. Regardless, I shall ask you to refrain from making Indian references in the class. It undermines my authority in English literature."

I was crestfallen. How then, could I show her how much I had studied about her culture? I could hardly pursue her up and down the halls, the way the infantile boys did their latest passion.

She continued. "However, if you maintain the utmost discretion, I would be honoured to have you to my house, my auntie's house, for dinner. Your parents are also welcome."

I shook my head, horrified at the thought of my Kraft Dinner-14oz.-beefsteak-eating father negotiating his way through a rich palette of curries. My mother had hightailed it off with the dry wall guy and I hadn't seen her in months. It was the third such flight of *goddamn selfish fancy* and my father swore he would not take her back yet again, should she return to him. Or me, her only daughter.

"No!" I exclaimed. "I mean, I promise to tell them, but I really don't think they would be comfortable. With the spices," I added hastily.

"Very well." She glanced at the clock over the chalkboard. "Go eat lunch. Perhaps next Friday, at seven? I'll see that you get my, my auntie's, address."

"Can I, *may* I, still call myself Roop?" I entreated.

"Oh, dear. We'll see, shall we?"

I backed away, afraid that taking my eyes off her would nullify the invitation.

"Going *where?*" asked my father during dinner that night, his mouth half full of roast. "To your teacher's house? A class thing?"

I considered lying, but my father, in his new dual role of parenting, had been known to confirm fishy stories. "No, just me." *Be cool*, I instructed myself. *Be nonchalant.*

He refilled the gravy boat from the coagulating mass on the stove. "This teacher is a woman, right? I'm sure I don't need to tell you what a man would do to a young girl, alone in a house." He shot me a pointed look. A man could teach a woman to drywall and whisk her away.

"Yes," I answered, feeling impatient. "It's a woman. Miss Chowdhury."

He paused to consider the name. "Chowdhury? There's getting to be a whole pile of them in Sage."

"Dad, that's so gross."

After further strained discussion—I was grateful it was based more on the peculiarities surrounding a student being singled out for a teacher's personal attention, than on Miss Chowdhury's heritage—I found myself knocking on the auntie's door, the designated Friday night.

It was answered by Auntie, an older woman, Indian of course. Her staccato, jilted movements contrasted with the graceful gestures of my Miss Chowdhury like oil and vinegar. She was plain old fat, not remotely bodacious, and decidedly garish. Still, I was determined to ingratiate myself.

"*Namaste*," I greeted.

Her face remained stern, but she returned the greeting.

"Anita!" she shouted, still looking at me. "The girl is here." Auntie summoned me forward, her arm plump and scaly but resplendent with jangling bangles. "Come."

I followed her into the living room, disappointed that it did not match the opulence of the picture books I had pored over. I longed for brick red walls with gold appliqués and chunky mahogany furniture. Instead, the eggshell-white walls and the blue brocade upholstery were similar to those in my own home. I had to be satisfied with two bright, velveteen wall hangings depicting Ganesh, Shiva and languishing women surrounded by tigers.

"*Namaste*," said Miss Chowdhury, vaporizing into the room wearing a soft pink sari, edged with intricate silver stitching. Her smile was genuine and warm, and I wanted her to take me in her arms. "You met Auntie?"

I nodded and Auntie grunted. "Don't mind her," Miss Chowdhury assured, "she is put out because Friday is usually Kentucky Fried Chicken night, and I insisted we eat traditional." Her voice poured over me as I imagined *jelabi* syrup might do.

"Please sit down. I shall put on some music. Would you prefer Bollywood style, or classical?"

"Whatever suits you, Miss Chowdhury," I replied in my most formal voice, thrilled that she assumed I knew the difference. My studies were not in vain after all!

Lilting sitar music soon filled the room and then I was left alone while they finished dinner preparations. The air was thick with heady aromas, as thick as I anticipated the savoury sauces would be.

During dinner, Miss Chowdhury answered my spray of cultural questions with patience, only becoming irritated when I inquired about her plans for marriage. Auntie snorted but Uncle, who had slid into his chair as we were sitting for dinner, did not even look up from creating his next ball of rice and *dal* and popping it cleanly into his mouth like a peppermint.

"I have no plans to marry at this time," she clarified. "It's part of the reason I came to Canada, to remain independent. Now, let's give you a lesson in eating with your hands before any more of your dinner lands in your lap."

I so wanted to ask more, but sensed the topic was closed. Indeed, my coated hand and slops were testament to my Western incompetence. By the end, I was stuffed, though still using four fingers.

"There's more," Miss Chowdhury informed when we'd emptied the stainless steel bowls. She dabbed her lips. "Auntie is no Mother Hubbard, to be sure."

For dessert, when Miss Chowdhury served us shallow bowls of rice pudding, a panicked look must have crossed my face for Auntie began chortling with glee.

I was just about to admit defeat and ask for a utensil, when Auntie stopped laughing and produced four spoons from the sideboard drawer behind her. She handed me one, a smile still playing at her lips.

"Auntie insists on playing that trick on any non-countryman who joins us for a meal. It perversely pleases her to have people think we are barbarians, not Indians, right, Auntie?"

"*Chi, chi, chi*," tsked Auntie.

Several weeks later, a Saturday, I knocked on Miss Chowdhury's front door just before noon, hoping my timing for the impulsive visit might include lunch. My mouth was already watering in anticipation of tasting the delicate nuttiness of basmati rice, a searing vindaloo. I hoped there was no left-over fried chicken.

Auntie's voice barked out to come in. When she saw it was me, uninvited, she growled lowly, "Your teacher is not here."

I ignored her usual gruffness; she would not come between Miss Chowdhury and me. "What happened?" I asked, for Auntie's left foot was propped up on a hassock. Her ankle was swollen to the diameter of a fat cassava.

"None of your business, nosy girl."

"Is your husband home to help you?"

She made a disgusted hissing sound. Perhaps he was off with his cronies, chewing and spitting *paan*, as Miss Chowdhury had confided before our dinner. "Do you want me to get you anything?"

Her eyes flicked to the stairs as she debated letting me help or not.

"Fetch my bedpan. Under my bed. Don't touch anything else."

"Your bedpan?" I repeated, hoping I wouldn't have to empty it first.

"Aach. Typical spoiled and fickle girl. Like Anita. First you want to do something, then you change your mind. Off and on like electricity."

"No, no. I'm going," I'd be foolish to miss this opportunity to explore.

I dashed upstairs and grabbed the bedpan, fortunately unfouled. Then I called down about having to use the bathroom and entered Miss Chowdhury's room.

Oh, Miss Chowdhury.

The whole room smelled like her: intoxicating sandalwood. The bed was unmade and I leaned into it, inhaling her essence. Clothes were all over and I was charmed that she was messy, like me.

"Girl! Bring the bedpan."

"Yes. Coming."

My heart pounding, I snatched up a poof of teal material. It was the pants and tunic of one of her suits. But I couldn't find the matching scarf, despite a mad search.

Auntie's voice was shrill from the foyer. "Girl! You pass water slower than a dying old man. What are you doing up there?"

At last I spied a streak of teal, just under the bed. I rolled the three pieces into a tight wad, stuffed it into my backpack and dashed out of my love's room.

Indeed, Auntie was teetering on the bottom stair, her face ferocious. I gripped her elbow and guided her back to her chair.

I left after she settled her bulk, afraid she would demand I place the stainless steel pot under her gigantic bare bottom.

On Monday, Miss Chowdhury greeted me with a peculiar look. I mouthed *Namaste* to her and took my seat. When she handed out the previous week's essays, I was doodling Bic pen renditions of Ganesh, the elephant-man god, and thinking about drinking sweet *chai* with Miss Chowdhury on a rooftop terrace during the camel races in Jassailmar.

I was flooded with shame when I saw the fat, red D on the top of my assignment and fought back tears.

"The essays ranged from mediocre to quite thoughtful. We'll discuss them in more detail next day. Class dismissed. Gillian, please stay behind."

There were definite sniggers in my direction as my classmates shuffled out.

"I will explain why you received a D," she began. Her melodic rhythm separated my indignation and longing like clarifying butter and I forgave her the undeserved mark. "Gillian, the assignment was to compare and contrast two pieces of English literature from different periods. Your choice of *The Canterbury Tales* and the Hindu Holy Scriptures, therefore, did not meet the criteria. Furthermore, your interpretation of the sacred *Bhagavad Gita* was ill-researched. Incorrect, in fact, to the point of near-blasphemy."

Blasphemy?

I fought back tears.

I had worked hours—days!—on the paper, wanting to impress her so much.

The tears won out and began rolling down my cheeks, big droplets like the first signs of monsoon.

She did not acknowledge my pain, but chose instead to focus somewhere over my left shoulder. "If you wish to redo the paper —properly—I shall accept it before next Monday only."

How was I to ever get my adoration reciprocated?

"Questions?"

She was looking at me less severely now, her gentleness having returned.

"I have a question, yes. Would you care to come to my house for dinner on Friday night?"

Her exasperated expression was mixed with degrading pity.

"*Dhanyavad.* No. My parents and brothers are coming from India, as well as my mother's youngest sister from Toronto."

"Saturday, then? Sunday."

She exchanged her genteel aura for irritation once again.

"Gillian! This must stop. It is not appropriate."

gilliangilliangillian. Why was she trying to hurt me?

I nodded but inside, *inside*, like rotting fruit, my blood, my mind, were fermenting. I gathered my books and shoved them haphazardly into my pack. I was almost out the door when Miss Chowdhury said, "I understand you paid a visit to Auntie on Saturday."

I couldn't trust myself to speak. I just stood there like a palm tree, swaying from internal turmoil.

"I also understand you've had some family difficulties this fall."

My goddamn mother! How could she be so embarrassing, hundreds of miles away? Again, I couldn't reply.

Miss Chowdhury said nothing more. Her peculiar, pitying look haunted me all day.

I skipped English Lit. on Thursday, too mortified to attend.

Plus, I wanted to shut up the student body. I wanted to punish Anita.

Still, while I bided my time in the bathroom until the period bell, I knew I couldn't let things go.

Couldn't let *her* go.

Perhaps things would not have gone the way they did, had not Carla and Deb confronted me Thursday after school by following me home and barricading me in my own bedroom.

"You're, like, totally weirding out on us," Carla informed me between mouthfuls of Wagon Wheel. "People're calling you the new Gabbi Varvarinski."

Gabbi. Sage High's resident daughter of a nut. Her mother'd tried to commit suicide by lighting herself on fire.

Deb murmured her agreement.

When I didn't protest, or even reply, Carla continued. "So, first it was this name change thing. Weird, but you picked a cool name. Then we have to listen to this bullshit screeching every time we come over. Get out the Rick Springfield, will ya?"

I could see it was driving her crazy that I wasn't reacting so I continued imagining myself as a serene priestess dispensing wisdom on the shores of the Ganges.

"But lately," she glanced at Deb. "Lately, it's really bad, all the language. And have you even taken off those stupid pajamas things since Chowdhury gave them to you?"

I felt myself flush, embarrassed I'd stolen, then lied about, my outfit. "*Salwaar* suit," I interrupted smugly, to cover my shame. "And you know I don't wear it to school, only after. I don't want to draw attention to Anita's generosity."

She rolled her eyes. "Whatever. Here's the thing, people are starting to talk."

I raised my eyebrows to prompt her onward, though my heart was thudding.

Carla exchanged a satisfied smirk with Deb.

"Kids are saying you've got a crush on Chowdhury and if you don't be careful, you're gonna turn into a Paki-lesbo."

I sneered. "She's Indian, not Pakistani."

Deb and Carla gaped at me.

"You see what we mean? You care about what stupid nationality she is, over turning lezzie? See what's happening?"

I decided my two friends were actually enjoying themselves, playing saviour. I'd always been on the fringe with them anyway. My new devotion to India was a delicious way to oust me.

"Are you asking me to choose?" I challenged.

They looked surprised, but could hardly back down now.

"Well," said Carla, "we've got our reputations to protect. You're dragging us down."

"Fine," I said, trying to sound smug. "Consider yourselves free."

They hauled themselves off my bed and sauntered to the door.

"Give us a call when you wanna be Canadian again," Carla sniped.

"Yeah," said Deb, ever loquacious.

Following this ostracism, I rapped on Auntie's front door on Friday night. Mother Nature saw fit to pelt down rain and I was a sopping, pathetic figure in the doorway.

She grunted at me as usual, then waddled off. Her ailing foot seemed cured. I took her retreat as invitation to enter.

The living room contained Uncle and another rather morose-looking older man—her father, perhaps? There were young men, the brothers she had spoken of, I assumed, and two women of Auntie's generation. Mother, the dignified one and *chota* Auntie, the little aunt.

Miss Chowdhury was not to be seen.

"*Namaste*," I whispered, my former bravado gone.

The men continued their conversation in Hindi and the boys only nudged each other, but the woman I suspected was *mata*, motioned me to sit down.

"*Mira nam Roop, hai.*"

Auntie mumbled something to the woman who had at least acknowledged my presence.

"Ah, one of Anita's students. How very lovely. I am Anita's mother." She smiled, as gracious as her daughter.

I sensed I had little time. "Please, *shrimati* Chowdhury, please tell me about your daughter when she was younger."

Mrs. Chowdhury looked pleased to be asked, despite Auntie's groans besides her and the third woman's indifference. She took a deep breath and I hoped she was going to launch into a long, juicy history, when Miss Chowdhury appeared from the kitchen. She was dressed in an exquisite tumeric-coloured sari, far more formal than those of the other women. The dips and swirls and folds of silk covered her lusciously and I wanted to lick the soft flesh of her back and belly that peaked out under her rib-tickling *choli*.

"Gillian!" she exclaimed.

"Roop," I reminded, my silent threat of causing a scene veiled except to her.

She looked around the room of inquiring faces.

"Do come upstairs. I must show you the new jewelry Mummy gave me." Miss Chowdhury flashed me a smile, as discreet as the Hindu goddess Lakshmi's, and beckoned me to follow.

In her bedroom, she shut the door behind us before whirling about like a pinwheel and letting her real feelings show.

"How dare you? How dare you invade my privacy, my family like this? You simply must stop this behaviour; it's becoming ... it's becoming, well, psychotic! You cannot be my friend, my sister ..."

Lover.

"... my daughter."

She smoothed the glossy, coifed hair at her temples. "You are my student. Only. And you cannot simply *become* Indian." She shook her head at me, now almost pitying.

"Gillian, I want you to transfer out of English literature class. In fact, I have already arranged it with the principal. I told him there were special circumstances you didn't wish disclosed and he agreed to give you a study period for the remainder of the term, at no penalty to your academic standing."

"But I don't want to transfer," I protested.

"Ah, but I wish you to."

Now there would be nothing. No one.

The urge to be within her arms was overwhelming. I flung myself at her and nestled my body into hers. Its warmth against my damp cotton blouse was soothing. She struggled to disconnect from me, but I was stronger.

The scent of sandalwood filled my body and I wanted to crawl inside her, to be suffused with her spirit.

"Damn you, Gillian!" she trilled. "Do I have to scream downstairs to get you off me?"

"But you won't," I murmured into her neck. While my right hand pressed into the small of her back, I pivoted her face into mine with my left.

Bobby Mac had taught me to kiss in eighth grade.

Oh, how I yearned to explore Miss Chowdhury's mouth slowly, to savour her certain succulence as I would a bite of butter chicken. But I knew there would not be the time, or compliance, and parted her lips, her ivory teeth with aggression.

Her tongue was as sweet and slippery as a ripe mango.

I liked to believe, given one more second, that she would have relented. One more moment of intimacy and she would have requited my passion.

But the door flew open, revealing Mrs. Chowdhury and one of the brothers.

"*Mata-ji!*" cried out Miss Chowdhury. I was shocked into releasing her and she wrenched herself away. "Please, Mummy, Rashid, help me!"

My lips were wet with saliva, though perhaps it was just my own. I wiped them on my sleeve and saw I had drawn blood.

No.

It was only her smeared lipstick, bright as pomegranate seeds.

Mrs. Chowdhury gripped the doorframe for support, Rashid grasped his mother around the waist.

Angry Hindi pelted me like bullets. In seconds, the other faces peered in and joined the cacophony.

"Get out, Gillian," shouted Miss Chowdhury, pushing me through the crowd and down the stairs. "Get out! You've no idea what you've done."

No, I didn't.

Not really.

Not even when Principal Jones announced Miss Chowdhury's resignation, Monday morning. Not even when a new Indian family moved into Auntie's house and claimed no knowledge of the former owners each time I pounded at the door.

On what I calculated was the first day of *divali*, the late autumn Light Festival, my mother sent divorce papers from Red Deer by courier. That January, we moved to Ontario for a fresh start.

In Sears, now, almost a decade later, I tremble. The right side of Miss Chowdhury's face, and down her neck, is as dark red and shiny as tamarind chutney. Her right eye does not blink, the skin is so tight and deformed.

"Miss Chowdhury," I begin. "I am ..."

"Gillian," she completes.

Her look of hatred pees over me, hot and vile.

"I have always wanted to know what happened. I've worried so."

Her good side jerks spasmodically into a scoff. "Really, Gillian? It's been a few lifetimes. Do you remember my last words to you?"

My head spins. I've tried to remember only the delicious feelings. I bow my head, shamed. "You said, 'You've no idea what you've done.'"

She holds her gaze steady.

I want to resume our last encounter. I want to peel off her hideous mask and attach it to my own face. I want her forgiveness for being a mere child who only wanted someone beautiful to love her, for this is how I now understand my obsession.

"Please, I want to know what happened. I need to know. Consider hearing of your obvious pain, part of my punishment."

She looks to the left, so I can only see the scar. Yes, punishment.

"I was to marry, in Delhi. He was abusive. I knew he was, that's why I refused the arrangement and begged my parents to send me to Canada. They are very, very traditional."

I feel nauseous and my bowels are alternately rumbling and clenching. "Why did you return then? If you knew what India held?"

She fixes her good eye on me, resigned now to the fate of meeting me again. She waters down her loathing expression, like a tourist curry dish and sighs. "Once Auntie and *mata* saw us, and the others, they made me. I knew they would. It didn't matter who pursued who: family honour was at stake. They whisked me back to marry the fiend before being single, in the West, could further corrupt me. They threatened to tell the school. What choice did I have? Regardless, I could not continue to teach at that school, with you there."

Oh please God, tell me you felt . . .

"If I had quit, to escape you, my work visa would have been revoked. I would have been deported and destitute."

No. It had never been. Not for a moment. Never even if the gods had granted a thousand more moments.

"And your face?"

She shrugs. "I tried to leave him after a few years. His brothers hunted me down and set me on fire. If I lived, my punishment would be for life, every time I looked in the mirror. If I died, Sudha would be free to marry again, to collect another dowry."

"But that was, what, 1986, '87?" I exclaim. "Surely to God such . . ."

The mobile side of her face grimaces. "I told you, we have very traditional families." She traced a long finger down her plasticky throat, like a lover might. "Look what it took before my father would allow me to return to Canada."

A harried, matronly clerk sweeps by. Her nametag says HERA. "You ladies need help?"

"We're fine, thank you," we answer as one. Models of Western decorum.

She glances at Miss Chowdhury's face and cannot suppress an expression of discomfort before bustling away, perhaps grateful she does not have to serve the monster-face.

"I must go," Miss Chowdhury says, thrusting the yardage she has been kneading like chapatti dough back into its chrome cage.

"No! Please. I must find a way to apologize..."

She laughs, cackles really, and shakes her head. "There is nothing to be said, or done. Perhaps you should refresh your studies about karma, Gillian. I find it very comforting myself."

And my Miss Chowdhury leaves me again.

The bed sheets are damp where I have clenched them. I stuff them into the bin and pick up her discarded curtains.

I bury my face in the folds. The folds catch my tears.

Maybe it's only my memories, but I draw in the heady scent of sandalwood, the essence of Miss Chowdhury.

THIS SIDE OF BONKERS

Ki Young found a low knothole in the fence shared with the neighbour. He found it crawling under the lilac bush, while playing a lonely game of war.

Now, whenever he can, between Canadian Mummy's plodding through English picture dictionaries and some-mornings play group, he watches Neighbour Lady in her kitchen. Once he saw her abandon a perfectly good batch of sweets, take off all her clothes and dance around naked.

He's only four, but he's been waiting for a repeat performance ever since, sensing the act's naughtiness. It would be the same in Korea.

"Ki Young! Come, Ki Young!"

It's Canadian Mummy. She talks to him like the dog, complete with the hand gestures. Cuddles him like the dog too—maybe a fraction less—but the dog is bigger than him, so that makes sense. Ki Young can't understand Canadians and their dogs anyway. It's crazy. Back home, before Grandfather died, a big mean Doberman had guarded their little grocery and Ki Young was told to keep his distance. No cuddles there. His only other contact with dogs was going with Grandfather to slurp *soo yuk.* Yummy stew, as tender as the Kraft Dinner Canadian Mummy served.

"What were you doing?" Mummy asks, imitating his squat beside the fence. She's a bit wobbly.

He thinks. Ah yes! "Looking."

"Looking? Yes. Looking. At what? Looking at what?" Mummy's eyes are glassy and her breath is fermented smelling. But not as bad as Grandfather's after a waxy little green box of *soju.*

"Look at lady."

"The lady. Looking at *the* lady. Well, don't do that. That lady is strange. Like a witch. You know *witch?* Bonkers." Mummy twirls her finger at her temple.

Ah! michi nom. Grandfather, in the end.

He goes off to play with the toy cars, wishing they were Hyundais, but not daring to risk offending and losing his collection, triple to the assortment he had to leave behind. There is an abundance of everything in the house, from shiny magazines with curvy—*jjut bbong*—yellow-haired girls, to flats of Campbell's tomato soup, to used tissues. Mummy cries a lot. Some of the magazines are Mummy's, some Daddy's. The soup is for him, everyday, for lunch. He is going through "a stage," apparently. That is what Canadian Mummy said to Daddy at dinner. "Our boy is going through a tomato soup phase."

The funny thing is, it isn't really about tomato soup. It is that Mummy is slopping it into the pot before she asks what he wants anyway. Besides, faced with the gargantuan icebox and the walk-in pantry, to eke out a nod is all Ki Young can manage. It isn't as though his culinary tastes run to the exotic, or even varied. Grandfather's apartment in a disintegrating district of Seoul was far more humble and there, for as long as he could remember, they ate breakfasts and lunches of spicy *kimchi* and bland sticky rice.

Bonkers Lady comes over later that morning. Ki Young wets himself, terrified she has finally come to report his spying, perhaps the naked dancing incident specifically.

No. She wants a ride to the C-Train. Her car is broken.

"Hello, Little Man," she says, leaning against the doorframe while Canadian Mummy searches for her keys. "What's your name again?"

He understands, but says nothing, just stands squirming behind the umbrella stand trying to hide the dark patch at his crotch, down his left leg.

Canadian Mummy will be angry. Maybe. Sometimes he is a Good Boy and a Bad Boy for the same thing. Like the second day of his New Canadian Life, when she discovered him squatting over the toilet, the way Grandfather had taught him. First she scolded, plucked him up by the armpits and deposited his backside squarely over the bowl. Then she stood guard, a smile playing at her lips.

Ki Young climbs into the back seat and decides he'll say his accident occurred in the car. She could hardly fault that. She hadn't even asked if he'd had to go before jabbing her keys in the direction of the back seat. "In, Ki Young. In the car."

"The air's a bit, uh, stale. May I open the window?" asks Bonkers Lady. Ki Young is certain she's referring to his acidic urine smell and cowers into the corner of the back seat. But it's Canadian Mummy she's looking at. Yes, pee and the old fruit smell; they could easily be mistaken.

"Of course," says Canadian Mummy airily. She is always very nice to Bonkers Lady in person, whether across the lawns, or now, as chauffeur.

They leave the subdivision, which Ki Young recognizes: it's the route to the playgroup. Soon though, they are coasting through unfamiliar territory. He strains to see out the back window, to absorb the buildings, the terrain, and struggles to translate at least some of Canadian Mummy and Bonker Lady's words.

"Karli, across the street? About to pop, eh?" says Bonkers Lady.

"I guess. Ooops, sorry," adds Canadian Mummy, bumping them over a corner curb.

"I offered to read her cards for her, give her some of my home-brewed ginger tea, but she said she'd stick to science."

Canadian Mummy swerves the car away from a bicycle.

"Goodness," gasps Bonkers Lady, one handing gripping the door, the other a large pinkish stone hanging on a leather strap around her neck. "So you and Will are done trying?" asks Bonkers Lady. "Now that you've got him?"

Him. She's looking at him. Ki Young equals Him.

Canadian Mummy lifts her shoulders up and down. "Well, I've heard of women, lots of them, who get pregnant after adopting. Like the pressure's off, or something."

Bonkers Lady adjusts her messy ponytail. "Hmmmm. Drop over for some herbs if you want."

The car lurches to a stop.

"And I've got remedies for other things too," she adds, opening the door. "Really. For anything that ails you."

"Well, I've my hands full now. We have to get enough English into him before regular pre-school starts in the fall."

Ki Young spots a man who looks like a fat Grandfather with a straighter, surer walk, crossing in front of them. Was that right? Were there other Koreans to be seen, to eat with, to speak with and show he is no moron, in the New Canadian Life? He'd have to keep a lookout. There certainly were none close to the house.

"Thanks bunches for the lift. It's Tracey, right? I wouldn't have asked, but it's the Big Gyno appointment. You know how it is."

Canadian Mummy blinks and holds onto the steering tight. "It's Trudi. Yes, Belinda. I've had my share of Big Gyno Appointments, believe you me."

Bonkers Lady covers her mouth and gasps. "Sorry, hun. Of course. How rude of me."

"You're sure you don't need a pick up?" asks Canadian Mummy sharply.

"No. Thanks. Sorry. Thanks."

Canadian Mummy sniffs loudly and wipes her right eye with
her shirtsleeve before starting the car. Ki Young unsnaps his seat
belt and puts his hand on Canadian Mummy's shoulder.

"No cry. Bonkers Lady," he whispers.

This makes Canadian Mummy cry harder.

At home, she sighs when she discovers his wet pants. She
sends him into the tub (but he just had a bath the night before!)
and gives him clean Spiderman underwear, stiff jeans and then
tortures them both with forty-five minutes of picture dictionary.

Hhhhhhhouse. Ki Young lives in a hhhhhhhhouse. Ba-bee. Big
tummy ladies will have a baby. Canadian Mummy points across
the street. Baby. Ki Young touches Canadian Mummy's stomach.

No baby. Only him.

Canadian Daddy is called Will. He is a tiny, tiny bit Korean,
which is why he, Ki Young, was noticed. Chosen. That is what
Korean Temporary Mummy said. That is what Canadian Busy
Woman in the Red Jacket said. And now what Canadian
Mummy and Daddy say.

"Ki Young. Look at me. You are a special boy. Understand?
Special. Canadian Daddy, see his black hair? Canadian Daddy is
a little bit Korean. You are our special son." The dog receives
less laborious dissertations.

Canadian Daddy speaks no Korean, doesn't eat with chopsticks and enjoys fluffy, long-grain rice. Canadian Little Bit
Korean Daddy was not so convincing. He doesn't see him that
much anyway. Daddy works until after Ki Young has eaten dinner. Daddy eats fast and then goes down to play with his trains.
He has miles and miles of tracks that run all over the basement.
Ki Young can look, but not touch.

Bonkers Lady comes home by taxi.

Ki Young goes to the knothole. Bonkers Lady is at her big
kitchen window, talking to herself. Well, he sees no one else. She
is washing dishes, holding them up to the light of the window
and occasionally scraping off reluctant bits with her fingernail.
Suddenly, she stops and stares at his fence. His knothole.

Ki Young freezes.

This is definitely not a Good Boy thing.

She beckons with a long finger that matches her long, long body. Four of Ki Young's, at least.

He keeps staring through the hole.

Bonkers Lady keeps motioning.

After nearly having his second accident of the day, Ki Young scrambles away, into the relative safety of his New Canadian Life house. He plays Car Collection fervently, until his Campbell's tomato soup lunch is ready. Canadian Mummy is impressed he is Such a Good Boy.

Still. Still, there is the chance of the naked dance again, better yet the throwing cookies spectacle, and the knothole draws him back. When she beckons this time, he reports to her front porch where she presents him with cookies on a plastic plate. Many cookies. Big Ones.

She has all her clothes on. This both relieves and disappoints Ki Young.

While he sits on her porch munching cookies (from the floor, a box or the oven, Ki Young doesn't know), a man comes in a big truck.

Red. Rrrrred. All apples are red. Some trucks are red.

"Hey little buddy. I'm here to fix the car." He air-punches Ki Young.

Ki Young jumps to his feet and gives his best Tae Kwon Do kick in response.

Car Fixer Man is impressed. "You know Kung Fu, huh? Guess it's in your blood."

Ki Young retreats into the corner with his cookies.

Bonkers lady answers the door. She still has her clothes on. Well, that makes more sense. Canadian Mummy always has many clothes on, the same ones, for days in a row. She wouldn't, however, let Ki Young wear his Winnie the Pooh T-shirt on back-to-back days.

"Thanks for coming so fast, Jimmy. You know where

everything is. As usual, I don't know what's wrong. My powers only get me so far." She laughs.

The man goes into the garage to look at the car and Bonkers Lady gives Ki Young four more cookies. She closes the door and Ki Young eats the cookies on her front porch. Canadian Mummy doesn't call out for him. Perhaps she is asleep on the couch, that is where she goes after serving Campbell's tomato soup lunches.

At his seventh cookie, Ki Young's stomach starts to churn. He remembers the feeling, knows what will soon happen. Grandfather did it all the time at the end. Ki Young did it in the airplane, twice, on his way to his New Canadian Life.

"Toilet," he says aloud. It is clearly enunciated, but there is no one to hear. He is overcome with nausea. What seems like twenty cookies and five Campbell's tomato soup lunches are vomited all over Bonkers Lady's porch.

Then he feels better. Shamed, but better. But Canadian Mummy! Peeing in his pants and spewing lunch all in one day— surely she will send him back to Korea. There would be no Good Boy/Bad Boy angle to this at all.

He runs into his own yard, to the hollow spot under the lilac bush where the knothole is and begins to sob.

After maybe ten minutes, when his outburst has ebbed to sniffles and hiccups, he hears Car Fixer Man call out, "Jesus Christ! Somebody's puked all over your porch, Belinda! That Chinese kid."

Ki Young trembles. He hears Bonkers Lady open her door and gasp.

Bonkers Lady comes to the side of her house for the water hose. When she returns the hose to its special hanger, she squats down at the hole and meets Ki Young, eyeball to eyeball. He is too terrified to move.

"It's okay, Kyung," she soothes, her voice ever so gentle. "It's okay. Come out. Come out from there. It's my fault for giving you so many cookies."

He extracts himself from the lilac bush and she meets him at the end of the fence. She takes his hand. It's warm and dry. Canadian Mummy's hands are cold. Always cold.

"Poor little bastard," she says to Car Fixer Man. "He's been in the country but a month. His mom's a bit nutty." She twirls a finger around her temple.

Canadian Mummy, michi nom? Was everyone michi nom in Canada?

"Well, not nutty exactly, just a lush. She smelled like a distillery when she drove me to an appointment this morning. It's not right, her driving around with Kyong, here." Speaking of him seemed to remind them both of his presence.

"How's your tummy? That was a big tummy full of cookies and ..."

"Campbell's tomato soup," he finishes, pleased for the chance to articulate.

She grimaces. "Yes. I figured."

Car Fixer Man has drifted back to the car.

"Do you want to come in, Kyun? You can play with my magic crystals, if you're very careful."

Ki Young nods, though he does not know why except going inside with Bonkers Lady is better than playing alone, or staring at Canadian Mummy lying on the couch.

He happily sorts a glass bowl of coloured stones as Bonkers Lady babbles away beside him. "This one's for headaches. You know headaches? That one, the greeny one? For staying power." She cackles a little, like a cartoon witch, but smiles nicely at him after, so he feels okay.

They both hear Daddy's car next door. Instinctively, Ki Young slides off the chair and pads toward the door.

Bonkers Lady accompanies him across the lawns.

Canadian Daddy eyes her suspiciously. "Hello, Missus ... Madam. Hello, son. What have we here?"

"Forgive me. Your wife, Trina, isn't it? She was feeling ill. I saw her lie down on the couch. To be candid, I have a clear line to your living room from my kitchen window, when neither of us draws the curtain. I just took Kyoon off her hands for a spell. We've had a lovely afternoon counting crystals."

Canadian Daddy looks sad and mad and grateful all at once. Confusing.

"I see. Well, thanks are in order. Come, Ki Young." He extends his hand. It's a big hand, quite warm and a little wet. Bonkers Lady keeps standing there.

"If there's anything I can ..." she starts.

Canadian Daddy pauses before their front door and clears his throat. "Ah. No. There's nothing." A little sharply he adds, "I'll see my wife draws the curtains, so that you don't feel obliged to ..." He stops talking and pushes open the door.

Ki Young is able to quickly wave goodbye before Daddy pulls him in. Bonkers Lady looks pretty, standing there in her long pink dress. It has feathers on it. She looks pretty and kind. Not bonkers at all.

My special, special thanks to Turnstone Press.
I always believed in the women of ... *Bonkers* and am so
grateful to Turnstone for being the publisher that
came to believe in them too.

Also, a huge thanks to my eagle-eyed editor Wayne Tefs
who sharpened my technical skills immeasurably—
a wonderful gift I humbly accept.

Before Debbie Sue could respond, all six feet and two inches of James Russell Overstreet, Jr., the most beautiful man in Texas, walked through the doorway. The powerful legs of the horseman he was filled his starched, knife-creased Wranglers. A silver badge hung on the pocket of his white-on-white striped shirt. His skin was as tanned as his alligator boots, he had a thick black mustache Tom Selleck would envy, and his lean jaws shone from a fresh shave.

Her heart thumped. Every female cell in her body squealed and fainted. She resisted the urge to look down, certain the soles of her boots had melted. Still, she forced an act of cool detachment. She had to. If the dike damming up her emotions ever sprang a leak, anything could happen.

Buddy's finger touched the brim of his gray Resistol. "Ladies." He turned to Debbie Sue. "My secretary said a crazy woman called and insulted her. I figured it had to be you."

Dixie Cash

*Since You're
Leaving Anyway,*

Take Out
the
Trash

AVON BOOKS
An Imprint of HarperCollinsPublishers

This is a work of fiction. Names, characters, places, and incidents are products of the author's imagination or are used fictitiously and are not to be construed as real. Any resemblance to actual events, locales, organizations, or persons, living or dead, is entirely coincidental.

AVON BOOKS
An Imprint of HarperCollins*Publishers*
10 East 53rd Street
New York, New York 10022-5299

Copyright © 2004 by Dixie Cash
ISBN: 0-06-059536-1
www.avonromance.com

First Avon Books paperback printing: September 2004

Avon Trademark Reg. U.S. Pat. Off. and in Other Countries, Marca Registrada, Hecho en U.S.A.
HarperCollins® is a registered trademark of HarperCollins Publishers Inc.

Printed in the U.S.A.

10 9 8 7 6 5 4 3 2 1

I dedicate this book to everyone who has ever told me I'm funny and to my sister and writing partner, Jeff, who kept telling me, "You can do this." Without her, I'd still be funny, but thanks to her, now I'm a funny author.

—Pam

I dedicate this book to my sister Pam, who loves to laugh and whose very dreams must be comedies.

—Jeffery

One

Debbie Sue Overstreet sat at the payout desk of the Styling Station, staring at the balance column in her big black checkbook. From the bottom line of check stub #938, a fat goose egg glared back at her. She groaned. The payment on her pickup truck was past due again.

Okay, so opening a beauty shop—that is, a salon—in Salt Lick, Texas, hadn't been the most profitable decision she had ever made. But couldn't anything go right? She was twenty-eight years old and had been a failure at everything she had tried. Marrying, mothering, rodeoing, and now, beauty shopping. Maybe she should have finished college.

Her mental calculator churned into action. If she could do a dozen perms and/or coloring jobs between now and the end of the week, she could get the pickup payment in the mail on Saturday and at least avoid the tacky phone calls from those collection people. Add a few drop-in haircuts, and she might even be able to buy a pizza and a six-pack Saturday night. Or maybe she would get *really* lucky, and Pearl Ann Carruthers would come in for the works, head-to-toe. If that happened, she might make *two* pickup payments.

A disc jockey blathered from a radio in the background. "Sun's up, folks. Eight-thirty, temperature's ninety-two degrees, no rain in sight. Here's a blast from the past by Joe Diffie, all about the devil dancing in empty pockets. How many out there in our K-Country audience can relate to that one?"

Debbie Sue stared at the radio. Was that DJ psychic?

Eight-thirty. Ninety-two degrees. Another hour and the salon's air-conditioning system would be taxed to the max by the relentless September heat of West Texas. The little dial adding up kilowatts on the electric meter would be spinning out of control, kicking the power bill into the stratosphere.

Thank God for the blue-hairs who came in once a week, rain or shine, hell or high water. Their big hair, dyed and teased to the extreme, paid the utility bills.

She slapped the revolting checkbook closed and walked over to the four-foot-square mirror in front of her station. Her chestnut hair with its carefully placed sun-in highlights hung to the middle of her back and felt like a horse blanket. Hot. One of these days she intended to cut the mane on her head within an inch of her scalp.

She grabbed up a giant plastic clip and pinned most of the thick mop into a twisted roll. Instantly a few sheaves escaped, giving her the bed-head look. Oh well. Some of her best customers strove for the popular style.

She had left the house without makeup this morning, so she dug in a drawer for cosmetics. The owner of one of the only two beauty salons in Salt Lick couldn't appear before her customers looking like something the dog dragged in. She applied a few flicks of black mascara and a swipe of Coral Reef lipstick. She gave up on herself then, snatched a bottle of Windex off the shelf under the counter, and turned her attention to the smudges on the mirror.

As she fogged the mirror with cleaner, a car door slammed outside. That would be Edwina, Debbie Sue's only employee and one of her two best friends in the whole wide world. Edwina Perkins manned the Styling Station's second chair and was as much a fixture in the salon as the row of four dryers with teal padded seats or the two maroon shampoo bowls in the back room.

Edwina had been a hairdresser in Salt Lick for over twenty years. Debbie Sue hired her hoping she had a following, and indeed she did, but putting the Styling Station's books in the black would take a heck of a lot more customers than either she or Edwina could pull in. Maybe she could set off a bomb under the competition down the street.

The front door flew open. The Christmas bells

tied to the knob whacked the door and clattered as if in pain. Edwina charged in, super-sized plastic cup in hand, cigarette clamped between her teeth. In addition to a following of loyal salon patrons, Edwina had an addiction to Marlboro Lights and Dr. Pepper.

The five-foot-ten brunette's wooden platform heels clomped like horse hooves across the vinyl-covered floor. Panting for breath, she placed her cigarette on the edge of her station's counter in front of her mirror, then set down her drink and purse. "She finally done it. She's gone."

"I don't believe it." Debbie Sue rose on her tip-toes and swiped Windex off the top of her mirror.

"Well, believe it, girl. I heard Harley's brother at the Kwik-Stop tell Marsha while she rung up his coffee. She didn't come home last night."

The fact that she and Edwina could read each other's thoughts and carry on gossip without using names came from living a lifetime in the same town, knowing the same people and places and recycling the same rumors year after year. "Humph. Just because she didn't come home doesn't mean she's gone. She could be shacked up somewhere."

Edwina gave her a flat look. "With Harley in town? I don't *think* so."

Edwina's smoldering cigarette was searing a brand onto the teal Formica counter. Debbie Sue glowered at it and doused it with a squirt of

Windex. "Cri-ma-nee, Ed, you're gonna set this place on fire."

"Hey, I might've won the bet." Edwina ignored both the reprimand and her extinguished smoke and rummaged in her tray of permanent wave rods and brightly colored curlers. She came up with a folded paper on which a wagering grid had been drawn. The Styling Station's faithful customers had maintained a pool, betting exactly when Pearl Ann Carruthers would finally leave her husband.

For ten years the richest, unhappiest woman in Salt Lick had told the town's citizens that "someday" she would leave Harley Carruthers and move to Cowtown. Fort Worth, where skintight Wranglers and good boots were the only real necessities of life. Moving to Fort Worth was better than going to heaven, according to Pearl Ann. In heaven you might be promised eternal peace, but in Fort Worth, you were *guaranteed* fun and sin.

If anybody could appreciate the latter, it was Pearl Ann.

The Christmas bells jangled again, and Debbie Sue's other best friend dashed in, frantic and as out of breath as Edwina. "Did y'all hear, did y'all hear?"

"We're ahead of you, C.J. We already know about Pearl Ann. She's probably gonna be at happy hour in Fort Worth this very afternoon, guzzling margaritas with some tight-assed cowboy."

Carol Jean Anderson's blue eyes flared wide. "Fort Worth! Where she went is the great happy hour in the sky."

"The Petroleum Club?" The posh private club on the top floor of the Frost Bank Building in downtown Fort Worth was the only elevated bar Debbie Sue could think of.

"She's *dead*, Debbie Sue. She killed herself. She blew her brains all over the front seat of her new Cadillac."

Silence hung in the room for several heartbeats. Edwina broke into a coughing spasm.

"It's true," C. J. said, beginning to sniffle.

Edwina's upper lip skewed up under her nose. "Eee-yew! Ain't that Cadillac a pale yellow?" At the stunned look C. J. aimed in her direction, Edwina added, "Okay, excuse me. I think it's awful, but I also have a vivid imagination. That's all I meant."

Tears gathered in Debbie Sue's eyes. She had known Pearl Ann her entire life, and unlike most of the women in Salt Lick, had liked her. Oh sure, Pearl Ann was obnoxious at times. Well, to be honest, she was obnoxious damn near *all* the time. Lord, she never missed a chance to let everybody know her clothes came from Neiman-Marcus or that her husband bought her a new Cadillac every year. Her jewelry was equal to the economy of a Third World country. Even more intimidating was her Victoria's Secret face and body that were the fantasy of every red-blooded man and nightmare of every woman in Salt Lick.

But she had been a loyal, generously tipping customer since the day of the Styling Station's opening. Debbie Sue and Edwina had cut miles of her hair, dyed it a rainbow of colors, and applied a thousand protein packs. "But—but that's just not possible. She just got a new perm and had her lips and—"

"We need details." Edwina pried out a Marlboro and lit up. "I'm fixin' to call Buddy." She clomped to the payout desk and picked up the phone.

"Wait a minute," Debbie Sue set down her Windex bottle with a thud. "If anybody's calling my ex-husband, it's gonna be me."

C. J.'s brow arched into a knowing look. Edwina made no attempt to hide an exaggerated eye roll as she handed over the receiver. It was just pure hell having people know you so well. "What?" Debbie Sue growled to throw them off track.

"She just happens to know the number by heart," Ed said to C. J.

"Will y'all stop it?" Debbie Sue keyed in the sheriff's office number. "I'm a businesswoman. I'm supposed to know how to call the law. In case I get robbed or something."

"Yeah," Edwina said. "I was just thinking that very thing. Beauty shop robbery is a real threat in Salt Lick."

An exaggerated Texas drawl came on the line. "Good morning. Sheriff Overstreet's office. How may I assist you?"

Oh puh-leeze! Since being promoted from "the woman who would recognize the ceiling tiles in motels across West Texas" to sheriff's office dispatcher, Tanya had taken on a condescending attitude. Unsavory rumors about her and the sheriff had swirled through Salt Lick like an Easter Sunday sandstorm, but Debbie Sue was unaffected. Tanya herself had probably started the tall tales. If Debbie Sue knew anything about her ex-husband, it was how seriously he took his job as county sheriff. He would never take a chance of smearing his reputation by having a fling with an employee.

Debbie Sue put on a professional, no-nonsense voice. "Sheriff Overstreet, please."

"Buddy, er, uh, Sheriff Overstreet is, uh, uh . . . in-dis-posed. Is there anything *I* can do for you?"

"Only if I had a hard-on and a ten-dollar bill. Just tell him to call me." Debbie Sue slammed down the receiver. "Slut," she muttered.

Edwina blew out a stream of smoke. "Tact is one thing I've always admired about you, Debbie Sue. Tell me again how you no longer care a thing about that man."

C. J.'s brow crinkled into a bewildered look. "What does a hard-on and a ten-dollar bill have to do with anything?"

"Well . . . She said he was *in-dis-posed*. You tell

me. Where'd Tanya Metcalf learn a three-syllable word?"

Her blond friend's eyes bugged. "He was into what?"

"C. J., one of these days you're gonna drive me to drink."

"But you already drink."

Debbie huffed an exaggerated gasp. "Holy cow, C. J. Look, I don't want you to take this the wrong way, but shouldn't you be at work?"

"I called in sick. When I heard about Pearl Ann, I just couldn't make myself go."

Before Debbie Sue could respond, the door opened again, and all six feet and two inches of James Russell Overstreet, Jr., the most beautiful man in Texas, walked through the doorway. The powerful legs of the horseman he was filled his starched, knife-creased Wranglers. A silver badge hung on the pocket of his white-on-white striped shirt. His skin was as tanned as his alligator boots, he had a thick black mustache Tom Selleck would envy, and his lean jaws shone from a fresh shave.

Her heart thumped. Every female cell in her body squealed and fainted. She resisted the urge to look down, certain the soles of her boots had melted. Still, she forced an act of cool detachment. She had to. If the dike damming up her emotions ever sprang a leak, anything could happen.

Her thoughts flew to that schoolteacher in Odessa she had been told he was dating. Debbie

Sue had never met her, never seen her, but she was sure the woman was too short, too tall, too fat, and too thin, and wouldn't know a good saddle horse from a hobby horse. What could Buddy possibly have in common with her?

Buddy's finger touched the brim of his gray Resistol. "Ladies." He turned to Debbie Sue. "The office radioed that you called me?"

Debbie Sue willed her tongue to untie as chocolate-colored eyes bored into hers. "I did?"

Buddy opened his palms and gave her a questioning look. "Tanya said a bitchy woman called and insulted her. I figured it had to be you."

The nerve! Debbie Sue gathered her composure and hoisted her chin. "We heard about Pearl Ann."

"And what?" he snapped. "You want the gory details to yak about in the beauty shop all day?"

Debbie Sue extended her air of wounded pride. "We were friends of Pearl Ann's. We saw her at least once a week, sometimes more. We're entitled to know what happened."

"Entitled?" He glared down at her for a few seconds, then started for the door. "If you don't need anything, I gotta go. People are waitin' on me."

She marched behind him, all the way to the driver's door of the county's white Tahoe parked in front of the Styling Station. "Well, 'scuse the hell out of me, Wyatt Earp. I have some information you might like to hear, but now I'm not even gonna tell you."

"Oh, I don't believe that or you wouldn't've followed me out here."

"Well . . . well . . . Ed just tattooed Pearl Ann's lips and eyelids a few days ago."

Buddy's eyes squinted into a pained expression. "What the hell does *that* mean?"

"Well, dammit, Buddy, it hurts to get tattooed. Would somebody do it if she was planning on blowing her head off?"

Buddy sighed. "Give me a break, Flash. I'm up to my ass in alligators on this. By noon the press will be filling up the motel and I'm still trying to figure out what happened." He yanked open the Tahoe's door.

Debbie Sue could see the man to whom she had been married for five years, who wasn't easily shaken, was just that. Shaken. Why wouldn't he be? The oil-rich Carruthers family were icons in West Texas. Harley Carruthers and Buddy had been in school together, had played on the same sports teams. And Pearl Ann was . . . well, what *had* Pearl Ann been? Besides being high school homecoming queen once, her claim to fame was marrying Harley. "You mean you don't think she killed herself?"

"Hell, I don't know. I called in the forensic boys from Midland. We'll hear in a day or two." He cranked the engine. "By the time this spreads around, the whole town will be in an uproar. I don't need any more headaches, so you girls just cool it." He backed in an arc, stopped and looked back at her, his hat brim set just above his eyes, his elbow cocked on the windowsill. "Please?"

The county rig roared out of the parking lot, spraying sand and caliche.

Debbie fanned away a cloud of white dust and stamped her foot. "Dammit, I just hate him."

She hesitated before going back into the salon. *Flash.* The pet name her dad had given her when she was a little kid winning barrel-racing competitions in Little Britches rodeo. Buddy was the only one who still called her Flash. From him, as from her dad, it had been an expression of affection. The memory made her heart hurt.

The county SUV's taillights disappeared from sight, and she couldn't keep from thinking about another day three years ago when she had stood in this same spot and watched his taillights. The day he had said if she didn't calm down and give up rodeoing, it was over between them. She told him to go to hell, get out of her life, and take his badge with him.

And he did.

The painful irony was that the divorce did force her to give up rodeoing, and she hadn't even missed it. The only thing she missed was Buddy.

Two

As Buddy pulled away from the Styling Station, his eyes kept stealing to his side mirror and the woman who had cost him damn near everything, starting with his heart and ending with most of his material possessions. He couldn't keep from remembering three years ago, the day he drove out of this same parking lot and left her standing in that same place.

He wished she didn't get better looking every time he saw her. This morning she wasn't wearing so much black gunk on her eyes, and he liked her without it. Green eyes as pretty as hers didn't need that beauty shop crap. Her body had never had an ounce of flab anywhere and still didn't. Her tight Wranglers and those little T-shirts she had always worn never failed to set off an urgency in his groin.

As burdened as he was by all that was going on around him, he still smiled at her calling him Wyatt Earp. She had never let him get away with being too full of himself.

He guessed she still hated him as much as she had that day he handed her an ultimatum and she told him to go to hell. Little did she know that after he left her, hell was exactly where he went. He had lost himself in a harem of women, some of whose names he couldn't even recall. If he hadn't been sheriff, forcing Debbie Sue out of his heart and mind might have driven him into some even more perverse activities. Moving on had taken a long while, but he *had* moved on, and now life was a lot less complicated.

Until this morning, that is, when he walked up to a new yellow Cadillac and saw a pretty woman with a quarter-sized hole in her head, a woman he had known as long as he could remember.

How had Debbie Sue and her goofy friends found out about Pearl Ann so fast? It wasn't even ten o'clock.

A crackle on his two-way broke him out of his mental meandering. "Sheriff Overstreet, some people from Midland are here waiting on you."

The message snapped his mind back to his job. "I'm on my way, Tanya. Be there in three minutes."

At his office, three crime scene investigators introduced themselves, and he led them out to the landfill a couple of miles out of town. There he had left Salt Lick's one deputy, Billy Don Roberts, with instructions to surround the area with crime scene tape, then stand guard over the corpse and the Cadillac.

As he brought the Tahoe to a stop, he saw the deputy had strung enough yellow tape to stretch from Dallas to El Paso. It draped from sage bush to sage bush, the perimeter bigger than a football field. Billy Don wasn't the sharpest knife in the drawer, but at least he had followed directions—if to the extreme.

Buddy had already made his own limited investigation of the death scene and taken pictures, so he turned it over to the CSI team. They started work at once, attempting to beat the deterioration caused by the scorching heat. He helped as much as he could, but mostly he stayed out of their way. Hours later, one of them approached him. "We'll take the body and the samples we collected back to Midland. I'll call you later today with our progress. We'll have a formal report after the autopsy."

"Any preliminary thoughts?"

"I'd say you were right, Sheriff. I don't think we can call this suicide. We've done a gunshot residue test. As you probably know, that may or may not help you discover who did this. It's not a contact wound. Quite a bit of tattooing around the entrance. Shot probably fired from the passenger seat."

Buddy had made the same observations and reached the same conclusion. His heart pumped hard as he recalled walking up on the death scene and the 9mm automatic pistol lying on the passenger seat. His very first thought had been that the pistol lay in an odd location for a self-inflicted wound. "I saw," he said. "You get the pistol?"

The expert squinted up at him, blinded by the brilliant sunlight reflecting off the white caliche landfill. "Know who it belongs to?"

"I'm checking on it. I'm guessing it belonged to her or her husband. They both had permits to carry."

"Doesn't do as much damage as some guns, but the result is the same."

"Yep. Dead is dead."

Whoever had shot the wife of Harley J. Carruthers obviously had more bullets than brains. While Harley and Pearl Ann might not have had a perfect marriage, the powerful Carruthers family was close-knit. None of them would appreciate somebody putting a bullet into Harley's wife's head.

Buddy's mind sorted what he knew about the victim, whose appearance and personality reminded him of old Marilyn Monroe movies. She was twenty-eight, the same age as Debbie Sue. When his ex-wife and Pearl Ann had been girls, to say Pearl Ann's family was poor was a compliment to their standard of living. For Pearl Ann and her siblings, there had never been enough of anything—food, clothing, or reasons to hold up their heads.

Still, she'd had a way about her that could make a man feel he was more than he was. With little regard for boundaries, tangible or intangible, and while still a teenager, she had managed to lasso one of the richest men in Texas.

Every Salt Lick citizen whispered about her liaisons outside the marriage, but Buddy had personal knowledge of just how predatory she could be. An invitation had been extended to him personally on more than one occasion, and he had been tempted a time or two. Thank God, good sense and respect for her husband, a man he had called friend most of his life, had prevailed.

No telling how many men Pearl Ann might have slept with or which ones could be suspects. Besides men, plenty of wives or girlfriends would be happy to see her gone.

Then there was her husband, and two questions Buddy was duty-bound to consider. Did Harley know she cheated? And if so, did he hate her enough or love her enough to shoot her?

Earlier Buddy had instructed the owner of the only tow truck in Salt Lick to stand by and wait for his call. He flipped open his cell phone and called him to come for the Cadillac and take it to the impound yard. Then he headed for the Carruthers ranch.

It was late afternoon by the time he passed over the cattle guard that was the doorway to the Flying C's sprawling fifty sections. The thirty thousand acres-plus wasn't the biggest spread in West Texas by a long shot, and it wouldn't run many cows, but it was big enough, especially when oil wells were scattered all over it. Multiple pump jacks sawed up and down on the horizon pumping precious black gold from deep in the ground. Buddy thought back to childhood when he and his friends climbed astraddle and rode them like bucking broncs.

Located more or less in the middle of the ranch, the main house was a ways from the cattle guard. Buddy wended up a wide caliche road that took him through a pasture dotted with Hereford, Black Angus, and Brahma steers. Any day now, they would be hauled to market. For a brief moment he wondered what price these premium animals would bring this year. Back when he had owned a few acres and a few head, he kept up with the daily price of prime beef-on-the-hoof. He no longer bothered. After his small herd had been sold during his divorce from Debbie Sue, he no longer had the heart.

Some five hundred feet before reaching the house, he passed the large party barn Harley built soon after marrying Pearl Ann. Its interior was patterned after the old Stage Coach Inn in Stamford, which had been a bowling alley before it became a dancehall. Harley's barn had seen countless revelers. Food and liquor had always been abundant, and dancers logged a thousand miles on its concrete floor. Some of the biggest names in country music, personal friends of Harley's, had entertained from an elevated stage inside.

As a kid, Buddy hadn't had a concept of how rich Harley was, but the party barn and the shindigs that occurred there put into perspective just how much money a man could piss away when he had more than he knew what to do with.

Lord, how many evenings had he and Debbie Sue danced away in Harley's barn, then gone home and made love 'til daylight or lay in each other's arms laughing about the events of the evening? Bittersweet memories better left stored in the far reaches of his mind.

At the rambling Spanish-style ranch house, he was surprised to find the owner absent, particularly after he had told Harley he would come to the ranch as soon as the CSI team left. The Mexican housekeeper said, in a mix of broken English and fluent Spanish, Harley had gone to the pueblo to take care of business. The gist of it, Harley had gone to the funeral home.

Taking a look around outside, Buddy drove along the two-track driveway that took him to the corrals and pens surrounding a series of barns. In the distance he could see three small houses, homes to the Flying C's manager and the ranch hands, and he pondered what kind of relationship Pearl Ann might have had with the ranch's employees.

By five o'clock Debbie Sue had a headache the size of Houston. The day had been a virtual tornado of women coming and going, leaving bits and pieces of gossip, sucking up something new and blowing on.

She couldn't find it in herself to participate in the talk. Her mind was preoccupied with a nagging question. Why would a woman who loved two things beyond all else—money and her own good looks—commit suicide when she had a bounty of both? And why would she choose to mar those good looks by putting a gun to her head? The scenario just didn't fit.

Off and on all day, her thoughts drifted back to the evening when, a few months ago, she had stayed late to give Pearl Ann a last-minute trim and perm. The voluptuous blond kept lifting a flask from her purse and doctoring her Diet Coke. The more Diet Coke she drank, she looser her tongue became.

She told a bizarre story. Having signed a prenuptial agreement as an ignorant child, she feared a divorce from Harley would leave her as poor as she had been when they married. Years of collusion with one of the Carruthers accountants in Midland, plus a cash kickback, had resulted in her squirreling away a sizable sum from her monthly allowance and any other place where cash could be removed unnoticed, not excluding the kitchen and housekeeping budgets. Her "getaway fund," she called it.

And if what she had hidden wasn't enough to pay for her freedom, she would resort to other means. She had lived with Harley long enough to know where the bodies were buried. If the IRS knew the methods by which Carruthers money was relocated, reinvested, and reinvented, they could be busy for years.

With Pearl Ann having sworn her to secrecy, Debbie Sue had never told anyone of the late-night revelations, but the conversation gave credibility to the notion that the restless wife *would* someday leave Harley. Where had Pearl Ann's plan gone awry?

After the last customer left, Debbie Sue went to the payout desk and began to sort the day's receipts. She took payment from customers by cash, check, and credit card, even laughed and told a few of them she would take pigs and goats if they didn't have cash. Unfortunately the joke was frighteningly close to being on her, because if someone wanted to hand over livestock, she did have a place to house it out at her mom's.

Edwina finished up a cursory cleaning effort, then stuffed a partial pack of cigarettes into her purse and picked up her Dr. Pepper cup. "I'm outta here," she said. "Why don't you come by the trailer this evening. Vic's cooking up something good, and he gives the best neck and shoulder massages this side of Dallas. If that doesn't unwind you, there's always the other man in my life, Jose Cuervo."

Debbie Sue hadn't eaten since she downed a strawberry Pop-Tart for breakfast. Edwina's significant other could impress anyone with his home cooking. While in the navy, he had been all over the world and knew how to use exotic spices and seasonings. Debbie Sue's mouth watered, thinking what he might be cooking compared to what she had in her own refrigerator. "Guess I'd better pass. I really need to drive out to Mom's. I'm sure she's heard about Pearl Ann, and she might want to talk."

"Your mom hasn't been in to have her hair done in nearly two weeks."

"I know. That's why I have to go see her. And Rocket Man."

Edwina tsked and shook her head. "Most people would have sold that horse a long time ago, Debbie Sue."

"Bite your tongue, Ed. Rocket Man's my pal. He's won me a roomful of trophies and belt buckles and even a little money. He's earned the right to roam the pasture and get fat and lazy."

Besides her mother, the brown and white paint horse had been the most constant living being in her life since she was fifteen. He had seen her through the loss of her dream of a pro-circuit barrel-racing career, the loss of her precious baby boy and her husband. Hell, he had even been there the night of her seventeenth birthday, when she lost her virginity to Quint Matthews behind the horse trailers at a rodeo in Lubbock.

But most important of all, the horse had been a gift from Buddy. She would keep him until he died. Or *she* died. Whichever came first.

"Okay, hon, but don't work too much longer. You look tired. Tell Virginia *and* Rocket Man hello for me. You know I love them both."

Debbie Sue locked the door behind Edwina. One good thing had come from the day's exceptional number of customers. She had more than enough money to make her pickup payment. She plopped down in the chair at the payout desk and pulled her checkbook out of the bottom drawer.

Edwina threw her purse in the back of her car and removed the bath towel that covered the driver's seat and steering wheel. Leather upholstery exposed to the Texas sun all day could burn a blister on your butt before you knew what happened. And turning the steering wheel using only your fingertips was frowned on by the law.

She had left all the windows down to allow ventilation, but the Mustang still felt like a sauna. God, how much longer would this heat hang on? As a native, she knew how to deal with the West Texas weather, but there came a time when enough was enough.

Pulling out of the parking lot, she made one last glance at the silhouette of Debbie Sue bent over her bookkeeping. *Bless her heart.* The news of Pearl Ann's death had been a double whammy for her. Debbie Sue was nice enough to have really cared for Pearl Ann, and the self-centered blond's death meant a financial blow to the salon.

Sometimes being the older, more experienced

friend wasn't easy, Edwina thought. She had been in Debbie Sue's shoes and knew how uncomfortable they could get. Broke, but independent and hardheaded, was a combination that could depress the pope.

Then there was Buddy. Debbie Sue still loved that good-looking sucker. Edwina had always thought Buddy felt the same, really, but now that he was seeing a schoolteacher from Odessa, she feared his feelings might have taken a turn. She had known about the woman in Buddy's life for a while now—hell, everybody in town probably knew—but she wouldn't mention it unless Debbie Sue brought it up first.

Maybe something or someone would come along and change things for Debbie Sue, someone like Vic Martin. After three worthless husbands, Edwina had sworn off men forever until she met Vic.

Thinking of her live-in partner reminded her of the message left on voice mail last night by his ex-wife, Brenda. Vic and Brenda had been divorced ten years, but their history went back twenty. She appeared to be two-stepping her way through another twelve-step program, which always prompted a phone call in which she begged Vic to meet her and take her back.

Vic always returned her calls, talked to her sometimes for over an hour. No way was Edwina not going to eavesdrop, especially when she heard him speaking in soft, soothing tones. He always sounded like a parent talking to a small child, but that didn't keep Edwina from chewing on her skillfully sculpted acrylic nails.

Edwina was puzzled by Vic's attitude toward his ex-wife. From what she knew of Vic, he had little tolerance for weak people, was a firm believer you didn't let destructive circumstances determine your fate.

Even with that philosophy, he had sympathy and mind-numbing patience with Brenda and her alcohol addiction. He had never said why, but Edwina rationalized he blamed himself for leaving her alone on naval bases while he played war games.

Edwina worked at not letting the periodic phone calls rock her world, but she had been to a rodeo or two and stayed for the dance. She knew a woman who became overconfident and thought her man wouldn't leave her was a fool.

She closed her eyes and thought about the day she and Vic had met and the happy years between then and now. He had brought more stability to her life than she had ever known. She turned the key in the ignition, anxious to get home and show him how much he meant to her.

Three

Debbie Sue closed the checkbook and left the shop for another day. On the way out of town, she dropped the day's receipts in the bank's night deposit and slid her pickup payment into the mailbox in front of Salt Lick's tiny post office.

Afterward she stopped off at City Grocery & Market, the town's only grocery store, and picked up some apples and carrots, then added Twinkies and a six-pack of Coors. The carrots and apples were for her, the beer and junk food for the horse. Rocket Man had always been an unconventional animal.

Debbie Sue's mom lived on twenty-five acres ten miles out of town in a vintage clapboard house where Debbie Sue had grown up. As a grade school kid she had hated covering that ten miles in a school bus that had no air conditioning, hated arriving at school covered with dust. As a teenager the drive had been a pain in the ass, and she usually had been in such a hurry to get from home to town or vice versa, she never noticed her surroundings.

Now, driving through the stark, treeless landscape, she thought of something she had heard a rodeo announcer say once: In West Texas you could look farther and see less than anywhere else on earth. More truth than not to the words.

In recent years she had come to realize she loved the miles of unfettered visibility and the big sky and the sense of boundless freedom the landscape gave her. She loved the endlessly shifting sand, wasn't put off when it dusted her dishes inside the cupboards. She even loved the tumbleweeds plastered against the barbed-wire fences. Why would *anybody* want to move to Fort Worth?

Nearing the turnoff to her mother's driveway, she spotted the first fence post where her eighteen-year-old horse grazed. She eased the Silverado to the shoulder of the road and began tapping the horn in staccato beeps. Ears at half mast, Rocket Man ambled to the fence and blew through his nostrils. Uh-oh, he was unhappy.

She climbed down from her seat and met him at the fence. When his gentle brown eyes with their spidery long lashes met hers, she scratched his neck, then placed her cheek against his, whispered her apologies for letting two weeks lapse since she had seen him, and reminded him of his beauty and stature. The horse soon warmed up, rubbed his head against her outstretched hand, and nibbled at her hair.

The bond between them was simple. Debbie Sue provided all his needs, or at least the ones she knew about. He, in turn, gave her unwavering loyalty and affection. In their barrel-racing days, he had performed to the utmost of his ability and never disappointed her. Her relationships with people—well, with men—had been less successful.

She carefully climbed through the barbed wire fence. Rocket Man nickered when the Twinkies and beer surfaced from the grocery sacks. She fed him the spongy cakes one by one and watched in amusement when he clasped a can between his teeth, tossed his head back, and guzzled the sudsy stream of cold beer. "One more for you, ol' sot," she said, laughing, "and that's it."

She placed a hand on the paint's side, and together they walked the quarter mile to her mother's modest house, which sat in the shade of huge pecan trees planted decades ago. A warm breeze touched her cheeks, and she glanced toward the sinking sun. "Red sky at night, old friend," she said, patting her horse's side.

Soon flowering plants in beds at the edge of the front porch came into view, adding to the welcoming appearance of her childhood home.

A laughing Virginia Pratt stepped out onto the wooden veranda. "Are you with the posse or are you the bank robber?"

Mom had greeted her with a laugh and that

same question since Debbie Sue was a little girl. "That depends on whose side you're on" was the standard comeback.

The woman who looked closer to forty-two than fifty-two walked toward the fence, wisps of blond hair stirring in a gentle wind. Debbie Sue met her and offered her the remaining four cans of Coors. "Want a cold one?"

"Sounds good. Hot today." She reached for the cans. With her other hand, she rubbed Rocket Man's face, then gave him a kiss on his nose. "I hope you weren't feeding this horse Twinkies and beer."

Debbie Sue squeezed through the fence wires. "Does he need more hay?"

"We're okay for now." Her mother started for the house, popping the top on a beer as she walked. "All day I've been hearing about poor little Pearl Ann."

Debbie Sue fell in step beside her. "Yeah. Me, too."

Her mom passed her a beer. "Just goes to show you, money doesn't buy happiness."

"Maybe not, but it sure buys a heap of other stuff." Debbie Sue took a swig of the cold liquid, letting it cool her from the inside out.

Entering her mother's dimly lit, air-conditioned house felt like stepping into a time warp. Pictures lined the walls and sat on tabletops chronicling Debbie Sue in every stage of growing up.

Above the sofa, in the mix of life captured by

camera, was a faded rectangular outline on the aged green wallpaper, evidence that something had hung there at one time. Virginia Pratt had left the empty spot on purpose, her way of saying something was there and now it was gone. The picture that had filled the space, the *only* picture of Debbie Sue and her dad, was tucked between quilts in the linen closet.

Tom Pratt had walked off when Debbie Sue was eight years old, taking nothing and leaving everything, including a note that said, "Sorry. You both deserve better." Well, he had been right about that.

Next to the empty rectangle hung Debbie Sue and Buddy's wedding picture. Smiling back from the frame were two young people in love, with a baby on the way and happy times ahead of them.

She wished the wedding picture was hidden away, too. She couldn't look at it without remembering the day she made a special trip home from her sophomore year at Tech and told Buddy she was pregnant. She had been so nervous, dreading his reaction.

His plans to become a Texas Ranger had already been sidetracked by his dad's unexpected death. But he had erased her fears when he knelt in front of her, wrapped his arms around her waist and placed a tender kiss on her stomach. "We'll call him Luke," he said. She laughed and asked, "What if it's a girl?" He assured her it would be a boy because a big brother would be needed to defend the honor of the beautiful sister who would follow.

They had made love that evening. He had been afraid of hurting her and the baby, but she urged him on. Buddy was a man's man and strong as a plow horse, but no lover could ever be more tender than he had been that night.

Then the baby came premature and lost his struggle for life en route to the neonatal unit in Midland. The scar left by losing Buddy was a scratch compared to the bleeding slash left by losing their baby boy. That period of her life was too unbearable to ever dwell on. Suffice to say, she no longer fussed over babies of friends or otherwise. Even now the sight of a little boy waddling alongside his mother, dressed in tiny Wranglers and a too-big hat, could, in an instant, plunge her into a pit of sadness.

She didn't need any more pain today, so she halted her detour through the halls of her memory and glanced toward the den at the Post-it notes plastered all over a bulletin board and an upright piano. Her mother supported herself as a part-time surgical assistant at the vet's office, but the other part of her life she spent writing country-western songs. She'd had small success. A few Texas bands played her music in honky-tonks. "What're you working on, Mom?"

"I've got one in my head I'm still fiddling with."

Her mother walked to the bright yellow and white kitchen and placed the remaining two cans of Coors into the refrigerator. "I'm calling it, 'Since You're Leaving Anyway, Take Out the Trash.'"

Debbie Sue laughed for the first time all day. Her mother composed tongue-in-cheek lyrics because she found most country songs too sad and depressing. "Here's one for you, Mom. 'I Miss My Ex, but My Aim's Getting Better.'"

"Awww, you must have seen Buddy today." Her mom slid an arm around her waist. "I guess he's got his hands full, doesn't he?"

Debbie Sue sighed inwardly. Her mother adored Buddy. She mentioned him at every opportunity. He must still think a lot of her, too, because he stopped by from time to time to visit her. A moment of silence followed. "What Buddy's got his hands full of is a schoolteacher from Odessa."

"Maybe you just *think* that. He's never said anything to *me* about her."

"Now why would he say anything to you about his girlfriend? You're my mother."

"You might be surprised at some of the talks Buddy and I have had over the past three years. I think he gets lonesome for someone to be open and honest with. You were his sounding board before. You should talk to him. I know he's strong, but with Harley being his friend and all, I'll bet he could use some moral support right now."

"Buddy and I haven't had a real conversation since before he left me."

"Then maybe it's time you did." Her mother released her and moved to the refrigerator. "Had supper?"

Behind her mother's back, Debbie Sue wiped away a tear. "No, but that's okay. I'll find something at home. I'm exhausted. I'm gonna collapse in front of the boob tube with my feet up. I just came out to check on you and Rocket Man. You haven't been into the shop. You're due a cut and color, you know. Want me to bring the stuff out here this weekend and do it for you?"

"Heavens, no. The last thing you should be doing on your day off is my hair. You work too hard. Always have." She smiled and patted Debbie Sue's shoulder. "Okay, so much for the sermon." She went to the refrigerator door and began taking out food. "I fixed myself some chicken-fried steak and fresh black-eyed peas for supper. I'll just send the leftovers home with you."

Without allowing Debbie Sue time to protest, her mother pulled a brown paper bag from a crevice between the refrigerator and the end of the cabinet and began adding to it emptied plastic margarine containers of leftovers. Black-eyed peas, mashed potatoes and gravy, and a foil-wrapped package of meat. Also a hunk of fresh cornbread. A banquet. Debbie Sue's stomach rumbled and growled.

She said good-bye, promised to come back when she could stay longer, and walked with Rocket Man back to the Silverado. And a flat tire.

"Shit. This day just gets better and better," she told her horse.

Rocket Man snorted and ambled off.

She couldn't remember if the spare had been repaired after her last flat. With night rapidly approaching, there wasn't much time to debate her options. She lay down on her back and scooted under the rear end where the spare was bolted to the chassis. A vehicle crunched to a stop on the gravel shoulder. A door slammed.

"Debbie Sue?"

She recognized the voice and thought a word too bad to say. "What?"

"You got a flat?"

She twisted around to look at the boots. Yep, tan alligator. "Is a snake's ass close to the ground?"

Buddy chuckled. "God, I needed that. Come out from under there."

She inched out and clambered to her feet, brushing off dirt and debris. "Well, I didn't need this."

Her bed-head hair-do and clip sagged halfway to her shoulder. She loosened the clip and ran splayed fingers through the thick tresses.

He plucked a dried grass stalk from near her temple. "Your hair looks pretty."

"It does not.

"Okay, it looks like shit. I'm too tired to change this tire. I'll take you back to town and we'll get Leroy to tow it into the station."

"I can't afford for Leroy to tow it."

"Don't worry about it."

"Well . . ." She hesitated, but the idea of some-body else changing her flat tire and Buddy paying for it was too tempting to resist.

From behind the fence, Rocket Man whinnied. Buddy walked over to the fence, and Debbie Sue followed. "How's the ol' boy doing?"

Rocket Man's head sawed up and down and he nuzzled Buddy's shirt pocket. As Buddy rubbed the long neck and apologized for having no pep-permints in his shirt pocket, Debbie Sue hid a smile. Horses fell in love with Buddy as often as women did. "He's in better shape than I am."

Buddy's eyes locked on hers. "I wouldn't go *that* far." He turned back to the horse. "Gotta go, sport. You behave yourself." He gripped Debbie Sue's arm and herded her toward the county rig. "Let's go. I've had a long day."

She freed her arm. "Wait, I've got to get a sack out of the cab."

"I'll get it."

She settled an admiring gaze on his butt in his tight Wranglers as he walked toward her pickup and reached into the cab. As he sauntered back to-ward her, his wide shoulders blocked out the set-ting sun's neon orange, shoulders that hadn't been built in a gym, but sculpted by years working on ranches and in the oil fields. Buddy had never shirked hard work.

A memory crashed down on her—his naked, near-perfect body crossing their bedroom. She used to lie in bed and take pleasure from just watching him and knowing that only she had the right to trace the whorl of black hair that traveled down his stomach to the thick curly thatch of his groin or touch the little brown mole hidden just at the edge of it.

As he came nearer, strands of jet black hair curled from beneath the sweatband of his hat. He inhaled deeply and grinned. "Lemme guess. Your mom's chicken-fried steak. I'd walk ten miles in worn-out boots for Virginia's cooking."

I'm not sharing it. Debbie Sue gave him a squint-eyed evil grin and grabbed the sack. Served him right for planting erotic memories in her head.

She hadn't been alone with Buddy in years. If her feet didn't ache, she wouldn't accept his offer for a ride. Uneasiness intact, she approached the sheriff department's Tahoe and threw a glance at the heavy steel mesh separating the driver from the backseat. "I'll ride in back."

"No, you won't. That's for prisoners. Get up front."

She eyed the shotgun braced between the dash and the front seat. *Okay, he's protected, but what about me?*

Except for the radio hissing and sputtering, they rode in uncomfortable silence for a mile. Finally she could no longer stand it. "Been out to Harley's, huh?"

"Yeah."

"I expect they're all real torn up."

"Yeah."

"Everybody's wondering about the funeral."

"Probably."

"Humph. I had a better conversation with Rocket Man."

"Don't be horsey, Debbie Sue. I got a lot on my mind."

She shrugged. "Fine. Whatever."

The last sliver of sun sank below the horizon, leaving them in semidarkness. She stared at his movie-star profile, marred only by his mustache. "Are you worried, Buddy? Aren't you scared?"

"Scared? Of what?"

"What happened with Pearl Ann is awful. I know you. I can tell when you're uptight and scared."

She could see a faint sag of his shoulders as he braked at the intersection with the highway. "If I tell you this, you have to promise me you won't blab it in that *damn* beauty shop."

"You know I won't blab."

"It's not official, but it looks like Pearl Ann didn't kill herself."

Fuck! Debbie Sue drew a sharp breath. It was hell to always be right. "Is that what *you* think?"

"I'm not thinking. I'm waiting for science to tell me." His thin smile was almost, but not quite, hidden by his mustache. "I should have known that head of yours was busy when you made that tattooed hip remark. Pretty sharp of you to catch that."

"Tattooed *lip*, Buddy. *Lip*."

He reached across and brushed her bottom lip with his finger. "Lip. Yeah, I got it."

She jerked her head backward as if his finger delivered an electrical shock. "Don't do that." Her own fingers flew up and covered her mouth.

His cell phone warbled and she jumped again.

"You're sure spooky. What are *you* scared of, Debbie Sue?" Pulling onto the highway, he unclipped the phone from his belt, flipped it open, and stuck it against his ear "This is Overstreet. . . . Hey, there . . ." He turned his head left and spoke toward the side window, the tenor of his voice softening. "No, uh, I'm not finished yet . . ."

Rat!

He gave a soft laugh. "Yeah, uh, so did I. . . . Sure, that'd be great. . . . Okay, see ya then." He snapped the cell shut and replaced it on his belt without another word.

Rat bastard!

Within seconds he turned off the highway onto her street, but Debbie Sue scarcely noticed. She was now focused on how his phone voice changed from curt and professional to warm and engaging. The Tahoe rolled to a stop in front of her small tan brick house, the home her driver and she had shared for the duration of their five-year marriage. Every part of her wanted to ask who called on the goddamn phone. What *woman* had his *private* cell number?

Damn his overtanned hide. Damn his ever-loving cowboy charm. Damn his intense eyes that could undress you and make you love it. She couldn't get out of this SUV fast enough. When she jerked the door handle, it didn't respond. Realizing control of the doors and windows was under the direction of the driver made her even angrier. She glared at him. "Well?"

Buddy released her locked door. She shoved it open and all but sprawled onto her sparse lawn. She caught herself and climbed out. "Thanks for the ride, Don Juan. And just for the record, that *damn* beauty shop is my livelihood."

She slammed the door and stomped toward her front door, heard the squeal of tires as he dug out and roared away.

Inside the kitchen she stopped. She was empty-handed. *Well, fuck.* She had left her sack of food with Buddy.

Dirty rotten double-rat bastard.

Four

Debbie Sue stood in front of her open, vintage refrigerator, which did *not* have an ice and water dispenser on its door, and stared at the sparse contents inside. *Where the hell is that TV chef when you need him?*

The thought of Buddy sitting down to enjoy her mother's chicken-fried steak and fresh black-eyed peas was galling.

"I could call his cell phone and demand that he bring my food back," she grumbled, bobbing her head to the empty refrigerator, "but *I* don't have the number."

She didn't dare let herself think about the lacerations inflicted on her heart from hearing Buddy talk on the phone to another female in that tender voice once reserved for her.

She pulled out a jar of dill pickles and a bottle of Corona. She had read a magazine article that told her beer was full of vitamin B. She found a half sack of Fritos in the cupboard and placed all three items on the lamp table beside the distressed leather reclining chair that had cost a month's wage from the salon.

By now it was debatable if her stomach or her feet protested the louder. She returned to the kitchen and dragged out a plastic dishpan, filled it with hot water and dumped in some Epsom salts, then carried it, too, to the living room and placed it on the floor in front of her chair. Last she grabbed her portable phone, found the TV remote between the sofa cushions, and settled in front of the screen. With a groan, she tugged off her boots and socks, then immersed her feet in the warm water. They nearly sighed.

Surfing channels, she found a mariachi band, high school football scores, a lot of preaching, and a *whole* lot of news. Her feet hurt too badly to dance, she couldn't care less about the football scores, and preaching would only worsen her headache. And God knew she'd had enough news for one day. A hundred damn channels and nothing to watch.

She had just chomped down on a pickle when the phone rang. Buddy, calling about her food. She didn't need caller ID to tell her. She keyed the *on* button. "Just leave it on the front porch and hurry up, while it's still hot."

After a pause a male voice replied, "Well, okay, but aren't there laws against that kind of thing?"

Fuck. Quint Matthews. She hadn't talked to him

since last December at the National Finals in Las Vegas. He had shared his box seats with her, Edwina, and C. J. After the show he took her to dinner in one of the most obscenely opulent restaurants she had ever seen in her life, then took her to his room, which was the most luxurious hotel room she ever *hoped* to see.

Oh, he'd called since then and left messages on her voice mail, but she hadn't returned the calls. It wasn't that she didn't find him interesting or attractive. *Au contraire*. After seven or eight margaritas one night, she had declared to Edwina that "Clint made her wees neak." And he was available. *Texas Monthly* had named him one of the Lone Star State's most eligible bachelors.

Only one thing was wrong with Quint. When she had opened her eyes in that king-sized bed in Las Vegas and looked into the face above hers, there was no black mustache and no chocolate brown eyes.

"Well, my Lord, Quint. I've been wondering how you are."

"I'm just fine, darlin'. Can I use my imagination about what's still hot or are you fixin' to tell me?"

Debbie Sue couldn't help but grin. She had a propensity for bad boys, the badder the better, and Quint was the baddest. "It's too long a story and I'm too tired to go into it. Just talk nice to me because I've had a really rotten day."

"I can do better than that. I'm gonna be in your

part of the country Saturday. How 'bout I take you out for dinner and some boot scootin'?"

Danger. Danger. World champion bull rider. Moving in perfect rhythm, thigh to thigh, breast to chest. Hard muscles against soft flesh. "That sounds terrific. Call me when you get to town."

"Call you? I've been leaving you messages for over six months. I know when a woman's playing hard to get." He laughed. "I'm not accustomed to it but I recognize it."

She laughed, too. Quint was nothing if not cocky and ornery.

"I'll get there early enough to come by your shop. I've been wanting to see your operation, and I'd like to say hello to Ed and that pretty little C. J."

My operation? Yikes. "Great. Ed will be thrilled to see you, too. I nearly broke my leg tripping over her dropped jaw when she met you in Vegas."

Debbie Sue and her two friends had been buying programs at the rodeo when somebody yelled, "Hey, Debbie Sue Pratt!"

It had been years since anyone called her by her maiden name, and she almost hadn't responded. When she did, she saw her old boyfriend from her teen years. In the eleven years that had passed since their last face-to-face, he had transformed from seventeen-year-old heartthrob to full-grown hunk who made other places throb. Edwina had gone into a complete twitter when he winked at her and kissed the back of her hand.

Debbie Sue's life had been full since she and Quint parted. She had fallen in love and married. Had buried a baby and divorced. His life had probably been more entertaining, but she didn't see how it could have been more real.

"Okay, darlin'," he said on a laugh. "Saturday. Where'd you tell me your shop is? On the main drag?"

"You can't miss it. It's on the corner. It used to be a gas station. You know those old-fashioned round gas pumps? There's two of them out front, dressed up in women's clothes."

"Say that again?"

Debbie Sue felt her cheeks flush. The explanation for the gas pumps in costumes was too long and too difficult. "Never mind. Just take my word. You can't miss it."

A guffaw came across the line.

Well, what was so damn funny?

After she disconnected, her thoughts lingered on Quint. Most people wouldn't describe him as handsome, but he had a presence so potent and undeniably male, no woman's hormones could resist a sudden upsurge—especially if said woman hadn't been touched in all the right places since she saw him nine months ago.

She had a sexual history with Quint all right, starting at the beginning of her seventeenth year. She and Rocket Man had been racing barrels, and he had been riding bulls. It had taken only a few hours for his twinkling blue eyes and easy laugh to charm her right out of her underwear.

Since then he had parlayed his ability as a first-rate bull rider into a pro rodeo career and three world champion bull-riding titles. He had snagged multiple endorsements and the hand of 1998's Miss Rodeo America. Fourteen months later, they divorced. At the time his quote to the press had been, "Guess she was ready to cut me from the herd." *Poor Quint.* He deserved better.

Feeling upbeat for the first time since morning, she transferred from her chair to the bathroom, mouthing a song. "If you got the money, honey . . ."

She ran a bath and sank into a tub of imaginary bubbles. Just because West Texas water was so hard that bubble bath refused to bubble didn't mean she couldn't use it. If she ever got rich, one of the things she would buy was a water softener.

Her thoughts drifted back over the three years since Buddy had told her he wanted a divorce. She had been a different person each year. She spent the first year of freedom cursing the day she laid eyes on Buddy Overstreet. The second year she partied and enjoyed the singles scene.

The third year had brought a reality check in the form of the chance encounter with Quint in Vegas. That night he made several references to "we" and "us," speaking of the future and including her in it. It was then she realized that while in Quint's company it seemed easy to dismiss Buddy from her here and now, she could *never* imagine him absent from her future.

She told C. J. and Edwina that her uncustomary silence on the flight back from Vegas to Texas was exhaustion, but in fact she was fully alert and had a plan. She could hardly wait to tell Buddy she had changed. She knew her own destructive behavior had destroyed them, and racing Rocket Man around three barrels at breakneck speed wasn't a solution to anything. She had grown up. She would stay home, do laundry, and learn to cook.

Back in Texas, the fifty miles from Midland International Airport to the outskirts of Salt Lick felt like five hundred. As soon as she dropped Edwina and C. J. off, going against all rational thinking and logic, she drove to the sheriff's office. When she burst through the door, a startled Tanya Metcalf looked up and informed her Buddy was out with his girlfriend from Odessa. "Oh, surely you've heard about them by now," Tanya said, looking smug. "They've been thick as pea soup for the past month. Guess he's got it pretty bad."

Debbie Sue had muttered something incoherent and backed out of the office, swearing to herself and God she would never come that close to humiliating herself again for Buddy Overstreet.

And she wouldn't.

It was over between her and Buddy. She had to deal with it, and what better way to do that than with a sexy, rich hunk like Quint.

She dropped an oversized nightshirt over her head, her thoughts flying to Pearl Ann and what Buddy had told her. She left the bedroom and checked the locks on her windows and both doors.

"Can you come by and pick me up?"

"I sure can, hon." Edwina's yawn came over the receiver. "What's wrong with Big Red? Throw a shoe?"

"It's at the Texaco. Buddy had it towed last night."

"Ohmygod. Did you have a wreck? Was anyone hurt? Were you arrested?"

"Ed, Ed, calm down. I had a flat out near Mom's. Buddy came along and gave me a ride home. He had my pickup towed because my spare was flat, too."

"You were alone with Buddy? Please tell me you bit him on the neck, right where he has that little scar under his chin."

Debbie Sue steadied herself, thinking of the position from which she had last seen that scar. "No biting. Not even close to his neck. Just as I thought we might be starting up a decent conversation, that whore of a schoolteacher called."

Debbie Sue repeated Buddy's telephone dialogue, filling in what she hadn't heard with what she imagined. She concluded with "You might know Odessa would hire somebody sorry and no-good to teach in their schools. How could Buddy not see right through her?"

"How do you know it was her?"

"Well, who else could it have been?"

"Why damn near anybody, from Tanya Metcalf to Liz Taylor. Buddy ain't chopped liver, you know."

Debbie Sue frowned. She hadn't thought of *that*. No, he definitely wasn't chopped liver. To her dismay, at thirty-one, he was even better-looking than he had been at twenty-one. Why couldn't he grow ugly?

A shower, a wrestling match with her Wranglers and boots, and a half hour later, she heard Edwina honk. She dashed out the door and into her pal's royal blue '68 Mustang where she was met by the reek of stale cigarette smoke. Debbie Sue cranked down the window to keep from gagging. Why would Edwina stink up a classic car with toxic fumes? They flew past Salt Lick's only drive-through eatery. "Times like this, I wish Hogg's opened before eleven. I'm starving. I had pickles and beer for supper."

"*Blech*. I'm surprised your mom didn't have something delicious for you."

"Chicken-fried steak and all the trimmings. It went home with Buddy." Debbie Sue related how her ex-husband's conversation with somebody with whom he obviously had more than a passing relationship had sent her into such a fit, she forgot her food and nearly fell out of his pickup.

"You poor thing. Don't worry. I can fix you up

with breakfast. What you need is to find a good man who can cook."

"What I need is to make enough money to hire a maid."

Edwina dug her cell phone out of her monstrous black and white cowhide purse and keyed in a number. "Hey, Poodle, could I ask you for a big old favor? If Debbie Sue and I pull up out front, would you bring us a couple of those biscuits you made this morning? And throw a sausage patty between them." She paused and turned to Debbie Sue. "Do you want an egg on that?"

"No egg and I don't want fries with that order, either, but I would looove some coffee, cream and one sugar."

Edwina placed the order, made a U-turn, and headed toward her trailer.

"I'm not believing this," Debbie Sue said. "I *would* say Vic has you spoiled, but that is such an understatement."

"Don't think it doesn't go both ways, hon. If I've learned anything in my forty-five years on this earth, it's how to give as well as take. Lord, I've run off a lot of good men with my hardheaded ways."

Debbie Sue couldn't tell if Edwina was making small talk or preaching. They pulled in front of a cream-colored double-wide with blue shutters. Vic Martin trotted out the front door with a small paper sack and a Styrofoam cup. He was a huge

man, an ex-navy SEAL, complete with shaved
head and muscles on his muscles. And right now
his chest and belly were covered with a red ruffled
apron that said "Kiss the Cook" in white letters.
Seeing him deliver breakfast curbside made Debbie Sue giggle.

"I fixed one for you, too, Mama Doll." He
grinned and gave Edwina's cheek a loving brush
with his thumb. "Since I made you late this morning, it was the least I could do."

As they pulled away, Debbie Sue munched on a
biscuit and mulled over Edwina's remark about
hardheaded ways. Maybe the old smokestack had
a point. "Now I've seen everything. Does he do
windows, too?"

Edwina's mouth turned up in a sly smile. "You'd
better believe it, hon, but that's not what he's best
at."

"Don't tell me. I don't think I could stand it."

Well after six o'clock in the evening, Debbie Sue
and Edwina washed and dried the last customer
and locked the door. They hadn't had such a busy
day since the high school prom. Weddings, funerals, and proms always bumped up the salon's
gross numbers.

Most of the day's customers had come for gossip about Pearl Ann's death. Walking out with a
new hairdo covering a head full of information
was a bonus.

The five customers who had invested five dollars each in Edwina's pool, betting on when the murder victim would leave her husband, were especially eager to learn who had won the twenty-five-dollar prize. They agreed among themselves that whoever wrote "when hell freezes over," "when chickens need lip gloss," and "whenever" had disqualified themselves. "Before I sleep with George Strait" was the winner, hands down. Charlene had come close to winning with "When I grow a mustache," but menopause had sneaked in since she placed her bet and she was no longer eligible.

Edwina dragged out the push broom and began to sweep sand into a pile. Keeping the fine West Texas sand out of the shop on any day was impossible. When the door opened and closed as often as it had today, the white vinyl floor looked like someone had poured cupfuls of the tan grit on it. "When you saw Buddy last night, he didn't say anything about Pearl Ann, did he? It just haunts me why that woman would put a gun to her head."

"Just that he called in the forensic lab from Midland. I'm not sure, but I think he *has* to do that."

"Even if he didn't say anything, he's bound to *think* something. Last I knew, Buddy wasn't stupid. If I thought you were holding back on me . . ."

Debbie Sue gave her a shrug and upturned palms. She wouldn't dream of betraying Buddy's confidence, even to a good friend.

Edwina put away the broom, went to her station, and tapped a Marlboro from a crushed pack. "What I'm trying to say here, girl, is our reputation is on the line." She lit up. "On. The. Line. Think about it. When it comes to spreading the news, we've never been outdone. You don't need film at eleven if you've got the Styling Station twenty-four-seven."

Debbie Sue's mind wandered off to visualizing how that slogan would look on matchbooks. She could see the cover as a glossy pink, with burgundy letters and maybe a little logo. "Buddy said he'd hear something from Midland in a couple of days. We'll just have to wait. Every customer I had today thinks the whole thing is somehow Harley's fault."

"Too bad you missed Ruby Cantrell. She thinks aliens had something to do with it. Said they left a crop circle behind her house Monday night."

"When did a backyard full of dead weeds become a crop?"

"What can I say? You know Ruby. Sharon Douthitt said one of their pumpers told her husband he saw Harley going into the Starlite Inn in Odessa with a blond."

"Really? Somebody told me it was a redhead . . . Edwina, speaking of blonds, did C. J. ever say how she knew about Pearl Ann? I was so blown away by the news I didn't even think to ask her who told her so early in the morning. I mean, Pearl Ann must have just been found when C. J. raced in here."

"I asked her when you followed Buddy outside, but she just broke down and bawled like a baby. I never knew she and Pearl Ann were close."

On Friday the official story appeared in the *Salt Lick Weekly Reporter*, alongside Buddy's picture and a quote. Pearl Ann Carruthers had died from a single shot to the head by a 9mm automatic pistol, inflicted by persons unknown. Her husband had offered a fifty-thousand-dollar reward for information leading to the capture and conviction of the killer. The funeral was scheduled for Monday at the Calvary Baptist Church.

So much gossip flew through the Styling Station the thin white curtains Debbie Sue had hung on the windows didn't fall lax all day. She was half listening to the talk with one side of her brain, and focused on the reward with the other. Lord, with that much money she could pay off her debt to the bank and rid herself of the salon's monthly mortgage payment that was eating her lunch.

Soon after she and Buddy had divorced and he deeded the service station to her, the great State of Texas sent her a notice ordering her to dig up and either dispose of or replace the station's aged gasoline storage tanks. The bid for the clean removal of the tanks turned out to be staggering enough, but the cost of replacing them and upgrading the station to current EPA requirements was astronomical. The six-digit number put the quietus on her or anybody else making a living from selling gasoline from the old service station.

She couldn't think of any viable use for a limestone rock gas station building constructed in the forties. She couldn't think of a business she could operate in it or a service she could provide from it to compete with existing businesses in Odessa. The locals enjoyed making the forty-five-mile trip to the bigger town too much.

And worst of all, she couldn't think of a living person who would buy the relic from her. Buddy wouldn't even take it back for free. Ownership had passed to his mother when his father had dropped dead at age fifty from a heart attack in the midst of an oil change. Buddy had quit college to operate the station for his mother's benefit as well as to provide a living for himself and Debbie Sue, but he had hated the thing from the get-go. When the Salt Lick sheriff met an untimely death during his term, Buddy ran for the office unopposed. After being elected, he had closed the service station down for good.

A beauty salon was the solution Debbie Sue finally landed on, and she enrolled in the beauty college in Odessa. She had never been sorry, really. She found she liked the creativity required by hairdressing and cosmetology. The only difference from horse grooming or maintaining her steers back when she had been in 4-H was the horse and steers had usually been better company.

Converting the gas station to a beauty salon didn't prevent the state's demanding cleanup of the soil surrounding the old storage tanks when they were discovered to have leaked. Even if she tore down the building and pulled out the storage tanks, she would still have to clean the soil. Who knew the great State of Texas could be so mean?

As the company she hired out of Odessa worked at digging out contaminated dirt and replacing it with fresh, the cost soon exceeded the original estimate by more than double. Buddy had shown the better part of valor and assumed as much of the cost as he could. Even with that, her part amounted to over thirty thousand dollars.

She'd had no choice but to mortgage the station building. Her only other option was to walk off and turn her only asset over to the state, as many of the mom-and-pop service station owners had done after EPA legislation brought them bankrupting cleanup costs. Buddy urged her to do just that, but with typical Debbie Sue stubbornness, she refused.

After adding to the loan the cost of converting the interior, then purchasing salon equipment, she was fifty thousand dollars in debt and hadn't even torn out the antique pumps out front. Edwina solved that problem by dressing the pumps in women's clothes. She even went so far as to coordinate the costume to the season.

Nor did the salon have a decent sign. Debbie Sue quashed calling it the Styling Boutique as planned. With the words "Service Station" already visible in bright red letters, she simply bought a quart of white enamel and one of red. She covered over "ervice" with white, then in red, painted in "tyling."

No one in Salt Lick seemed to notice the mismatched or unaligned letters or even care. That was one of the nice things about living in a town as small and removed from urban culture. People didn't have high expectations.

So why *couldn't* she solve Pearl Ann's murder and get fifty thousand dollars? The chances she'd succeed were probably better than winning the lottery. Her instincts were good. Hadn't she had that gnawing hunch from the beginning that the woman didn't commit suicide?

Saturday dawned with Debbie Sue having cogitated all night. She left her bed determined to put Buddy Overstreet in a far, far corner of her mind where he belonged and concentrate on Quint Matthews. By hooking up with Quint, she wouldn't have to worry about solving a murder mystery to get enough money to pay off her debt. Despite the fact that the only time she had slept with him in more than ten years had conjured up her desire to reunite with her ex-husband, she had to admit Quint was an extremely capable and unselfish lover. Piles of money and great sex. What was not to like? *Solving a murder mystery? Phfft.* What had she been thinking?

Yep, hooking up with Quint was, by far, the smarter thing to do. With her mind set on the notion, all she had to do was convince her heart to follow.

She molded her breasts into her Wonderbra and pulled out of her closet a knit robin's egg blue shirt with a plunging V neck and her favorite Rockies, not too new, but not too faded, either. They fit her like a coat of paint.

Around her waist she wrapped a brown leather belt adorned with engraved sterling silver squares and enhanced it with one of her medium-sized trophy silver belt buckles. Then she pulled on beige Tony Lama boots and hooked sterling and turquoise drops in her earlobes.

A Navajo bracelet made of tortoiseshell inlaid with a coral cardinal and mother-of-pearl flowers cuffed her wrist. The piece was what they called "Old Pawn" in Albuquerque, and she considered it a treasure. Not just because it was old and it was against the law to make jewelry out of coral and tortoiseshell nowadays, but because Buddy had bought it for her. Last, she hung a silver chain holding a tiny turquoise heart around her neck. Buddy had bought it, too. The heart fell to a strategic place just at the top of her Wonderbra cleavage.

At three o'clock the last customer was sent out the door with new honey-colored frosting and a cut that had appeared on a model in *Glamour*. Debbie Sue locked the door. "Okay, Ed, this is it. With the commotion all week, I didn't get around to telling you Quint Matthews is stopping by and taking me out to dinner."

Edwina gasped. "He's not!"

"He is. He called me Tuesday night."

"Debbie Sue, I ought to take a hairbrush to your backside for depriving me of news like that."

"Just make me good-looking. It's plumb dumb for me to keep pining over Buddy. I need fresh meat."

Edwina gave her a sour look. "I'll try not to take that literally."

"I'm going for the *sophisticated bitch* look to-night, Ed."

"You got it, hon." The veteran beautician crushed out her cigarette and went to work. She shampooed Debbie Sue's long silky hair, then plopped her down in her styling chair, ignoring that the starched, tight Rockies made it binding to sit or bend. Edwina dried and combed and twisted and rolled. When she finished, Debbie Sue's red-brown hair was slicked back from her face in a smooth do with the blond highlighted streak showing down the middle and a sexy-as-all-get-out knot at the crown.

"Wow," Debbie Sue said. "I look like a fancy skunk."

"As long as you don't smell like one," Edwina quipped.

For a finishing touch to the topknot, Edwina added a little wispy hairpiece, then dragged out a satchel filled with cosmetics.

"No face makeup." Debbie Sue halted Edwina's hands. Except for a few freckles on her nose, her skin was flawless and smooth. "Just do my eyes and cheeks."

Edwina bronzed Debbie Sue's eyelids and mascaraed her naturally thick lashes. She added Antique Rose blush to her cheeks and Rosewood Frost lipstick to her full lips. When she finished, Debbie Sue almost didn't recognize herself. "You're a vision, girl. Want me to put some acrylics on those nails? We've got time."

"No fingernails. I won't be able to stuff my shirttail into these jeans." Debbie Sue rose and looked closer into the mirror, made a few brushes to her eyebrows with her fingertips, adjusted the heart hanging around her neck. She dug into her handbag, brought out a purse-sized atomizer of Paloma, and sprayed behind each ear and between her breasts. Family and friends called her a tomboy, but that didn't mean she couldn't smell like a sexpot. "Don't ever mention Buddy Overstreet's name again, Ed. Tonight I'm going for the gold. I'm tired of this town, tired of this beauty shop, and tired of being broke."

"Um-um," Edwina said. "I can see it now. You'll be walking bowlegged for a week." She propped an elbow on the payout desk, gave Debbie Sue a head-to-toe. "Just don't make any sudden moves in those jeans unless you've got an extra pair somewhere."

Five

At five o'clock a car door slammed and Debbie Sue's heart lurched. She felt seventeen again. Her pulse was racing, and she had a sudden urge to pee. She darted to the storeroom and peeked out from behind the burgundy and pink floral print curtain that hid the storeroom from the salon. "Ed, just act cool. I'll come out casually, as if I didn't realize he had gotten here."

She stood in the cramped area rehearsing an act of surprise. The last thing she wanted was for a bad boy like Quint to think her future depended on the outcome of this date. Some of her nervousness was for good reason. How often did a hick from Salt Lick go out with the Most Eligible Bachelor in Texas? Taking one last look in the mirror, she sucked in her gut and parted the curtains.

"Goodness, I didn't—" She clamped her mouth shut and tried not to gape. "Buddy. What are you doing here?"

Her ex laughed. "Between you and Ed I'm beginning to feel unwelcome. She 'bout jumped out of those funny-looking shoes when I came in. . . . Hey, Ed. You okay?"

Debbie Sue's gaze darted to Edwina, who had just lit the wrong end of her cigarette. A tiny flame burned beneath her nose. She tamped out the cigarette in an ashtray.

"You two sure are nervous. Somebody hiding out in the back holding a gun on us?"

"I'm, uh . . . we're just surprised to see you, that's all. Why are you here?"

"I got to feeling bad about not returning Virginia's food to you the other night. I forgot it was in the Tahoe until after ten o'clock. I figured it was too late to bring it back so I heated it up and ate it. Lord, your mother can cook."

Debbie Sue tried to block out the sight of Edwina waving her arms and pointing to her watch behind Buddy's back. It wouldn't be the end of the world if Quint came in, but she didn't relish the thought of being picked up for a date with her ex-husband present, especially a date with Quint Matthews. Buddy knew she and the ex-rodeo star had once had a fling. She turned Buddy around and pushed him toward the front door. "Don't worry about it. I didn't need all those extra calories. Glad you enjoyed it."

"Whoa. I may be a country boy from a small town but I know when somebody's trying to get rid of me. Is everything really all right?"

"Dammit, Buddy, would you quit trying to find something wrong in every situation? Sometimes your insatiable need to fix everything is such a pain in the ass. Maybe I'm just plain ol' tired and want to get out of here or maybe I've got plans."

"Okay, I'm leaving. I came by to tell you Mack Humphrey's got some extra hay he'll give away. Thought you might could use it. Sorry I bothered you." He blatantly looked her up and down. "I can see you've got somewhere to go." He nodded to Edwina and stamped out the door.

He had no more than driven away before a shiny black Lincoln Navigator turned into the parking lot. "Ohmygod, he's here. Look at that rig he's driving." She made a mad dash for the back room again, then stuck her head around the floral curtain. "Ed, just talk to him for a little bit, then I'll come out."

Words were wasted on Edwina because she wasn't listening. She had her nose plastered to the window that took up the upper half of the front door. "Now there's a man who makes a woman feel proud to be female. Um-um. I'd be on him like cheese on nachos."

The bells on the door clattered as Quint entered. He swept off his hat and extended his right hand to Edwina. "I hope you remember me, darlin', 'cause I remember you. I'm Quint Matthews." The statement was on a par with "I hope you remember me. I'm Troy Aikman."

"Why, as I live and breathe," Edwina said and

fluttered her heavily mascaraed eyelashes. "Las Vegas wasn't it, Quint?"

"Yes, ma'am. Did Debbie Sue tell you I was coming by?"

"Seems like she mentioned it. I hope you didn't have any trouble finding the shop."

"It was hard deciding which service station with old gas pumps wearing dresses to stop at, but I finally just picked one and went with it."

Debbie adjusted her boobs in her Wonderbra and made her entrance with a gasp. "Why Quint, I didn't hear you come in."

Quint's gaze roamed her up and down and stopped at the little turquoise heart just as she had hoped. He broke into a wide grin. "Now that's what I'm talking about. You look good, Debbie Sue, real good."

Debbie Sue's brain shut down. Her tongue begged her to do something, but all she could produce was a giggle. She thought she heard Ed mutter "Pitiful" under her breath, but she wasn't sure.

Finally the gears clicked in, "I hope you don't mind if we drive over to Odessa to eat. I know a terrific restaurant, and it has a good house band that plays on weekends."

"Why honey, that sounds just great." He turned back to Edwina. "It was a pleasure to see you. I hope it's not so long before we meet again."

Buddy walked out of Nelson's Rexall carrying the latest edition of the *Odessa American* and a sack holding razor blades, shooting a glance across the street at the Styling Station's parking lot. A cowboy wearing a big hat was helping Debbie step up into a new black Navigator. And the man was? . . . Shit!

A pang sliced through Buddy's gut. Where in the hell had Quint Matthews come from? The last time Buddy saw him was at the Fort Worth Stock Show and Rodeo when a mean-ass bull named Bodacious had bucked his showoff butt in the dirt.

Buddy's queasy feeling made no sense. He had been divorced from Debbie Sue three years and he was seeing Kathy. His ex-wife was a beautiful woman. No reason why some guy wouldn't want to take her out, and she was free to see whom she wanted. But as hard as Buddy tried to rationalize, the cold hard truth couldn't be denied. The thought of her with Quint Matthews knocked the props right from under him.

He stood back under the drugstore's awning and watched the fancy SUV pull away from the Styling Station's parking lot, hoping Debbie Sue didn't spot him and think he was spying on her. The vehicle headed out the Odessa highway, and Buddy figured he knew its destination.

He threw his newspaper and sack into the Tahoe, scooted in and checked his watch. Kathy was expecting him in an hour. He scarcely had time to shower, shave, and change clothes. His original plan had been for a nice dinner somewhere, maybe a dance or two and a sleepover at

Kathy's apartment in Odessa. Suddenly the plan took on tarnish and his own empty bed in his tiny apartment held an awful lot of appeal.

The forty-five-mile drive in Quint's luxury SUV flew by as he caught Debbie Sue up on the last few months' rodeo news. He didn't mention Pearl Ann's murder, which Debbie Sue found to be a relief. It was all she had heard for the past five days.

The rodeo stock business was bigger than ever, he told her. Even parts of the country where rodeos had never been held, much less been popular, were now seeking him out for bookings. "I've been thinking ever since December, Deb. It'd sure be great to have you with me on the road. As much as you know about horses, you could find the best ones for me while I check out cattle. I fly first-class all over the country, darlin'. Stay at only the best hotels, got a bottomless expense account."

Debbie Sue felt herself grinning like an idiot. She didn't trust herself to comment for fear she might scream an exuberant "Yes!"

Following her directions, he drove them to Kincaid's. The well-known Odessa dining establishment was housed in a building designed to look like an old barn, inside and out. On the lower floor, small tables surrounded a dance floor and a raised bandstand. The serious dining occurred on the mezzanine, which could be reached by either elevator or a wide staircase rising up one side of the room, its handrails supported by massive carved balusters. The decor might be rustic, the dress code casual, but everybody in West Texas knew Kincaid's was no cheap steak joint.

Dining at Kincaid's with any man besides Buddy was a part of Debbie Sue's exorcism process. The restaurant had always been their special place. If she could manage an evening there without breaking down and weeping, she would wake up stronger for it in the morning.

Quint guided her into the packed foyer with a hand on the small of her back. Debbie Sue basked in the envious glances of women they passed. Not only was her escort a good-looking sonofagun, he might as well have had hundred-dollar bills sticking out of his pockets. Anybody in his (or her) right mind could see the shirt on his back had probably cost a minimum of two hundred dollars. And his boots . . . well, what he paid for the boots would buy her groceries for half a year.

Quint spoke to the maître d', and at the same time made a smooth move into his pocket, pressed something against the young man's hand. Immediately they were led upstairs to the mezzanine dining area that looked down on the dance floor below. The room's acoustics were so well tuned, meals were undisturbed by the band music.

The cocktail waitress appeared, and Debbie Sue ordered the restaurant's signature drink, a Margarita Mortal. Along with Jose Cuervo, grenadine, and triple sec, the concoction was topped off with a full jigger of Grand Marnier and served in a grandé margarita glass. Compared to the margaritas Debbie Sue made at home, it was an atom bomb.

Quint asked for a shot of Crown Royal. A large diamond mounted inside a gold horseshoe glinted from his left ring finger as he chose hors d'oeuvres from the menu. Debbie Sue gloated with wicked pleasure. Having money was so much fun.

They discussed the things they had in common, which mostly included livestock and rodeo. He picked up her hand and circled the back with his thumb, looking at her with a penetrating gaze. "I didn't drop into Salt Lick because I'm passing through, you know. I'm serious about wanting you to travel with me."

She felt both exhilarated and confused. Travel with him as what? A horse buyer? His mistress? Did a salary and benefits come with the package, or was her intended pay to be sleeping with him? "I don't know, Quint. I have responsibilities. And debt. I can't just walk off from everything. And I have Rocket Man."

"I can't believe you've still got that horse." He leaned back and finished off his drink. "Well, selling a horse is no problem. What kind of debt? Pretty good wages come with the job, you know."

Sell Rocket Man? Inside she scowled, but she made an effort to home in on the more positive parts of the conversation. She made a long-winded explanation of the service station's environmental cleanup and the expense of opening the salon, during the middle of which he ordered another shot of Crown.

"You mean ol' Buddy didn't help you pay for all that?" he said at the end of her story. "What kind of a chickenshit is he?"

Her spine jerked a little straighter. She had never heard *anybody*—except herself, of course, and she had a right to—call Buddy Overstreet a chickenshit. And as far as helping her, he had sold his horses and cows and paid every dime he had in savings toward the cleanup. "Of course he helped me. As much as he could. We were divorced, you know. He didn't have to do anything at all."

"I know why you married him, but how come you divorced him? I never heard."

"I didn't. He divorced me."

Quint's blue eyes landed on her cleavage again. "Well, if he isn't a chickenshit, he's at the least a dumb bastard. So tell me what happened."

How could he speak of Buddy in such a disrespectful way? Buddy had given up a lifelong dream to marry her. Her spine stiffened a little more. She went from sipping her margarita to gulping the last of it. "We had issues. It was my fault."

"I'll bet. If you hadn't been pregnant, you never would've married him in the first place."

"Why, that's not true. We loved each other. We wanted the baby, but I lost it. And afterward, I had this . . . depression. I made our lives so miserable, he couldn't live with me anymore."

What was she doing? Why was she telling Quint Matthews all of this?

He released her hand and leaned back, cocked his elbow on the back of his chair. "Jesus Christ, you're still in love with him, aren't you?"

"Well, no. I just . . . I just don't see what's to be gained by talking bad about him all the time. Can I have another margarita?"

"Sure." He summoned the waitress. "I still say he's a chickenshit. Let's go ahead and eat."

A chill settled between them. The conversation about her and Buddy's relationship had caught her off-guard, but she regrouped, keeping her eye on the prize. How could she have wound up defending Buddy to Quint? Had she lost her mind?

A different waitress came with menus, and she ordered a T-bone and a baked potato, but Quint ordered some kind of grilled gourmet chicken and a salad. When she gave him a questioning look, he patted his stomach and said, "Gotta watch my waistline. I don't get the exercise I used to."

They ordered more drinks while they waited for the food. Quint swallowed a sip of whiskey and leaned forward, resting his forearms on the table. "Debbie Sue, I haven't forgotten Las Vegas. I've been thinking about it for over eight months. Don't think I don't know why you hightailed it out of my room before sunup that morning. I said I want you with me and I meant it, but I don't want your ex-husband in bed with us again."

Help! Where was the waitress? She wanted a Margarita Mortal in each hand. It was one thing to spend the night with Quint on a lost weekend now and then, but to commit to a more permanent arrangement suddenly seemed like adding a fourth barrel to the barrel-racing course. She gulped a large swallow of her drink. "Bed?" she squeaked.

"Bed. We spent the night together, remember? And as I recall, you had a hell of a good time. I was thankful the room was soundproofed."

Yikes! Her scalp began to sweat. "Well, I—"

"Darlin', I can make you forget Buddy Overstreet ever lived. I can show you—"

"Why, Quint Matthews. I haven't seen you in years."

Debbie Sue and Quint looked up at the same time, and there stood Buddy.

And a woman. Without a doubt, the schoolteacher from Odessa. How *dare* he bring her to Kincaid's?

"Mind if we sit with you? The place is a little crowded tonight."

Before Quint could reply, Buddy dragged up two chairs and placed them at the end of their table. "Have a seat, Kathy," he said to the woman. She sank to the chair seat like a robot.

Buddy sat down himself and called the waitress over, ordered a glass of white wine and bottle of

Coors. "Bring these folks another round, too. Keep 'em coming." He winked as he instructed the waitress, "Put it on my bill."

Debbie Sue and Quint both sat speechless through the drink ordering process. Buddy made introductions—Quint, an old acquaintance. Debbie Sue, ex-wife. Kathy Something, a resident of Odessa.

Debbie Sue, Quint and the woman nodded to one another.

"Lemme see, Quint," Buddy said, grinning and pushing his gray hat back with his thumb. "I think it was the rodeo in Fort Worth the last time I saw you. You were trying to ride that mean sucker. I believe they called him Bodacious."

"Might have been," Quint said, unsmiling.

Buddy turned to Kathy. "Ol' Bodacious is the only bull they ever retired unridden. Isn't that right, Quint?"

"Might be."

Debbie Sue inhaled half her drink. The schoolteacher from Odessa blinked, and Debbie Sue stared at the bangs that crossed her forehead like a wide-toothed comb. Her dark hair brushed her shoulders when she moved her head. *Split ends.* The woman could use a hot oil treatment.

"Buddy tells me you're quite the horsewoman," Kathy said.

The first word from the woman's mouth, and Debbie Sue knew she wasn't a Texan. She managed a blurry glare at Buddy. "I know a horse or two."

"I've been telling Buddy he has to teach me to ride." Kathy batted her eyelashes at Buddy and squeezed his arm. "How hard can it be? Even children ride horseback."

Debbie plopped a forearm on the table and leaned forward. "I'll tell you this much—"

"You folks ordered yet?" Buddy's dark brown gaze drilled Debbie Sue. "Try the chicken-fried steak, Quint. That's my favorite. Beef's real good here."

Bastard. Debbie Sue ducked his eyes and pasted on a smile as wooden as the schoolteacher's.

The food came. Hers filled a platter, Quint's, a saucer. The steak was bigger than her hand and an inch thick. Her potato was the size of Idaho. No telling when she might get to eat here again, so she intended to ask for a doggie bag.

The waiter came for Buddy's and Kathy's orders. As Buddy started to order, Kathy placed her hand on his arm, stopping him, and began speaking to the waiter in Spanish. The young Mexican seemed delighted, and they carried on a conversation in Spanish for several minutes. After he left, Kathy turned to Buddy and told him their order would be done to perfection.

Big deal. A lot of Texans speak Spanish, especially if they teach school. "So, Karen," Debbie Sue said, "how long have you lived in Texas? Where'd you learn Spanish?"

"It's Kathy, dear. I've been here a little over a year. I'm from Chicago. Growing up, I learned

Polish and German. After those, Spanish came easily."

"Uh-huh." *Fuck*.

Buddy led the conversation into a discussion of fine performance horses about which he knew a lot, but Quint said little. The ex-rodeoer probably didn't know much about fine horses. His only real interest was broncs and bulls. In fact, she remembered from their rodeoing days, Quint hadn't much liked animals of any kind. His focus had always been only on winning money.

Kathy Something didn't say a dozen words. She mostly blinked until she turned to Debbie Sue and said, "Would you like to go with me to the little girls' room?"

Little girls' room? Please tell me she didn't say that. Debbie Sue wrinkled her nose and mouthed a no. When Kathy excused herself and crossed to the restrooms, Debbie Sue watched her backside. The woman was a bottle-butt, pure and simple. And she had on a *dress*. Where had Buddy found her?

The cocktail waitress appeared again with Kathy trailing behind. Debbie Sue opted to skip the middleman and go to straight tequila. Quint liked the idea so much he ordered a shot for himself. When the waitress queried Buddy and Kathy, they both declined. Buddy said he was on duty twenty-four-seven, like it or not, and Kathy never drank more than a glass or two of white wine, in case she ran into some of her students somewhere. Quint asked Kathy what she taught, and when she replied high school honors chemistry and yoga at night at the college, Debbie Sue ordered a double.

Her vision began to blur, and in her head, she was practicing Spanish verses she had learned in high school when a slurred statement from Quint interrupted her thoughts. "Let's dance, Susie. I promised you boot scootin'." He stood up and looked over the wrought-iron railing, down at the dance floor in the atrium below. He swayed forward. "Where the hell's the floor?"

Susie? Who the hell was *Susie?* "Downstairs. I'll show you." Debbie Sue scowled at Buddy and grabbed Quint's arm. "Excuso por favor," she said to their uninvited table guests. "We'll be backo uno momento."

Quint picked up his hat and set it on his head at a cockeyed angle. Debbie Sue led him from the table to the wide stairway. A few treads from the bottom, he missed a step, tumbled the rest of the way, and landed face-first on the empty dance floor. His hat popped off and skidded all the way to the foyer. Two waiters dropped their tasks and rushed to his aid.

Debbie Sue stopped, grabbed the rail above the melee, and called down to him. "Quint? Did you fall?"

He mumbled and muttered as the two waiters, babbling in Spanish, lifted him to his feet and escorted him to the men's room. Debbie Sue turned and climbed the stairs, hanging on to the rail with both hands as she started back to the table. Her surroundings seemed to be floating. She placed her steps with deliberate care as she returned to her chair and picked up her purse.

Buddy looked up. "That was quick. How's the band?"

She tossed her head so hard her neck popped. She lost her balance and wound up with her feet crossed at the ankles. "It was terrific, thank you. Now we're going home."

"Where's the champ?"

"He's waiting downstairs." She concentrated on uncrossing her feet.

Buddy broke into a loud laugh and slapped his thigh. "That landing at the bottom of those stairs was better than the one he made off of ol' Bodacious."

"Fuck you, Buddy Overstreet." Making a deliberate effort to avoid falling forward, she turned to Karen, or Kathy, or whoever. "It's very nice to have met you, ma'am."

At the bottom of the stairs, Debbie Sue found Quint doing something to his hat. The brim had a distinct impression of a boot heel. "Let's get the fuck outta here," he slurred.

Debbie Sue sensed a presence and turned. Buddy was right behind them. "Say, hoss," he said to Quint in a firm voice, "you're not planning on driving, I hope."

Oh shit. Debbie Sue opened her mouth to speak, but Buddy pointed his finger at her. "You're not driving, either."

"I'll get a cab," Quint mumbled.

"Doubt if you'll find a cab that'll drive you clear to Salt Lick." Buddy adjusted his hat and pulled car keys from his pocket. "I'll take you home myself."

Debbie Sue couldn't put two sentences together to argue. As if they were under arrest, Buddy herded them to the county's Tahoe and opened the back door. Quint fell onto the backseat and Debbie Sue followed him. Both knees of his Lucchese khakis were ripped and one tear had a bloody spot. She bent forward and took a closer look. "Ohmygod, Quint, you're hurt."

Even through the black mesh partition that separated them, Debbie Sue could see Buddy's eyes glued to Quint in the rearview mirror. "Where you staying, Slick?"

"My house. Just take us to my house," Debbie Sue said.

A moment of silence followed, then they peeled out of the parking lot with such a jolt their heads jerked backward.

"Why don't you drop me off first, sweetheart," Kathy said. "I can see you have your hands full."

"Shit," Debbie Sue muttered, staring through the black mesh at the backs of her ex-husband's and Kathy Something's heads. "Shit, shit, shit."

Edwina was looking at the TV, but her mind was miles away. Odessa to be exact. She intended to watch the situation between her good friend and Quint with a skeptical eye. Debbie Sue wasn't the type to sleep around, and it was real obvious Quint had ridden more at the rodeo than a few bulls.

Edwina's second husband and the father of her middle child had been a rodeo cowboy. He had never reached the lofty level of world champion. He had been involved more in the lower level of partying and carousing. She had always suspected he only married her because it was cheaper than having his Wranglers and shirts starched and ironed by the cleaners.

Even after all these years she still wished she had been there when he came home and found those precious shirts cut into confetti and his custom-made boots filled with cement.

The surface reasons to approve of Quint Matthews were all there—looks, charm, and money—but who knew what lay beneath? She had been lured by the same three demons herself and learned the hard way there was a big difference between having character and being one.

Six

Buddy awoke at daylight horny, as usual.
For the past dozen or so Sunday mornings, Kathy
had been beside him, more than eager to assist
him to a pleasant satisfaction of his morning call.

This morning, he was glad to be alone. Debbie
Sue's memory filled the other side of the bed, and
a threesome had never appealed to him.

He hadn't slept worth a damn. All night, images
of her and Quint Matthews invaded his sleep.
And his nightmares. Without opening his eyes, he
yawned and stretched and locked his hands behind his neck, thinking about how it had poleaxed
him when he walked into Kincaid's and saw his
ex-wife and that showoff jerk holding hands
across the table.

And she was wearing the bracelet he had
bought her in Albuquerque when she and Rocket
Man won the barrel-racing competition and set a
record. After the show, they and the horse had

celebrated by sharing a six-pack. He and Debbie Sue celebrated in private later that evening and set what they had laughingly called a record of their own.

Sex between them had always been white-hot. Neither divorce nor time had diminished the memory of her body, honed and firmed by a lifetime of athletic activity, pressed against him. Her mouth—sweet as a ripe plum—kissing, biting, sucking . . . *Shit.*

How could a man ever get a woman as vibrant as Debbie Sue out of his system? They went so far back, all the way to when she was a raw-boned little girl of eleven in an oversized hat and he was fourteen and they had been in 4-H. He had never seen a girl so good at handling horses, something he considered then to be the exclusive bailiwick of boys. She'd had no fear of an unruly knothead and soon had him nuzzling her pocket for a chunk of carrot. When the other boys weren't around to hear, he found himself consulting her about how to deal with his own mare.

By the time she had reached fifteen and he was a senior, anybody could see beauty would be added to her spirited personality and go-getter attitude. The same boys who teased him about the crush she'd had on him for four years were envious of the friendship he had forged with her.

She was competing and placing in barrel races in high school rodeo. Virginia hauled her from show to show in an old pickup, pulling a rusty, beat-up one-horse trailer housing a too-old horse that didn't even belong to them. The bay belonged to a ranching family who said Debbie Sue could ride him in exchange for grooming and training.

Everyone who saw her performance said all she needed was a good horse and she would be a champion.

It just so happened Buddy had what he believed was a good horse. He had been cowboying for a rancher up out of Lubbock when he came across one of the ranch's brood mares in trouble while attempting to deliver. He stayed with the exhausted animal and helped her leggy, wobbly offspring make his appearance at four o'clock in the morning. The rancher, on hearing Buddy had saved the mare's life, made him a gift of the foal.

Debbie Sue had been foremost in his mind even then. He countered the rancher's offer with a request the grateful man didn't even hesitate to agree to. Instead of the foal, Buddy asked for the five-year-old paint gelding the rancher's daughter had used for barrel racing. The girl had lost interest in the sport and the horse, and left the animal to roam the pastures. The horse's smarts, quickness, and speed hadn't escaped Buddy, and he had long known nothing was worse than a good, smart horse with nothing to do. With the right rider, the paint had the makings of a champion, and Buddy knew the right rider.

As if it were yesterday, Buddy remembered approaching Debbie Sue with his predicament. He would be leaving in the fall for college. "Fixin' to be a Texas Ranger," he told her. Would she like to have the barrel horse for her own?

When Buddy took her to see the brown and white horse he had named Pete, it was love at first sight. She laughed and cried and hugged the horse, promised to sleep in the barn with him. She renamed him Rocket Man on the spot. Then she threw her arms around Buddy's neck and said, "Buddy Overstreet, I will love you forever."

He winced. Forever had turned out to be too damn short.

For him, survival kept getting in the way of college, not to mention his dreams, and his education turned into a hit-or-miss proposition, punctuated by cowboying on cattle ranches and roughnecking on drilling rigs. He stayed in touch with Debbie Sue, using Rocket Man as an excuse for phone calls and visits.

Then Quint Matthews entered the picture. Buddy didn't know him personally, but he knew his reputation. A comer in bull riding, he had a showy style and in the arena, wore loud-colored shirts and bright red chaps. The buckle bunnies always went for the bull riders, and Quint took full advantage of that fact. It had taken some doing to win Debbie Sue back from a guy like Quint, but Buddy, in his typical plodding fashion, had done it and never looked back.

The question he faced today was, did he want to do it again?

And if he did, what was he going to do with Kathy?

He threw off the covers and sprang from bed. He couldn't lie in bed any longer thinking about old times and new problems.

"Aarrgh." The sound echoed from the bathroom.

Debbie Sue opened one eye to blinding sunlight and scanned the room. She was in *her* bed, in *her* bedroom. Her Rockies were folded and hanging neatly across the back of a chair. *What the hell . . . ?* She ran her hand over the mattress beside her. She was alone. *Thank God.*

Before taking the risk of raising her head, she lay there piecing together the previous night's events. She remembered getting up to dance, then being led to a backseat. Why would she and Quint be crawling into a backseat when he had driven his classy Navigator? Gradually things began to unfurl—stopping in front of her house, being carried inside and laid on the bed, jeans and boots gingerly removed, covers tucked around her body and . . . Buddy? Had Buddy kissed her?

Ohmygod. She had been brought home from her first date in years by her ex-husband. She threw back the sheet and saw, to her relief, she was wearing panties and her T-shirt.

A string of expletives from the bathroom vibrated the walls. She swung her legs over the side of the bed and pushed to her feet. Something dark, and fuzzy as a tarantula, covered her eyes. Just before she screamed, she remembered the hairpiece Edwina had stuck in her hair.

She stumbled to the narrow hallway and saw Quint in the bathroom doorway, hanging on to the doorjamb as if he had been crucified. He was wearing his wrinkled shirt and boxers. His hair looked like it had been combed with a skillet. Both his knees were cut, bruised, and swollen.

"Oh my Lord, Quint. Do you want something for that swelling?"

"Normally that's a question I can't wait to hear a woman ask early in the morning."

"I'm sooo sorry."

"Hellfire, Debbie Sue. You're more dangerous than bull riding ever was. I think my back's broke."

"Where did you sleep?"

"I woke up in the bathtub." He stared down at the tub with bloodshot eyes.

Debbie Sue bit her lip. He had to be looking at the orange ring of mineral rust that made a narrow circle around the white enamel sides of the old tub. No cleanser would remove it. The only way to get rid of it was to do away with the tub, but on her list of priorities, a long way from the top was a new bathtub to replace one that was perfectly good except for a little rust. "It's clean," she blurted. "You know how West Texas water is."

He grimaced and grunted. "What the hell happened to my pants?"

"You mean we didn't get home with them?"

"Fuck. I had to cut 'em off me with my pocket knife so I could take a leak."

"What?" Debbie Sue glanced at the floor and saw the wrinkled wad of khaki cloth. She might not survive bending over, but she took a deep breath and went for it, retrieved the pants from the bathroom floor, saw the ragged edges where the zipper had been carved out of the fly. She looked around. On the edge of the sink lay the khaki zipper with all its teeth interlocked. She picked it up and looked closer. It was sealed shut with something hard and clear. She lifted it to her nose and sniffed.

Fingernail glue!
Dammit, Buddy, I just hate you.

While Quint showered, Debbie Sue threw on a robe and padded to the kitchen. With every step, a gong crashed in her head. Her stomach rolled. She knew a country song from years ago about Jose Cuervo being a friend, but she intended to kill the sonofabitch if she ever saw him again.

She rooted around in a catch-all cabinet drawer looking for a safety pin for Quint to use to close his pants. All she found was an empty tube of fingernail glue and a pink plastic clothespin. Going back to the bathroom and hearing the thrum of the shower, she eased the door open and placed the clothespin on the vanity. "Quint, I couldn't find a safety pin, but here's a clothespin."

His soaked head jutted past the edge of the shower curtain. "A clothespin?"

"It's all I could find." She gave him a weak smile.

He grunted.

She returned to the kitchen, glad he didn't appear to be interested in a morning session of sex. She certainly wasn't up to it. Besides, seeing Buddy with a date last night had soured her on men in general and sex maybe forever. She didn't have a clear memory of everything that had happened, but she distinctly remembered hearing Karen Something call Buddy sweetheart.

She set coffee on to drip, then opened the refrigerator. She stood there studying the contents and letting the cold air cool her body. The morning temperature had to be ninety again.

She had bought bacon and eggs and frozen biscuits for this morning's breakfast, intending to do the domestic routine and cook for Quint. She even bought a half gallon of orange juice with the outrageous notion she would use the bottle of champagne aging in her cabinet since New Year's and make mimosas for breakfast.

Now the very idea made her want to hurl. She reached for the half-gallon jug of Tropicana, unscrewed the lid, and drank deeply. The cold orange juice hit her stomach like one big ice block.

Quint came out of the bathroom, sweating and trembling, and wearing his wrinkled khakis with the fly held together by the pink clothespin. When she told him it looked like a tiny penis, he tried to cover it with his wrinkled shirttail. "Do me a favor," he said, "and don't use the words 'tiny' and 'penis' in the same sentence." When she asked him if he wanted an egg for breakfast, he glared at her, turned and rushed back to the bathroom.

She drank more orange juice and ate a piece of stale bread. Then she squeezed herself into a pair of Wranglers, threw on a yellow T-shirt, and put her hair up in a ponytail.

They left her house in her pickup, headed for Odessa and Quint's Navigator. She had been forced to dig out her darkest sunglasses to combat the blinding white sunlight and focus her eyes on the road. By the time they reached the city limits of Salt Lick, Quint, leaning against the passenger door, was sound asleep and snoring like a foghorn.

When they reached the Navigator, Debbie Sue was relieved to see the luxury SUV hadn't been vandalized while spending the night in Kincaid's vast, empty parking lot. Quint limped to the driver's door, mumbling as he fumbled for keys that he would call her, and drove away. No doubt she had seen the last of him. It was just as well. Maybe she didn't have what it took to tie herself to somebody for the sake of money.

That, and seeing Buddy escorting a woman, reinforced that she *had* to collect that reward from Harley, pay off the bank, shut down the Styling Station, and leave Salt Lick, Texas.

It was past noon when she arrived back in Salt Lick, and she was hungry as a weaned calf. *Mom.*

Her mom always had something good cooked and ready to eat. She stopped off at City Grocery & Market and picked up a Rocket Man treat.

When she reached her mom's, the paint met her at the fence corner. He shied away when she tried to give him a hug, showing his independence. But when she dragged out the Cheerios, he couldn't resist. "You are such a pushover," she told him as she fed him handfuls of Cheerios.

As soon as she walked through the front doorway of Mom's house, she smelled food.

I would have made a lousy mom. I don't even cook.

She found her mother at the cookstove, an apron covering her church clothes, and Debbie Sue felt a twinge of guilt. As a good Southern Baptist little girl, she had always gone to Sunday school and church and even vacation bible school in the summers. Another lifetime, another world.

"There was a prayer for the Carruthers family before the sermon today," her mother said.

"Really?

"The women's auxiliary posted a request for food for the dinner after the funeral service Monday. I signed you up for a meat loaf."

"Mom, no. The last meat loaf I made, even Rocket Man wouldn't eat."

"I remember. I'll make the meat loaf. Do you think Edwina will want to bring something?"

"I wouldn't count on Ed. Until Vic came along, she used her oven for extra shoe storage."

They sat down to fried pork chops, fried potatoes, fried okra, red beans simmered with chili powder and a big hunk of salt pork, and hot fresh cornbread and a tub of real butter. Debbie Sue made a mental groan. Only in West Texas were bacon drippings as common an ingredient as salt and pepper. Someday she intended to have a conversation with her mother about health food, but not today.

"I wish I had known you were coming out," her mom said. "I've got some lemons. I would've baked a pie." She started to rise from the table. "I could—"

"Mom, I don't even know if I can eat all this. Where would I put a pie?"

"Oh dear. Are you having your period?"

Debbie Sue dropped her forehead to the tabletop, letting the cool Formica surface ease the fire in her brain. "Mom, do you have an aspirin?"

Her mother hurried from the room and returned with a bottle of aspirin tablets. "Your problem is you work too hard and you're under too much stress. Dr. Phil says—"

"I know, Mom." Debbie Sue washed down two tablets with iced sweet tea. She did feel better after eating and broached the subject weighing on her mind. "Bet you can't guess who was in town last night."

"Quint Matthews."

Damn small towns. "How'd you know?"

"Sweetie, when a celebrity comes to town, everybody knows. What's he doing in Salt Lick?"

"Oh, you know. Checking out livestock. Counting his money . . . Asking me to go traveling with him."

Her mother's brow arched. "Traveling where?"

"Everywhere. He thinks I'd be an asset to his business, helping him pick horses for rodeo stock."

"Of course you would. The only person I can think of who's better with horses than you are is Buddy."

"Well, trust me. Buddy won't be offered the job."

"Humph. I suspect a horse buyer is not what Quinton Matthews is *really* after. I remember him."

Her mother would never forget Quint was the male who deflowered her teenage daughter or that Debbie Sue and he had spent a summer screwing like rabbits.

"Oh, Mom. That was a long time ago."

"A leopard doesn't change his spots. Rodeo cowboys are all the same, all the time. Even if they get rich."

"He was a kid, Mom. We were both kids."

"Don't forget, I knew his daddy. I would hate to see my only little girl involved with a Matthews."

"Mom, he's filthy rich. Can't you overlook a few character flaws?"

"What answer did you give him?"

"None, I don't think. I may never hear from him again. You won't believe what Buddy did." Debbie Sue repeated the previous night's events.

Her mom laughed so hard her eyes teared. "That Buddy. I knew he still loves you."

"He got me drunk and humiliated me in public."

"But that doesn't mean he doesn't love you. I wonder if I could work that story into a song."

"Don't you dare."

On Sunday evening Debbie Sue called Edwina and told her that out of respect for the Carruthers family, she wouldn't be opening the beauty salon on Monday.

"Oh, come on. Tell me the truth. Quint's still there, isn't he? And you can't talk. I saw the chemistry between you two. Yesterday was the first time I saw Buddy Overstreet as past tense in your life."

Chemistry. Honors chemistry. As she thought of Buddy's date, Debbie Sue's stomach rolled again. "I met Buddy's schoolteacher last night. She's a Yankee. She's an honors chemistry teacher. Teaches yoga at the college at night. And she speaks perfect fuckin' Spanish."

"What does she look like?"

"Remember Ramsey's fifteen-year-old son, Todd?"

"She looks like Todd Ramsey?"

"No, she looks like Todd's horse."

"Now, now. Buddy wouldn't date someone who looks like a horse. Were you nice? Did you make a good impression?"

"Let's just say I, er, *we*, made an impression.

Buddy and Quint had a real pissing contest, and I think Quint lost."

She told the parts of the Saturday night disaster she could remember, including the details she had refrained from telling her mother. When she said Quint had left her house wearing his battered Resistol, wrinkled clothes, with a clothespin holding his pants together, Ed screamed with laughter for a full minute.

"It's not funny, Ed. He didn't even kiss me good-bye."

"Fingernail glue? Hold on. I have to tell Vic." Edwina yelled away from the phone. "Vic, Buddy didn't want Debbie Sue screwing Quint Matthews, so he glued his pants shut with fingernail glue."

Debbie Sue heard Vic's deep, rich laugh in the background and stared at the ceiling. "Maybe you should yell that again, Ed. I don't know if all the neighbors heard it."

"I can't believe Buddy did that," Edwina gasped between guffaws. "You gotta love a man with a sense of humor."

"I still have the zipper. I think I'll hang it on the rearview mirror in my pickup."

"If you don't, I want to," Edwina said and broke into peals of laughter again.

"I hate to change the subject when you're having such a good time," Debbie Sue said, "but have you talked to C. J. lately?"

"I haven't seen her since she came in the shop Tuesday."

"I've called her twice to see if she wants to go with me to Pearl Ann's funeral, but she doesn't answer. I don't know where she keeps herself these days."

"Hmm. Guess we'll see her at the funeral."

Seven

Buddy and his deputy arrived at Wilkins Funeral Home at nine o'clock Monday morning to escort Pearl Ann Carruthers's coffin to the Calvary Baptist Church. Already, no empty space could be had in the old rock church building's small parking lot. A couple of troopers from the state Department of Public Safety were on hand to help unsnarl traffic.

Buddy was disappointed to see so large a crowd gathered so early. He had wanted to be positioned in time to watch the mourners as they arrived. Now, so many had arrived before him, he was forced to stand at the back of the church.

There were too many unfamiliar faces to learn anything new anyway. The Carruthers family tentacles reached far and wide, and friends from everywhere had come to pay their respects. The curious, Buddy suspected, outnumbered the grief-stricken by an embarrassing ratio.

Though the September day was hot, most of the attendees were dressed up. Not much occurred in Salt Lick that called for putting on dress clothes, especially on a ninety-degree day, but a funeral was just such an occasion. Debbie Sue arrived alone and sat with her friend Carol Jean. She actually had on a dark green dress and high-heeled shoes, clothes she rarely wore.

Buddy liked seeing her in a dress. She had great legs and slim ankles. Her dress wasn't frilly with bushels of billowing fabric like the ones Kathy wore. Debbie Sue's was plain and form-fitting. That thick, long hair he loved to burrow his hands in was piled on top of her head with a pretty clip, and she was wearing the little emerald earrings he had bought her once because they reminded him of her eyes. She looked every inch the woman who still haunted his nights if he didn't grab control of his mind, which was exactly what he had to do now.

She didn't glance his way. He guessed if she hadn't hated him before, Saturday night should have been the clincher. What he had done to her and Quint had been childish, but all he could think of at the time was keeping that bull rider out of her bed.

The eulogy was short, delivered by a preacher who had never seen Pearl Ann in his church. Nevertheless, as they did for any Salt Lick citizen, the women of the church auxiliary served lunch after the service in the reception hall. Buddy put in a cursory appearance.

Afterward he returned to his office in front of the jail and waited. The Midland CSI team had returned Pearl Ann's personal effects in a large manila envelope. Harley was due in to pick them up, and Buddy had questions for him.

The widowed man appeared on time, wearing a dress shirt and slacks and a loose tie. He hadn't changed clothes since the funeral. He looked pale and grim. Distress lines set off his mouth. At this moment he was Buddy's number one suspect. Hell, he was the *only* suspect.

Buddy dumped the manila envelope's contents onto the desk, and Harley sorted through the evidence of a well-heeled victim—a leather purse and matching wallet with fancy initials printed all over it. Driver's license. Credit cards from upscale stores. Three hundred dollars in cash. In addition, there was a diamond-faced Presidential Rolex watch, a diamond tennis bracelet, a wedding ring holding a diamond the size of a marble, a diamond and ruby cocktail ring, and gold and diamond hoop earrings. Robbery was obviously not the motive.

"Everything there?" Buddy asked.

Harley shuffled through the dozen or so credit cards. "I didn't even know she had all these." He turned his attention to the jewelry pieces and moved them around on the desk. "Best I can tell, it's all here. I didn't see her Monday evening, so I don't know what she was wearing. Nothing seems to be missing at home."

He picked up the tennis bracelet and studied it a few seconds. "Wait a minute. Was there a gold bracelet, with a charm on it? One of those cheap Texas things, had a diamond chip?"

Buddy assumed the forensics bunch had gone over the car's interior thoroughly. He shook his head, making a mental note to drive out to the landfill and look around. Even with crime scene tape stretched around where the car had been parked, so many people would have tramped through the site by now, his searching for a bracelet probably would be a waste of time, but he felt obligated to do it. "Guess they didn't find it. I'll take another look."

Harley walked over to the window, stuffed his hands into his pockets. "Are you going to call in some help on this?"

Buddy stayed in his seat, ignoring the slap at his ability to do the job to which he had been elected and wishing he could see Harley's face. "Before you start asking *me* questions, Harley, I've got a few for *you*."

The millionaire turned back, his expression startled. "Me?"

"You weren't home Monday night? When did you see Pearl Ann last?"

"Early Monday. She was still asleep when I left the house. I went to the Midland office. I came back when they called me Tuesday."

"Can anybody vouch for that?"

"I was at the condo. You know, the one I keep in Midland."

Buddy did know. He had been in the luxury condo. Harley had kept it for years to avoid the sixty-mile daily commute between Midland and Salt Lick. None of the Carruthers clan actually lived in Midland, even though their company offices were there.

Harley dragged a hand through his hair and looked at Buddy from under an arched brow. "I wasn't alone if that's what you're asking."

"That's part of what I'm asking. I'm gonna need your companion's name."

"No can do, my friend. It wouldn't matter anyway. She doesn't have anything to do with this."

"It's not her I'm asking about. She's not the one who needs an alibi . . . Or is she?"

"Goddammit, Buddy, just cool it." Harley strode back to the front of the desk and jabbed his finger on the desktop. "You've known me forever. You know I didn't do any harm to Pearl Ann. Jesus Christ, she did what she damn well pleased. Had everything money could buy."

"Simmer down, Harley. Who do you think *would* harm your wife?"

Harley laughed bitterly. "A better question is who wouldn't." His head tilted back, and he closed his eyes. "There were so damn many. I didn't even care enough to keep up with them anymore."

Buddy stood up and began to place Pearl Ann's baubles back into the manila envelope. "You might as well take this stuff on home. Give the matter some thought, 'cause I'm still gonna need that name."

As Harley left the office, Buddy stared after him, his mind traveling back to their school days. Buddy had been an athlete, played on Salt Lick's football team. Harley had been small and clumsy, a wannabe who mostly got in everybody's way and was the brunt of cruel jokes behind his back. The kids who hung out with him did so because he always had money to spend. The true poor little rich kid.

Feeling sorry for the way the jocks snubbed Harley, Buddy had been one of the few who tried to befriend him. Until the day the wealthy oilman's son left home for college at A&M, he had hung on to the association with Buddy.

As was traditional, Harley, upon graduating from Texas A&M, took over the family's oil and gas business and managed it with ruthless finesse. He might be a "good ol' boy" who drank and caroused with the best of them, but no one laughed behind Harley Carruthers's back now. And they wouldn't dare laugh to his face.

These days, he and Buddy had so little in common, their relationship had to be defined as one of mutual respect more than friendship. But there was a connection nevertheless. Buddy's gut told him Harley hadn't murdered his wife, but who was the man protecting?

Buddy donned his hat and headed for the Tahoe. He might as well look for that gold bracelet with a Texas charm.

Approaching the landfill, even from a distance, he recognized a familiar red Silverado. "Dammit," he muttered.

He climbed up the dirt mound surrounding the landfill and looked down. The crime scene tape had been torn askew. Since the announcement that Harley intended to pay a fat reward, people had milled through the dump like cattle. Gawkers, busybodies, ghouls. Keeping the scene pristine had been impossible.

And standing right where the Cadillac had been parked, despite the warnings written on the yellow tape, he saw Debbie Sue and Edwina. They had no idea he was near. He blew out a long breath, then dug in his heels and hiked down. "What in the hell are you doing here, Debbie Sue?"

His ex-wife turned toward him. Her pointed chin hoisted. "Nothing. I'm just looking."

He gripped both her and Ed's upper arms and half walked, half ran them beyond the sagging crime scene tape. "You have no business behind this tape."

"Ow, ow," Debbie Sue said. "Who do you think you're manhandling? Get your hands off."

"This is a crime scene."

"Big deal. A heck of a lot of people were here before we got here. I'm investigating. I'm fixin' to collect the reward Harley put up."

"Debbie Sue, this is serious. It's murder, forgodsake."

Her eyes began to shimmer. *Tears?* "Please, Buddy. I have to. I need that money."

He had never been able to stay angry when she cried. He preferred her cussin' and spittin' and kickin' any day. He guided her and Edwina around the toe of the hill, to the Tahoe. He sat Debbie Sue, now engaged in all out weeping, down on the passenger seat and squatted in front of her. "Tell me the big financial emergency. What's happened?"

"I'm tired of slaving for the bank. I don't have a life. I work six days a week. I'll be an old woman by the time I get out of debt."

He reached back for his handkerchief and dabbed her eyes. "Everybody's in debt, Flash."

"It's more than the debt. I don't know if the shop's gonna make it. I can't lose the shop. I can't have another failure."

He pulled her to her feet and into his arms, rubbed her spine with his fingers. "You've never failed at anything, and I doubt if you're gonna fail at that beauty shop, either."

She wailed louder. He looked across her head at Edwina, pleading for help with his eyes.

Edwina stood there with a cigarette cocked between the fingers of one hand and the opposite fist planted on her hip. "It's been a tough week."

He set Debbie Sue away, wiped her eyes, and stuck his handkerchief under her nose. "Blow," he ordered, and she did. "Now you two listen to me." He stuffed his handkerchief back in his rear pocket. "I want you to stay out of this. You could do more harm than good. There's not a chance in hell you're fixin' to collect that reward. You could even end up like Pearl Ann. And I don't want to have to worry about you."

"We'll behave. We promise." Edwina dropped her cigarette into the sand and ground it out with her shoe. She reached for Debbie Sue's arm and coaxed her away from Buddy. "C'mon Debbie Sue. We've got fish to fry."

Buddy wasn't sure if he should take her last remark as a positive or a warning of things to come. The two women returned to the red Silverado with sobs still hitching from Debbie Sue's throat. Buddy watched them leave, a plume of white caliche dust spewing behind the pickup. God, what was he gonna do with the mess of feelings Debbie Sue aroused in him? He already knew he couldn't live with her, but living without had turned out to be just as hard.

He hadn't had his arms around her in over three years, had forced from his mind just how damn good he felt when he held her and when she acted like she needed him. She wasn't the type to cry over just any ol' thing. There had to be a lot of emotions running deep for her to show tears. She had always been so strong and independent, the very characteristics that made her both a pain in the ass and an irresistible partner.

He knew about her debt. Even after he had sold his scanty cow herd, his six horses, and the land he had made payments on for years to help her meet the expense for the service station cleanup, she had, against his advice, borrowed to the max.

Debbie Sue had never done anything half-assed. She had been determined to turn the sixty-five-year-old albatross into something profitable. He admired the effort and time she put into the task. Every time he drove past the beauty shop she was there, working. Her competitor opened only four days a week. Not to be outdone, Debbie Sue opted for a six-day week, taking Sunday as her only day of rest. No wonder she was emotional. She had to be exhausted.

If she was desperate enough to consider something as crazy as going after Pearl Ann's killer, would she consider attaching herself to someone as rich as Quint Matthews? The thought was unsettling, but quickly dismissed. *I know Debbie Sue,* Buddy told himself. Now that she was grown, she would never take up with somebody as shallow and egotistical as Quint.

"I know Debbie Sue," he repeated aloud. "I know Debbie Sue."

Each time he said it, the conviction seemed to dwindle.

* * *

Debbie Sue slashed away tears with the back of her hand. "I need your help, Ed."

"You know you've got it. What are we up to now?"

"Regardless of what Wyatt Earp says, we're fixin' to solve this crime. We can split the reward money. With twenty-five thousand dollars, I'll be able to pay down the loan on the shop. I can get the bank to lower the payment to an amount I can live with."

From the corner of her eye, Debbie Sue saw her pal shake her head. "I don't know, Debbie Sue. Buddy said—"

"Ed, it's more than the money. It's a matter of principle. He talked *down* to me, like I don't have good sense."

"Baby doll, sometimes you're your own worst enemy. Maybe you oughtta think about things."

"What ought I think about?"

"Buddy was awful nice to you just now. And what he said wasn't unreasonable."

Debbie Sue braked to a skidding stop as they reached the intersection with the highway. "Nice? He treated me like I'm ten years old. His concern is I might solve the crime and tarnish his image. And with a scratch on the great Buddy Overstreet's saddle, he might not get hired by the DPS."

"Hmm," Edwina said. "That's not the way I see it. He showed real concern. Besides, what do we know about solving a crime?"

Debbie Sue pulled onto the highway and barreled toward the Salt Lick city limits. "I already know more about this case than he does. If I tell you something, will you promise not to lecture me? And more important, promise you won't tell anyone, and I do mean *anyone*."

"I promise I won't lecture and I promise to keep this to myself. Now, is this the part where we cut our fingers and mix our blood?"

"Dammit, Ed, I need you to be serious about this."

"Sorry, hon. I can't help trying to turn a serious moment into something light. Dysfunctional upbringing, you know? Why don't you pull into Hogg's so I can get a Dr. Pepper and have a smoke."

"I'm fixin' to buy you nicotine patches for Christmas, Ed."

Debbie Sue wouldn't allow smoking in her pickup, but she knew Edwina's addiction. She careened into Hogg's Drive-In, barely missing the pink "Elvis Ate Here" sign out front.

No one of the current generation of Salt Lick citizens knew if Elvis had really eaten at Hogg's or what a rock-and-roll icon might have been doing in such a tiny, remote town in West Texas, but in honor of "The King," Barr Hogg kept the drive-in painted a vivid pink trimmed in black and had a jukebox that played *all* of Elvis's songs. Besides old-fashioned malts and milk shakes and other fattening treats, he served a unique array of hamburgers to consumers who drove from a hundred miles away to eat them. So maybe Elvis really *had* eaten there. Stranger things had happened.

Debbie Sue stopped at the drive-up window and ordered two Dr. Peppers, then drove to Salt Lick's community center where the city used precious water to keep a small lawn green. It was the closest thing to a park Salt Lick had. They left the Silverado and sat down at the one concrete table huddled under a spindly elm tree.

Edwina lit up, took a long draw from first her cigarette, then her Dr. Pepper. "Go ahead. I'm listening."

For the first time, Debbie Sue repeated the story Pearl Ann had told her about hiding money from Harley. Since Pearl Ann had gone to the great honky-tonk beyond, Debbie Sue figured an oath of secrecy no longer mattered.

"And all this time I thought she was dumb as a rock," Edwina said, shaking her head. "Where did she put the money?"

"That I don't know, but I know who does."

"You do?"

"Think about it. This is money only two people knew the whereabouts of, and one of them is dead."

Edwina's jaw dropped as realization struck her. "The accountant."

"Bingo."

"We gotta tell Buddy."

"Forget that. Don't you dare tell him. Or *anybody*. The reward is a big temptation, really big, but that's not all that's stuck in my craw." Debbie Sue stood up and began to pace around the concrete table. "Ever since I saw that woman with Buddy I've been thinking about how accomplished she is. She's college educated, she speaks several foreign languages, she teaches *advanced* classes and even knows how to do yoga, which takes concentration and self-discipline. Hell, I can't even spell self-discipline."

Edwina glared across her shoulder. "Don't you think you're being a little hard on yourself? Don't take this as an insult, but you were a professional barrel racer. You trained yourself and your horse to be champions in a tough, competitive business. You won money. You broke records."

"What's riding a horse around three barrels? Good Lord, Ed, a well-trained horse can do it by himself."

"Maybe so, but somebody has to teach him how."

"Even little kids can barrel race, Ed. I can't stand to have Buddy think a schoolteacher from Chicago is a step up from me."

"And how does solving this murder and collecting the reward change any of that? Not that I believe Buddy would ever think of you as a step down from anything or anyone."

"It would prove I'm no dingbat small-town nobody. It would prove a lot *to me*." Debbie Sue patted her chest with her palm. "I need to know I can start something and finish it. I need to feel like I've accomplished something besides having my husband divorce me and going bankrupt in a beauty shop. Until now, I've never felt ashamed of myself, and I hate it."

Edwina let out a gusty sigh and lit another cigarette. "So what are you planning? You and me going out chasing killers?"

"No. You and me are fixin' to go see that accountant."

"Hooo-ly shit! How do we find out who he is?"

"You've been sniffing too much spray net, Ed. Think. Who do we know who works for Carruthers Oil & Gas Company?

"Ohmygod." Edwina banged her forehead with the heel of her hand. "C. J."

"I don't want her to get suspicious though. We're going to have to be careful how we go about getting information from her."

"That'll be a trip you don't have to pack for. C. J.'s the most accommodating person I've ever met. She would've given Santa Anna the keys to the Alamo."

"If I recall seventh-grade history, I don't think he needed them. Anyway, that little personality quirk is why we can't let her in on what we're doing, which means we have to keep it a secret from *everyone*. Can you keep it from Vic?"

"You know I tell him everything, but I can try. But I won't lie to him, Debbie Sue. That's the quickest way to ruin a relationship. One lie leads to another, and before you know it your tongue's all tangled up."

Debbie Sue dropped back to the concrete seat at the table. "You know so much, Ed. You should put some of that wisdom to work for you. You should write one of those self-help books on relationships."

"Yeah, right. Everybody wants to read how a forty-five-year-old three time loser at marriage holds a relationship together."

"Is writing a book any more far-fetched than us finding Pearl Ann's killer?"

"I guess not. My downfall's always been not recognizing far-fetched when I see it."

Debbie Sue frowned and bit down on her bottom lip. "That's something we both could work on."

The drive back to the Styling Station was quiet. Debbie Sue couldn't stop thinking about how good it had felt to be in Buddy's arms. It was embarrassing she had cried and become so emotional in front of him. She had always prided herself on being strong and stoic, but it had seemed that everything came crashing down at that moment. Her debt, seeing him with a girlfriend, being in the place where Pearl Ann had died.

Buddy's girlfriend. He had moved on. Debbie Sue knew he had gone on a binge of women and sex after their divorce, but she excused him for that. He had been as lost as she. But having *one* girlfriend to whom he was loyal and with whom everyone associated him had to mean he was serious.

She had to move on, too. Somehow, like it or not, she had to move on, too.

But how?

* * *

Twenty-five-thousand dollars. Edwina couldn't wrap her mind around that much money. She dug in her purse and came up with a grocery store receipt and an eyebrow pencil. Scribbling figures, she calculated that if she put back a dollar bill a day, it would take over sixty-eight years to save twenty-five-thousand dollars.

Sixty-eight years. Motherofgod. The realization surged in her mind like a geyser. The reward took on new meaning. Good idea or not, she was now fully engaged in a new game, and the name of it was "Let's Spend the Money."

It would be nice to do something for her three daughters. Lord knew, there were more years than not when she hadn't been able to do anything but put three meals—*most of the time* three meals—on the table. Between sorry husbands, she had worked sorry jobs for even sorrier wages.

Billie Pat, Jimmie Sue, and Roberta Jean were the products of three separate unions. She had given them their respective fathers' names, and the men had given them little to nothing. Yet somehow all three had become well-adjusted, responsible women. They had met and married men who were good husbands and enjoyed productive lives. What more could a mother ask for?

How about three daughters who get really terrific souvenirs from their mother's trip to Barbados? *Now you're talkin'.* She and Vic had spent many nights talking about places they wanted to go and things they wanted to see. He had spent time there, tracking down bad guys. He spoke often about going back as a civilian.

Okay, that settles it. After everything Vic had done for her, the least she could do for him was to take him back to his beautiful island retreat. As a civilian. As a *first-class* civilian.

She would help Debbie Sue solve the mystery of Pearl Ann Carruthers's death and reap her half of the reward.

Eight

A week had passed since the biggest funeral ever held in Salt Lick. Other than register in her brain every miniscule crumb of gossip she heard in the salon about Pearl Ann and Harley, Debbie Sue had done nothing toward solving the murder mystery. Well, not exactly nothing. She *had* watched or taped every episode of *CSI, NYPD Blue, Cops,* and all the *Law & Order* hybrids and studied the investigating techniques of the various TV detectives. She paid particular attention to the guilty characters and zeroed in on their mannerisms.

Buddy was outpacing her. Salon patrons reported daily on his investigative activities. With a badge and access to official reports, *he* had an overwhelming advantage.

Unidentified fingerprints had been found in Pearl Ann's car. When Buddy's deputy's wife came in for a trim, she revealed that the gun that killed

Pearl Ann had been her own. *Yikes!* How awful was that, being murdered with your own gun?

Buddy had questioned two dozen people, including all the hired help out at the Carruthers ranch. He had asked Harley to take a lie detector test with the Odessa police polygraphist, but Harley's lawyer had squelched that. Instead, Harley would hire his own technician. Salt Lick citizens awaited the results with held breaths.

Buddy was right about one thing. This was serious. If someone killed once, wouldn't he or, ohmygod, *she*, be likely to kill again if someone came close to discovering his or her identity? The ability to jump on a horse and gallop to safety didn't feel nearly as comforting as it had looked when Dale was helping Roy. Debbie Sue wished she had taken that Tae Kwon Do class when she lived in Lubbock.

Friday morning she decided she was as ready to begin as she would ever be. "It's time we did something," she told Edwina. Her sleuthing partner gave her a thumbs-up, and Debbie Sue called C.J. at work. "Hey, kid, where you been hiding? Ed and I were just talking about you. We haven't seen you in nearly two weeks. What's up?"

"Oh, Debbie Sue, it's so good to hear your voice. I've been trying to find the time to stop by the shop and I've been meaning to call, but crazy doesn't come close to describing the way things have been around here since . . . well, you know."

"I can only imagine. The whole thing seems like

a nightmare, doesn't it? Listen, Vic's on the road, so Ed's coming over to my house tonight after work for happy hour. I'm mixing a pitcher of killer margaritas." Debbie Sue laughed. "Killer, get it? We'll throw some burgers on the grill and kick back. You up for that?"

"Margaritas sound wonderful. I'll bring the rum."

Rum? Debbie Sue grinned. She had really missed C. J. "No, that's okay, sweetie. I've got a half gallon of tequila, and Ed's bringing the meat. See you around seven."

At the notion of interrogating a friend who was under the influence of tequila, Debbie Sue felt a twinge of guilt, but only a twinge. She didn't dare tell C. J. any of the plans she and Edwina had made. C. J. was loyal and trustworthy, but she blurted secrets without even knowing she did it.

By six-thirty Debbie Sue had donned cutoffs and a halter top and done the domestic thing— peeled off lettuce leaves, sliced onions, tomatoes, and cheese, and had them waiting under plastic wrap in the fridge. After dumping potato chips into a large wooden bowl, she walked outside to start the fire in the grill. Even with the house shadowing the eight-by-ten-foot concrete patio off the dining room, the ninety-plus temperature still had the whole backyard sizzling. Hell, it would probably be easier to just fry the meat on the patio's concrete.

The phone warbled. Probably Ed calling to ask if she needed to bring anything besides the hamburger meat. Debbie Sue picked up and cradled the receiver under her chin while she used both hands to squeeze another stream of fire starter onto the coals. "I had to start without you, but I can keep it hot 'til you get here."

"Darlin', I'm gonna call you for the rest of my life just to hear what you say when you answer the phone."

Fuck. She had to learn to check that damn caller ID. "Quint Matthews. I didn't realize it was you."

"Now don't go disappointing me."

"Are you in town?"

"I'm in Seguin at the ranch. I've been thinking about our last evening together. I'll say one thing for you, darlin', you certainly know how to keep a man guessing." He laughed. At least he was a good sport. "You know, I come across a lot better when the ex-husband doesn't show up and when my zipper's working."

She chuckled, too. "Well, I've come across a little bit better myself."

"I know. I haven't forgotten Vegas."

Debbie Sue felt a sudden flash as hot as the coals in the barbecue grill. She hadn't forgotten, either. "How are your knees? Were they badly hurt?"

"Nah, I've had worse injuries. Not as embarrassing, but worse. Listen, I've got to take a look at some calves up in Andrews in a couple of weeks. October fifth. How about I pick you up at your house, say seven o'clock two weeks from tomorrow night? We can finish our conversation. But let's find a one-story eating joint where we won't run into your ex-husband."

Debbie Sue chewed on her lip, deciding what to do. The Saturday night at Kincaid's hadn't been fair to Quint or her, either. He had always been a lot of fun, and she couldn't complain about him as a lover. And there *was* all that money, with which he was generous. "That sounds great. Two weeks from tomorrow, seven o'clock. I'm really glad you called."

Edwina arrived with the hamburger patties shaped and ready to cook and took over the barbecue grill. Debbie Sue made a pitcher of margaritas, carried it outside to the patio, and relayed the news about the pending date with Quint.

"Good, I'm glad," Edwina said. "I can't wait to hear what happens next."

"Hellooo." C. J.'s voice came from the front doorway.

"We're in the backyard," Debbie Sue yelled, "soaking up the heat."

The three friends went through their usual routine of hugs, kisses, and comments on clothes and hair and how good each one looked, as if months instead of two weeks had passed since they had seen each other. C. J. wore capri pants and a tube top that would have fit a Barbie doll. Debbie Sue noticed glittery studs bigger than pencil erasers stuck in her earlobes. "Hey, kid. New earrings. CZs, huh?"

"Uh, yeah," C. J. tittered. "Who can afford diamonds on *my* pay?"

Debbie Sue told C. J. of the disastrous date with Quint and the blond friend laughed until she cried. When Debbie Sue produced Quint's ragged and glued zipper, the three of them collapsed in laughter.

Edwina removed the cooked patties from the grill and Debbie Sue refilled C. J.'s glass. After gorging on hamburgers and gossip and plying C. J. with four margaritas, Debbie Sue felt the time was right. "So C. J., I was floored when Harley put up a fifty-thousand-dollar reward. I can't even imagine that kind of money. I knew the Carruthers were rich, but wow."

A loose spiral curl hung between the tipsy blond's eyes. She flopped one wrist. "Oh, rich isn't even the word. I'm surprised he didn't put up more."

"Any nibbles on that bait?" Edwina refilled C. J.'s glass with one more margarita.

"Not a one. One of the accountants assigned to handle the reward fund thought it would bring informs . . . informers, uh, ants out of the woodwork, but no one yet."

Uh-oh. C. J. was getting too snockered to talk. "One of the accountants? Just how many accountants does Harley have?" Debbie Sue shot a look at Edwina, who was holding her Bic lighter suspended beneath her cigarette.

"There's a dozen." C. J. began to list them on her

fingers. "One for land, one for oil, one for investments. Harley doesn't want to give the responsibility to just one or two. He says he doesn't want his whole empire crashing because one guy decides to make a career move."

"That Harley. Shrewd dude. No wonder he's rich."

"I don't think he's rich 'cause he's sssrude," C. J. slurred and leaned forward. "I think," she whispered, "it's 'cause his daddy gave him a lot of money."

"Hell of an allowance," Edwina put in, and the three of them cackled in unison.

"Pearl Ann told me once she didn't know a thing about the family business," Debbie Sue said.

"Guess it would have been tough screwing her way through a dozen accountants," Edwina cracked and they cackled again.

"Oh, Pearl Ann didn't have to do it with a bunch of accountants," C. J. said, sloshing her drink over the back of her hand, then licking away the wetness. "She had her own personal one. Harley wouldn't even dish . . . disscuss money with her. He just told her to see Eugene."

"No kidding? I'm betting Pearl Ann convinced Eugene to up the ante, if you know what I mean." Edwina's perfectly tweezed and shaped black eyebrows bobbed up and down.

"You mean sex? With Eugene?" C. J. giggled and held out her glass for a refill. Debbie Sue complied.

"You wouldn't think about Pearl Ann with Eugene if you saw him." C. J. sipped and licked her lips. "He's short as me and skinny. He has a comb-over that starts just a little above his right ear." C. J.'s finger pointed at her left temple. "His glasses look like bottle bottoms and he's chewed his fingernails to the nubs. I think his only intres' iss—iss hiss numbers." C. J. frowned, then giggled again. "Besides, he's swish . . . swissy. Naw, Eugene was safe from Pearl Ann."

"Are the accountants in the same building you work in?"

"Yeah, but different floors. I'm on two. They're on four, five and six. Hey, why don't y'all come see me sometime. We could do lunsh."

"Maybe we will," Debbie Sue said. "It's hard to get out of town when you work six days a week, but maybe we'll just mosey up there for lunch someday."

Debbie Sue excused herself, walked back into the kitchen and the notepad by the phone. "Eugene. Floors four through six. Short, comb-over, swishy nerd."

She returned to the patio, stepping into the middle of a conversation between C. J. and Edwina. C. J.'s eyes were round as marbles. "You mean you can do that with your mouth?"

Debbie Sue relaxed. For a split second she had feared Edwina had spilled the beans, but after C. J.'s comment, she knew her sleuthing partner was only lecturing on sex, which she was prone to do after she passed her margarita limit. Edwina the sex expert had the floor and the evening went forward without another word on the Carrutherses.

On Monday Debbie Sue canceled all appointments and hung a sign on the salon's front door. "Closed for Inventory." She drove to Edwina's trailer, twisting the radio knob until she found tolerable music—Merle Haggard singing about prison walls. She hoped Merle wasn't trying to tell her something.

Once Edwina was seated in the Silverado, Debbie Sue looked over at her and grinned. "Of all the adventures we've had, Ed, this may be the best."

"And if it's not," Edwina drawled, "it damn sure should be in the top ten. I just hope we haven't bit off more than we can chew. And I hope Buddy doesn't find out we're doing this."

"How would he find out? And what if he does? We have a right to go for the reward money."

"I know, but it makes me nervous. He told us to keep our noses clean."

"Look, we've already gone over it. Everything's perfect. This Eugene whatever-his-last-name-is had the perfect motive to murder Pearl Ann. Money. Green greed. The root of all evil. The path to destruction."

"Okay, now you're scaring me. You sound like the Baptist preacher."

"Sorry. I'm a little nervous, too. The thought of that reward money makes me crazy. What are you gonna do with your half?"

"I'm praying I don't have to use it for bail or a lawyer. If I get past that, I'm planning on a long romantic vacation for me and Vic."

Debbie Sue entered the Midland city limits and began looking for a pizza joint. She spotted a neon pizza whirling on the palm of an animated Italian chef. She stopped and ordered a large pepperoni. Twenty minutes later she walked out with the box.

"Lor-deee, that smells good," Edwina said. "I didn't think I was hungry until now. Let me just take a little peekie-poo."

Debbie Sue slapped a hand on the top of the box. "Oh no you don't. We don't touch the pizza, got it? Now start getting ready."

Edwina reached into a brown paper grocery sack she had placed on the seat between her and Debbie Sue and pulled out a bright orange shirt with "Pizza Slut" screen-printed in black across the back.

"Wait a minute," Debbie Sue said, spotting the back of the shirt. "What is this? I thought you said you had an old pizza delivery shirt?"

"This is it. What's the problem?"

"Pizza *Slut*? Where were you wearing this, a red-light district somewhere?"

"It's part of a Halloween costume. I don't think anyone'll notice. Have a little faith in me, sugar."

"You're right, Ed. No one will notice a skinny, five-foot-ten woman with a coal black beehive, cat-eye glasses, and leopard stretch pants. Especially if she's wearing three-inch wooden platforms and a shirt that says 'Pizza Slut'. I'm feeling better already." Debbie Sue sighed and shook her head. "It's too late to worry about it now. Here's the building."

She turned into the visitors' parking lot of the Carruthers Oil & Gas Company, a six-story building of reflective glass glittering in the sun. She looked one last time at Ed. "Okay, old friend, this is it. Are you ready?"

"Does a fifty-pound sack of flour make a big biscuit?" Edwina scooted out of the pickup, dug a crumpled pack of Marlboro Lights from her purse, pried out a bent cigarette, and lit up.

"Edwina! What are you doing?"

"I'm smoking, dammit. You won't let me smoke in the pickup."

Debbie Sue gasped and swung out the driver's door. "Well, hurry up. Someone may see us."

"Okay, okay." Edwina clamped the cigarette filter between her teeth and reached into the pickup cab for the pizza.

"Edwina, put that cigarette out."

"What, you want me to drop it right here, on this nice, clean concrete?" She tottered toward a butts receptacle outside the building entrance, balancing the pizza on one hand. Debbie Sue held her breath until Edwina dropped the cigarette into the receptacle, then the two of them passed through the wide entrance.

They stopped in front of stainless-steel elevator doors. "You know, Ed, we really should take the stairs. Someone we know could see us on this elevator."

Edwina stared down at her high-heeled shoes. "Are you out of your mind?"

"I keep telling you to quit smoking."

"Godalmighty." Edwina held up one foot and thrust it forward. "Even if I quit, I couldn't climb six flights of stairs in these shoes."

"Okay, okay. We'll take the elevator. We'll start at the top and work our way down. I've never liked starting at the bottom."

Debbie Sue kept her fingers crossed there would be a reception area. When they exited the elevator they found themselves peering across the hallway into a glass-fronted office suite where they could see burgundy high-backed chairs lining the walls and long, low-slung tables with magazines and elaborate floral centerpieces. A mahogany desk the size of a four-horse trailer was parked in the middle of the room, and a young woman sat behind it, staring intently at a blue computer screen.

"Okay, Ed, when you see me sit down and pick up a magazine, you come in with the pizza."

Edwina nodded.

On a deep breath, Debbie Sue opened the door.

"Good afternoon, may I help you?" The receptionist smiled, overfriendly. Even so, she succeeded in making Debbie Sue feel as if she had tracked manure onto the pearl gray carpeting. The scent in the air was woodsy potpourri, but Debbie Sue smelled money.

"I'm supposed to meet someone here, but I'm a little early. Do you mind if I just have a seat and wait?"

"No, not at all. May I offer you some coffee or other beverage?"

"No, thanks. I shouldn't be here that long." Debbie Sue picked up a *Newsweek* and began flipping through the pages.

When Edwina entered carrying the pizza box, the receptionist robotically looked up and smiled. "Good afternoon, may I help you?"

"I hope so," Edwina said between gum smacks. "I got a pizza for Eugene. The kid working the phones didn't get a last name."

"I'm sorry. We don't have a Eugene on this floor. Could that be the last name? We do have a Juan Eugenio. Let me call him."

The receptionist made a move to pick up the phone, but Edwina stopped her. "No, no, it was definitely a first name. I'll just try the other floors."

"Nonsense. Let me make just one call." French-manicured fingers lifted the receiver. "Hi, Carol Jean."

Debbie Sue's heart stuttered and Pizza Slut threw her a bug-eyed stare. Rapid-fire gum smacks carried all the way across the room.

"Someone's here looking for an employee

named Eugene," the receptionist was saying into the phone, "but she doesn't have a last name. Do you have the company directory in front of you? . . . No, you don't have to bring it to me. I've got a copy, but someone borrowed it . . . okay . . . un-huh, yes I have it, thanks." She hung up and smiled at Edwina. "You're in luck. There are only two Eugenes in the building. One on five, Eugene Thomas, and one on four, Eugene Grubbs."

"Thanks, hon, I really appreciate it." Edwina turned and breezed out as if she were wearing skates.

Debbie Sue stood up. "I think I'll go call the person I was going to meet. Thanks for everything."

She made for the door before the receptionist could offer to help her make the call. She found Edwina waiting in the hall, the pizza box braced against her hip.

"I thought I was gonna die, Debbie Sue. What if C. J. had come in? We didn't discuss that little detail."

"You're right. That was a close call. We'll take the stairs to five. You can make it. It's downhill."

Edwina's wooden heels clanged and echoed every step down the steel stairs until they reached the fifth floor. "I hope nobody heard us," she said.

Debbie Sue gave her a wry look. "I hope you remember the names."

"Hell, no, I don't. I'm concentrating on not losing my bladder." The same scene, minus the call to C. J., replayed on the fifth floor. Robotic receptionist, extremely helpful, informing Pizza Slut that Eugene Thomas had called in sick and wasn't available.

By the time they tramped to the fourth floor, Edwina's nervousness and impatience had tripled, a condition Debbie Sue had seen degenerate into disaster more than once. But it was too late to back out. She rejected the receptionist's syrupy friendliness again—apparently Carruthers Oil & Gas employed the Stepford Wives—and took a seat in the reception area. She held her breath as Edwina entered.

"Good afternoon, may I—"

"Help me?" Edwina dropped the pizza box on the receptionist's desk and bent forward, her palms on her knees as she heaved for breath. "Yeah, do me a favor, sugar. Tell Eugene his pizza's here."

Oh dear. Not only had Edwina run out of air, she had definitely lost some of her motivation for the required theatrics.

"Eugene?"

"Eugene Whoever. Don't you have a Eugene on this floor?"

With a puzzled expression, the receptionist picked up the phone. "Mr. Grubbs, there's a delivery person here from"—she waited while Edwina straightened and turned her back—"from, uh, Pizza . . . Pizza Slut? . . . Yes, maybe you should, sir. Thank you." She hung up, and the cheery demeanor returned. "He'll be right with you. Say, are you one of those singing messengers? You know, like they have for birthdays?"

Edwina shot her a wilting look. "Oh that's just part of my act. Wait 'til you catch my tap dance."

Before the conversation could turn into a scene, Mr. Comb-Over came out of a hallway to their right. "I'm Eugene Grubbs. May I help you?"

"Godalmighty," Edwina said, "you people are polite."

Debbie Sue mouthed for her to shut up.

Eugene was just as C. J. had described him. Short, skinny, thick glasses, but C. J. had failed to mention Eugene had a face so handsome, he could be called pretty.

"Here's your pizza." Edwina picked up the pizza box and shoved it toward him. Reflexively his hands came out and took it. "That'll be fourteen bucks," she told him.

"But—but I didn't order a pizza. There must be a mistake."

"All I know is some guy named Eugene at this address ordered a pizza and this is the third floor I've been to. You owe me fourteen bucks."

"I was planning to work through lunch, but—okay, what kind of pizza is it?" He opened the box and peeked inside. "There's a slice missing! You can't expect someone to pay for a pizza with a missing piece." He slapped the pizza box down on the receptionist's desk and prissed up the hallway from which he came. Yep, C. J. was right. He was definitely swishy.

Edwina shrugged at the even more puzzled receptionist and picked up the pizza box. "Looks like I'm out fourteen bucks. And a tip. You want a pizza?"

The receptionist shook her head.

Edwina shrugged again, scooped up a slice of the pizza, and chomped down on a big bite as she strode through the entrance doorway.

Debbie Sue followed straight to the elevators. As the steel doors glided shut, she opened her mouth to speak, but Edwina stopped her with a raised palm. "I don't want to hear it. If you'd said we had to take those stairs, I would've had to sit down on this pizza box and slide."

"Why in the hell did you eat a slice?"

"I got hungry. You made me leave the house so early I missed breakfast, remember?"

Debbie Sue scowled. "I doubt if it was *me* who made you miss breakfast, *Mama Doll*."

Edwina flipped a palm in the air. "Do we really care if ol' Eugene gets a pizza? We've got his last name and that's what we were after."

She was right. The last name was all they needed. They should have asked C. J. the night of the hamburger and margarita party, but unfortunately, their blond friend hadn't been the only one guzzling tequila.

She knew from C. J. that CO&G employees had reserved and labeled parking in the basement parking garage. On the elevator keypad, she chose "G." All they had to do was locate Eugene's slot.

As soon as the elevator doors opened again, there it was within their view, "Reserved for E. Grubbs." And occupying the parking place was an immaculate, new Mercedes-Benz.

"Wow," Edwina said. "Would you look at that? Instead of becoming a makeup artist, I should have taken some bookkeeping classes."

Debbie Sue dug in her purse and produced a note she had written earlier:

Meet me Sunday morning. 9 o'clock. Denny's on I-30. Don't worry about recognizing me. I know you. It's about a mutual friend, Pearl Ann Carruthers.

A second look at the gleaming Mercedes revealed recessed wiper blades. *Rats.*

"Ed, give me your gum. I want to be sure this note doesn't blow away."

Nine

From the seat of his personal pickup truck in front of the CO&G building, Buddy made a phone call to Harley Carruthers's office. "This is Mr. Overstreet. I'd like to see Mr. Carruthers this afternoon, maybe around three-thirty."

"I'm sorry, sir, but his last appointment of the day is at three, and that time is already taken. May I take a message or may I offer you another time?"

"No, I'm from out of town. Maybe I can catch him after his appointment. Will he still be there at four?"

"No, sir. He leaves between three-thirty and four."

Buddy's dash clock showed two-fifty. "Guess I'll have to catch him later. Thanks for your help."

He had awakened determined to learn whom Harley was protecting. And he *was* protecting someone, of that Buddy was certain. He pulled into the visitors' parking lot and chose a slot that gave him the most advantageous view of the basement exit and took off his hat. Even if Harley saw him, Buddy doubted he would recognize him without his hat and out of the county's Tahoe. He left the motor running to take advantage of the air conditioning and put a George Jones CD in the player.

At precisely four o'clock, Harley's silver Lexus sedan pulled out of the parking lot. Dark tinted windows made it impossible to identify the passengers, but Buddy could see two silhouettes. Staying a safe distance back, he changed lanes and eased in behind the luxury car.

When the Lexus drove through the wrought-iron entrance into the gated condominium community where Harley owned a unit, Buddy swore under his breath. He badged the young woman at the security gate, and she waved him through without a word. Some security for a bunch of condos that were anything but low-rent.

He knew the location of Harley's unit in the warren of condos and townhouses. By the time he reached it, the Lexus had stopped in the driveway. Buddy parked behind a scrawny tree a comfortable distance back, but in perfect view of the two people exiting the vehicle. The woman had on sunglasses. Her long hair was the color of a roan horse he had owned once. A blue dress that looked like a work dress failed to hide a small but curvy body.

He didn't recognize her and was disappointed. He had figured Harley's mistress would be someone he knew. Now he realized she could have been his three o'clock appointment or one of his employees.

She and Harley kissed briefly when they reached the condo's front door, then disappeared inside. Buddy sat for another hour, but no one came out. He checked his watch. Kathy had invited him to dinner at her apartment, said she had something to discuss with him. He didn't want to be late. She insisted on punctuality.

A strain had been hamstringing their relationship ever since they had run into Debbie Sue and Quint Matthews at Kincaid's. They hadn't slept together since. He had been too busy to drive to Odessa for recreation.

For the whole thirty-mile drive from Midland to Odessa, he thought about the woman he had seen with Harley. He didn't know if it was her half-hidden profile, her walk, the curve of her backside, or what, but there was something familiar about her that he couldn't quite put his finger on.

Buddy arrived on time at Kathy's modest duplex apartment with a box of chocolates he had bought at a Midland drugstore tucked under his arm. Showing up for a date bringing candy was a new experience, but he couldn't think of anything else she might like, and he thought a gift might ease the tension between them.

She answered the door, barely giving him a

chance to remove his hat before both of her arms slid around his shoulders and her body pressed against his. Maybe things had settled down. He started to kiss her, but she turned her head. "Oh, careful. My lipstick."

Well, maybe things were still a little tense. He set her away and handed her the box of candy, accompanied by a hopeful smile. "Brought you something."

She made a little gasp and clasped her hands in front of herself. "Oh, thank you so much. I'm on a diet, but my students will love these."

Buddy was taken aback, but managed to laugh. "Gosh, if I'd known I was buying for students, I would've got a six-pack."

Her mouth tipped up into a smile. "Now, now. You don't want me to lose my figure, do you?"

Kathy was always concerned with her appearance, always wanted to look pretty. And she did. She kept her dark, shoulder-length hair neat, and she wore pretty dresses printed with flowers. She even smelled like roses. Tonight was no exception.

She smiled as she left his embrace and took his hat. "You look tired. Can I mix you a drink or get you a beer?"

She was always polite and hospitable. "Sure," he said, "beer will be fine."

She laid the box of candy beside a tall vase of flowers standing on a table by the front door, then placed his hat, crown up, on top of the candy box.

He winced. As soon as she turned her back and headed toward the kitchen, he turned the Resistol over to rest on its crown.

Delicious-smelling food aromas filled the apartment. "Sure smells good," he called to her. He walked over to the sofa, noting dark blue upholstery printed with big pink and white blossoms. At one end sat a little white table that looked like straw, holding a lamp and a bouquet of flowers. As he sank onto the puffy cushions, he felt like the grand marshal at the Rose Parade.

Her small living room looked nice. Cozy and feminine. A teacher's pay didn't afford expensive decorations, but the room was immaculate—as if something as messy as a person didn't live there. The gold lamp gave off light too dim to read by. He felt like a bull in a china closet in such fragile surroundings, but it beat the heck out of the bare one-bedroom apartment located above a garage he rented back in Salt Lick.

Soft, classical music that wasn't country-western played in the background. Yessir, he was a lucky man that a woman of Kathy's culture and refinement put up with him. She had come closer than anybody since Debbie Sue to capturing his heart. In fact, she was the first one to whom he had gotten close who didn't have something to do with horses or cows.

Kathy reappeared with a frosted glass of beer in hand. She placed a coaster on the table beside him and set the beer glass on it, then handed him a little square napkin.

"I hope you like lamb. I had a very difficult time finding it. The stores here don't stock it."

Buddy had never knowingly and willingly swallowed a bite of lamb in his life. "Sure," he said.

She took a seat beside him, her knees touching his, and set her own glass on a coaster on the table in front of the sofa. "I hate to hit you with this the minute you walk in, but I've been practicing what I want to say all day, and if I don't do it now I don't know if I ever will."

A tinge of worry flickered in Buddy's head. "You know you can talk to me about anything, Kathy."

Her lips tipped into a hint of a smile. "Okay, here goes. I've been thinking about us. Especially since we ran into your ex-wife at Kincaid's."

Buddy nearly choked on a gulp of beer. He grabbed his handkerchief from his rear pocket and wiped his mouth. "Nothing like good, cold beer on a hot day."

"It's clear Debbie Sue's getting on with her life," Kathy said, ignoring his cough.

Buddy felt a tic in his right eye. "It appears she is."

Kathy drew a deep breath. "But I wonder if *you* are."

"Me?"

"I don't know where I stand with you, Buddy." She rose and moved to the other side of the room.

"What I mean is, if you have unresolved feelings for your ex-wife, I'm wondering if maybe you want to explore those."

Buddy's mind raced. So that was the problem. Kathy felt insecure. They had been dating on weekends for almost a year, when he could get away from his job. He didn't mind driving to Odessa. In fact, he liked escaping the gossip and busybodies in Salt Lick. If he slept over at Kathy's apartment on a Saturday night, he didn't have to worry about somebody driving by and recognizing his pickup. He was content with the arrangement. He had thought she was, too.

"To be honest, I haven't thought too much about the future in the way you're talking about, Kathy."

Though she was standing a few feet away, he saw her eyes brighten with tears. She looked down, toying with her nails. "I've never told you," she said, "but I had a job offer to work in Austin the past school year. I turned it down, but now I don't know if I made the right choice."

He rose from his seat and walked over to her.

She looked up at him with eyes filled with emotion. "How can you be so obtuse? Don't you know I'm in love with you?"

Obtuse? Her hands slid up his chest and around his neck, but he grasped her wrists. "Kathy, I—" Her mouth covered his, stopping his words. She kissed him deeply, and he could feel the shiver than ran through her body. In spite of the panic mushrooming inside him, he returned her kiss.

"I feel so much better," she said, drawing back, "If you can kiss me like that, you must feel something, too. My parents are coming from Chicago for Thanksgiving. I'd like to be able to tell them we're talking about marriage."

"Marriage?" The tic in his eye grew worse.

"You plan for the future, don't you? We're both getting to the age we should think seriously about children we might want someday."

"Children?" The word came out a croak, and Buddy knew he wasn't carrying his end of the conversation. He didn't dislike kids, but the memory of losing one was stuck in his chest as permanently as a burr in a cow's tail. He had never been, and would never be, able to erase the image of a tiny white coffin and a tiny grave and a tiny human being he and Debbie Sue had called Luke. He hadn't had a driving desire to expose his heart to that much feeling again. For *any* woman.

"It's simple, really. When you think about your future, Buddy, am I a part of it? Do you or do you not see me in your plans?"

Buddy was having trouble seeing anything at all except a Texas Ranger's badge on his shirt and Salt Lick, Texas, in his rearview mirror. In rare moments, he had thought perhaps he should make some decisions concerning Kathy, but marriage wasn't exactly one of the things he had considered. So what *was* he considering? She had asked a fair question, but he couldn't force an honest answer from his mouth.

"Is this something you'd rather think about for a while?"

Her voice brought him back to the conversation. "Uh, Kathy, I don't want this to sound like a tired old saying, but I really do think the world of you. I'm caught off-guard is all."

"I thought the best part of our relationship is that neither one of us has to be on guard. No games, no pretenses."

"You're right. Just give me some breathing room, okay? I need to clear my head. I've got a lot going on."

"I know. I shouldn't have brought it up when you're so involved in this horrible murder investigation, but I have to think of myself, too." She paused for a few seconds. "You said breathing room. That doesn't mean you want to break things off, does it?"

"That's not what I mean." Buddy put his hands on her shoulders, looking into her eyes. "I just need some time. This is an important decision. We shouldn't be hasty making it."

"I don't want to lose you, Buddy." She began unbuttoning her dress.

Buddy checked himself to keep from groaning aloud. A cold shower couldn't have doused his libido any quicker than the conversation that had just occurred. Oh, he had to admit he had come here for sex, as much as anything else. He was human, wasn't he? He had anticipated a grilled T-bone, a relaxing drink or two, then a night in

Kathy's arms in Kathy's bed. The last had lost all its appeal, and he had no desire to eat cute little fluffy animals.

He headed for his hat. "Kathy, I think the best thing I can do is just go on home."

"But dinner—"

"I know you've gone to a lot of trouble and I appreciate it, but I'm feeling a little unsettled. I think it would be wrong if I stayed."

She looked up at him, her dark lashes blinking rapidly. "It's Debbie Sue, isn't it?"

"I didn't say that."

"But it's what you meant." In the low light, her eyes glistened with moisture.

He set his hat on and reached for the doorknob. "Don't be upset." He leaned down and brushed her cheek with his lips. "You've already hashed this out with yourself, but I'm a little slow. I need to do some thinking. Let me call you."

Rolling down the highway, Buddy chastised himself for getting into this situation with Kathy. She had asked how he could be so obtuse. Man, he had to agree with her on that one. He had been out of the dating game for a long time. In truth, he had never even been *in* it. He had known as a kid that Debbie Sue was the partner for him, and the encounters he had with women after her and prior to Kathy couldn't be called dating. It was more like buying a few drinks, then paying for a room.

He felt like a jackass for not seeing the signs Kathy had been putting up. He hadn't stopped to remind himself that most self-respecting women wouldn't be satisfied for an indefinite period of time with a casual arrangement built mostly on sex.

Maybe it wasn't fair to continue seeing Kathy if he didn't have plans to include her in his future.

His future?

That was another thing he hadn't succeeded in doing—putting together his future.

Introduced as a fiancé by Thanksgiving? Damn.

Well, it was still September. He didn't make snap decisions or form snap judgments. Even though he had to solve Pearl Ann's murder, there was still plenty of time before Thanksgiving to reflect about Kathy. He wasn't avoiding the issue, he told himself. He simply had time to think about it.

Debbie Sue was glad to see the name Maudeen Wiley on her appointment list for Thursday. Maudeen, who thought hair color was to be used like lipstick, came into the shop once a month, or more often, for a new shade.

Maudeen was just what Debbie Sue needed to lighten up the week. The octogenarian approached life full-throttle, didn't mind telling you she considered it her responsibility to dispense common sense, whenever necessary, to the less fortunate who appeared to have none.

Debbie Sue loved her attitude and always gave her undivided attention, extra time, and a special senior citizen's discount. She didn't mind lowering the fees because she enjoyed Maudeen's company and the hilarious words of wisdom the elderly woman left behind.

"Have you ever known someone you thought might be capable of murder?" Debbie Sue asked her as she applied a stripe of Fiesta Red color along Maudeen's part line.

"Funny you should ask. I went out with Bart Jenkins last week, and he has *killed* any chance he ever had of getting me in bed again."

Debbie Sue had to stop and think, searching for the link between the murder of a human being and Maudeen's social life. "Bart is such a sweet little man. What could he have done to upset you?"

"He told everyone at Peaceful Oasis I was easy. Every time I walk into a room, all the other women stop talking."

Debbie Sue stifled a grin as she parted the back of Maudeen's hair into sections. "Oh, they'll get over it. They're probably jealous. Maybe those ladies should come in and have their hair dyed. New hair color would give them something different to talk about."

"They already dye their hair. Pink, blue, purple. Looks like a damn Easter egg hunt when the old crows get their heads together."

Debbie Sue laughed. "You're a trip, Maudeen. I hope I still have as much fire as you when I get to be your age."

"Well, honey, I hope so, too. The worst part of getting old is how people think you *should* be acting. They want you dead before you die."

Debbie Sue spotted a gleam in the elderly woman's eye. "Tell me something. If you were going to go after this reward money Harley put up, how would you go about it?"

"Is that what you're thinking about? Lands, child, you do remind me of myself when I was your age. That's exactly what I would have done. Sounds like fun. First off, in your shoes, I'd make damn sure my evidence was rock hard before I gave it to the sheriff."

"I don't follow you."

"Why, honey, you're the sheriff's ex. You don't think you can just waltz in and claim the reward without everyone in town raising hell, do you? You'll have to all but catch the killer all by yourself and drag him up the road by the collar so it'll look like you're the one who really got him. Otherwise everybody will think you and your old sweetie are in cahoots."

Holy shit. Debbie Sue had been so focused on the amount of the reward money, she had never thought of what the town would think. She helped Maudeen from the hydraulic chair to a dryer chair and handed her *Globe* and the *National Enquirer*.

Maudeen had hit on something. It was like one of those sweepstakes drawings you enter where family members of the sponsor weren't eligible to win. Now she had one more reason to keep her activities a secret from Buddy.

After styling the older woman's bright red hair into a thick roll and lacquering it until it felt like plastic, Debbie Sue gave her favorite customer a kiss on the cheek and told her she would be hard for the men at Peaceful Oasis to resist.

"I do look good, don't I? Wish I could afford a boob lift. I'd go after that new guy that just moved into E-7. He's a younger man. Sixty-eight. And his grandson works for that company that makes Viagra."

"You don't worry about a boob job. If he hears you're easy, he'll probably be looking you up. Maybe even tonight when he sees your new hairdo."

"You're right. I'd better hurry back. It's almost four. Most of those old codgers will be shuffling into the dining room for supper. They'll all be in bed by seven, but if E-7 likes my new hair color and I'm lucky, I could be there by six."

As Maudeen was driven away by her great-granddaughter, Debbie Sue waved good-bye. As usual the sassy older woman had given her food for thought.

The remainder of the day was less entertaining. The Coca-Cola delivery man came and refilled the struggling seen-better-days Coke machine. A group of Boy Scouts came by selling raffle tickets for a drawing at Benton's Monuments and Home Accessory Emporium. The winner got either free headstone engraving or a silk flower arrangement. Debbie Sue bought three two-dollar tickets. What the heck? Where but Salt Lick could you go into a business to order a grave marker and come out with a toilet seat cover?

Ivalene Buchanan, the local Avon lady, made her deliveries. Ivalene felt her job called for her not only to sell Avon's products, but to be a walking billboard as well. Her eyelids were always at least four different colors. The deepest, richest shades of lipstick were always freshly applied to her lips, and her cheeks were wild with streaks of color and highlighter. Each wrist and bend of the elbow wafted a different fragrance, and she wore enough costume jewelry to sink an ocean liner.

Though nearing seventy, she proudly boasted that thanks to the miracle of Avon she didn't look a day over thirty-five. Edwina was always quick to agree, pointing out only to Debbie Sue that Ivalene truly didn't look *a day* over thirty-five, but she looked every bit of the twelve-thousand-plus days that she was.

Debbie Sue observed all of it with lazy amusement. She loved everything about her world. The eccentric octogenarians, the slow pace of life in a small town. Even the people who weren't her favorites fueled Edwina's mock standup comedy routines. Leaving Salt Lick forever wouldn't be easy. The only thing harder would be making the decision to do it.

Only two things were missing in her otherwise acceptable life—money and Buddy. She had two viable chances at money—the reward or Quint.

But she didn't have a chance in hell to recapture Buddy. Whoever said it was better to have loved and lost than to have never loved at all was a dumb-ass. A plain and simple dumb-ass.

Ten

Saturday night Debbie Sue went to bed early. She wanted to be rested and at the top of her game for the Sunday morning meeting with Eugene Grubbs. Edwina had promised to accompany her, then slide into a neighboring booth and listen. They had agreed early on to never leave each other alone with a suspect.

When sleep finally came it was filled with distorted images. A nightmare scared her awake and she sat up, her heart racing. In the dream, she had been sitting in a restaurant booth with a tall stack of hot pancakes in front of her. An unidentifiable man across the table suddenly grabbed her head and attempted to smother her by forcing her face into the pancakes. As she fought frantically for breath, the Odessa schoolteacher appeared in a waitress uniform and poured syrup on her head, ruining her blond highlights.

Oddly enough, she wasn't too worried about

the faceless person, but if she saw that bitch Kathy what's-her-name again, she would kill her for ruining her hair color.

Unable to return to sleep, she rose and showered and shampooed her hair. Though the morning temperature hovered in the high eighties, she dressed in black clothing—black Wranglers, black T-shirt, black boots. She banded her hair into a ponytail and tucked it under a dark blue "LaMont's Feed & Supplements" gimme cap. To finish her disguise, she covered her eyes with a pair of sunglasses with mirrored lenses she had bought at The Galleria the last time she visited Dallas.

She left her house in plenty of time to pick up Edwina and reach the Denny's in Midland by nine. Her stomach was tied in knots. They rode in silence as the endless landscape of scrubby pasture, leafless brush, and sawing pump jacks flew by.

"Did Vic wonder where you were going so early on a Sunday morning?" Debbie Sue finally asked, breaking the tension.

"Vic's on a run to Phoenix. I don't expect to see him before Tuesday night."

The owner of an eighteen-wheeler, Vic was a contract trucker. He hauled everything from cattle to cabbage. Driving the interstate satisfied his need to be on the go, and Edwina satisfied all his other needs.

"Vic had a phone call from Brenda the other night," Edwina said suddenly.

Uh-oh. Debbie Sue already knew Vic's ex lived

somewhere in Southern California. To a trucker, a short hop from Phoenix. "Oh? Same situation as before?"

"Yep. She's drying out and wants to use Vic as a towel. I swear to God, if—"

"Ed, you can't be seriously worried about her. This woman doesn't mean anything to Vic. He's just being . . . he's just being Vic."

"And I'm just being Edwina. If she doesn't leave him alone, her next recovery program may be done from a hospital bed."

Debbie Sue didn't want to make light of Edwina's feelings, but if there was a better relationship around than Vic and Edwina's, she wasn't aware of it. Still, she couldn't blame her old friend for being concerned. If the shoe were on Debbie Sue's foot, she would feel the same way. Sometimes she wished it had been another woman whom she could blame for Buddy divorcing her. Maybe she could fight another woman and win him back, but how could she wage war against herself?

Denny's came into sight. "Tell me we're doing the right thing, huh, Ed?"

"Ab-so-fuckin'-lutely. I've already made a list where I'm gonna spend that money."

"I mean, you don't think anyone has ever been stabbed or had his throat cut with a butter knife, do you? Or what about a spoon or a fork? A fork could really do damage. A fork could put out an eye."

"Eugene doesn't look like he could stab *toast*.

Besides, it's broad daylight, and Sunday morning in Denny's is a mob scene."

"You're right. So all I have to worry about for the rest of my life is darkness and being alone. Terrific."

To be certain she could make a quick exit, she found a parking slot away from the view of other diners and backed into it with the skill of one who had backed a horse trailer into a tight spot uncountable times.

Inside, she and Edwina separated. She took a seat at an end booth near the emergency exit, and Edwina sat down at the next table over. No one but Edwina could overhear her conversation with Eugene.

A harried waitress came to Debbie Sue's table with coffee pot in hand. "Our special today is the all-you-can-eat pancakes."

"*No*. No pancakes. I don't want *any* pancakes. Just coffee. Here, you can take the silverware, too." Debbie Sue gathered up the knives, forks, and spoons arranged at four place settings and handed them to the waitress. "No pancakes, no silverware. Just coffee." To the pile of eating utensils in the waitress's hands, she added four pitchers of varied flavors of syrups. "Here, take these syrups. I don't need syrup because I'm not having pancakes."

The puzzled waitress left, arms laden with silverware and syrup pitchers.

At nine o'clock Eugene entered and looked

around. He was dressed impeccably. Beige shorts, starched beige shirt with a brown and gold scarf at the neck. He had a leather fanny pack belted around his waist and he wore loafers, no socks. He looked nervous and strung out.

It was then Debbie Sue knew she had *The Power*. She was suddenly self-assured and calm. She was suave, she was classy, she was Renee Russo in *The Thomas Crown Affair*. And he was *not* Pierce Brosnan.

Rising from her seat she approached her quarry, noting the look of bewilderment on his face, as if he were trying to remember where he had seen her before.

"Thank you for being prompt, Eugene. Won't you join me at my table?"

Before sitting down, Eugene pulled a handkerchief from his back pocket and thoroughly wiped the seat on his side of the booth. He reached into his fanny pack and brought out a squeeze bottle of gel hand sanitizer and rubbed it onto his hands and wrists, making sure the cuticles of each fingernail were thoroughly cleansed. It became even clearer what C. J. meant when she said Eugene was swishy.

Finally he turned his attention to Debbie Sue. "You knew Pearl Ann?"

"Yes, we were friends. For a long time."

"I doubt that. You might have thought she was your friend, but I guarantee you that little hussy was never a friend to anyone." He raised two fingers and wiggled them at the waitress.

"You don't sound like you liked her very much."

"I didn't dislike her. I was ambivalent about her. Mr. Carruthers gave me an assignment. She was part of it."

The waitress reappeared and poured Eugene's mug full of hot coffee, refilled Debbie Sue's. "Are you having breakfast, sir?" she asked Eugene. "Our special today is all-you-can-eat pancakes."

"Oh, no thank you. I'll have dry toast, whole wheat, and hot tea with a small sliver of lemon. And could I please have a spoon?"

Yikes! "Can you make that a metal spoon, not plastic?"

The waitress glared at Debbie Sue. "Sure I can." She stamped away.

Eugene's eyes darted about the room as if he feared someone might sneak from a hidden place and grab him. "What, exactly, do you want from me? Why the cloak-and-dagger routine? I've already told the sheriff from Salt Lick everything I know."

The last statement took some wind from Debbie Sue's sails. So it was true. Buddy *had* left no stone unturned.

The waitress returned with a full set of silverware for Eugene, along with his toast. Debbie Sue gulped and tried to discreetly examine the sharpness of the knife blade. "Did you tell the sheriff about the little kickback Pearl Ann's been tipping you all these years, or the getaway fund that is bound to be sizable by now?"

Small beads of sweat broke out on Eugene's forehead, and his left leg began bouncing hard enough to shake the table. *Yes!* She had hit a nerve.

"I don't know what you're talking about." His voice came out too shrill for an innocent man.

"Oh, come on. I know the arrangement. What did you do with the extra money, Eugene?" She leaned across the table and drilled him with a laser stare from behind her sunglasses. "Or better yet, what are your plans for the mother lode?"

"I've told the *authorities* all I know." He started to rise. "You're crazy. This conversation is over."

Debbie Sue whispered, "She made a tape. She had a file. And I have both of them."

Eugene sank back to the seat. "I don't believe you. I want to hear the tape. I want to see the file. Until I do, you're a liar and this meeting never happened."

"I'll let you choose. Who do you want present when you hear the tape, Sheriff Overstreet or Harley? The only way you're going to hear it is with one of them present. Besides, I don't even need the tape or a file." She tapped her temple with her forefinger. "I have enough details right here to set the law onto an investigation."

Eugene's shoulders fell and he looked down at his chewed fingernails. "What do you want from me? Is this extortion? Do you want money?"

Debbie Sue thought she might shriek with delight. Good Lord, this was easier than she had imagined. "Oh, I want money all right, but I don't want it from you. I want to collect the price on your head."

"Price on my—" He gasped. "Forevermore, you think *I* killed Pearl Ann?" He let out a nervous cackle.

Diners at other tables turned and looked, and Debbie Sue felt uneasy. She had expected him to break into tears and confess at this point. Then she would retrieve her cell phone, call Buddy, and ask him to come pick up the killer. That's how it happened on *Law & Order*.

"Maybe you did, maybe you didn't. In any case I think we have motive. Why don't I call Sheriff Overstreet? I think he'll be a lot more lenient if you turn yourself in. If he has to come after you, he might not be as civil. He's a big guy, you know."

"Oh, I know. And he is *sooo* yummy."

Yummy? She could think of a dozen adjectives to describe Buddy, but "yummy" wasn't one of them. "You could claim temporary insanity," she went on. "Harley would probably even back you up on that one. If the sheriff has to come after you, it's going to look bad for you. Premeditated." She pursed her mouth and nodded.

Eugene stared back at her, bug-eyed. Debbie Sue wished she could read minds because there was clearly a thought process in action. He sprang to his feet and glared down at her. "There's another legal term you might look for when you read your next crime novel. It's called 'circumstantial evidence.'" He turned and prissed to the front door, his mincing steps making his butt twitch.

Debbie Sue sat stunned. And confused

Edwina eased into the spot Eugene had vacated. "What was it he said about circumcision?"

"Circumstantial, Ed. He said my information is circumstantial. He doesn't think I have enough proof to do him any harm."

"He's just blowing smoke. I've seen a lot of men who were scared. Usually my exes when I threatened them with bodily harm, but that's beside the point. He was scared all right. When a man makes an exit that quick, it's because he doesn't want you to see his fear."

Debbie Sue looked at her friend with awe. "Ed, I am constantly amazed at your knowledge of the human animal, men in particular."

"Trust me, honey, it's both a gift and a curse. Speaking of blowing smoke, let's get out of here. I'm having a nicotine fit. Or did you want to have some of that all-you-eat pancake special?"

"I'd rather stop at Sonic for a breakfast burrito and a big Dr. Pepper. We should decide what to do next."

"Now you're talking."

Halfway to Salt Lick, Debbie Sue told Edwina she would call Eugene at work the next day and ask if he'd had time to think about their conversation. "You know," she said as an afterthought, "there's one thing about the meeting that really bugged me. It was all I could do to not stare at his eyebrows."

"Eyebrows?"

"Yeah, didn't you notice? They were perfectly plucked and dyed. Best job I've ever seen, too. And he thinks Buddy's yummy."

Edwina blinked a few times, then slapped her own cheek. "Well, rope my ankles and call me dogie."

By the next morning Debbie Sue had replayed her meeting with Eugene Grubbs over and over in her head. Her instincts told her he was guilty of *something*. At this point she wasn't sure it was murder, but then again, she didn't feel comfortable saying it wasn't. Being a detective was too hard. She couldn't wait to give up this second job she had taken on.

Before picking up the phone to call Carruthers Oil & Gas, she flipped over the week-at-a-glance calendar and let out a soft whistle. "Oh my Lord, Ed. I don't know how I let time slip by me, but homecoming weekend's coming up."

In Salt Lick, homecoming was more than a high school football function. It was a reunion of current and past residents. Starting on Thursday, parties would be slated in homes all over town. The weekend culminated Saturday night at a huge dance in the high school parking lot following the football game. "We're both booked solid starting Thursday, and right through to Saturday."

Edwina sighed and began to sort curlers in her tray. "Seems like it comes earlier every year. It won't be the same without the big to-do at the Carruthers place. Remember last year's party when C. J. and Pearl Ann got into that catfight over that really good-looking cowboy from San Angelo?"

Debbie thought back to a year ago and the dance at Harley's party barn. She had never seen mild-mannered C. J. so upset about *anything*. "Lord, yes, I'll never forget it. He wasn't a cowboy, though. Wasn't he the chef Pearl Ann insisted on bringing in for the party?"

"C. J. wasn't mad, as I recall. It was Pearl Ann who was fit to be tied. Poor C. J. was just defending herself."

"All I remember is when the guy and C. J. were dancing and Pearl Ann cut in. I thought Pearl Ann was going to pull C. J.'s hair out."

Edwina shook her head and sucked up a long drink of Dr. Pepper. "C. J. was so embarrassed."

"I know. She still doesn't like to talk about it." Debbie Sue propped her elbow on the payout desk and rested her chin on her palm. "You know, that's when I remember seeing another side to Harley, too. He was so nice to C. J. He took her outside and talked to her. He was trying to make her feel better. I'll bet he was always making some kind of apology for Pearl Ann's actions.

"Yep, Pearl Ann was always good for new gossip. Hell, what she *wore* was good for a week's worth. Homecoming this year's gonna be dull."

"Face it, Ed. Not only will there not be a party at Harley's this year, maybe there'll never be one again. But I can probably liven things up for you for a short while. I've got a date with Quint Saturday night."

"Shut up! Do you really?"

"Too bad he never made it to one of the Carruthers parties. He would have been right at home."

"So what're your plans? He's already been through the public humiliation routine. Why don't you save some time and just yank his dick off when he comes to the door?"

Debbie Sue fixed Edwina with a bland expression. "Why, Edwina Perkins. You act like what happened that night was *my* fault. I really want this evening to be calm and normal. I'm trying to convince myself I want to get involved with Quint, you know?"

"If you have to *convince* yourself, then do both of you a favor and forget it. I dated a really, really rich man once. He had so much money he misplaced more than most people make in a lifetime. I wanted to make things work so damn bad."

"So what happened?"

"I threw up every time he wanted to screw. Once or twice I made it to the bed, but every time I had to make him stop so I could throw up. Nothing shrinks a man's dick like vomit breath. I even tried telling myself I was allergic to him, and with enough exposure I would build up a tolerance."

"Good Lord, Ed, he *must* have had a ton of money."

"Well, I said he did. One good thing came of it though. I lost about fifteen pounds dating him, never looked better in my life."

"It's not quite that extreme with Quint. I really do like him and he does stir up some feelings in me. I just think he wants things to move a little faster than I do."

"If the man is really interested in you, he'll give you space. Look, Vic will be home this weekend. Why don't y'all come over? My honey can throw something on the grill that's sure to impress Quint. It'll be fun. We can eat early and still have time to go to the dance."

Vic could impress anyone with his home cooking and if there was any trouble, the six-foot-three martial arts expert could rip the instigator's heart from his chest. A man with those skills was a plus to have around at a drunken homecoming dance.

Besides that, with having dinner at a friend's house, she could postpone the inevitable decision about Quint—would she or wouldn't she? "Hey, thanks so much, Ed. He's picking me up at seven. We can be over soon after." She picked up the phone receiver. "Now don't interrupt me. I've got to make this phone call before anyone comes in." Debbie Sue keyed in CO&G's number.

A Stepford Wife answered. Debbie Sue asked for Eugene. A professional female voice told her Mr. Grubbs was out of the office ill. Debbie Sue swore under her breath. He was probably at home hiding behind the sofa.

"I'm a friend of his and thought I'd say hello. Do you have his home number handy? I'll call him there."

"I'm sorry, ma'am, but Mr. Grubbs has an unlisted number, and we aren't allowed to give out employees' phone numbers. If you'll leave me your name, when he retrieves his messages, I'll tell him you called."

"No, thanks. I'll just call back."

Okay, fruity hotshot, you've escaped me for now. She would allow him one day to make a decision. She would call again tomorrow morning, and he had better be there or . . .

Or what? Well, she didn't want to think about *or what* right now.

At the end of the day Edwina bid Debbie Sue a good evening and headed home. She had tried to put Brenda's message out of her mind but Vic was on the road, and what if he decided to just follow the interstate on out to California? In the commonsense recesses of her mind, she knew he wouldn't do such a thing, but in the battle-scarred regions of her heart, she feared he might. She knew the male animal only too well.

She had seen pictures of Brenda. Once when

helping Vic search for his discharge papers, among old military mementos, documents of commendation, letters to and from home, photos of a naval station, and numerous medals and ribbons, they found a snapshot of a young beauty, a stark contrast to his other pictures that were so military. Looking to be no more than eighteen, blond and tanned with a drop-dead gorgeous body covered only by a ruffled bikini, she seemed to be the perfect Valley Girl stereotype, lying on the beach, head propped on her hand to pose for the picture.

"Wow, is she one of your medals too?" Edwina had asked.

Vic looked at the picture for what Edwina felt was a little too long before answering. He explained the woman was his ex. Edwina had tried to imagine her after the ravages of time and alcohol abuse had taken their toll. But each time the image of the beauty on the beach assaulted her. Judging from the photo the only thing she and her live-in lover's ex-wife had in common was they were both females. And one other thing—they both loved Vic.

She decided right then and there, when she got home tonight if there was another message from Brenda, she intended to accidentally erase it. No sirree, she wasn't giving up Vic without a fight.

And if Miss California wanted to come and get him for herself, she'd better pack a lunch and bring an army.

Eleven

Buddy sat behind his battered desk in the sheriff's office and rocked back in the Naugahyde upholstered chair. He had drunk so many cups of coffee, he wouldn't blink for three days.

In front of him lay a yellow legal pad. On each line he had written the name of a person he had talked to casually or interviewed formally about the Carruthers murder. He had scribbled notes beside the names and in the margins.

Doodles and drawings of a Texas Rangers badge filled in the blank spots beside the names of the employees of Carruthers Oil & Gas. They had stonewalled him. Even Carol Jean had clammed up. He understood their attitudes. Working for CO&G was the best job in West Texas. Excellent benefits, outlandish perks, and a salary not even in shooting range of other area employers.

With flying colors, Harley had passed the lie

detector test arranged by his attorneys. Deep down, Buddy had never *really* believed he killed Pearl Ann anyway.

The only person he hadn't talked to was the mysterious redhead he had seen accompanying Harley to his condo.

He was at the end of his rope when it came to fresh ideas or clues. He reached for his hat and walked from his office into the reception area. "Tanya, I'm fixin' to run and take care of something. Be back shortly."

"I just put Kathy on hold for you."

Damn. He didn't want to get into a conversation with Kathy now. "Did you tell her I was here?"

"No, I told her I wasn't sure where you were."

"Good. Tell her I'm out. Thanks, Tanya."

Walking toward the Tahoe, he made a mental note to call Kathy later. He didn't know what he would tell her, but maybe an answer would come to him by the time he returned from his errand.

He pulled alongside the Styling Station, grinning as he passed the two gasoline pumps dressed in black and orange Halloween costumes. Salt Lick citizens didn't notice the oddity anymore, but it always made him laugh. A magazine in New York had even published pictures and done a small article about the pumps. Guess that was the kind of thing people up North liked to read about Texans.

Debbie Sue was just hanging up the phone

when Buddy entered. She looked up, hoping she had hidden a startled expression.

"Ladies. I didn't catch y'all at a bad time, did I?" He looked around the empty shop.

"Nope," Debbie Sue said, attempting to make her voice sound innocent. "We're just waiting for the herd to stampede. What's up?"

Edwina sauntered over to Buddy. "I think this boy's here for a haircut. Look at these curls." She lifted off his hat and combed her long red nails through his black hair. "How 'bout it, babycakes? Want me to give you a trim? Or how about something more personal?"

Buddy's face turned from tan to red. Edwina had always engaged in verbal foreplay with Buddy, and most of the time Debbie Sue laughed about it, but this morning it irritated her.

"Ed, one of these days I'm gonna put Vic in jail for about three days," Buddy said with a laugh, "and you and I are gonna get to know each other better."

"I'd ruin you for other women, cowboy. I'd give you two days, then break Vic out of jail and leave you heartbroken."

The two laughed. Debbie Sue tried to join in but sounded phony. "What are you doing here, Buddy? You don't usually come by just to say hello."

"I need your help, Flash. Is there someplace we can talk?"

"You can talk right here," Ed said. "I've got to

run to Kwik-Stop for some smokes and DP. I can't bear to face the day without them."

Liar. Debbie Sue knew Edwina came in every day with plenty of cigarettes and a gallon of Dr. Pepper.

"Always good to see you, hon." The skinny brunette trailed her fingers across Buddy's wide shoulders. "Come back when it's just the two of us. I want to show you some uses for these multi-position hydraulic chairs."

Debbie Sue didn't want to dwell on the mental picture that flew into her mind. She had imagined she and Buddy christening one of the salon chairs. She planted a fist on one hip. "Okay, you've got my full attention 'til ten o'clock. This doesn't involve Super Glue does it?"

Buddy frowned. "Huh? Uh, oh yeah. Sorry about that. It seemed funny at the time."

"Maybe to a sadist."

Buddy grinned and rested his forearms on the payout counter. His teeth were as perfect as new piano keys. Debbie Sue loved seeing him smile.

"Listen," he said, "I've hit a dead end on this murder. Pearl Ann left a string of people with a motive, but none I can find who would have actually killed her. Everybody's either got solid alibis or solid lie detector tests. All I've got is one fingerprint that doesn't match anybody's. That reward money hasn't raised so much as a whisper."

Despite her determination to maintain her silence about what she knew, Debbie Sue was moved by Buddy's straightforward admission. "So what do you want from me, a confession?"

"I don't mean for this to become beauty shop gossip, but Harley's got a redheaded girlfriend. Have you and Ed seen a woman around him with long red hair?"

"The only redheads I see are the ones who get their roots colored, and none of them are younger than sixty-five. Something tells me that's not who you're looking for."

"No, Harley's alibi is young and hot. He won't give me her name. I followed them, so I've seen her."

Debbie Sue couldn't keep her eyes from bulging. "You followed Harley and a girlfriend? Ohmygod, Buddy. This is serious. What if he finds out?"

"Murder *is* serious, Debbie Sue."

"Ohmy*god*, Buddy. Do you think Harley did it?"

Buddy's brow crinkled into a frown. "No, no, no, Debbie Sue. Don't blow this all out of proportion."

"Can't you use your authority? I mean, you're the sheriff. Don't you have ways to make him cooperate? Thumb screws? Electric shock?"

"Cut it out, Flash. This is getting to be a real problem. I wouldn't admit it to just anybody, but—"

He stopped and looked past her. She could see the tumult in his eyes. "What, Buddy?"

"I've pressed Harley as far as he's gonna be pressed. If I don't come up with a genuine suspect soon, he's threatening to bring in the Texas

Rangers or some other outside outfit. He's already asked why I don't call in help. I've got to find Pearl Ann's killer. I can't be known as the sheriff who couldn't solve the only murder that's happened in Salt Lick in sixty years. Christ, I'll never get hired by the DPS." He straightened his shoulders and gave her a direct look. "Kind of a selfish reason, huh?"

He look so beleaguered, Debbie Sue wanted to put her arms around him and whisper soothing words, but she struggled to maintain her grip on reality. "Don't be so hard on yourself, Buddy. We all do things for selfish reasons. Is the redheaded woman someone you think could be guilty?"

"Only because I can't find anybody else."

"If Harley passed the lie detector test, why is he still protecting his girlfriend?"

"That's my question, too. That's why the red-head has become my top suspect."

At that moment, the door opened and Edwina's first customer of the day entered. Debbie Sue directed her back to the shampoo area and told her Edwina would be back any minute.

"Looks like you're about to get busy," Buddy said. "I'll go. I didn't mean to bother you. It was a shot in the dark that you might know something that could help me."

"Hey, I'm not through talking, but you're right. It is about to get a little crowded in here. Can I call you tonight at home, say about eight o'clock?" She caught a quick little breath, fearing he might say no. "I might think of something between now and then."

"Sure, uh, I mean, yeah. Eight o'clock's fine. Hope you *do* think of something. And Flash?" He picked up her hand and kissed her palm. "Thanks."

A football-sized lump lodged in Debbie Sue's throat. Before they married and especially after, she and Buddy had been best friends, had always solved problems together until she screwed everything up. She felt the weight of the world on her shoulders as she watched him drive away. She had key information to the case and hadn't shared it with him.

Damn you, Buddy, for making me feel guilty.

By the end of the day Debbie Sue had made up her mind to tell Buddy everything she knew about Eugene Grubbs. Crime solving was best left in Buddy's hands anyway. At home, as she changed into cutoffs and a faded Dallas Cowboys T-shirt, she was surprised by a knock at her door.

It was only seven-thirty. Maybe Buddy was dropping by instead of waiting for her call. She hoped so. She had resisted the urge to kiss him this morning. He had been so open and honest, it had touched a deep place in her heart, and the thought of kissing him touched a deep place somewhere else. She intended to greet him with a kiss that would never end. Caution, pride, and ego be damned. Trying to rebuild her life without him wasn't working. One moment of kissing Buddy again was worth any price she might have to pay.

For thirty seconds, she worried about her appearance, then flung open the front door.

Kathy Something was standing on her doorstep, smiling like a possum. "Debbie Sue? Do you remember me?"

Debbie Sue's brain scrambled to recover from shock. "Sure, yeah, of course I do. It's Karen, isn't it?"

The woman was wearing black slacks, an old-lady blouse with seed pearl beading on a round collar, and black patent T-strap shoes. And she was clutching with both hands the strap of a small shiny patent leather purse. Where was she headed, Old Maid's Night Out?

"No, Kathy. Kathy Boczkowski. I was with Buddy at Kincaid's in Odessa the night we were introduced."

Kathy offered her hand, Debbie Sue shook it and winced. She hated pumping a hand that felt as if it had no bones.

"I'm sorry to drop by at this time of night. I went home from work to change into something more comfortable or I'd have been here earlier. I wonder, would you mind talking to me about Buddy?"

"Buddy? Has something happened to Buddy?"

"Oh no, nothing like that. Do you mind if I come in?"

Debbie Sue stepped back and gave Buddy's girlfriend entry to her home, trying to remember when she had last run the vacuum. *What in the hell kind of name is Bosh-cow-ski?*

As Kathy passed in front of her, Debbie Sue caught a strong whiff of roses. *Blech!* She rolled her eyes, slammed the door, and followed Kathy to the living room.

Her visitor perched on the edge of the couch, and Debbie Sue rushed to pick up scattered reading material—*Western Horseman, American Cowboy,* PRCA newsletters.

"It's very important to me that you and I have a good relationship, Debbie Sue. Buddy thinks the world of you, and I respect the years you've known each other."

Kathy might as well have been speaking Polish for all the sense her conversation made. Or for that matter, her visit. *What in the hell is she doing here?* "I'd offer you coffee, but I only have instant. You want some"—Debbie Sue's mind inventoried what she had in the house to serve—"some orange juice?" She still had half of a half-gallon of Tropicana from when Quint came.

"Instant coffee would be fine. I sometimes resort to using it myself when I'm in a hurry."

Debbie Sue dredged up a phony smile and retreated to the kitchen. *What in the holy hell is she doing here?* As she rummaged through the cupboard looking for the jar of instant Folger's she had bought last winter, she sensed someone behind her and turned around, found herself nearly nose-to-nose with Kathy.

"I know you and Buddy went through a lot together and I'm not foolish enough to think, just because you're divorced, those years don't count."

What in the ever-loving, holy hell is she doing here? Debbie Sue found the coffee and placed a cup of water in the microwave. "I never drink coffee when the weather's hot." While the microwave ran, she set about searching a different cupboard. "Sugar. Want some sugar? Oh, here. I've got some of those little flavor pills you put in coffee. Um, let me see, I think it's Irish Cream. Yep, it's Irish Cream."

The microwave pinged and Debbie Sue dragged out the mug of hot water, dumped in a heaping teaspoon of coffee granules, then a flavor pill. She added a second one for good measure before handing the steaming mix to Kathy.

Kathy took the mug and went on talking non-stop. "Buddy and I talked about this and he agrees that when we run into each other again, there should always be friendship and warm wishes between us."

Friendship and warm wishes? When we run into each other again? Definitely not words that came from Buddy Overstreet's mouth. Enough was enough. "I'm sorry, but I don't understand where you're coming from or where you're headed. Let's cut to the chase."

"Well. You are upfront and forthright. Buddy said you would be direct. I assured him the best way to handle this was woman-to-woman. We thought you should be the first to know. He and I are going to be married. We intend to make the announcement at Thanksgiving."

All the air left the room. Debbie Sue felt as if her head had been injected with Novocain. "Oh" was the word that fell from her mouth.

"Are you all right? I'm so sorry. Can I get you something? You really don't look well."

"No, no, I'm fine. Just surprised. Uh . . . Buddy knows you're here?

"Oh, it was his idea that I come. He didn't want you to hear it like beauty salon gossip." She winced, a tight little frown squeezing between her brows. "Oh, I'm sorry. That was insensitive of me. You work in a salon, don't you?"

"Well, yeah. Actually I *own* it, but that's beside the point." Debbie Sue despised herself for feeling the need to offer a defense. "God love that Buddy, always thinking of my feelings. You know, I don't want to be rude, but . . ." Debbie Sue marched to the front door and opened it. She pasted on a smile. "I'm expecting company."

"Oh, well I don't want to intrude. Promise me you're fine."

Debbie Sue gave her a horse grin. "I promise."

After Kathy Bosh-cow-ski gathered her handbag and left, for what seemed like an hour Debbie Sue sat in the same spot staring at nothing in particular. She could feel her blood rushing through her body, hear her own breathing. Had she developed superhuman powers, or was the breaking of her very human heart what had brought on this phenomenon? She thought back to seeing Buddy earlier in the day. He had been so sweet, affectionate even. His kiss on the palm of her hand had almost made her faint.

She had bought his "poor me" routine, hook, line, and sinker; had nearly told him her fifty-thousand-dollar secret about Eugene Grubbs. And that wasn't all. She had made up her mind to . . .

Bastard!

She reached for the phone and stabbed in Buddy's number.

He answered on the first ring. "Hey you, I was afraid you might have changed your mind about calling."

"Buddy Overstreet, you're a limp-dicked motherfucker. If you ever come in my shop again, I'll poke you with a cattle prod." She punched off the call and threw the phone across the room.

As God is my witness, I will never understand women.

And just when he thought things had softened up between him and Debbie Sue, too. Buddy sat motionless holding the receiver to his ear. Until he heard a knock. He felt safe opening the door because his angry ex-wife couldn't possibly have made it to his house since she hung up in his ear just moments earlier.

To his astonishment there stood Kathy. "Kathy. What are you doing in Salt Lick?"

"I'm so sorry to bother you. I know you said you need some time, but I felt terrible about the way things ended yesterday. I feared you would think I was trying to use sex as a tool to sway your decision. I would never stoop to doing something so crude and unladylike."

"No need to apologize. I didn't think that at all." Buddy looked down at his socked feet. If he had known she was coming, he would've at least put on his boots.

"Oh good. I do feel better. Now I have a little confession. I went by Debbie Sue's house and—"

"You did what?" A mild panic zinged through his chest.

"I know, I know. It was a mistake. I only wanted to tell her I was glad to have finally met her and that you had all the respect in the world for her."

"Come on in," he said. "It's a little chilly out there on the porch."

"Oh, thank you." She stepped through the doorway, and the scent of flowers filled his small entry.

"Here, put your purse down." He took her purse, laid it on an end table by the couch. His place was a mess. Newspapers strewn all around, a plastic tray left from the TV dinner he'd had for supper, his boots lying in front of the couch.

She looked up at him with pleading eyes. "I also asked her for help. You know, tell me something about you that might help me improve our relationship. Since she's involved with another man, I didn't see the harm. I know it was stupid, but I felt so desperate after yesterday."

He felt a little desperate, too. Debbie Sue had called him names before, but he couldn't recall if she had ever called him the one he just heard. Cussin' was part of West Texas vernacular, even among women, but sometimes Debbie Sue took it to new heights. Clear back at age eleven, she'd had colorful language. When they were married, he had threatened a dozen times to wash her mouth out with soap.

"You're not angry with me, are you? I've already been thrown out of one house tonight."

"Debbie Sue can be a handful if you don't approach her just right. She can be . . . well, headstrong."

"Yes, I can certainly see that's true." Kathy smiled. "Living with her must have been trying. She's very juvenile for someone her age, isn't she?"

Juvenile? Buddy had never thought of Debbie Sue as juvenile, even when she had been one. As for living with her, when things had been good between them, he had never had so much fun in his life.

"I thought since I've driven over here, we might have some dinner together," Kathy went on.

Buddy was still lost in thought, and Kathy caught his attention only because he realized she had stopped talking. "I'm sorry, Kathy, you were saying?"

"Oh, silly, I asked if you wanted to go have some dinner?"

"Gosh, uh, wish I could, but I've already eaten. Plus I've got some things I need to look into, some phones calls to make."

She cocked her head and looked up at him from the corner of her eye. "Okay, I'll let you off the hook this time. But don't forget"—she rose on her tiptoes and placed a peck of a kiss on his lips—"I'm waiting for an answer."

Then her hands slid around his neck and she all-out kissed him. Her body came against him and she moved her pelvis against his fly. He could feel himself growing firm. Damn, this wasn't what he wanted. He took her wrists and unhooked her hands from behind his neck. "Kathy, I—"

She kissed him again, then gave him a teasing smile. "I know when I'm not wanted." She kissed the tip of her finger and touched his lips. "Bye, for now."

And she was gone.

He stood stupefied in the middle of the living room. He had a hard-on. Debbie Sue hadn't left his thoughts, but Kathy had turned him on. All he could do was sigh.

Experience had taught him that leaving Debbie Sue alone until she settled down was the best thing. He wished Kathy hadn't gone to see her, but it was too late now. Maybe it was fate.

He had no doubt the small kiss on Debbie Sue's palm had spawned a reaction, and he had made up his mind the next time the opportunity arose, he intended to give her more to think about. But Kathy stopping by her house probably had ensured the next opportunity was somewhere between next year and never.

Twelve

Debbie Sue spent the greater part of the night vacillating between crying in despair and raging in anger. A part of her had known the day would come when Buddy would find someone and remarry, but another part of her refused to accept it. She couldn't remember much of life without him.

She stewed over two big decisions. With Kathy's announcement, she had no choice but to continue working toward collecting the reward money so she could pay off her debt and leave Salt Lick for good. She might go back to Lubbock to Texas Tech. Twenty-eight wasn't too old to start over in vet school.

If collecting the reward and reenrollment in college proved impossible, she would take Quint up on his offer. Either option would take her away from Salt Lick and a daily view of Buddy happy with a new wife.

She arrived at the salon uncustomarily late. Edwina's Mustang was already parked in its usual place. When Debbie Sue opened the door, she found the lights and the air conditioner on and she could smell a strong dose of brewing caffeine. A Toby Keith tune blared from the radio and Edwina was dancing in a circle with the broom, singing at the top of her voice.

Edwina froze mid-step. "What the hell happened to you? You look like you bawled your eyes out all night."

Debbie Sue rounded the payout desk and stuffed her purse in a drawer. "I don't want to talk about it, Ed."

"Only two things can turn a woman's eyes into road maps. Either a man or something she's allergic to."

"In my case I think they're one and the same." Debbie Sue sniffled. She walked over to her older, wiser friend, laid her head on her shoulder, and began to sob.

"Now, now, hon. It can't be as bad as that. Did you and Buddy get into a scrap again? Was it over this reward business? Was it Quint or Kathy?"

At the mention of Kathy's name, Debbie Sue's volume amplified. "She—she came by my house last night and—and—" Debbie Sue broke into racking sobs and couldn't continue.

"And—and what? You hit her? You threw her out? What in the hell does she mean coming to your house? She has no business—"

"She came to tell me she and Buddy are getting married."

"What? I don't believe it."

Between sobs, Debbie Sue recounted the story to Ed.

"Did you talk to Buddy?"

"Well . . . sort of."

"Uh-huh, I know what *that* means. I wouldn't believe it 'til I heard it from Buddy's mouth." Edwina set her away, yanked a tissue from a box on the payout desk, and handed it over. Debbie Sue dutifully dabbed her eyes.

"She wants you out of the way. Clear and simple. Hell, hon, one woman will say anything to another if she sees a threat."

Debbie Sue sniffed and blew her nose. Edwina stroked her hair. "Remember my ex Jimmy? I once told his girlfriend I had only a week to live and my last wish on earth was to spend that week with Jimmy. I had her going to the point she was bawling. She told me to have a wonderful week with him. I guess it was. We ended up married by Wednesday."

"Edwina, that's just awful. How could you do such a thing?"

"You've never heard the old saying, 'All's fair in love and war'?" Maybe that's what this Kathy person is thinking. Maybe she'll say and do anything to get the man she wants. I'd drive a tractor over one of my kin if—well, that's not a good example. I'd drive a tractor over *most* of my kin just because I had the opportunity."

Debbie Sue laughed a little. Edwina was good for a lot of things in life, including cheering up a friend.

"When you think with your emotions instead of your head," Edwina continued, "you always get the short end of the stick. We should talk about this later, after you've had some rest and a little more time to collect yourself. Don't make any decisions when you're heartbroken and haven't slept."

"No, Ed. I've been carrying that short-ended stick my whole life. I'm turning over a new leaf. From here on out, it's going to be about *me* and what *I* want." Debbie Sue squared her shoulders with renewed determination and went to the desk to check the appointment schedule.

The rest of the day went without interruption. She worked as if on automatic pilot. Customers came and went. She bleached, curled, teased, and sprayed nonstop, didn't even pause for lunch. Her first break came at two o'clock. She stepped into the back storage area for some privacy while she ate a Snickers bar and made her second call to Eugene in Midland.

After a transfer to Eugene's extension, a recorded female voice announced, "You have reached the office of Eugene Grubbs. Mr. Grubbs is no longer with our organization. If you care to leave a message please wait for the tone. If you prefer to speak with the operator please stay on the line."

What the hell? What had happened to Eugene?

Did he get fired? Did he quit? Was he on the run? Was he running in *her* direction?

Another voice broke into her scrambling thoughts. "This is the operator. May I help you?"

"I hope so. I'm calling Eugene Grubbs and I got a recording that said he no longer works there. There must be a mistake. I just spoke to him Sunday."

"I'm sorry, ma'am, but Mr. Grubbs submitted his resignation yesterday, effective immediately. Is there someone else who can assist you?"

Debbie Sue's head spun. She had the uneasy feeling that if she looked over her shoulder Eugene would be standing there. "If you can just tell me where he's gone, I'll call him there."

"I'm sorry, but he didn't leave a forwarding number."

"Can you give me his home address or phone number?"

"I'm sorry, ma'am, but that—"

Debbie Sue hung up. She had known the question was off-limits before she asked.

She must have had a dazed expression on her face when she walked back to the front of the shop, because Edwina said, "God, I have *got* to get you in a poker game someday. You look like you just saw a ghost."

"I've lost him. He's gone."

"Buddy's gone?"

"No, Ed, Eugene Grubbs. He quit his job. They don't know, or they're not telling, where he is. He was so scared Sunday he's probably in Canada by now. Or Mexico. Shit. My only suspect."

Debbie Sue sat down in her styling chair and rested her elbows on her knees, propped up her head with her hands. "I'm such a lousy sleuth. I didn't even get his license plate number. I have no way in hell of finding out where he lives, much less where he is."

"My sister's kid can find out anything you want to know on the Internet. He's a weird little sonofagun, but smart as a whip. Honestly, it would scare the stuffing right out of you if you saw what he can dig up on people. There's no such thing as not knowing where a person is anymore. If I'd had him and the Internet around fifteen years ago, I'd have saved a bundle on lawyers."

"Can you give him a call?"

"Sure."

"But be sure you don't tell him *why* we're looking for this guy."

Debbie Sue finished up the day and did her routine cleaning. She had never been so glad to see a workday end. When she stepped outside the shop to go home, she noticed for the first time the distinct smell of fall in the air. The summer heat still hung on, but there was the promise of autumn and lower temperatures.

And something else just as enticing—the aroma of burgers cooking on the grill at Hogg's Drive-In. All at once, her stomach didn't care about finances or love lost. It registered hunger with enough angst to get her attention.

Debbie Sue mounted the Silverado and wheeled into the drive-in, went inside to the front counter, and ordered a cheeseburger, a large order of onion rings, and a tall milk shake to go. Her bruised ego needed feeding, and there was nothing like grilled fat doused with ketchup and washed down with sweet ice cream to fill that ticket.

While she waited, she turned and gazed over the room full of tables and booths and diners and she saw him—Buddy, sitting at a table in the back corner with his deputy, Billy Don. She watched as he slipped a half teaspoon, never any more, of sugar into his coffee and lifted the cup to his lips. His tongue flicked a drop of coffee from his mustache. She felt light-headed, and the pain she had pushed to the recesses of her brain all day came full frontal.

She could hear his deep baritone voice, and when he tipped his hat back with his thumb and laughed, it became too much. She spun around and dashed for her pickup, fumbled the key into the ignition. She cranked the motor, backed up, and floored the accelerator. The Silverado lunged and came to a jolting stop. She had failed to press the clutch. Before every eye in Hogg's could land on her, she restarted the pickup, pulled away, and charged home.

Is this the way it's going to be every time I see him? I can't handle this. I simply cannot handle it. Yes, leaving Salt Lick was the right decision.

She parked in the driveway in front of her house and reached for her food. *Well, fuck.* She'd left it at Hogg's.

The minute Debbie Sue walked into the familiar surroundings of her home, before she even snapped on a light, she knew something was wrong.

Intuition in full gear, the hair stood up on the back of her neck and arms. She resisted the urge to turn and run and reached instead for the light switch closest to the front door. A small gasp passed her lips as she viewed the wreck that had once been her living room. Her reclining chair was overturned. Her sofa cushions had been thrown off, and the sofa bottom was cut into gaping openings with stuffing protruding.

Everything was in disarray. Drawers emptied, magazines and books scattered and torn. She found the same wreckage in every room. Even her bathroom had been trashed, and, most puzzling of all, some of her cosmetics appeared to be missing.

Instinctively she knew who had done this. Eugene Grubbs, looking for the fictitious tape. Well, he didn't find it, did he?

She spent the remainder of the evening putting everything back in order, adrenaline driving through her veins. It had been a while since she had done any deep housecleaning, so she incorporated that into the chore of straightening and reorganizing, which made for a really long day. By midnight she was spent. With exhaustion added to the sleeplessness of the previous night, she fell sound asleep as soon as her head hit the pillow.

The ringing of the phone seemed far away and dreamlike. She floated to the receiver. In her dream, Buddy was on the other end, calling her to thank her for a passionate evening together.

She giggled into the receiver. "Hi, sugarfoot—"

"Debbie Sue? Are you alone? Dammit, I must be getting old. I can't keep up with everything that's going on."

Oh crap. Edwina. Debbie Sue lifted herself from the haze. "What time is it?"

"It's late. Damn near eight o'clock. Still got time to have your coffee. I called to let you know what Curtis found."

"Did I know Curtis lost something?" She fought off the cobwebs clouding her thought process. "Who's Curtis?"

"My sister's kid. You know, the Internet geek?"

Debbie Sue was suddenly awake and alert. "Good, I'd like the chance to talk to that prissy little pissant again."

"When did you ever talk to Curtis?"

"Not him. Eugene Grubbs."

"Oh *that* prissy little pissant."

Debbie Sue explained to Edwina the condition in which she had found her home the previous evening.

"Did you call and report it to Buddy?"

"I wouldn't call Buddy if a whole damn wall

was torn down. It had to be Eugene looking for the tape, the one I told him I had."

"I've got his home address right here. You can make him a tape and mail it to him. Tell him you're gonna pull his ears off and stuff 'em in his pockets so he can hear you kicking his butt if he ever comes near your house again. You know, be subtle."

"This is serious, Ed. If he'll destroy my house, there's no telling what else he's capable of doing. I'm almost afraid to go into the shop today. He might have gone there, too."

"How does he even know who you are and where you live?"

"You said it yourself. There's no such thing as not being able to find out who someone is anymore. Now, tell me what Curtis told you."

To Debbie Sue's amazement, Edwina supplied Eugene's Social Security number, address, unlisted phone number, date of birth, education and employment history. He had no criminal record, not even a driving violation. One of his employers was Kisses Lounge.

Kisses Lounge? The only gay nightclub in Midland—or possibly in all of West Texas?

"Maybe you should give this information to Buddy," Edwina said. "I'm worried over your safety."

"I've been thinking about it, too. If we go into the shop today and the limp-wristed little shit has been there, I'll tell Buddy. If he hasn't, I won't. What do you think of that plan?"

"Like all your others, well thought out and clearly based on sound reasoning."

Debbie Sue arrived at the salon to find everything in the order in which it was left the night before. So what was her next move? Did she go to the home address provided by Curtis or try phoning again? She opted for the phone call. She would be braver over the phone. At this point, perceived bravery was all she had going in her favor.

After five rings she was ready to hang up when an answering machine picked up. "Hi! This is Eugene. If you want to tell me something, wait for the beep. If you're calling Janine, press two now."

Janine? Good Lord, was Eugene married? Did he have a female roommate?

"Surprise, Eugene," she said to the voice mail. "It's me again. You didn't find the tape, but then I guess you know that already. You didn't really think I'd be so stupid as to leave it at my house, did you? It's locked away in a safe place. It's time you gave up. I'll give you one day to think about it. I'll be waiting in front of the sheriff's office tomorrow night at six o'clock. We'll go in together, and you can turn yourself in. If you don't show up, I'm going in without you. I'll be giving the tape to the sheriff and I'm telling him everything else I know, too. See you tomorrow night."

She was shaking so hard, it took two attempts to hang up the receiver. The shakiness had to be from pure adrenaline coursing through her veins because she felt an odd sense of sudden strength and confidence.

The only thing to do now was decide what action she would take if he didn't show. All she had for evidence was a story relayed to her by a now-dead woman. If there was a paper trail of Pearl Ann's money and accounts, Eugene had probably disposed of it before he left the company. The tape would be the only concrete piece of evidence she had against him—that is, *if* she actually had a tape. The chance was looking good that the only thing she would collect in the way of reward was the dust the fund had accumulated.

Oh please, dear God. Let him turn himself in or I'm up one of your creeks without a paddle.

When Edwina arrived Debbie Sue told her about the phone call to Eugene.

"Janine? Who's Janine?"

"Maybe it's his wife or girlfriend."

"Nah, unless my instincts have gone south, I pegged that guy for being light in the loafers. Just for the hell of it, let's call back and listen to Janine's message."

"I don't know Ed, I'm—" Debbie Sue didn't finish her sentence because Edwina was already keying in the fifth number.

Edwina listened a minute, then pressed number two, keyed on the speaker phone, and waited. The soft strains of "Strangers in the Night" drifted through the phone, followed by a sultry feminine voice. "Well, hello. This is Janine. I'll be doing my show at Kisses tonight at nine. If you can't make it, please leave me a message. But trust me, honey, it'll be your loss if you don't come see me. Buh-bye."

Edwina hung up the receiver with a blank expression.

"That almost sounded like Eugene," Debbie Sue said.

Edwina's blank stare evolved into a big grin. "What're you gonna be doing tonight around, oh say, nine?"

"What am I ever doing any night around, oh say, nine? I'll be getting ready for bed."

"Not tonight. We're going to catch a show. I'm not sure, but I think we just might have located the elusive redhead you told me about."

Edwina's explanation of the voice mail message left Debbie Sue with a sick feeling in the pit of her stomach. Buddy's questions about a red-haired woman came back to her. Had the world gone crazy? Pearl Ann had been murdered, Buddy was engaged, and Harley was gay? "Eugene would recognize us. We'd be sitting ducks in a strange place."

"You don't get it, do you? We're going in drag. Dressed as men. The fort will be standing, but the little general and his troops won't be there."

"The fort? But why? Why do we need to do this?"

"What if Eugene goes underground and becomes Janine permanently? We have to know what he, I mean she, looks like, don't we?"

"Oh man. This wasn't supposed to get this complicated."

"You're right, there shouldn't be anything difficult about solving a murder. What a drag." Edwina chuckled. "Drag. Get it?"

"Ed, that's not funny. I'll go only if Vic goes with us."

"Ab-so-fuckin'-lutely. This would be like Christmas morning to him. Happy hour material for years to come."

Kisses Lounge was located in downtown Midland in an office building abandoned long ago by a defunct oil company. At eight-thirty Vic and his two new buddies walked in. The club was low lit with small tables and intimate booths surrounding a dance floor, with a stage at one end. Couples were in various stages of activity—dancing, sitting, or observing.

Looking around, Debbie Sue didn't see anything hugely different about this bar from any other she'd been in. The people, music, clinking drink glasses all looked and sounded the same until she looked closer and saw a day's growth of chin stubble barely visible beneath heavy makeup and chest hair instead of cleavage. The women were handsome men and the men had become beautiful women. Or something.

Debbie Sue and Edwina had achieved the

proper look without a lot of fuss. Edwina had trimmed some wisps of hair off an old wig and used her skills to make mustaches. Double-backed tape held the disguises in place. Once they scrubbed their faces of makeup, donned their usual weekend clothes, gelled their hair back and put on bill caps, the effect was startling in its authenticity.

Debbie Sue did go to the trouble of taking a couple of Ace bandages and pressing her breasts to a flat profile. Edwina achieved the same look without doing a thing. Vic suggested a more masculine walk for Debbie Sue and a rolled up pair of socks to stuff into her jeans for authenticity.

"I look like something crawled under my lip and died there," Debbie Sue complained.

"Well, excuse the hell out of me," Edwina retorted. "I did the best I could. I happen to think it looks real. Does *mine* look bad?"

"No, yours looks really good. Well groomed."

"Just listen to you two," Vic said with an eye roll. "Even when you're going out in drag you're worried about how you look. Unless you're hoping to get lucky it doesn't matter."

"Well, what's wrong with having a little pride in yourself?" Edwina whispered to Debbie Sue. Debbie Sue gave a thumbs-up.

"This place should be called Don't Judge a Book by Its Cover," Debbie Sue said.

"I never thought I'd hear myself complaining about a penis," Edwina said, adjusting the accessory in front of her jeans. "No wonder men are so hard to get along with." She grinned at Vic. "Excluding you, Poodle."

"I know," Debbie Sue replied. "If I had one of these things bunched up in the front of my pants all the time, I'd be disagreeable, too."

"Maybe that explains why they're always so eager to whip it out," Edwina said.

They chose an inconspicuous table that was private, but still allowed a good view of the stage. Vic ordered three beers just as the house lights dimmed from low to dark as a cave and the stage lights came to full voltage. A voice came on the sound system and announced that the lovely Janine would be making her appearance shortly and directed all to take their seats. The waiter—or was it waitress?—delivered their drinks and winked at Edwina.

"See," Debbie Sue said with a laugh, "I told you how good you looked. Maybe he or she will slip you a phone number before the night's over."

Edwina turned to answer, but just blinked instead. "What?" Debbie Sue asked. "What's wrong?"

"There's a hair in your beer."

"There is not. I just had a sip. You're being childish." She picked up her mug and it was all she could do not to squeal. Her perfectly formed mustache was floating on the surface of her beer.

"Don't worry about it," Vic said. "I'll lay odds that's not the first false anything that's been left in this joint at closing time."

Within minutes a ravishing redhead sauntered onto the stage. Her/his red sequined gown caressed her/his curves. Debbie Sue could see only a slight resemblance to Eugene, but to the unsuspecting eye she/he was all gorgeous woman.

Janine performed an ambitious routine of lip-synching to Aretha Franklin's "Respect," Peggy Lee's "Is That All There Is?" and brought the house down with Tammy Wynette's rendition of "Stand by Your Man."

At the end of the act, Debbie Sue and her coconspirators made a hasty exit. Vic drove them to a truck stop on the way out of town. Bored waitresses watched with no expression or reaction as the two men went into the ladies' room and emerged as women. Now, sans two "penises," they enjoyed strong black coffee and warm apple pie.

"Do you think you'll recognize Eugene again if you see him as Janine?" Edwina asked as they walked to Vic's pickup.

"I don't think I'll have a bit of trouble. He's one of the most beautiful women I've ever seen."

"Sweet baby," Edwina said to Vic, blowing a stream of smoke in the opposite direction, "did you ever find yourself alone with someone like that? You know, all promise and no delivery?"

Vic fished in the pocket of his jeans for his pickup keys. As he zapped the doors unlocked, his gaze shifted between Debbie Sue and Edwina. "Just once," he answered.

Something in the delivery of those two words

silenced Debbie Sue as well as Edwina for the ride home.

When Vic pulled up in front of Debbie Sue's house he volunteered to walk her to the door, but she declined.

"Just don't drive away until I get inside. No need for you to come in. Had fun, you two. Strange, but fun."

Debbie Sue blew them a kiss. As they pulled away, she waved one last time and pushed open the front door. She reached for the light switch. A hand covered hers. Before she could scream, pain exploded in the back of her head and her own lights went out.

Thirteen

Debbie Sue awoke disoriented and confused, with a dull pain in the back of her head. Her head felt cold. She reached to touch the tender spot and was surprised to feel an ice pack. "Sonofabitch—what the hell—where—"

"Oh thank God, you're alive. Lie still, don't move. I am sooo sorry," Eugene/Janine blabbed on. "I had no idea I had that kind of strength. You surprised me when you came in. I only wanted to stun you. Are you okay?"

The events of the evening began to unfold in Debbie Sue's crimped brain. She took note that she was lying on the floor, with a pillow under her head and her horse-design afghan across her body.

She twisted in the direction of the voice, and, despite the fact that she'd had the snot knocked out of her, she was taken aback by what she saw.

Eugene/Janine was dressed like a Ninja—black

running shoes, black sweatpants, and a black turtleneck top. He had removed the long wig but hadn't removed the stage make-up, the red lacquered nails or the four-inch chandelier rhinestone earrings.

"*I* surprised *you*?" She made an attempt to creak from the floor to the sofa and saw a gun in her attacker's hand.

"Don't move or I'll hurt you," her assailant warned.

"You've already hurt me, you little shit."

"Oh dear, I had this speech so well rehearsed. Now you've thrown me off. Give me a second." He cleared his throat as if auditioning for a part. "I got your little message. I'm not meeting you anywhere and you're not giving that tape to anyone but me. If you don't want to cooperate, maybe I'll have to make a call on your mother or your horse."

Under other circumstances Debbie Sue might have been terrified by the appearance of the intruder, the gun, and the warning, but her head hurt and it was hard to be too afraid of someone rehearsing a speech meant to instill terror in her heart while she watched. Still, she didn't want to underestimate him.

"Answer some questions for me first," she said. "Do you really think you're going to enjoy money you got at the expense of another person's life?"

Eugene/Janine gasped. "I've already told you, I didn't kill Pearl Ann. Just the thought of it—" He closed his eyes and shivered. "All that blood and . . . stuff. I can't even swat a fly. Are you sure you're okay? Can I get you something?"

For the first time Debbie Sue began to consider that he couldn't have murdered Pearl Ann, and he didn't have it in him to shoot *anybody*. She relaxed a little. "Okay, let's say I believe you. Why are you doing this? Why are you so afraid of the tape?"

His eyes teared and he began to sniffle. "I've worked for the Carrutherses since I left college. I have deep respect for all of them. They've treated me and the other employees in exemplary fashion." Debbie Sue reached for a Kleenex from the end table and handed it to him. He dabbed at the corner of one eye. "Oh dear, my mascara's running."

"You should use waterproof. Maybelline's the best. Finish your story."

"I *did not* respect or even like Pearl Ann. She was a greedy gold-digger. Why, Harley did everything in the world to make her happy. If I had someone who treated me just half . . ." His voice began to trail off, and Debbie Sue feared he might break into sobs.

He gathered himself and went on. "Excuse me, I'm trying not to be so emotional, but I've had one of those days when absolutely everything goes wrong. I've screwed up my entire life, and I can't seem to figure out how to stop this avalanche of despair closing in on me."

Avalanche of despair closing in on me. She had to remember that one for her mom. She fought the urge to lean forward and pat the knee of the man who had knocked her unconscious and was now holding a gun on her.

"When Pearl Ann approached me about helping her put back a little nest egg, I just couldn't resist the money. I'm so ashamed. The Carrutherses were so good to me."

"I can see where you'd be tempted. Five thousand dollars a month is a lot of money to anyone, but can we clear up one thing?"

Eugene/Janine looked up at her with a quizzical expression.

"Pearl Ann told me part of the payoff was sleeping with you."

He sprang from his seat as if he had been goosed. "That cheap, overdressed, over-made-up tramp. Why, the very thought makes me want to just put this gun to my head. I swear it does. How dare she besmirch my reputation."

"Calm down, Eugene. At this point, I don't think your reputation is what's at stake here."

"You're right." He dropped to the couch. "Oh God, what a mess I've made." He laid the gun on the cushion, hid his face in his hands, and burst into tears. Debbie Sue scooted closer and put her arms around him, patting his shoulders and saying an occasional there, there.

With her free hand she picked up the gun. Its featherlike weight told her it couldn't be real. Had to be a stage prop. On closer examination she saw it was plastic.

Her only suspect was no killer. *Fuck!* Now *she* felt like crying.

"The worst part of this whole thing, Debbie Sue, uh, may I call you Debbie Sue?"

She flipped up a palm and shot a glance at the ceiling. "Sure, why not."

"The worst part is—do you have another tissue? I hate it when my mascara runs."

Debbie Sue plucked a bouquet of tissues from the box and handed them over. "What's the worst part?"

He blew his nose with a loud snort. "I didn't stop with hiding the five thousand a month from Mr. Carruthers. I embezzled the nest egg for myself. That tape will start an investigation, and I'll end up in jail for embezzlement or a murder I didn't commit." He began to sob again.

"There, there," Debbie Sue said again and patted his shoulder. She couldn't keep from wondering just how much money Eugene/Janine had stolen.

"I'm too pretty to go to jail," he wailed. "I have delicate features. I don't want to end up as someone's prison bitch. I have a Ph.D. in finance from SMU, forgodsake." He placed a fist against his mouth and bit down on his knuckles.

"Give the money back. And what you can't give back, Harley will probably let you pay back. Don't you think that's worth a try?"

"It's gone. Not a cent is left."

"All of it? I mean, we must be talking thousands here."

"All of it. I've given it to a team of surgeons, the best money can buy, in Las Vegas. I'm going, or I *was* going to have a sex change operation."

"No shit?" It was all Debbie Sue could think of to mutter.

"Yes. I've known for as long as I can remember I was trapped in the wrong body. Can you imagine what it's like walking around as the wrong sex? It is hell, a living nightmare. I've spent my whole life in love with men I can't possibly have."

"Well, honey, who hasn't? I mean, really."

"When I saw the financial opportunity, I couldn't resist it. It's not like I really hurt anyone." Eugene/Janine burst into great gulps of weeping. "Damn these hormones. I've been taking hormone shots for weeks now preparing for the surgery. I cry all the time, and when I'm not crying, I'm eating. I'm not so sure being a woman is such a great idea after all. Oh, my life is crap."

If the scenario were not so tragic Debbie Sue could have burst into laughter. "Just so you'll know, I caught your show tonight at Kisses Lounge, and I thought you were terrific."

"You did? You thought the show was good? Do you think they'd like me in Las Vegas?"

"Why not? You knocked everyone out at Kisses, and you looked stunning."

"Really? You're not just saying that? You didn't

think I went a little overboard on the eye shadow?"

"It worked great under the lights."

"The hair, you didn't think the hair was too big? I could get another—"

"The hair was fabulous and the dress was to die for."

"You're just so nice to say such sweet things. You know, my mom made that dress."

"Get out."

"No, *you* get out." The two fell against each other in laughter, like old college roommates.

"Seriously," Debbie Sue said, "you need to come by the salon and let us do your colors for you. With your blue eyes and fair complexion—"

"Debbie Sue, are you in there?" The voice was Edwina's and she was yelling and pounding on the front door. "Debbie Sue, if you don't answer me, Vic's fixin' to tear this door off of its hinges. Debbie Sue, are you all right?"

"Ed, I'm okay," she shouted to the closed door, then turned to Eugene/Janine. "You better scram. Go out the back while I keep Ed and Vic busy. Trust me, you don't want to mess with either one of them. Vic's got a *real* gun. He knows how to shoot, and Ed will tear your arm off and beat you with it."

"Oh my gracious." Eugene/Janine covered his mouth with his fingers. "No offense, sweetie, but maybe you should find some new friends." He stood. "You're right. I'd better dash. Thanks so much. You're such a lamb. I'm so sorry I hit you. Oh, about the tape . . ."

"Don't worry. There never was a tape. Or a file. I only told you that to get your attention."

"Why you little hustler. You're quite the tease, aren't you? I could get really angry at you if I didn't feel like I've found a new friend." Eugene/Janine made kissing sounds in her direction and headed for the patio door leading to the backyard.

As soon as he was out of sight, Debbie Sue went to the front door and opened it. Edwina and Vic stumbled through.

"Where is he? Where'd he go?" Edwina pushed past her carrying a flowerpot of dead begonias from the front porch, poised to whack somebody. "Are you all right?"

"What are you doing here?"

"Your neighbor Mrs. Sanders called us and said she saw a man or a woman, she couldn't be sure, holding you at gunpoint. Why are you hanging on to an ice pack? Are you hurt?"

"I'm fine. Eugene Grubbs was here. I accidentally hit my head. Things are fine now. He didn't hurt me."

"See, Vic? I told you it wasn't necessary to call Buddy."

Oh no! "You called Buddy? Why would you do that? I don't want to see him. I have nothing to say to him."

"You have nothing to say to who?" Buddy entered the room in full professional mode. He looked around the room, his deep brown eyes taking everything in, his hand resting on the pistol riding on his belt. One eyebrow climbed up his forehead at the sight of the pot in Edwina's hand.

She looked down at the brown dried plant, too. "This needs water. I was just bringing it in to give it a drink."

Buddy strode toward the patio door Eugene had left open a few inches. Before reaching it, he stopped, bent over, and picked up something lying on the floor. He turned back to them, dangling a glittery long earring between his thumb and finger. "This belong to anyone here?"

Vic stood by, no expression at all, chewing on a toothpick. Edwina and Debbie Sue spoke in unison. "It's mine."

Buddy's eyes shifted between them. "So which is it?"

"It's hers," Debbie Sue and Edwina said in harmony and pointed at each other.

Buddy's fists jammed against his belt. "Okay, you two, I'm in no mood to play games. I want to know what's going on here. Debbie Sue, are you all right? I got a report a man and a woman were holding a gun on you. I want to know who and why?"

"It's a misunderstanding. You can see I'm fine. There was no gun. It was a hair dryer. I was fixin' a friend's hair."

"But your neighbor—"

"Mrs. Sanders is blind as a bat. Last Wednesday night she watched her aquarium for an hour before she realized it wasn't the TV."

Edwina flipped a wrist at Buddy. "Yeah, she's failed the eye exam at the DMV the last five times she's gone to get her driver's license renewed."

Debbie Sue could see Buddy wasn't buying it. His posture showed no hint of muscles loosening.

"Okay, that's enough," Vic said. "I'm not letting this go any further." He fished a small piece of notepaper from his jeans pocket and handed it to Buddy. "Here's the name, address, and phone number of the man who was here this evening. This is probably the second time he's been here. The first time he broke in and trashed Debbie Sue's house. I'm not sure what happened tonight."

Every drop of blood in Debbie Sue's body drained to her feet. She forgot her anger and that Buddy had hurt her heart. She forgot he was marrying the schoolteacher from Odessa. Truth be known, she'd come close to forgetting her name. She was a wreck.

Buddy studied the name on the notepaper for what seemed like an eternity. Debbie Sue could see he was so mad his hands were trembling. He folded the note and slid it into his shirt pocket, turning to face her. "Anything you want to tell me?"

"Eugene is a friend of mine. Since when did it become a crime to have a friend over? My house was broken into, but I don't know who did it. Nothing was taken. It was probably some kids looking for beer."

"Rest assured, all of you, I'm gonna get to the bottom of this. I'm gonna call the police chief in Midland and tell him to pick up this Eugene for questioning. If there's nothing to hide, then there's no problem, but if I find out you've kept something from me—"

"Oh and you'd be just the one to recognize someone keeping secrets, wouldn't you, *Sheriff* Overstreet." Debbie Sue glared up at him. "Yep, let's just all tell the secrets we're keeping."

"I don't have a clue what you're talking about, but I'm not finished with you." Buddy turned to Vic. "Thanks for the information. I appreciate your help." He touched his hat brim. "Ladies," he said, and strode into the night.

"Saaay," Edwina drawled, "that went real well."

Debbie Sue explained Eugene's visit to Edwina and Vic. By the end of the story, they were all in agreement that Eugene most likely had nothing to do with Pearl Ann's murder.

The moment the friends drove away from her house, Debbie Sue called Eugene and warned him he would soon be picked up by the Midland police. "Just stick with the story that we're friends and I was doing your hair." Debbie Sue pictured Eugene's bald head and bit down on her lip. "Believe me, if you can carry this off, you'll be getting that surgery."

"Thank you so much for your faith in me. I don't know how I can ever repay you." He/she burst into sobs.

"I didn't even ask if you have an alibi for the night Pearl Ann was killed."

"I *do* have an alibi. I was performing at Kisses. I had three shows and didn't leave there until almost daylight. It'll be easy to check out. We had a full house that night."

"You'll have to lie to the sheriff about taking the money. Do you think you can manage that?"

"Oh, honey, my whole life is a lie. Did you say the sheriff, the Salt Lick sheriff? Is *that* who I'm going to be talking to? Oh honey, put the cuffs on and take me in. That man is gorgeous."

"That man is a chickenshit. And my ex-husband."

"Are you kidding me? Uh-oh, I see lights flashing. Oh dear, I see two men in uniform coming to my door. Guess I better go. Let's keep in touch, sweetie." He made an exaggerated sigh. "I'm ready for my close-up, Mr. DeMille."

Driving away from Debbie Sue's, Edwina sweet-talked Vic into stopping by Hogg's for a pint of ice cream. It had been a stressful evening, and she wanted a diversion before returning home. Four cars were ahead of them in the drive-through line, leaving them time to talk.

"What's your take, Poodle? Do you think Eugene had anything to do with Pearl Ann's murder?"

"He sure had the motive. That's a lot of money, but the guy is no killer. If he was, he would have taken Debbie Sue out instead of looking for the tapes. Removing her from the picture would ensure that no one would know."

Taken Debbie Sue out? The gravity of those words struck Edwina hard. What in the hell had she and Debbie Sue been thinking, trying to find a murderer? Godalmighty, she couldn't find the remote control half the time. With Eugene/Janine being cleared, it pretty much put them out of the bounty-hunting business. That was fine with her. Nothing was worth one of them getting killed.

The next morning Buddy drove to Midland and interrogated Eugene Grubbs for two hours. He felt like a bully. The accountant was no bigger than a bar of soap after a hard day's washing. When Debbie Sue had first said she was doing a friend's hair, Buddy hadn't believed her, but he did believe she could have been doing the guy's, er, the girl's, uh . . . well, makeup.

Eugene was honest and upfront about the animosity he felt for Pearl Ann. He had an explanation for the sudden departure from his employment and the visit to Debbie Sue's house. When the call came in from the manager of Kisses verifying that Eugene had performed on stage the evening in question, Buddy had no choice but to erase him from the list of suspects.

"Say, Sheriff Overstreet," Eugene said as Buddy departed. "You should come by the club and catch my show sometime."

"Yeah, well, I don't get to Midland—"

"I'll do a special number just for you. Got a request?"

"Yeah, I do, Eugene. How about, 'From Now On, All My Friends Are Gonna Be Strangers'?"

"Ooohh, Merle Haggard. You've got it, cowboy." Eugene looked up at him like a bull yearling turned loose in a herd of heifers. "That and anything else you want, cowboy."

Buddy wasn't sure, but he thought Eugene batted his eyelashes.

Fourteen

Debbie Sue came to semiconsciousness the next morning with memories of waking beside Buddy drifting through her mind. When they had been married, mornings had always been special. She would snuggle in close to him, he would wrap his strong arms around her, and even if they didn't make love, they would hold each other until they both were fully awake.

Her arm flopped over to the empty opposite side of the bed and found the unused pillow. Whispering his name, she pressed the pillow to her body. She imagined her hand wrapping around his hard, thick penis, teasing him awake with her thumb and hearing his soft groan. She imagined his work-hardened hands kneading her bottom and her sliding her leg across his belly. She shifted positions, waiting for the next part of the vignette when he would pull her astraddle him and . . . ohdeargod. She had forgotten how Buddy felt inside her. She could remember his intense eyes locked on hers, remember his outcry when he came and her own earth-shaking orgasms, but she couldn't remember how he *felt*.

She opened her eyes and sat up in her misery, wiping away tears with the corner of the bed-sheet. Why couldn't someone magically appear and give her the date and time that Buddy Over-street would no longer haunt her dreams? If she knew that five, ten years from today, his memory wouldn't arouse her body or stir emotions in her heart, she would buck up and endure until that date. It was the daily ache that left her depleted, the fear that this pain might never end, that it had become part of her unchosen destiny.

The thought of him waking beside Kathy Bozo and doing with her what Debbie Sue had just imagined sent a pain so sharp through her brain, she couldn't bear to lie in bed any longer. Well, she simply wouldn't allow herself to think about it, she told herself in the bathroom mirror. She would fill her head with all forms of minutiae. If she needed to whistle "Dixie" and tap dance, she would do that, too. Whatever it took. Her heart couldn't stand this overload of grief.

In keeping with that strategy, she stopped at a produce stand a family of migrant workers had set up on the side of the road between her house and the salon and bought a couple of pumpkins to carve into jack-o'-lanterns.

Then she made her way to the Kwik-Stop a

block from the salon. With Eugene Grubbs cleared of the murder of Pearl Ann, she had decided she had better resort to Plan B for her retirement portfolio: lottery tickets. Saturday night's pot was up to twenty-four million. A win, coupled with a date with Quint Matthews, wouldn't be a bad way to end the week, especially considering the week's beginning had been a chapter right out of a Stephen King novel.

At the salon, lifting the pumpkins out of her pickup bed and positioning one under each arm, she kicked open the front door, ready for another day of glitz and glamour. The jingly bells on the doorknob whacked the door with a vengeance.

Under Edwina's watchful but wary eye, she placed the pumpkins at her work station, then marched to the back of the salon. She donned her smock and returned to the front. "Ed, you and I are fixin' to do some carving."

Edwina inhaled a puff of smoke and shifted her weight from one leg to the other. "A few days ago you were crying your eyes out. Yesterday you were assaulted by a cross-dressing fruit, and today you want to carve vegetables. You're either handling things really well or you've gone clear off the deep end. Which is it?"

"Eugene is not a fruit, he's a woman trapped in a man's body, Ed. A pumpkin is a fruit, not a vegetable. Now, listen carefully. I cannot, I *will* not, talk or think about Buddy and Kathy Bozo. If I do, I'll lose my mind. Do you want to see me lose my

mind, Ed? Is that what you want? Are you interested in helping me carve these friggin' pumpkins
or not?"

"Okay, okay. I woke up this morning with a
driving urge for a horticulture lesson. You think I
can work miracles with hair? Wait 'til you see
what I can do with *fruit*. I haven't done one of
these since my kids were little."

"It'll be fun. When I was in high school a bunch
of us would ride out to Fiddler's Road on Halloween night. The guys would build a big fire and
we would all sit around telling horror stories
while we carved jack-o'-lanterns. Times were so
simple then. Buddy would help me with my
pumpkin because he always had a sharp knife
and—"

Before she knew what hit her, Debbie Sue was
crying. Buddy had been a part of those Halloween
festivities for two of her high school years. How
do you stop thinking about someone who penetrates every memory you've stored in the past seventeen of your twenty-eight years?

Edwina came over and smoothed strands of
hair from Debbie Sue's forehead. "I know you
don't want to talk about him, but since you're already crying, there's something important I have
to ask."

"What?"

"Vic feels real bad about calling Buddy into that
situation last night. He wouldn't do anything to
upset you, but he thought the report of someone

holding a gun on you was no joking matter. He hopes you're not mad at him."

"No, I'm not mad at Vic. Please tell him being mad at him never even entered my mind." Debbie Sue pulled herself together.

"Good, that's a relief. We're both looking forward to having you and Quint over Saturday night."

"Do you think Vic will like Quint?" Debbie Sue plucked a Kleenex from a box on the end of the payout counter and dabbed her eyes.

"Hell's bells, hon, you know Vic. He pretty much treats everyone the same. He thinks the world of you, and if Quint is someone important to you, then Vic will treat him as such."

Debbie Sue had to admit, at this point Quint *was* important to her. He could be holding the key to her future. Or she could be holding the winning lottery ticket. Either way, the gamble held comparable odds.

Buddy stopped in the middle of the main street to allow a carload of teenagers to pass. Jaywalking wasn't a concern in Salt Lick. To find a crosswalk, you'd have to drive clear to Odessa. The driver honked and all the teens shouted and waved. Buddy smiled and tugged at his hat brim.

Being a teenager—high school homecoming, football games, Halloween—man, what a great time that had been. The teenage problems that had been typical then seemed small and insignificant compared with what he faced now. He wondered if, in twenty years, he would feel the same way about his current predicament. Something, probably the dull headache that had not eased up since Pearl Ann's body was found, told him her murder would never be small and insignificant, but his most fervent prayer was that it didn't remain unsolved.

Buddy thought back on this morning's interrogation of Eugene Grubbs. If the man's alibi hadn't checked out, Buddy would have been tempted to arrest him on the spot and bring Debbie Sue in on general principle. She hadn't told him the truth about her relationship with Eugene. Buddy had no proof to back up his gut feeling, but the fact that Eugene was Pearl Ann's accountant smelled of trouble. Be it fornication or cooking the books, there wasn't a better dealer at the table than Pearl Ann had been.

Thinking about the victim made him remember there would be no get-together this year at the Carruthers party barn following the football game, a first in a good number of years. One year he remembered in particular when homecoming fell on a Halloween weekend, Harley announced the party would be a masquerade ball. Debbie Sue and he hadn't been married long, and he wasn't sheriff. Partying had been more fun when he was only a law-abiding citizen and not the law.

Debbie Sue was pregnant and couldn't drink alcohol, but they hadn't needed booze to have fun.

They had gone to the party as a football player and a cheerleader, only they added a twist. *She* dressed up like the football player and *he* the cheerleader. He took a lot of teasing about his hairy legs and the enormous prosthetic boobs that kept traveling from the front of his sweater to his shoulder blades. They both had laughed until they cried. She had gone a little overboard in painting him up with eye shadow and gluing on false eyelashes. The final touch had been the addition of a wig of long red—

Buddy stopped dead in his tracks. He felt as if someone had just put a fist in his gut. *Good Lord. The red wig.*

The sudden recognition of the elusive redhead nearly toppled him. Retracing his steps, he crossed the street and hot-footed to the Tahoe. A glance at his watch told him she should be home in twenty minutes, providing she didn't have a rendezvous planned with Harley. He drove to his office, grabbed some notes off his desk, and headed out, intending to be there when she pulled up.

Debbie Sue carved on her pumpkin between customers. She cut an opening in the top and scooped out the insides, all the while making sounds and exclamations of disgust. She had forgotten what a yucky job pumpkin carving was. Edwina dove into the project wholeheartedly. She chose painting a face over carving one and with the cosmetics on hand, was able to produce a jack-o'-lantern face worthy of a prize.

Just as they were admiring their artwork, the Christmas bells on the front door jangled and Eugene/Janine entered with the subtlety of a wild bucking horse. He/she was wearing designer clothes with all the accessories and looked every bit the part of a rich, well-kept woman.

"Eugene! I didn't know if I'd ever see you again. You look fabulous." Debbie Sue rushed over to meet him and kissed air beside his cheek.

"I just couldn't leave without saying good-bye," he said.

"Ed, c'mere. I want you to meet someone. Eugene, this is one of my best friends in the world, Edwina. We all call her Ed."

Edwina advanced slowly as she and Eugene/Janine sized each other up.

Eugene/Janine let out a gasp of recognition. "Well, my stars. If it isn't the Pizza Slut."

"I'm surprised you remembered me. We met only the once." Edwina actually blushed. Debbie Sue couldn't believe her eyes.

"Why, how could I not remember you? You have one of the most original looks around. I haven't seen anyone wear cat-eye glasses with rhinestones in years. You are truly one of a kind."

Debbie Sue glanced at Edwina, who today was wearing black and orange striped leggings, a black oversized sweater, and black high-heeled boots to her ankles. In addition, she had on orange glass bead earrings the diameter of a Dr. Pepper can and a black and orange cha-cha bracelet. Debbie Sue had become so accustomed to Edwina's colorful dress, she scarcely noticed it anymore.

"That's true enough," Edwina said.

"You're leaving?" Debbie Sue asked Eugene/Janine.

"Oh, sweetie, I'm on my way to Las Vegas. To be born again."

"I've heard people give a lot of reasons for going to Vegas," Edwina said, "but being born again wasn't one of them."

"I'll explain it later, Ed," Debbie Sue said.

"Oh my goodness. Who did the makeup on the pumpkin?"

Edwina spoke up. "That would be me."

"Oh my heavens, girl, you are so good. You certainly answered your calling as an artiste, didn't you?"

Debbie Sue broke in. "So Eugene, I guess everything went okay with the questioning by the sheriff. You're cleared?"

"Oh yes. I just left Sheriff Overstreet about four hours ago. My alibi was airtight. Kind of a shame, too. I wouldn't have minded spending a little more time with that luscious man. For whatever reason you two broke up, get it behind you, girl. That man is a keeper."

"That man is a—"

"Now listen to me, Debbie Sue, I've had more experience with men than both of you. Well"—he hesitated, looking in Edwina's direction—"maybe not *both* of you, but I know a real gentleman when I meet one. I've heard every homophobic remark in the book, and Sheriff Overstreet treated me with the utmost courtesy. Believe me, in this cowboy corner of the world, he is a rarity."

Debbie Sue was anxious to change the subject. She didn't want to talk about Buddy and she sure as hell didn't want to talk about his outstanding virtues. "You left one of your earrings at my house. I wish I had known I'd be seeing you. I would've brought it to the salon today."

"Don't worry about it. When I get settled in Vegas I'll send you my address and you can mail it to me. I guess I'd better go. I'm flying out tonight at seven forty-five. I just wanted to thank you again. Wish me luck?"

"You know I do."

He opened the door, then stopped and turned back. "Debbie Sue, you were right about paying Harley back. I will, as soon as I become a star. Or maybe I'll fall in love with a rich man."

"Wow," Edwina said when he/she had left. She dug a cigarette out of her pack at the payout station. "He's happier than a hog sleeping in the sunshine."

"Yeah," Debbie Sue muttered. "He did steal the money. I feel guilty. Should we tell somebody?"

"The money was gone a long time ago. At this point, what difference does it make whose saddlebags it's in?"

"But, Ed—"

"Shh."

She wasn't at home as Buddy had hoped. Not wanting her to see the Tahoe, he circled the block a couple of times and waited a safe distance from the house. Nothing about this investigation had gone by the book, but he was determined to fit at least one piece of the puzzle into place.

Approximately thirty minutes later her Camry approached. As soon as she disappeared into the house, he pulled into the driveway, took a deep breath, and slid out of the Tahoe. Walking up to the porch, he straightened his holster, removed his hat and punched the doorbell. The woman who opened the door did a poor job hiding her startled expression.

Buddy nodded. "Carol Jean, may I have a few moments of your time?"

He saw her quick intake of breath. "Has something happened to Mom or Dad?"

"No, nothing like that. I'm here in a professional role to ask you some questions."

"Professional role? Questions? About what?"

"I've talked to Harley several times about circumstances surrounding Pearl Ann's—"

"Circumstances surrounding—I'm sorry to be

so dense, but I don't understand. Harley's not in some kind of trouble, is he?"

"No. Listen, can I come in for a minute?"

"Oh, of course. I'm so sorry to be so rude." She stepped back and allowed him entry into her living room. "Please sit down." She led him toward her sofa. "Here, let me take your hat. Can I—"

He hung on to his hat, holding it against his stomach. "I'm not gonna be here long. Look, Harley submitted to a lie detector test and passed, but he won't give me the name of the woman he was with the night Pearl Ann was murdered. I need to know who the woman is and why he's trying to protect her."

"I don't see how I can be of any help. I don't know anything about Harley's personal life." Her enormous sky blue eyes grew even larger.

"You don't?"

"Why, no. I'm pretty low on the flow chart at CO&G, so to speak. I hardly ever see Harley. I answer to several people who may eventually answer to him, but I—" She smiled, showing a dimple. "Could I offer you something to drink? I've got everything from beer to Kool-Aid. How are you, Buddy? Are you still seeing that teacher from Midland? Or was it Odessa?"

She was talking faster than he had ever heard her, so he patted the air with his palm to calm her down. "Look, Carol Jean, we go a long way back. You stood up with Debbie Sue at our wedding. I'll

never forget the song you sang at our baby's funeral service. I'm not gonna play games with you.
I've followed Harley a couple of times when he
left his building and took a redhead to his condo.
I'm thinking the redhead is you."

Her eyelids flew open even wider. "Buddy, you
know I date a different guy every three months.
Once men figure out I don't put out, they dump
me. Up until a couple of weeks ago, Harley was a
married man."

"Maybe so, but I know his marriage to Pearl
Ann wasn't made in heaven. It wouldn't surprise
me to hear she cheated on him during their honeymoon. And if she didn't, it wasn't long afterward.
I'm not passing judgment. I've talked to every person in this town and beyond about the murder.
The redhead is the only one I've missed."

Tears suddenly welled in her eyes. She sank to a
chair and ducked her chin. "I'm so ashamed. You
mustn't misunderstand about Harley. He didn't
care who knew we were seeing each other. It was
me who made him lie. He was trying to protect
me." She looked up at him with troubled eyes.
"You know my folks. They would be so humiliated if they knew I had been seeing a married
man, especially Harley."

Buddy took a seat on one end of the sofa and
laid his hat on a sofa cushion beside him. This
could be a long, fruitful conversation. "They don't
care for Harley?"

"It's not that they don't care for him. But he has

a reputation for prowling around and they wouldn't want me to be included as one of the prowlees. They have higher ambitions for me, I guess."

"Have long have you and Harley been seeing each other?"

"A little over a year. He's so different from what people think. Pearl Ann told such awful stories about him, and we all believed her." She hunched forward, her fingers tightly interlocked. "Why do you suppose we believed her?"

"I don't know, Carol Jean, I really don't." He leaned forward, too, resting his elbows on his knees. "Can you tell me what happened? Start with the night of the murder."

She shuddered and wrapped her arms around herself as if she felt a sudden cold wind. "I'll never get used to hearing that word linked with Pearl Ann." She looked off into the distance as if she were seeing an instant replay. "He and I left the office about seven that evening. We always waited until no one was around or we would take off before everyone started leaving for the day."

She stood up and began to pace. "The wig was my idea. It's the same one you wore to the Halloween party that year you and Debbie Sue . . . Well, anyway, we went to the condo and I fixed supper for the two of us. It's such a novelty to him to have a woman other than a Mexican cook make a meal for him. The first time I did he was astonished. I think I fell in love with him that night."

She returned to her chair and sat down again, appearing to be less agitated. "His brother Justin—he and I are the only ones who have Harley's cell phone number—called early the morning Pearl Ann was found and told Harley."

Buddy had called the Salt Lick ranch house that morning and spoken to Justin, who assured him he knew how to reach Harley and would do so immediately.

"So Harley was with you the entire evening?"

"Yes. We didn't go out. We watched TV and read. Some evenings we just sat on the couch and talked all night long. You know how that is, don't you?"

Only too well. Buddy could see that Carol Jean was deeply in love with Harley, and judging from the reaction he had received from Harley when he questioned him, the feeling was mutual.

"They had no marriage. I'm not being the naive other woman. I've heard many conversations between the two of them. She didn't care what he did and he didn't care what she did, either. So many infidelities killed anything he felt. He actually hoped she'd meet someone and run off with him. He thought that would have solved his problems. I think she was too smart to do that. She liked having money and being named Carruthers."

"You've never heard Harley mention anyone he thinks could have killed her?"

"He said the list is so long it would probably never be solved. Honestly, I think she finally met up with someone a little meaner than she was. I'll always believe she told someone to kiss off one time too many." Her jaw tightened. "I only wish I did have a name," she said with more vehemence than Buddy had ever heard from her. "I wish this were all over and behind us. If Pearl Ann's murder goes unsolved, the stigma will hang over Harley's head forever. And mine."

Buddy didn't doubt it. A story as juicy as Harley and Carol Jean's would travel through Salt Lick faster than bad news at a church social. "I have one more question, Carol Jean. Why didn't Harley just get a divorce?"

"Being married to Pearl Ann didn't keep him from doing what he wanted to until he met me. I believe he would have divorced her eventually."

They sat in silence for a minute or more. Finally Carol Jean spoke in her childlike voice. "Being in love can be both a blessing and a curse, can't it?"

Buddy only nodded. She had said it all. There was no need for words from him.

Fifteen

Buddy plopped onto the seat behind the Tahoe's steering wheel. The weeks of twenty-four-hour days wondering and speculating, theorizing and deducting had taken its toll.

With no other leads and no other suspects he was stopped as surely as a wagon with a broken wheel. He sat with his fingers on the key, just a motion away from turning the ignition. *What now? Start over? Throw in the towel, call the Rangers and turn the case over to them, admit I can't solve Pearl Ann's murder?*

On a sigh, he started up the Tahoe. What he needed most was a decent night's sleep. Maybe he could manage that much now that he knew the redhead's identity. No, he couldn't give up. Tomorrow he would go at it again with a rested mind. It would take more than a dearth of clues and suspects and nowhere else to turn to make him quit.

He pulled into the uncovered parking space near his small upstairs apartment and clomped up the stairs, the mystery a lead weight on his shoulders. Inside he dropped his keys in an empty ceramic bowl adorning the center of the dining table, walked over and turned on the air conditioner perched in one of the living room windows. On the end of the kitchen counter, the red signal on his answering machine flashed persistently. He groaned, pressed the button, and listened to a computer-generated voice while unbuttoning his shirtsleeves. "You have seven messages."

Seven. He had spent the week talking to people, even some he usually avoided. How could there be seven people he had missed?

First things first. He retrieved a cold Coors from the refrigerator, pried off his boots, and sat down to hear what he hoped was something new.

The first call was from his mom, from somewhere up north. Devastated by the death of his dad, she had been Buddy's financial responsibility for four years following his dad's sudden death. When she remarried a high school boyfriend from Abilene, Buddy approved. Since their marriage, the two traveled the country in their RV. She called from time to time to give their location and to tell Buddy she loved him.

He said, "I love you too, Mom," to the answering machine and pushed the button for the next message. Two calls from telemarketers, two hang-ups, a quick "Call me" from Kathy.

The last message chased his exhaustion right out the door.

At first he thought the caller must be one of his old friends from his younger days, and he replayed it. There was the unmistakable sound of voices and Tejano music in the background. Bar sounds. He heard what he suspected was the fumbling of the receiver.

"Shit," somebody muttered. Then the caller was talking. "Hey . . . hey, Sheriff Overstreet? I wanna tell you something." The deep male voice slurred, but the touch of Spanish was unmistakable. "I luffed Pearl. She luffed me, too. She was sooo beautiful. . . . Need to tell somebody I'm sorry. I gafe her a Texas bracelet and—"

"Please deposit two dollars and twenty-five cents for one minute," a computerized female voice said.

By now Buddy was on his feet, hovered over the answering machine. He heard more fumbling and swearing, then the line went dead. "Goddammit!" He slammed his palm on the counter. He did nothing for a minute but breathe hard and cuss himself for not having subscribed to caller ID. The machine told him the call had been made at two o'clock in the afternoon, but not from where.

Buddy was certain he had never heard the caller's voice. Until the mention of the bracelet, he thought it might be a crank call, but only three people knew about the missing bracelet—himself, Harley, and Pearl Ann's killer.

The TV remote was in Debbie Sue's hand, but her mind was at Midland Airport. She looked at the clock above her TV. Seven twenty-five, Eugene/ Janine would be boarding soon for his/her trip to Vegas and a new life.

A new life. Debbie Sue envied anyone who had found the path to a new life. And the money to take them there. She felt lonely and thought of calling her mom. Nah. A heart-to-heart would only keep her mother awake all night. Edwina? Nope. Edwina's wisecracks wouldn't cheer her up tonight. Besides, Edwina was probably snuggled up to Vic, and why ruin a good thing someone else had going?

Then she thought of a voice she hadn't heard in a while.

Debbie Sue had strict telephone etiquette. She never called anyone after ten o'clock in the evening and she never allowed a phone to ring more than four times. An answering machine would pick up by then and if not, well, the conversation wasn't meant to be. Just as she was about to hang up, her old friend's soft voice with its Texas twang came on the line with a sweet hello.

"C. J., did I bother you? I was ready to hang up."

"Heavens no, I was running a bubble bath. How have you been?"

C. J. had always reminded Debbie Sue of a kitten. Everything about her was delicate and soft. Even her voice sounded like a kitten's mew. "Oh, you know. Same old, same old. Sometimes blond, sometimes red, sometimes a permanent wave."

"It's eerie that you called. I was just thinking about you."

Debbie Sue smiled. When they were teenagers, she and C. J. had often been awed that they shared the same thoughts at the same time. "Same wavelength, remember? If I called every time I thought about you I'd be on the phone all day."

"Oh, I know. I haven't been a very good friend lately. I don't even know what's going on in your life, I've been so absorbed in keeping my own on track."

Debbie Sue thought she heard a rueful tone. "Well, that sounds intriguing. You've *always* had your life on track. Since we were little kids you were on track and *I* was running *up* the track barely ahead of the speeding train."

C. J. laughed. "You managed to stay ahead of it, though. I'm afraid this time it's me who's running up the track. In fact, I feel like I've just been mowed down by that locomotive."

This kind of talk was uncharacteristic of C. J., the eternal optimist. C. J. had pulled Debbie Sue out of a quagmire of anxiety too many times to count. Having the tables turned left Debbie Sue speechless. Her reason for calling seemed selfish and petty now. It was clear that her friend was in need also. "C. J., what's up? Is there anything I can help you with? Do you want me to just listen?"

"Oh, Debbie Sue, I've done something I'm so ashamed of. Everyone in town will know about it soon. You know how Salt Lick is. I don't know how I'm going to handle the rumors, the backbiting and stares."

Debbie Sue allowed a moment of silence for C. J. to continue, but no words came from the receiver. "So what is this terrible thing you've done? Let me guess. You didn't take a book back to the library on time."

More silence, except for the sound of an occasional sniffle.

"I'm sorry. Don't mind me. You know I have to make a smart-ass remark about everything. I didn't mean to hurt your feelings. Are you still there?"

"Buddy just left my house, and I told him something I swore I would never tell another living soul. I won't be able to hold my head up around here. Once this gets out, Harley's life and mine will be as good as over."

"Buddy? Harley? C. J., maybe you just better tell me—Motherofgod, don't say another word to anyone. We'll get you a good lawyer."

"What are you talking about? I don't need a lawyer."

"Are you sure? The combination of Buddy, Harley, and admitting a secret isn't a good sign these days."

"Debbie Sue Overstreet, if you will just give me a minute, I'll explain."

"Well, you said you'd done something awful. Sorry. Jumping to conclusions is the only exercise I get anymore. Why don't I just shut up and let you do all the talking. Now, plain and simple, what's up?"

C. J. filled Debbie Sue in on the events of the past year. She told her how Buddy had figured out that she was the mysterious redhead and had come to her house to talk to her earlier.

Debbie Sue was stunned. She had never known Carol Jean Anderson to step outside the box. The overdue library book would have been an adequate surprise, but what Debbie Sue had just heard was a bona fide shock. "Did Pearl Ann know?"

"No, she rarely saw or talked to Harley. The only thing she knew about their marriage was what she wanted out of it. I don't know what you think of Harley, but he truly is a wonderful man. A lot of bad things have been said about him, but they're not true. Despite everything that's happened, this past year has been the happiest of my life."

"Hey," Debbie Sue said softly, "you don't need to defend your man to me. I always took what Pearl Ann said about him with a grain of salt. I've known the Carruthers family all my life. We all have. They're good people. I don't like to judge a person unless I've seen them do something with my own two eyes."

"Thanks, I really appreciate that."

"As far as what people will be saying, just remember it'll only be until the next juicy story comes along. You haven't done anything most of them haven't done or wish they could. People know you, they know you're no home wrecker. More important than that, they know Harley had no home to be wrecked. The only person's happiness you need to worry about is your own."

A long pause. A longer bout of sniffling.

"So just how serious is it between you and Harley?"

"I want to wait a respectable amount of time and then we're getting married. I hope the murder will be solved and we won't have to worry about it the rest of our lives. He wants children as soon as possible. Can you see me as a mother, Debbie Sue?"

"I can't see you as anything but."

C. J.'s crying resumed. "It's been so hard not telling you or Edwina. Thank you so much. I really do feel better. I knew I just needed to hear you say it's all going to be okay."

"Well, that's because it is. You, Ed, and I have to get together soon. I'm being nice and supportive tonight but I can assure you we're going to grill you for details of this lurid year you've been living, you hussy."

C. J. laughed and made promises Debbie Sue

knew she didn't intend to keep. "You're sure you're okay with this?"

"Okay with one of my best friends becoming one of the richest women in Texas? Yeah, I'm okay with that."

After hanging up, Debbie Sue sat quietly, letting C. J.'s conversation sink in. Suddenly it all made sense. The long stretches of time when they wouldn't see her. The lame excuses she came up with for her scarcity. Diamond earrings the size of aspirin tablets. Once Edwina had even said perhaps C. J. was involved with a married man, but then they had laughed it off as just too preposterous for somebody as innocent as C. J.

It just goes to show, things aren't always what they seem.

By midmorning Buddy had tracked the number and location of the pay phone from which the guilt-ridden murderer had placed the call. Unfortunately, he had paid with cash instead of a calling card.

Buddy wrote down the information, thanked the operator, and hung up. The call had been placed from a bar in Dallas called Luna de Neón. The Neon Moon. He intended to go to Dallas. With any luck, Luna de Neón would be a hole-in-the-wall bar, one of those places where the bartender knows everyone who comes and goes. He knew the chances were slim, but less than twenty-four hours ago they had been nonexistent.

He called Harley and asked him to stop by his office and listen to the tape. Harley listened several times, but admitted he didn't recognize the caller. As Harley headed for the door, Buddy stopped him. "Harley, I had a long talk with Carol Jean last night. I know she's the woman you've been protecting."

Harley dropped to the seat of the straight-back chair in front of Buddy's desk. "Thank God, that much is over. I promised her I wouldn't tell anyone. I hope you can understand why we didn't want anyone to know about us."

"You should've come clean from the beginning. It would have made everything easier all the way around for both of us. There's nothing anybody could tell me that would make me think ill of Carol Jean."

"You're right. We're old friends, Buddy. I should have trusted you more . . . But I just love her so damn much and I don't want anything to hurt her."

"It would've hurt her a lot more if I'd wound up having to throw your butt in jail."

Harley looked at the ceiling and shook his head. "Women drive us to do dumb things, don't they? Did I hear you say you're going to Dallas tomorrow?"

"Yeah, but first I want to go out to your place with this tape and let your housekeepers listen. Maybe one of them overheard this guy before."

"Juanita and Gloria? Go ahead. Good idea." Harley rose to leave. "Tell me something, how did you figure out it was Carol? I thought we were being pretty careful."

"It was the red wig, Harley. I wore it one year to a Halloween party out at your place."

"Damned if you didn't."

With those few words Harley was gone.

In the afternoon Buddy drove out to the Flying C and found both of the Mexican domestic helpers at the Carruthers ranch. They agreed the voice was not one they knew. Buddy thanked them and returned to Salt Lick to make arrangements for a quick trip to Dallas.

As he passed Virginia Pratt's place he scanned the pasture for a glimpse of Rocket Man. As if the horse knew Buddy would be coming by, he was standing at the fence facing the highway. While in the motion of slowing and pulling over to the shoulder of the road, Buddy scolded himself because of the daunting tasks that lay before him and the time constraints. But he had to say hello to an old friend.

He climbed out of the pickup and walked up to the fence. Rocket Man nickered and sawed his head up and down. Buddy rubbed a hand down the horse's sleek neck. "Hey there, ol' pal. How you doin' this evening?" Rocket Man snorted and sniffed Buddy's pockets. "I don't have anything for you today. Your mama has spoiled you rotten." Buddy scratched the horse's ears. "She's mad at me again. Take care of her while I'm gone."

Returning to the Tahoe, he made a mental note to call on Virginia when he returned. He had been too busy to drop by of late, and he didn't want her to think he had forgotten about her.

On the way to town, he radioed the office. "Tanya, is Billy Don anywhere to be found?"

"Yessir. He's out front roping the fire hydrant. Want me to get him for you?"

God, he wished Billy Don wouldn't do that. Having the citizens of Salt Lick see the deputy with nothing better to do than practice roping didn't give the sheriff's office the air of professionalism and serious law enforcement Buddy would have liked.

Buddy had inherited Billy Don. He had been hired by the former sheriff right out of the oil fields. Buddy had to remind himself that Billy Don didn't see his job as a career. To him, the job of deputy brought him a considerably smaller paycheck than the one he had earned on a rough-necking crew, but he would be the first to admit the hours were better and the work was safer.

"No, just tell him to stick around. I want to talk to him when I get in. Shouldn't be more than twenty minutes."

The thought of leaving Billy Don in charge of the citizens of Salt Lick for more than a day was worrisome. The deputy was a good enough kid. His heart was in the right place, but his heart wasn't what worried Buddy. His *head* was what Buddy could never quite figure out the location of.

Billy Don managed to muddle through day by day when most of the calls into the sheriff's office involved family disturbances or drunkenness. With Buddy never more than a short distance away, he had always been able to undo Billy Don's bungling. But on a homecoming weekend, the town would be filled with revelers, and few of them would be sober.

A look of panic spread across his deputy's face when Buddy explained he would be out of town from early Saturday until Monday. "It's important that I make this trip to Dallas, Billy Don, and I need to know you can handle any situation that comes up while I'm gone."

"You can count on me, Sheriff. I won't do anything stupid like I've done before, neither."

If the statement was meant to be a cradle of comfort, it missed its mark. "There'll be a lot of people in town for the homecoming. Lots of parties and drinking. All you have to do is keep the peace. Make sure everybody's safe."

"Keep the peace. Make sure everybody's safe. Got it."

"I'll be around 'til tomorrow morning, but I plan on leaving before sunup. Is there anything I can help you with before then? Any questions?"

"Just a couple."

Buddy was relieved and impressed that Billy Don showed enough initiative to have inquiries. "Sure thing. What?"

"Where do you store the riot guns? And are you going to leave me any bullets?"

Buddy didn't dare blink. If he did, he might cry.

"There's not fixin' to be any riots and you're not gonna need to shoot anybody."

If the deputy survived 'til Monday, it would be a miracle.

Sixteen

Debbie Sue awoke Saturday morning after a marathon night of bizarre dreams and restlessness, the tangle of her bed linens evidence of the aerobic workout. The bottom fitted sheet lay piled on the floor. The top sheet was rolled in a ball and tucked into the folds of the bedspread. One pillow was at the foot of the bed, and her left foot was stuck into the other pillow cover, along with the pillow. The last time she had seen a bed this tossed was when—*stop it*!

Thinking of Buddy in *any* context had to end. Thinking of him *and* sex in the same thought was suicidal. Why in God's name did she have to wake up every morning thinking of a man she could no longer have?

She was a firm believer in the powers of the mind. She had a perfectly good brain, well conditioned. She would turn that old memory off and turn on a new one. C. J. and Harley—now *there* was something to think about.

C. J. had always had her pick of beaus. Three or four had proposed, but the petite blond hadn't even come close to accepting. Debbie Sue and Edwina had speculated many times on what it would take to capture C. J.'s heart. Now they knew.

They? Holy shit! Edwina didn't know about C. J. and Harley.

Debbie Sue glanced at the clock and wondered if she had time to call Edwina and tell her the big news. No, telling it in person would be better. She headed for the shower.

Half an hour later, having applied a scant amount of makeup, secured her hair with a large clip, and squeezed into jeans, T-shirt, and boots, she grabbed her purse and was on her way.

In the drive through town, she noted more activity than normal for a Saturday morning. The Steers, Salt Lick's six-man football team, were enjoying a winning season, which added to the number of alumni returning for homecoming.

Years ago, during oil's heyday, Salt Lick had been busy and bustling. These days most of the graduating youth left and didn't return, choosing instead jobs that had livable paychecks and fashionable addresses in Austin, Houston, and Dallas.

It was hard for Debbie Sue to imagine herself anywhere but here, but if she elected to go with

Quint on his whirlwind stops around the country, this time next year, she herself could be one of the former citizens returning for homecoming.

A powerful need she couldn't ignore hit her. She was starving. She thought about the sugar-laden offerings from the Kwik-Stop, but dismissed them when she remembered the delicious sausage biscuits served by Vic. She still had an hour before time to open the salon. She could go by Edwina's, tell her the latest news, and if she was lucky, she would be offered breakfast. Even if Vic wasn't in town, a piece of toast sounded better than high-calorie pastries. She made a sharp U-turn and sped toward Edwina's trailer.

There was only one way in and one way out of Edwina and Vic's cul-de-sac address. Debbie Sue had no choice but to drive by the garage apartment Buddy rented on the corner. She wasn't worried about running into him though. He would have left for his office at least two hours earlier.

The radio DJ announced the next classic tune was a favorite from Dolly Parton, "Old Flames Can't Hold a Candle to You." *Well, that's appropriate.* She reached for the volume knob, cranked it up and sang along . . .

And nearly zoomed right past Edwina's and Vic's street. She stomped the brake and yanked the steering wheel. Before she knew what happened, the pickup skidded and fishtailed. When it corrected itself and came to a stop, a white cloud of caliche dust and dirt hung in the air like fog. "OhmyGod! Shit!"

As the thick dust settled, she saw a person in front of Buddy's place, covered in fine white dust. "Oh, shit." The mystery person was bent over beside a black Mazda Miata, coughing and sputtering. It was—*yikes!*—Kathy Bozo-whatever.

Maybe she didn't notice me. Debbie Sue eased past the dust-covered car. She pulled up in front of Edwina's trailer and dashed to the front door. When it opened, she practically fell in on top of her friend.

"Hey," Edwina said, "what's going on? You being chased by somebody?"

"Quick, c'mere. I want you to see something." Debbie Sue rushed through the living room to the window, pulling Edwina with her. "See that woman?"

"That's a woman? She looks like one of those tribal people from Australia. What are they called? I got it on the tip of my tongue . . ."

"Aborigine."

"No, that's not it."

"Yes, it is. Dammit Ed, I didn't come over here to give you an anthropology lesson.

"Well, professor, what's so interesting about an albino coughing up a lung?" Edwina parted the curtains for a better look.

"That's Kathy Bozonowsky. The woman Buddy's gonna marry."

"What?" Edwina pushed Debbie Sue out of the way for a better look. "What happened to her?"

"I turned the corner too fast and—"

"I swear to God, sweetie, if you'd been alive when they built the *Titanic*, they would've called it the *Debbie Sue*."

Debbie Sue stared with wide-eyed astonishment at her friend and coworker. "Why, Ed. You can't think I did that on purpose."

"No, you're right, if you'd had a purpose, you would've run over her. What the hell kind of a name is Bozonosky?"

"Not Texan, that's for sure. She must be just leaving." Debbie Sue felt a tiny sting behind her eyelids. "Do you think she stayed over?"

"Naw, Buddy left out of here around five this morning. He and I hollered at each other when I walked Vic out to his truck. That car wasn't there then. He looked like he was going out of town. He had a piece of luggage and some hanging clothes."

"Really? If she'd known he was out of town, she wouldn't have come by, would she? That's a good sign, isn't it? The fact that he went out of town and she didn't even know. Maybe they had a fight."

"Now there you go again getting ahead of yourself. Did you ever talk to Buddy about this engagement?"

"Well, no, I've been meaning—"

"The two of you make my ass wanna eat a biscuit. It's clear to anyone who comes in contact with either one of you that you're crazy about each other."

"*Were* crazy about each other, Ed. *Were*. What you're seeing between me and Buddy now is nothing but a lifetime of knowing each other. Concern and friendship. It's not so much his getting married that bothers me, but he's marrying a snotty goody-two-shoes. That really ticks me off. She'll make his life miserable."

A pang of conscience hit Debbie Sue. How could anyone make his life more miserable than she had made it with her cussin', dish-throwing fits, days at a time of bawling and bitching, and finally her absences of weeks at a time rodeoing, something he opposed. Well, she wouldn't think about it right now. If she did, she would wind up in tears.

"Oh, so that's how it is? Concern and what else? Oh yeah, friendship."

"I don't want to talk about it anymore. That's not why I came over in the first place. I have some really big news, Ed."

"Really big? Okay, shoot."

"Nope. First I want something to eat. I was hoping Vic was home."

"He went to El Paso, but I'll scramble you up some eggs. The coffee's still hot."

"I've got a nine o'clock. Let me have just some

toast and coffee. I'll tell you while you're getting dressed."

Perched on the end of Edwina's bed with toast and coffee, Debbie Sue told her pal about the phone conversation she had the night before with C. J.

Edwina stopped lining her eyelids and gaped at her in the mirror's reflection. "Why, I flat-out can't believe it. Why didn't you call me and tell me last night?"

"It was late and I didn't want to disturb you. I figured only one of us needed to lose a night's sleep over it."

"Well, no kidding. I wouldn't have slept a wink. How in the hell did we miss that?"

"I guess because it was the last thing we expected. We were so intrigued by Pearl Ann's love life, we didn't stop to think Harley might have one, too."

"And they're getting married?"

"As soon as a respectable time has passed."

"Respectable? Given what Pearl Ann knew about *respectable*, I'd say about thirty minutes should be enough."

"Ed, don't speak ill of the dead. She'll come back to haunt you."

"I wish ol' Pearl Ann would come back to haunt me. It'd be worth it just to tell her about C. J. and Harley."

* * *

Buddy's plane landed at Love Field and he rented a car. Salt Lick's budget wasn't flush, so he asked for the cheapest vehicle. He ended up with a compact he had to crawl in and out of and in which he couldn't wear his hat.

He headed for the Dallas Police Headquarters. As a professional courtesy and for the sake of safety, he wanted to let Dallas PD know he was in town and for what purpose. And since he had no idea where he was or where he was going, he hoped for some assistance from his fellow officers in finding Luna de Neón.

He parked in the slot assigned for visiting peace officers and joined the mass of pedestrians standing at the corner waiting for the traffic light to change. He was the only person dressed in Western-style clothes, and stood out like a sore thumb. In Fort Worth, he figured no one would have given him a second glance, but in downtown Dallas . . . well, he was *not* part of a pedestrian's normal day. He felt a tinge of sadness. Dallas had become so cosmopolitan it had lost the look of Texas. Most of the oglers were transplanted Yankees and foreigners who had never seen a real cowboy. Maybe they had never even seen a horse.

Buddy climbed the steep stairs and entered the law enforcement building. A real pretty young woman was sitting at a reception desk in the middle of the foyer helping some Asian tourists with a map. The moment she spotted him she diverted her attention and eyed him up and down. "Why, hello cowboy. Are they filming a movie downtown or are you with the rodeo?"

"No, ma'am." Buddy touched the brim of his hat in a gesture of greeting. "I mean, there *could* be, but I'm not part of it, the movie, that is. I've been in rodeos though."

"Really? I'll just bet you have. I wouldn't mind watching you perform in the saddle."

With Edwina, Buddy would have joined in the exchange of sexual innuendos, but with this beautiful stranger, who was obviously more worldly than he, a slow panic crept up his spine.

"I was wondering if you'd be good enough to show me—"

"I'll be happy to show you anything you want to see." She leaned forward just enough to give him full view of ample cleavage. "Do you see something I can show you?"

Buddy gulped so hard he thought he heard the sound vibrate in the elevator shafts. She was having a good time at his expense. He wished he could think of something glib and smart, but the truth was, he felt like a fifteen-year-old kid on a 4-H trip. "Could you please tell me where the office of the chief of police is?"

"Sure thing. Use the elevator just behind you. Go up to the fifth floor. When you exit, turn to your left and it's the third door on the right." She gave him a big red grin.

"Thank you, ma'am." Buddy tipped his hat and nodded in her direction. As he walked off, he heard her remark, "Now *that's* what I moved to Texas for." Women. He would never understand them.

When Buddy reached the police chief's office, much to his relief, seated behind the desk was a woman who couldn't be more opposite of the younger woman in the lobby. She weighed at least three hundred pounds and had frizzy gray hair. She was busy filing papers in an accordion folder and barely looked up when he entered.

"How may I help you?"

Buddy noted that the nameplate on her desk said "Ethel Price."

"Miz Price, my name is Sheriff James Russell Oversteet."

"Do you have an appointment, Sheriff?"

"No ma'am, I'm in town be—"

"Are you picking up a prisoner?"

"No ma'am, I'm in town—"

"Are you testifying in a court case today?"

"No ma'am—"

"If you don't have an appointment and if you don't have official business here, I'm afraid—"

"Miz Price, with all due respect, if you keep interrupting me neither one of us is gonna get what we need." Feeling ill-at-ease in canyons of tall buildings and throngs of rude people had worn Buddy's patience thin.

She stopped her filing and peered at him over

the top of her half glasses. A big smile replaced the sullen expression she had been wearing. "You're from West Texas, aren't you?"

"Yes ma'am, Salt Lick. Have you ever heard of it?"

"Sure have. A big unsolved murder took place there. Pearl Ann Carruthers. Salt Lick has the best six-man football teams in Texas and there's a beauty shop in that town that's located in what used to be a gas station. The owner put dresses on the old pumps out front. Do you know the place?"

"Yes ma'am, I sure do. Two women work there. You'd like both of them."

"I'm sure I would. Maybe I'll just drive out west one weekend and check it out. It'd be good to get out of the city. Kinda closes in on you after a while, know what I mean? Now, how may I help you, Sheriff Overstreet from Salt Lick?"

"I only want to report my presence here today. I'm headed to a place called Luna de Neón to ask some questions. Do you happen to know anything about the place?"

"Enough to know you need to give me more details. They don't pay me to just sit here and look pretty, you know. I decide when the guys in the back get involved. Why don't you just tell me why you need to go to the Neon Moon."

Buddy explained.

"You did the right thing coming by here first," she said. "I've worked twenty-five years in the police department. I could tell you some stories. Most yahoos come to town and don't check in. First thing you know they've gotten themselves into hot water and when they call us we don't know who they are, where they're from, or if the call is even legitimate."

"I don't want to end up as one of your stories, Miz Price. I surely don't."

"Well, Sheriff, it's too late now. Let me step into the back for just a minute and I'll get someone who can help you."

When Miz Price emerged, she had a young Hispanic man in tow. He looked to be seventeen or eighteen, but the detective shield around his neck meant he had to be at least ten years beyond that. He was dressed like a gang-banger, with the walk and posture fitting the role. Even through his disguise, Buddy sensed a strictly business attitude about the young cop.

"Sheriff Overstreet, this is Detective Efrain Gomez. He works undercover. He's going to accompany you to the Neon Moon."

Sober-faced, Detective Gomez extended his hand.

"It's good of you to offer, but I really don't need anyone to go with me. I have directions, and I think I'll be fine." Though it would be nice to have someone help him find the Neon Moon, Buddy wasn't eager to share his investigation with a stranger, detective or not.

"I understand what you're *not* saying, Sheriff Overstreet," the detective said, "but trust us, Luna de Neón is not a place you want to go into alone."

"I appreciate your concern—"

"Sheriff Overstreet," Detective Gomez broke in, "do you speak Spanish?"

"Enough to get by."

"Getting by won't cut it in Luna de Neón. The place is one-hundred-percent Mexican, ninety percent illegal. If they so much as smell *law*, they'll scatter. You gotta lose the gun and the badge. We'll go in my car. I'll explain on the way over how this is gonna go down."

The detective clearly had a grasp of the situation. Buddy believed a wise man knew his limitations. He decided it was time to follow the more experienced detective's advice.

"Miz Price, would it be okay if I leave my gun and badge here with you? I don't want to lock them up in my car."

"In town less than an hour and you're already thinking like a city boy. We'll make one out of you, too, if you hang around long enough."

"Thank you for the offer, ma'am, but I'll finish up my business and be heading home."

"One more thing, Sheriff Overstreet," the receptionist added. "How'd you get past Yvette?"

"Yvette?"

"The young gal who works the information desk in the lobby. She always has an eye out for a good-looking man. You want my opinion, *she's* the most dangerous thing you'll come across today."

Buddy laughed. "I hope you're right about that, Miz Price."

Standing beside Detective Gomez, Buddy rode the elevator to the underground parking garage in silence. The detective seemed to be concentrating on his own thoughts, and far be it from Buddy to disturb him.

Once in the garage, he led the way to a late-model Chevy. The car had been red at one time, but was now faded to a pinkish hue. The driver's door was turquoise. Duct tape secured the flattened side of a cardboard Clorox box to the passenger window.

The detective's wardrobe, the car, the cryptic warning—it all seemed a little melodramatic to Buddy. After all, it was still broad daylight. "Detective Gomez, is all of this really necessary?"

"All of what, Sheriff, the precautions? Trust me. I've done undercover work in the area around Luna de Neón for the past eight years. You do not fuck with these people. They would just as soon kill you as swat the gnat. Now, do me a favor." He opened the Chevy's trunk. "Please put your hat and wallet in here, roll your shirtsleeves up, and pull your shirttail out. You are going in as a jealous husband."

Buddy hesitated, reminded that it had been jealousy that prompted his behavior at Kincaid's when he saw Debbie Sue with Quint Matthews. Of all times for that notion to raise its head.

"Oh," the detective said, "and put a hundred bucks in your pocket."

Seventeen

Debbie Sue arrived at work Saturday with a swarm of people and thoughts colliding inside her head—Buddy, Kathy Bozo, Quint, Eugene/Janine, Pearl Ann, Harley and C.J., Edwina and Vic.

She almost groaned when she saw Maudeen Wiley waiting for her, sitting in her great-granddaughter's mini-van parked in front of the Styling Station. Debbie Sue had always maintained a policy of "walk-ins welcome," partly for snagging last-minute customers, but mainly because a majority of the Styling Station's patrons were elderly. Since they couldn't remember if they had made an appointment, they often showed up as if they had.

As she helped Maudeen out of the mini-van and into the salon, the granddaughter pulled away in a cloud of caliche dust, leaving her grandmother in Debbie Sue's care.

The octogenarian settled into the reclining chair in front of the shampoo bowl. "I think we need to tone down this red color. I look like an Irish setter. And besides, the men won't leave me alone."

Debbie Sue draped her with a black cape, removed her thick bifocals, then eased her back to the sink. "I thought you wanted the men to be attracted to you."

"It gets tiresome fooling with them. They're too old to get it up. I told the cook at the home she should put Viagara in the oatmeal."

Constantly surprised and amused by Maudeen, Debbie Sue hid a grin. "What did she say?"

"Who knows? She can't speak English."

The cowbells whacked the front door, followed by the clomp of Edwina's platforms, and the day began with four people showing up at once. If Pearl Ann's murder had done nothing else, it had boosted the Styling Station's business considerably. One by one new customers had drifted from the competitor down the street to the Styling Station to hear the latest scoop.

As had become the norm since the murder, the first question every customer asked was "Have you heard anything new?" They assumed the sheriff's ex-wife had an inside track to the investigation.

Out front, Edwina was sorting and organizing and offering a free conditioning or a free set of acrylic nails if at least two of the women would make an appointment to come back on Monday.

Among the voices Debbie Sue recognized was Edwina's twin sister from Big Spring, Earlene. She hadn't been in for a free hairdo since Pearl Ann's corpse had been found, but like kudzu creeping over Georgia, the grapevine's fingers had had time to crawl over the scrub grass and sand dunes of West Texas. They must have reached Big Spring a hundred miles away because Earlene, whose visits were always accompanied by an ulterior motive, had come all the way to Salt Lick for some spicy tidbit to take back to her friends and coworkers at Wal-Mart. Earlene was about as welcome as a cloudburst at a rodeo.

Maudeen recognized her voice, too. "I remember when those two girls were born. Their folks came from Oklahoma, following oil field work. It was right after the war, I think."

"Which war?" Debbie Sue rinsed the last of the shampoo from Maudeen's hair and covered her red curls with a towel.

"Why, honey, the big one. And I can tell you their daddy, Art Elrod, didn't spend the war fighting Germans and Japs. He'd already screwed himself out of a seat at the table when he got to Salt Lick."

Debbie Sue giggled.

"Him and Edna had six kids," Maudeen went on. "All boys, and Edna was pregnant and big as a horse. When twin girls popped out, she was in a state of shock. Why, she didn't even have names for them."

Debbie Sue knew Edwina had older brothers, but they were seldom mentioned. They were scattered over Texas, Oklahoma, and New Mexico. Not much more was known about Earlene except that Edwina and she had nothing in common, and sharing the womb was the last thing they had done together. Debbie Sue helped Maudeen to a sitting position. "Ed hates her name."

Maudeen slid her bifocals on. "I don't doubt it. Why, Edna had picked out boy names so many times she just naturally gravitated to Ed and Earl. I expect Edwina and Earlene was the best she could do in the exhausted state she was in." On a sigh, Maudeen shook her head.

Debbie Sue helped her to her feet and offered her arm for Maudeen to hang on to. "You're probably one of the few people in town who even remember Ed's got a twin sister."

"Who'd want to remember Earlene? I'll bet tonight's dessert she's green with envy Edwina's captured that sexy-looking truck driver."

As Debbie Sue guided Maudeen from the shampoo room, she wondered if Edwina *had* captured Vic, and how brokenhearted would she be if he made up with his former wife?

Looking around the salon's front room, Debbie Sue saw a half dozen more waiting customers and wished she had rescinded the "walk-ins welcome" policy for the day. A heated argument had arisen about whether Elvis had really dined at Hogg's Drive-In.

Maudeen stopped in her tracks and planted bony hands on her nonexistent hips. "Why, I know he did. Why, he tried to pick me up right there in the dining room and take me off to the motel, but I turned him down."

Debbie Sue directed her to the styling chair in front of her station before a catfight among eighty-year-olds erupted.

"I want something special for homecoming," Maudeen said as Debbie Sue ran a comb through her wet hair.

"You're going to the homecoming festivities?"

"Why, of course. It's the only thing that happens in Salt Lick and this may be my last year to go."

"You're not moving out of—"

"Lands, no, but two of my friends croaked this year. I may be next."

"Nonsense, Maudeen. You're gonna live to a hundred."

Earlene, parked in the next chair and waiting for Edwina to retrieve some supplies from the back, piped up. "Well, I for one doubt if Elvis ever ate at Hogg's. I wish they'd take down that ugly pink sign. I mean, really. A pink and black plywood sign? It makes Salt Lick look tacky. I'm embarrassed to tell people I grew up here."

Edwina remained unusually quiet, as she always did when her sister was around. Earlene hadn't been in the shop an hour yet, and already she had flaunted to the audience of six her husband's good job at the post office. Jobs with regular pay and benefits were scarce as hen's teeth in the declining West Texas economy.

Earlene had also thrown out a remark or two about her successful twenty-seven-year marriage compared to Edwina's three matrimonial failures and boasted about how well *her* kids were doing without so much as asking about Edwina's three offspring.

In addition, she had reported how her ten-year career as a cashier at Wal-Mart was really taking her places, and she and her husband had paid cash for a new Crown Victoria.

No wonder Edwina was so quiet. Long ago, Debbie Sue and C.J. had determined Earlene thought herself better than Edwina. Well, for that matter, Earlene thought herself better than Debbie Sue and C.J., too. Lord, wouldn't she just die if she knew C.J. was on the verge of marrying Harley and taking Pearl Ann's crown as one of the richest women in Texas. If it weren't for violating C.J.'s trust, Debbie Sue would love to tell it.

"Edwina," Earlene said, "don't take this the wrong way. You know yourself I was overdue a visit to you, but I promised the girls I'd come back to work Monday with the low-down on Pearl Ann Carruthers."

"There's no low-down. She was found shot in her car. We're all waiting to hear who and why."

"Oh come on. You *have* to know the facts. This is such a small town and one of your best friends is the sheriff's ex. Let me tell you what I've heard. I heard she was found naked, robbed of all her jewelry, and r-a-p-e-d." She whispered loud enough for everyone to hear.

Maudeen spoke up. "Well, you heard r-o-n-g, Earlene. Pearl Ann was one of our own. The *fact* is, she's dead. The *fact* is, no one knows who killed her but the one who killed her. And while we're talking about facts, I'll tell you another one—"

"Now, Maudeen," Debbie Sue said, lifting the old woman's red curls and examining them and hoping to hush her salty tongue, "this deep red isn't going to be easy to change. If we try to go blond, it's liable to turn pink. I could apply a dark brown rinse, which would give you brown hair with copper highlights."

"That's fine, honey. You do whatever you think is best. And while you're doing it, tell me about your love life." Maudeen raised her voice loud enough for Earlene to hear. "Been getting any lately?"

"Maudeen!"

"You kids think you invented sex? How do you think you got here in the first place?"

"For your information, I do have a date tonight, but I don't know if I'll sleep with him."

Earlene couldn't help but hear, especially when

she was straining so hard to do just that. "You shouldn't be planning something like that ahead of time. Why would a man buy the cow if he can get the milk free?"

Maudeen threw her head back and cackled. "I never cared where he got the milk, long as he didn't forget the liquor."

Well, there you go, Debbie Sue thought. If there was ever anyone to give it back to Earlene in spades, it was Maudeen. And on that note, she retreated to the back room to find a brown rinse.

When she returned, Earlene was speaking loud and slow to Maudeen. "You really shouldn't be drinking liquor at your age."

"Have to, honey," Maudeen said. "Can't afford cocaine on a fixed income."

Earlene's chin dropped. "You're teasing, right?" She tittered and glanced at Edwina in the mirror. "She's teasing me, isn't she?"

Quick as lightning, Edwina answered. "Naw. She's snorted three husbands' life insurance right up her nose."

A great sigh came from Maudeen. "Nose candy. Nearly killed me in '68."

"Nose candy? . . . Well, my good Lord. I never . . . I don't know why I waste my time coming over here. You people are all crazy."

Nose candy? Where did an eighty-seven-year-old woman learn such lingo? But at least Earlene stayed silent for the rest of her visit.

Debbie Sue walked Maudeen to the door when her great-granddaughter arrived. The older woman pulled her down close and whispered. "Get yourself some of those lacy pants like those Victor Secret women wear. Your ass looks as good as theirs. Nothing makes a man hotter than sexy pants."

Debbie Sue laughed and hugged her favorite customer. "Shh. And by the way, thanks for shutting Earlene up."

"Why, honey, it was fun. I always enjoy taking on rookies. Hope I didn't hurt Edwina's feelings."

"Don't worry. She's in the back calling Vic. She had to wait 'til she stopped laughing to dial the number."

Buddy was glad Detective Gomez was doing the driving. He moved along the city streets with the ease of someone long accustomed to doing it. Buddy had been given some directions, but they didn't say anything about streets closed for repair, a fire engine denying access to an avenue, or street markers ripped from poles.

"You lived in Dallas all your life, Detective?"

"I came from Los Angeles about eight years ago. I worked undercover. Got injured in a drug bust. My wife thought it was a good time to move closer to her family. Even as a little kid, I wanted to be a detective. Coming here allowed that to happen."

Buddy looked with respect on the profile of a

man who had a lifelong dream and had actually achieved it. "Any regrets?"

"Never. Well, maybe one. I hate I waited so long and let so many things sidetrack me. But better late than never, right?"

"Yeah, right."

They had reached a part of the city that evidently had fallen on hard times. The houses that were still lived in had iron bars on the windows, and wary onlookers moved in and out of doorways. Car carcasses decomposed in front yards. Among them, wild-haired, skinny children ran and played as if oblivious to their surroundings. Scowling people, mostly Hispanic, seemed to be everywhere, and day laborers lined the street waiting for contractors to hire them.

It looked more like a Third World country, Buddy thought, than a neighborhood in the shadows of a wealthy American city, and he found himself appreciating Salt Lick and its sparse population anew. He was struck with the perplexing question of how anybody associating with a woman married to one of the richest men in Texas could come from this environment.

"Here we are. Now, Sheriff, once again, let me do all the talking."

Luna de Neón was a square, windowless stucco building painted mustard yellow. From any angle, it was in dire need of repair. The words "Luna de Neón" were painted in red uneven letters on the building front. A Mexican flag served as a curtain on the wooden entry door's windowpane.

Detective Gomez pushed open the weather-beaten door, and Buddy followed him into a gloomy room that reeked of body odor. October had brought cooler temperatures. Buddy could only guess how the joint had smelled in July.

The bar, located on the left, was lit by multicolored Christmas lights draped nail to nail from the ceiling. It looked to have been a drugstore counter in another time. A pool table crouched on the immediate right. Beyond, in the back of the room's dark recess, was a small dance floor anchored by an ancient jukebox blaring a Tejano tune.

When Buddy's eyes became accustomed to the dim light he could see the place was full of men who looked as if they had survived the roughest blows life could deliver. The few women present looked no better.

He followed the detective to the bar, feeling the cold stares of dark eyes glued to him, though no one paid attention to the detective. He said a prayer of thanks he had listened to Gomez. Had he let his ego prevail, right now he could be in a lot of trouble. Of this he had no doubt.

Standing beside Gomez at the bar, he feigned a relaxed stance and listened intently to the conversation between the detective and the bartender, who had a thick black mustache that reminded Buddy of pictures he had seen of Pancho Villa. All he needed was a sombrero and a couple of bandoliers crisscrossing his chest. Buddy's knowledge of the Tex-Mex language was barely good enough to make out the exchange between the detective and the barkeep.

The detective explained that Buddy was *un buen hombre y un buen marido.* Buddy deciphered "good man and good husband."

Buddy was married to Gomez's girlfriend's sister, Maria, the detective continued, and some guy had called her from the pay phone in here yesterday afternoon around two o'clock. Buddy was looking to find out anything he could. He added that Maria was a *puta* who had cheated before and Buddy wasn't putting up with it any longer. He wanted three things—the name of the caller, revenge, and a divorce.

The bartender nodded solemn-faced, said he understood the situation completely. He gave Buddy the head-to-toe, then told Gomez he wanted fifty dollars for information.

Buddy nodded and reached in his pocket for the bills he had stuffed in it back in the parking lot at the law enforcement center. He sorted out two twenties and a ten, tore them in half, and handed the three halves to Gomez. The detective passed them to the bartender and told him, "If he thinks you're telling the truth, he'll give you the other halves."

The bartender said there was a man in yesterday he had never seen. Mexican, but not from the neighborhood. He was present less than an hour.

He came in very, very drunk. He asked for a shot of a brand of whiskey not kept in the bar. He used the phone. The waitress helped him put money in the coin slot. He fumbled and dropped the receiver. The waitress heard him tell someone he loved her.

Buddy nodded and Gomez relinquished the remaining torn halves of the bills.

The bartender went on to explain that the caller was well-dressed, looked like he belonged in downtown Dallas. He was very tall, as tall as Buddy. Several of the women tried to hit on him, called him handsome. He left shortly after making the phone call.

Gomez asked if he saw the man's car, and the bartender answered he did not. Gomez thanked him and turned and addressed the room. In a loud voice he told them he was looking for the *hombre* who had made a phone call in here yesterday. "*Muy, muy borracho, bien-vestido, hermoso. Alto*," he added and pointed at Buddy, which left Buddy confused. He thought *alto* meant halt.

Only stares came in response, wary and suspicious.

"They will not talk to you," the bartender said and chuckled as he wiped the bartop.

Gomez thanked him and they turned to leave. As Buddy reached the door, a hulking man stepped between him and the exit and placed a palm on his chest. He stood eye level with Buddy. His dark eyes glinted. Buddy took in the muscular arms covered with tattoos, a wide scar running along the right side of the stranger's face and disappearing into a black beard. Greasy hair hung past his thick shoulders.

The ominous stranger sneered, lifted his chin, and sniffed the air. "*Huelo el cerdo. Es usted un hombre del cerdo?*"

Buddy picked up on the words "smell," "pig," and "man," and that was enough. He knew one thing from working with wild horses. The biggest mistake you could make was showing fear. The same could apply to humans. He looked down at the hand impeding his movement and answered in the best street Spanish he could manage. "I smell an asshole. Are you an asshole?"

The big Mexican's black eyes bored into his, but Buddy refused to flinch. Suddenly the man laughed, showing gold front teeth. He turned to the room and raised both palms. "*Bastardo resistente,*" he declared.

Everyone cheered, threw back drinks, and slammed shot glasses on tables. The big Mexican threw his thick arms around Buddy, pressed him in an aromatic hug, and invited him to have a drink.

Buddy said no thanks and backed out of the bar.

"What'd he say to me?" he asked Gomez once they were back in the car and headed for the law enforcement center.

"The first time he said, 'I smell a pig. Are you a pig?'"

"I got that part of it. What'd he say that made everybody cheer? I understood bastard, but not the second word."

"He told them you were a tough bastard."

Buddy laughed. "Well, as long as they didn't know the truth. I was damn glad not to be there all by myself."

Gomez laughed, too. "It went okay. You did good. I don't mean to be disrespectful of where you came from, but have you ever thought about leaving Salt Lick? Pursuing law enforcement elsewhere?"

"I've had a dream of being a Texas Ranger. I can't remember ever wanting to be anything else."

"So what happened?"

"Life mostly. I was in college when my dad died of a sudden heart attack. He owned a service station. He and Mom hadn't been able to put much money back, especially helping me go to college and all. I quit school to run the service station and help my mom. About four years ago the sheriff in Salt Lick died in a car wreck, so I ran for the office."

"You still helping your mom?"

"Nope. She remarried."

"You married, got any kids."

"Divorced. No kids."

"How long did you go to college?"

"Two years."

"Then what's holding you in Salt Lick? You got enough college hours and experience to apply with the DPS now. Four years with them and you could be promoted to Trooper Class Two. Then you could ask for consideration for a Ranger position. You're what, in your early thirties?"

"Yeah, something like that."

"The average age of a Texas Ranger is forty-five. You're way ahead of the game."

The detective hadn't said anything Buddy didn't already know. "How do you know so much about the Rangers?"

"I looked into it myself. It didn't appeal to me and I didn't want to do four years with DPS. Like I said, I wanted to be a detective in a metropolitan area. Guess it comes with our upbringing, huh?"

"How's that?"

"A kid from LA wants to be a detective. A kid from Texas wants to be a Texas Ranger. Maybe we watched too much TV growing up."

Buddy laughed. "Maybe you're right."

The remainder of the ride back to the law enforcement center, Buddy was silent. He didn't want to disclose to anybody that the thing holding him back was really Debbie Sue. He didn't even like admitting the fact to himself.

All trainees with DPS had to complete a twenty-six-week training course in Austin. Once training was complete, consideration would be given to a request of assignment to a specific area in the state, but bottom line, a DPS trooper was sent where he was needed.

He had never been totally apart from Debbie

Sue, even when she had gone to college in Lubbock. Now, though they were divorced, he saw her often and usually knew of her activities. He hadn't been able to make himself leave her, and Salt Lick, behind.

Eighteen

The Styling Station's last customer for the day was Debbie Sue's mom. The minute Debbie Sue began telling her what a hectic day she'd had, in typical fashion Mom said she would schedule for another time.

"No, please. I've looked forward to seeing you. Don't cancel on me now."

"Well . . . I'll leave you a good tip."

Debbie Sue said it was a deal and urged her mother to the shampoo room. She had no intention of taking a tip or even charging her mother. Still, she knew she would find a ten-dollar bill stuffed in her purse or her smock pocket at day's end. It was a game they played.

"Have you noticed all the commotion at the sheriff's office?" her mom asked.

"Nope. Haven't paid any attention." Debbie Sue cradled her mother's neck with a towel and tested the water temperature "You want coconut or strawberry?"

"I had coconut last time. I'll take strawberry. I heard the FBI released a flyer on a suspected terrorist who might have crossed over from Mexico. Billy Don's pulling everyone over to do a photo check. There must be a dozen cars parked in front."

The pleasant fragrance of strawberry-scented shampoo filled the small space as Debbie Sue washed her mom's hair. "Good Lord. Well, I guess it keeps him out of any real trouble. I can just imagine Buddy's reaction when he gets back in town."

"Back in town? How do you know if he's out of town? Have you two been talking?"

"Don't get your hopes up, Mom. Ed saw him leaving at the crack of dawn with clothes hanging in the back. Must be official. He was in the Tahoe."

"Hmm, I find that interesting. Aren't you just a little bit intrigued?"

"Nope. Am not." Debbie Sue rinsed away shampoo suds and placed a towel around her mother's head. "Now, tell me what we're doing with your hair today."

They walked together to the styling chair. "Same old, same old. Have you heard any more from Quint?"

"As a matter of fact, he's coming back to town and we're going out this evening."

"Oh? What are your plans?" Her mother's tone was less than enthusiastic. "You should bring him by the house. I'd like to see him again."

"No hard feelings, Mom, but running into my ex-husband the last date I had with Quint didn't exactly make for a good evening. I don't want to jinx this one. I want everything to be normal." She picked up a brush and a hair dryer and began styling her mother's short hair.

"Normal? What's your idea of normal? Dinner, dancing, gluing flies together?"

No matter how much Debbie Sue wanted to be indignant at the memory, it was still funny as hell and made her laugh.

While Debbie Sue and her mom chatted, Edwina had been busy sweeping up. "Well, no one's asked me—"

"That's right, Ed, we haven't."

Being cut off mid-sentence had never been enough to seal Edwina's lips. "No one's asked me, but I think Quint is going to expect an answer on his job offer. Since your mom's here, I think this is the perfect time to discuss it."

"Oh? You do?" Debbie Sue glared at Edwina.

"We both have a vested interest in your decision." Edwina fished a slice of Juicy Fruit from the pocket of her smock, peeled it, and folded it into her mouth.

"A vested interest?"

"We both love you and want the best for you, but *I'm* employed here and would kinda like to know if you're gonna be around."

"Ohmygosh, Ed, you're right. I'm sorry for being so selfish. It's not an easy decision to make. I guess I was thinking if I delayed it long enough it would either go away or an answer would just come to me."

"Sweetie, why is it such a hard decision?" Concern showed in her mom's eyes. "Is it not what you expected it to be?"

"On the contrary, Mom. It's more than I ever dreamed of. More than twice what I'm making now. I'd be working with horses, traveling all over the country with all expenses paid. I'd be going places and seeing things I've only read about."

"Humph. Sounds too good to be true."

There was no mistaking the skepticism in her mother's remark. "Maybe that's what scares me. It does sound too good to be true."

"Can I make a suggestion?" Edwina busied herself brushing sand and hair clippings into a dustpan. "This whole thing is a decision, not a tattoo. You don't have to commit your life to it. I could keep working in the shop. Hell, what else do I have to do? With the money you'll be making, you can pay off your debt in no time."

"But I have obligations here," Debbie Sue said.

"Like what?"

"Well, there's Mom and Rocket Man, my house . . ."

"Sweetheart, those don't sound like reasons," her mom said. "More like excuses. Rocket Man and I will get along just fine. Ed and Vic would probably keep an eye on your house. Why don't you try it for a few months? If it doesn't work out, come home. Haven't you heard the old saying, nothing ventured, nothing gained?"

Debbie Sue looked at her mother in amazed silence. She had expected a stronger debate. With a sudden rush of tears, she bent down and wrapped her arms around her mother. "Thanks, Mom, for always being there for me. You always know the perfect thing to say."

Her mom kissed her forehead. "That's because I love you."

"Christ, this is getting ridiculous," Edwina said, dabbing tears from her eyes. She walked over to the payout desk and switched off the radio. "So Virginia, what new number are you working on? I went around here for a week singing 'I Found Love on the Internet, but He's a Felon Serving Time.'"

"Believe it or not, I'm writing something serious for a change."

"You're kidding." Debbie Sue spun her mom around to face her. "I've been trying to get you to do that for years. Why the sudden change?"

"That guy I've told you about in Nashville's been after me a long time now to write a love ballad. I figure I don't have anything to lose."

Debbie Sue grinned. "Wow, Mom. Well—" she lifted her shoulders in a shrug—"nothing ventured, nothing gained."

Later at home, as Debbie Sue dressed for the

evening, she mulled over the conversation with her mother. Was Mom giving her blessing to Debbie Sue's seeing Quint? Had she given up on Debbie Sue and Buddy ever getting back together? If so, wasn't that a pretty good sign it wouldn't happen? After all, Mom did know everything that was worth knowing. It was all so confusing.

Debbie Sue took one last look at herself in the mirror while she hooked silver loops into each earlobe. Tonight she had chosen to wear her favorite outfit—a long-sleeved white satin shirt tucked into a black suede rayon broomstick skirt secured on the side with silver concho buttons. The skirt struck her a few inches above the ankle, showing off her black lace-up boots.

She topped it off with her black leather fringed waist jacket to complete the long, lean silhouette. She had always loved the way the jacket, secured by a single concho at the waist, made her waistline and hips look smaller. She had snatched it from a sale rack seven years ago and it had become a staple in her wardrobe.

Just then the doorbell rang. Quint. When she swung the door open he looked her over with a lecherous gleam in his eye. Before she could say a word, his arm circled her waist, he pulled her close and kissed her. He was an outstanding kisser who had all the time in the world to give her pleasure and she couldn't keep from kissing him back. It had been a very long time since a man had kissed her on sight, and he smelled like Boss. She had always been a sucker for a man who smelled good. The fact that he also looked good didn't subtract from the equation.

Just as suddenly as he had kissed her, he set her away.

"Wow, what was that for?" she asked.

"That's the way I like to end an evening, darlin', but with you, I thought it might make more sense to start out that way. Who knows what shape I'll be in by the time I bring you home?"

"Quint, please don't give me a hard time about Kincaid's. I really did feel bad about how things turned out, but I'd be lying if I didn't tell you that I've gotten the biggest kick out of remembering you and that pink clothespin. To be honest, I didn't think I'd ever see you again."

"I've had a laugh or two about it myself. Seems funnier looking back on it than it was at the time. But you know me, I'm an adrenaline junkie. Dating you's an adventure, sugar. Anticipating what's gonna happen next, not to mention the way you look tonight, could keep me coming back for months." He took her hand and gave her a twirl. "Pretty. Ver-ry pretty. Fringe is sexy as hell on anybody, but on you . . ."

He moved forward for another kiss, but this time Debbie Sue placed both hands on his muscular chest and moved back. "Hold on there, cowboy. We're supposed to be at Edwina and Vic's about now. They've invited us over for a home-cooked meal."

"Hmm." He planted a quick kiss on her lips anyway. "Then what?"

She slid her arms around his neck and they kissed again. "Afterward," she said as he sipped at her lips, "I thought we might check out the street dance."

"Darlin', if you keep teasing me, I'm not even gonna be in the mood to eat, much less dance."

She stepped away from his embrace, laughing. "You're right. We have plenty of time. This is homecoming weekend and Main Street will be blocked off and there's a good band. The weather's just right for snuggling, too."

"It's been a long time since I've been to an out-door dance. I like the snuggling part."

"We'd better go. We'll be late."

The black Navigator gleamed in the driveway even in the dark. When Quint opened the passenger door, Debbie Sue stopped. Lying on the seat was a large rectangular box wrapped in gold paper tied with a rust-colored velvet bow. Her pulse quickened. Not wanting to be presumptuous, she asked with as light a voice as she could fake, "Do you want me to move that to the backseat?"

He came close behind her and placed his lips near her ear. "I'd rather you open it first."

The package was bigger than a breadbox. It had to be something to wear because she caught a glimpse of the store label on one corner of the box, an ultra exclusive Western wear store in Santa Fe. She drooled over its ads in magazines. Unless it sold socks, there was nothing she could ever afford in all its finery. She clasped her hands under her chin. "Ohmygod, it's so beautiful."

"You haven't opened it yet."

"The box . . . the box *and* the bow . . . I mean, this is such a surprise . . . It's just beautiful."

"Let's take it inside and you can get a better look."

"Let's," she said, grabbing up the package. She carried it toward her front door, weighing it as she went. Her hands trembled and she fumbled with the knob.

Once in the living room, she stood looking at the gift as if it might magically transform itself into something else.

"Well, if you're not going to—" Quint made a move to remove the bow.

"Don't you dare. I'll do it. Just let me enjoy the moment." On a deep breath she tugged the ends of the bow loose and lifted the boxtop. Nothing could have prepared her for the contents.

Tucked in sparkling gold paper was the most sumptuous jacket she had ever seen. She gasped. The fabric was smooth and black. She could see green leaves and beaded pink roses. "Ohmygod."

She lifted the garment out and held it away, viewing it. The intricate beadwork glinted in the amber light from her one living room lamp. The hand-sewn label told her it was a Manuel original. Oh, she knew the label all right. Manuel Cuevas was preferred couture for the rodeo elite and superstars. She had seen similar jackets, knew the cost had to be in the neighborhood of a thousand dollars. She gasped again.

"Let's see how it looks," Quint said. "I guessed at the size."

She lifted up her arms.

"Tell you what. Let's take off your other jacket first."

"Oh, shit. Now I'm embarrassed." Her cheeks burned as she caught herself behaving like a silly fool. She removed her treasured fringe jacket, replaced it with the designer model, then scurried to see her image in the hall mirror. The cascade of green, gold, and pink embroidery draped across the shoulders, down to the elbows and down the front beside the lapels. Her broomstick skirt and boots couldn't have been more perfect with it. For that matter, her nightshirt would have been perfect with it.

She ran her fingers over the Spanish-style embroidery, admiring the beadwork that accented it. "Quint, I can't possibly accept this. It's just too extravagant."

"You don't like it?"

"Are you crazy? This is the most gorgeous thing I've ever seen. I love it. But I can't keep it." She made no effort to remove it.

"I thought of you the minute I saw it. If you're going to be traveling with me, you've got to look the part."

The part? Part of what? Just how much was this vision going to cost her, she wondered, as she twirled in front of the mirror. She didn't want to linger on that question. Better to enjoy the look and feel of this piece of art around her shoulders. Quint was right. She couldn't accompany a big-shot rodeo stock producer wearing T-shirts and jeans. "Sounds like you're assuming I'll accept your offer."

"I'm not assuming. I'm hoping." He stepped closer and his arm circled her waist again. "Please tell me the answer's yes."

"Yep, the answer's yes." Tears burned her nose as the realization hit her just what her acceptance meant.

He turned her in his arms, and this time when he leaned down to kiss her, she didn't push him away.

On the way to Edwina and Vic's, Debbie Sue filled Quint in on the couple's relationship. Vic had rear-ended Edwina's classic Mustang at a red light four years ago. Edwina leaped from the car ready to give him a piece of her mind. Two days later, having given him that and oh so much more, she and Vic emerged from the Starlite Inn in lust and in love and had been there ever since.

"In a twisted way, that's kind of romantic," Quint said.

"It *is* romantic, Quint. They're made for each other. They're soul mates, and circumstances brought them together. They act like honeymooners."

"Don't get me wrong, darlin'. I've got nothing against honeymoons, love or lust as long as they're *not* in that order, but love that lasts forever just doesn't exist."

Debbie Sue was thinking about a reply to this when Quint interrupted her thoughts. "So I'm having supper served to me by an ex-navy SEAL? A man who's killed with his bare hands, who's strong as a bull and mean as a snake? And he cooks, too?"

Debbie Sue laughed. "Don't make fun of Vic. He's very serious about his military career."

Quint chuckled with her. "Okay. Just remind me to eat everything on my plate."

They stopped in front of Edwina's trailer, and Quint reached behind his seat and grabbed a plastic sack. He pulled out a bottle of champagne. "I brought this so we could have a toast to our new business arrangement, but I hate to go empty-handed to someone's home for dinner. How about we take it in and all four of us can share the news?"

"I've always liked men who were sure of themselves, but you take the cake. What if I'd said no?"

"I guess I would've had to use this four-hundred-dollar bottle of champagne to drown my sorrows."

"You're kidding, right? Nobody pays four hundred dollars for champagne."

"I do, darlin'. I do."

Wow. The decision Debbie Sue had made seemed to be more right with every minute. She turned toward the passenger window, looked out into the dark, and grinned.

Nineteen

Edwina was waiting for them. She greeted them enthusiastically as she dragged them into her cozy trailer and practically grabbed Quint's hat off his head. She graciously accepted the bottle of champagne. "Oh, thank you, Quint. I'm sure this is good stuff. I noticed right off it doesn't have a screw-off top or come in a box. We'll enjoy it."

The second Debbie Sue emerged from the darkness, Edwina let out a whoop. "Somebody slap me blind. What in the hell are you wearing and where did you get it?"

Debbie Sue filled her in on the details of the surprise gift. She felt like a little girl showing her best friend the new Barbie doll Santa had left under the tree.

"Sugar, do you mind if I just put it on for a minute?" Debbie Sue removed the jacket with great care and admired it again as Edwina slipped it on.

"Vic! Vic, honey. C'mere. I want you to see something."

Vic appeared in the doorway wiping his hands on a kitchen towel. Edwina struck a pose. Vic showered her with a look of pure adoration, then took three steps across the room to Quint. "You must be Quint. Welcome to our home." The muscles in Vic's arms and shoulders rippled under his knit shirt as Quint's hand disappeared in his grip. " 'Scuse me for just a sec," Vic said then, releasing Quint's hand. "Got something in the oven."

Quint leaned close to Debbie Sue, shaking his hand to bring back the circulation. "You don't need to remind me. I *will* eat everything on my plate and love every bite of it. I don't care *what* it is."

"Hold up, hon." Edwina grabbed the bottle of champagne. "Take this with you. Quint was nice enough to bring it."

Vic accepted the bottle and moved closer to the end table lamp and read the label. He let out a low whistle. "I know for a fact you didn't run by Pinkies in Odessa and pick this up. This is an extremely fine vintage. Where'd you get it?"

Debbie Sue spoke up. "Quint, I thought you were kidding. I didn't know you were a wine connoisseur. Where *did* you get it?"

"I'm not a connoisseur. I bought it online from an auction house that deals in rare wines. I've got this hang-up. I like to own things other people want. But once I've got it, I tend to lose interest and look for the next thing. I guess the excitement of the quest is what turns me on. I was saving it for a special occasion."

Vic's gaze shifted between Debbie Sue and Quint, then landed on Edwina. "Did I miss something?"

"You got me. What's the special occasion?"

"Debbie Sue has agreed to come to work for me." Quint smiled and slid an arm around her waist.

"No shit? Well, that *does* deserve a drink. I'll get the glasses." Edwina disappeared into the kitchen.

"When does this take place?" Vic asked.

Debbie Sue was alarmed to discover she didn't have a clue how to answer Vic's question. She had been so absorbed with the issue of yes or no and the designer jacket, the date she would actually start this venture hadn't entered her mind. And now she had to wonder if *she* was the "next thing" Quint had to have and would subsequently lose interest in. She looked at him and laughed. "Looks like there's one small detail we haven't discussed yet. When did you plan on me starting?"

Quint did some mental calculations before answering. "I thought we'd get you on board by December. This is the busiest time of the year for me, and I'll need you to meet with one of my secretaries and fill out paperwork and—"

"You have more than one secretary?"

"This is a business, darlin', not a hobby. I actually have *two* secretaries and a staff." He started counting off on his fingers. "Two secretaries, a director of marketing, two bookkeepers, a couple of ranch foremen, two vets, and a handful of cowboys. You've got a lot to learn yet."

Indeed. She did have a lot to learn—about Quint's business *and* about Quint.

Edwina reentered the room with four paper cups. Vic took them from her and stacked them into one. He lifted her hand and gently kissed the top. "Sweetheart, let's use some better glasses for this occasion."

"Oh, dumb me. Of course. Be right back." Edwina made another exit. She returned with four Tupperware plastic tumblers. Vic gave her a look of pure adoration. Stroking her cheek, he said, "Mama Doll, this bottle of champagne probably cost several hundred dollars. I'll go get the good stuff."

Before he could leave, a frown puckered Edwina's brow. "Several hundred dollars. Why, Quint Matthews, do you just piss away money all the time or are you trying to impress us poor ol' country folks? I've never had anything in my mouth worth several hundred bucks in my whole life." She turned to Vic and squeezed his arm. "Uh, that is, until I met you, doll. You're worth that and then some." She planted a kiss on his cheek.

More shocking to Debbie Sue than the sexual innuendo was the pinkish hue she noticed creeping up Vic's neck and face. She wouldn't have imagined anything making Vic blush. "Edwina!" she said, laughing.

"Oh, come on, we're all adults."

Vic went to the kitchen and brought out crystal champagne flutes. Edwina took them from his hands. "Let's have a toast."

"Here, Quint, I'll let you do the honors." Vic handed over the bottle.

"You obviously appreciate good wine, Vic. I'd be happy to defer to you."

"Godalmighty, are we civilized or what? We're fixin' to have to let some pigs loose in the front yard if this keeps up. Here, let me do it." Edwina set the glasses on the table and snatched the champagne bottle from Vic.

Grasping it between her knees, she worked on the cork. Like a shot, the cork flew from the bottle and headed straight for Quint's face. With catlike quickness, he dodged the missile, staring as it hit the wall just beyond him.

"Man, you've got incredible reflexes," Vic said. "I haven't seen anyone move like that since I left special ops. What branch of the service were you in?"

Quint stuttered for a second, so Debbie Sue spoke up. "Quint wasn't in the service."

Vic's eyes leveled on Quint. "Why not?"

"He was world champion three years running," Debbie Sue blurted. "Bull riding." She had forgotten that Vic didn't understand why every red-blooded American man, woman, and child didn't serve his country.

"Oh. Well, that's too bad. The country could have used somebody like you." Vic filled each glass with the golden liquid, handed each person a flute, then sniffed the bubbling libation. When he lifted his glass, everyone followed his gesture. "Here's to new adventures and roads less traveled."

As the four glasses met and clinked, Debbie Sue felt relieved Vic hadn't pursued grilling Quint about his lack of military service. The teenage Quint, Debbie Sue remembered, probably hadn't given thirty seconds of thought to patriotic duty.

She took a demure sip and her eyes almost crossed. Oh well, she had never been much of a wine drinker, preferring cold beer any day.

Edwina took a gulp, held it momentarily, then ran to the kitchen and spit in the sink. "Good Godalmighty." She hacked and gasped. "I got vinegar in the cupboard that tastes better than that. I'm sorry, Quint, but if you really paid several hundred dollars for that, you got screwed. Or maybe I don't have very refined taste buds. Y'all can have my share."

"Don't worry about it, Ed. I don't think Debbie Sue is that crazy about it, either. Vic and I'll finish it off."

Debbie Sue left the remainder of her drink to the two men, who evidently shared different opinions from hers and Edwina's. Once the bottle had been emptied, Vic excused himself once more to the kitchen.

Quint and Debbie Sue took a seat on the sofa, sitting close with fingers interlocked. Smoothing strands of hair back from her face, he kissed her temple. "I'm happy you're with me."

Debbie Sue blushed and began to think how easily she could grow accustomed to this treatment. True enough, she had found out more about Quint and his business in the past hour than she had known before, but wasn't that what time was for?

Vic announced that dinner was served. "Hope you three are hungry. I made a big Greek salad, a great main course, and a dessert that's decadent."

Debbie Sue sniffed the air. "It smells fabulous, Vic. What's the main course?"

"Shrimp dumplings in a ginger broth. It's one of my favorite dishes, but I don't make it very often. It takes a long time to prepare. Tonight, for *you* guys, I wanted something out of the ordinary."

"Wait," Quint said. "Shrimp dumplings? Is shrimp a description of the actual dumpling or is shrimp in the dish?"

Vic gave him a bewildered look. "Shrimp *is* the dish. Is there a problem?"

"God, Vic, I feel terrible. I should've said something. I'm allergic to shellfish."

"Quint, I didn't know you had food allergies," Debbie Sue said. "Do you take medication?"

"Not usually. I'm careful about what I eat. I rarely have a problem."

Add that to the long list of information she had learned just tonight, Debbie Sue thought.

"Well, honey, you don't have to eat a lot of it," Edwina said. "Just a little bit won't hurt, right?"

"I can't even touch shrimp, Ed, literally. I'm sorry, Vic. I'm sure it's delicious, but I'd better stick to the salad. I'll make up for it on dessert. I love sweets."

"No problem. Like I said, I made a big salad. Let's eat."

The rest of the evening was pleasant. Small talk was made, stories exchanged. Debbie Sue and Edwina heaped compliments on Vic's head for his culinary talents. Vic demonstrated how to eat practically anything from grasshoppers to sticky rice with chopsticks, and Quint told what he looked for in a good competition bull.

"I sure am having a good time," Edwina said, her gaze traveling around the table. "What are y'all doing after you leave here?"

Quint put his arm around Debbie Sue's chair. "We're going to a street dance. Aren't y'all going with us?"

"Thanks, but no." Vic covered Edwina's hand with his. "I travel so much, I don't get near enough time with this woman. I'm guessing you two need to spend some time alone. And I *know* we do."

Edwina stood to clear dishes from the table and kissed Vic on the top of his bald head. "Just because there's no fuzz on top doesn't mean he's not a peach. I'll go get dessert."

"I'm afraid you haven't had enough to eat, Quint. I hope you like cheesecake," Vic said.

"The salad was plenty and I love cheesecake."

Edwina returned with the enormous dessert. A caramel-colored sauce dripped down the sides. It looked good enough to eat without the cake. It was a beautiful creation, Debbie Sue thought. Vic had really outdone himself.

"Can I have two helpings?" Quint asked.

"Honey, you have all you want," Edwina said. "You've been a real good sport tonight."

Waiting just barely long enough for everyone to receive a slice, Quint dove into his super-sized portion of the homemade cheesecake. He wolfed down three large bites, rolling his eyes and making little hums. "Thith ith wiwwy good," he said between bites.

Debbie Sue glanced at Vic, who glanced at Edwina. Edwina stared at Quint.

"Thorry I'm aking wude," Quint said, obviously enjoying his cheesecake.

Debbie Sue didn't know what to say. Vic seemed stymied as well, but Edwina said, "Hon, why are you talking like Elmer Fudd? Are you okay?"

Quint laid down his fork. "Oh thit. Whas in thith, Wic?"

"Just the usual stuff. The main ingredient in the crust and glaze is Frangelico."

"Fwangewico? Whas Fwangewico?"

"Hazelnut liqueur."

"Fug. I cannn ee nuth. Fug. I go inoo anphawac-
kic thock. I nee a thot . . ."

Debbie Sue's eyes bugged as she stared at Quint.
"You go into what?"

"Anaphylactic shock," Vic said, alarm register-
ing in his voice. "Quint, do you carry epinephrine
with you?"

"Jus a willle doze. Goo for en or enny minith. In
my twug."

"I'll get it." Edwina sprang from her chair,
knocking it backward to the floor, and charged toward the front door.

"It's going to take longer than ten or twenty
minutes to get to help," Vic said. "The closest doctor's in Odessa. Debbie Sue, call your mom and
ask her if she'll call Dr. Miller and have him meet
us at his office."

Debbie Sue's brain had quit working. "But Vic,
Dr. Miller's a vet."

"That's okay. He'll have epinephrine. Enough to
let us get to Odessa."

Vic went to Quint and began to monitor his
pulse.

"You're thaking me thoo a ved?"

Debbie Sue noticed Quint's lips had swollen
and he kept pulling his hand away from Vic and
scratching himself. She dashed to the phone in the
kitchen.

"Hurry up, Ed," Vic yelled.

Debbie Sue's mother picked up and after hearing what happened, she agreed to call Dr. Miller.

"I found it." Edwina said, rushing back carrying a black leather zippered pouch, which she handed to Vic.

"Great. Quint, which one of these vials is the medication?" Vic displayed the contents of the case.

Quint's eyes flew wide. "Notthows. Notthows."

"Nachos?" Edwina asked. "Did he say nachos?"

"I think he's saying, 'Not those,' " Vic said. "Is that right Quint? Can you give me a hint?"

"Fuck. This is no time for charades," Edwina said. "Let's get to the pickup."

The phone chirped and Debbie Sue answered. Her mother informed her Dr. Miller was already at the clinic delivering puppies. "That was Mom," she told the group. "I said we're on our way."

"Not 'til we give him a shot," Vic said.

"What? I thought you already did."

Quint spoke up, "In tha gwuf bos. Ith wille. Wook inna gwuf bos."

Debbie Sue volunteered and dashed outside, needing to do something to overcome the panic racing around inside her. She found a small, single-dose EpiPen in the Navigator's glove box and ran back into the house. "I've got it."

Her toe stubbed on the threshold, she fell headlong through the doorway and met the floor with a painful whack. When she opened her eyes, the tiny syringe containing the single dose of medication was stuck in the linoleum of Edwina's entry floor, plunger pressed down, medication fully released into the white and gray tile pattern.

"Well, I'm just lost for words," Edwina said.

"Okay, that's that. Let's move out," Vic ordered, helping Quint to his feet.

Within a matter of minutes they were in Dr. Miller's office, where he handed Quint a minimal dose of epinephrine. Vic administered it while Edwina and Debbie Sue oohed and aahed over the litter of puppies Dr. Miller had just helped a small dachshund deliver.

"Ladies," Dr. Miller said, "I hate to throw cold water on your maternal instincts, but this dose won't last long and he needs to get on his way. Mr. Matthews, I'm sending another EpiPen with you in case you need it."

The doctor took Debbie Sue aside, speaking softly. "I'm a little uneasy about his heart rate. Granted, I'm not accustomed to humans, but I still think it's a little erratic. Be sure to mention that to the physician you see in Odessa, okay?"

"Sure. Of course."

Quint made several attempts to pay Dr. Miller, but the veterinarian wouldn't hear of it. "Nonsense, Mr. Matthews. I didn't do anything these folks here couldn't have done if they'd had the medication."

Debbie Sue gave Quint a guilty look and squeezed his arm, "You know I feel just awful about falling with your shot, don't you?"

"Cuh happen oo anyone. On't worry."

"And you know I feel bad about that dessert," Vic said. "Hell, I never thought something like this would happen."

"He understands," Debbie Sue said, mopping Quint's face with a wet towel she had picked up in Dr. Miller's delivery room.

"I'm sure there'll be something I should apologize for before the evening's over," Edwina said. "If it's all the same to you, I'll just wait 'til then."

Keeping in mind what Dr. Miller had said about Quint's heart rate, Debbie Sue asked Vic to drive. Quint crawled into the backseat without an argument and Debbie Sue followed. As they passed through town, they couldn't miss the commotion at the sheriff's office. Every light in the building was on and a dozen or more cars were parked in front. Whatever was going on couldn't be good.

They arrived at the emergency room just as Quint's shot began to wear off. After taking the rudimentary medical history, the doctor instructed the nurse to administer medication. The doctor seemed competent and in control of the situation, despite the fact that Edwina had described him as an "infant with a five o'clock shadow."

Before Debbie Sue even had the chance to mention what Dr. Miller had told her, the young doctor approached the waiting group. "I'm afraid I'm going to keep Mr. Matthews overnight, just as a precaution. His reaction to the allergens seems to be under control but I noticed something on his EKG that makes me reluctant to release him tonight. Especially since he isn't staying in the immediate vicinity." His gaze stopped on Debbie Sue, and she felt her cheeks burn red hot.

"I've given him something that'll help him sleep," the doctor went on. "There's no need for any of you to stay. I'll let you speak to him and then we'll send him to a room for the night. He's in treatment room number three."

Allowing no time for discussion, he was gone to the next patient.

"Well, my Lord, Debbie Sue," Edwina said, "what do you make of that? Has Quint ever had heart problems before?"

"I don't know. I don't know if any of this has ever happened before. This whole evening has been one scrap of new information after another. Do y'all want to go with me to talk to him?"

"Nah, you go on ahead," Vic said, taking a seat and pulling Edwina down with him. "We'll wait here."

Debbie Sue tiptoed to the curtain closing off room number three from the rest of the medical area. She wasn't sure why she felt the need to be stealthlike. Probably from her childhood when her mother shushed her in any hospital setting because of the "sick people."

She peered gingerly around the opening in the drape. "Quint? Are you okay?"

He was lying on his back, EKG leads still glued

to his chest. His head was tilted back slightly and his lips were moving.

"Quint, are you all right? Should I call the nurse?"

"I'm okay. I was just trying to figure out what it takes to stay conscious through an entire evening with you. I don't know how we ever hooked up in Vegas, I really don't. I should've shot some craps that night 'cause I was riding a lucky streak."

Debbie Sue bit her lip. There did seem to be some cosmic force keeping them apart. Their last encounter had sent her running to the unopened arms of Buddy. There was no running to Buddy this time, and circumstances had already made it apparent that option wouldn't be available in the future either. "I'm worried about your heart, Quint. Has this ever happened before?"

"I tried to tell that kid it was because I'd been drinking, but he wouldn't listen. If I take one of those epinephrine shots when I'm drinking, my heart rate goes through the ceiling. Now he's got me damn near sedated and spending the night. I should just get up and go." He threw back the covers and made an attempt to rise from the bed, but immediately fell back. "Fuck, I feel like I'm fixin' to puke."

Acting on instinct, Debbie Sue grabbed the first thing handy and shoved it under his face. Everything he'd eaten in the past few hours emptied into his silver belly Stetson that had probably cost four hundred dollars.

"Oh dear," Debbie Sue said, backing toward the drape. "I just grabbed . . . I didn't see . . . I'll call the nurse to clean that up. Maybe I should go now. I'll be back in the morning."

She made her exit, and as she walked toward Edwina and Vic they stood up. "Should we go in and say something?" Vic asked.

"Oh, I wouldn't just now. I called the nurse, and she's on her way in. He's really sleepy. I think we should just go."

The threesome returned to Salt Lick just before midnight. The homecoming festivities were breaking up. Debbie Sue woke Edwina and Vic as she pulled in front of their trailer.

"Do you need me to ride with you tomorrow morning when you pick up Quint?" Edwina offered.

"No, Ed. Thanks, but you sleep in. I'll get over there early. He's bound to have things he needs to take care of. Thanks again for the evening."

"Don't thank me. I've done less damage on a night raid," Vic said.

"Nonsense. I'll talk to y'all tomorrow."

At home, though she was exhausted, Debbie Sue went through the nightly routine of cleansing her face. She thought back on the evening and the events. As determined as she had been to have a normal evening, it hadn't gone much better than the dinner at Kincaid's.

The next morning she woke a little later than she had planned on. She didn't usually set an alarm on Sundays. She always woke at her usual time automatically. But here it was nine o'clock. She took special care with her makeup and hair. Instead of her usual jeans and T-shirt, she donned a soft red velour jogging suit. The color was a good contrast with her hair, and the fabric hugged her curves in all the right places. When she opened her front door, she was shocked to see her driveway empty. Where the hell was the Navigator?

Before she screamed in full-blown panic that a fifty-thousand-dollar automobile had disappeared from her driveway, a fluttering sound drew her attention to the mailbox mounted on the left side of her door. A note was secured with the pink plastic clothespin she remembered handing Quint to use to close his fly.

I left the hospital against medical advice. Does that make me a fugitive? I sweet-talked a nurse into giving me a ride. Tried to wake you up, but I guess you didn't hear me knocking. Got to get down the road. Call you later. Thanks for everything.

QM

Debbie Sue stamped her foot and covered her face with both hands. "Well, fuck."

Twenty

Buddy was up, packed, and out the motel room door by five-thirty A.M. He had never slept late a day in his life, yet he had set the alarm and left a wake-up call just to be sure he didn't miss his seven o'clock flight. The one-hour trip would put him in Midland around eight and in Salt Lick no later than nine-thirty. He was leaving a day earlier than he had planned. As soon as he reached home, he would start working his new leads.

Just outside the Love Field gates, he came to an IHOP. He had time to enjoy a leisurely breakfast. He was sipping coffee when he opened the complimentary newspaper and read the lead story. Several people had been shot at a local bar. A grainy picture of Luna de Neón was displayed beside the story. His heart made a little bump. He scanned the article for the name of Detective Gomez and felt relieved when he didn't find it.

Allegedly, the fight had started over a wife finding her husband with another woman. The club's only bartender tried to intervene and was shot dead, along with the cheating husband and his mistress.

Buddy finished the article a little breathless. If he had made the trip to Dallas one day later, he would have missed obtaining a valuable piece of information, perhaps the key to solving Pearl Ann's murder. Then it hit him, the only person who could identify the mysterious Mexican who had called him was now a dead man. And he had no clue who the waitress was who had helped the suspect deposit money into the phone. *Damn.*

For the hour-long flight from Dallas to Midland, Buddy felt like a caged animal. He turned the pages of a magazine for the whole hour, but didn't read a word. When the plane landed he was up and out of his seat before anyone else.

He was so anxious to get back and start working on the case, he had forgotten about his worry over Billy Don, but when he pulled within sight of the sheriff's rear entrance he knew something was wrong. Terribly wrong.

The few times they'd had occasion to make an arrest in Salt Lick, if the prisoner had a car, it usually had been parked in the rear, away from the street, to keep it from public view. Small-town talk moved faster than a racehorse, and he saw no point in creating unnecessary complications in anyone's life. Tonight the small parking area looked like a used car lot.

Buddy suppressed a groan. He would rather have walked back into Luna de Neón wearing a pink skirt than enter his own office. He circled around front and parked. He climbed out of the Tahoe and walked to the door.

Before he even turned the knob, he could hear the ruckus and above it, Billy Don's voice. "Everybody needs to just settle down. Yelling at me ain't gonna get you nowhere. And Maudeen Wiley, you should be ashamed of yourself. Do you eat with that dirty mouth?"

Buddy stepped inside. Looking beyond Billy Don, he counted seven people in the jail's two cells—two women in one and five men in the other. Besides Maudeen Wiley, he saw Brother Greene from the Calvary Baptist Church, the football team's coach, Jim Finley; and four other model citizens.

They were all talking at once. Maudeen was trying to rally a chorus of "We Shall Overcome." Buddy couldn't make out much of what they were saying, but he did pick up that they were threatening lawsuits and demanding to be released, *now*. "Deputy, do you want to tell me what's going on here?"

"Sheriff Overstreet, you're home! Man, am I glad to see you. We've had a crime wave since you left. A true crime wave."

Buddy summoned all the control he could muster. "Billy Don, open those doors and let those people go. Give them their car keys and send them home."

"But I haven't fingerprinted them yet."

Fingerprinted. Buddy rolled his eyes to the ceiling. "We know them all. We know where they live. Let's let them go on their own recognizance. I need to talk to you, and I can't even hear myself think with all this noise."

"But—"

Buddy took the cell keys from the desk drawer. "Folks, I'm sorry for the inconvenience. Please go on home now."

All the prisoners filed out with strong last words for Deputy Roberts, except Maudeen. She remained in the cell sitting on the bunk.

"Miz Wiley, do you need a ride?" Buddy asked. "Is there anything I can do for you?"

"Could I stay just a little while longer? I called the Peaceful Oasis and they're getting a vanload of residents to come down and see me in lock-up. This is the most excitement we've had in ages. I'm the only one there who still has a life. I'm kind of a celebrity."

A van full of senior citizens shuffling through his office like a band of tourists was the last thing Buddy needed. "How about if Deputy Roberts takes you back in handcuffs? He could even leave them on 'til he walks you back to your room. Would that be enough excitement for you?"

"Could he hold a gun on me?"

"No, ma'am. I can't allow him to do that."

Maudeen took a moment to mull over the offer. "Tell you what. If he'll give me a stern talking-to in front of the others, it's a deal."

"Did you hear that, Deputy? When you get Miz Wiley inside the Peaceful Oasis, tell her you're releasing her this time, but you don't want to have to come after her again."

Billy Don had an argumentative look in his eye, so Buddy added, "And when you get done there, Deputy, come back here. We need to talk."

"C'mon, Miz Wiley," Billy Don said. "I'll carry your purse for you if it's all the same to you. I don't think I could take any more blows to the head." Billy Don adjusted the handcuffs on her birdlike wrists and walked her through the door.

Buddy sat down at his desk, tamping down his annoyance. He had phone calls to make before Deputy Roberts returned. He laid his notes in front of him and retrieved his worn, crumpled list of people he had questioned about Pearl Ann's death. The first number he dialed was Harley's. After four or five rings, voice mail came on and Buddy hung up. He didn't want to talk to a machine. He had a hot lead, and he was anxious to move on it.

He keyed in Carol Jean's number. Another recorded message. He spoke quickly and with authority, asking her to call him as soon as possible and as an afterthought, he added he would like to talk to Harley, too.

It occurred to him he hadn't checked his messages at home. Perhaps the murderer had left another confession for him. He dialed his number, entered the code to retrieve messages, and heard the monotone voice announce he had six calls. *God, let one of them be the killer saying here I am, come and get me.*

This time he wasn't so lucky. He had four calls from Kathy and two hang-ups. No doubt the hang-ups were her, too. Her tone of voice changed with each communication, ranging from pleasant to pissed. He didn't want to face that issue now, but he might as well call her.

He was met with the cool demeanor he had halfway expected. She allowed him to explain where he had been and the reason for the sudden departure. Gradually her attitude mellowed.

"Goodness, Buddy," she said, responding to the news story about Luna de Neon, "if that shooting had happened just a few hours earlier, you would have been there and I wouldn't even have known where you were."

Buddy detected a catch in her throat and knew she was struggling with tears. He felt like an asshole. "Let me make it up to you, Kathy. How about tomorrow night? We'll go out to dinner someplace nice. I can be over there by seven."

"That sounds wonderful. It'll be so good to see you. I love you, Buddy."

Just then he heard Billy Don open the door to

the office. Perfect timing, as always. "Oh . . . yeah, uh . . . okay, thanks." Buddy hung up feeling more like an asshole than ever.

Buddy had always found it difficult to stay mad at anybody for very long, and his anger with the well-meaning deputy had already subsided. Billy Don sat down across the desk and went into great detail explaining that he had been stopping cars, looking for the fugitives targeted by the FBI flyer. When the citizens had resisted showing their drivers' licenses, and hadn't allowed their vehicles to be searched, Deputy Roberts had arrested them for obstruction of an ongoing investigation. He produced the flyer from his pocket and showed Buddy the faxed notice.

Buddy didn't bother pointing out the scatter fax, sent to every law enforcement agency in the United States, specified that the men were believed to be in the vicinity of Los Angeles. At this juncture, what was the point? "Tell me why you picked on Maudeen. She doesn't even drive."

"Yessir. You know, that's the meanest little woman I've ever come across. When I was putting Reverend Greene in the squad car, she came over and started cussin' and beatin' on me with her purse. I had to put her in the car just to get her off me. She's a menace, that one is."

"Billy Don, we're lucky there isn't a lawyer in Salt Lick. Every one of those people would be in his office right now. We need to do some damage control to make sure they don't call one in from Odessa or Midland tomorrow."

"But they wouldn't—"

"The flyer says, 'Be on the lookout.' I hope you didn't really search their cars."

The deputy shrank a little lower in his chair. "Uh-oh."

Buddy leaned back, let out a groan, and looked upward for guidance he knew wasn't going to be there. "Billy Don, without probable cause and a search warrant, you can't search their cars."

"No kidding? Why, I didn't know that. How do you know so much about the law, Buddy?"

Buddy looked into the face of the young man whose question rang of sincerity. He was touched by his deputy's obvious admiration, but unlike Billy Don, Buddy busted his butt to learn everything he could about being a good law officer. "I read, Billy Don. I go to school. Did you think I drive over to Odessa College two times a week just to meet pretty women?"

"Naw, I didn't think that. You've already got pretty women around you. I think Miss Kathy's real nice-lookin', and your ex, Debbie Sue, she's the best-lookin' woman I know. I saw her drive by Saturday night with that rodeo fella. She looked like a hundred bucks. I wanted to stop 'em so I'd have an excuse to get his autograph, but I was too busy. You think she'd get Quint Matthews to sign something for me?"

Buddy felt as if the floor had fallen from beneath him. *Debbie Sue had seen Quint Saturday night?* He couldn't explain why, but he thought the disastrous evening at Kincaid's in Odessa would have discouraged Quint, who was bound to be accustomed to easier prey than Debbie Sue. *Dammit, of course he's back. For him, the challenge of a woman like Debbie Sue would be a turn-on.*

"You'll have to ask her, Billy Don. I wouldn't know."

Suddenly chewing on Billy Don's ass seemed unimportant and following up on his new leads seemed less driving.

"That's a real good idea, Buddy. I just might do that. It's not every day a famous bull rider shows up in Salt Lick."

"Go on home and get some rest, Billy Don. You've had a busy weekend, and I've got to start making phone calls."

"Thanks, Buddy. That's real considerate of you. I *am* tired. There's a lot of upset to arresting people, ain't there?"

Left alone, Buddy ran his hand over his face, unable to shift his thoughts away from his ex-wife and Quint Matthews. How could Debbie Sue, or any woman, resist the world Quint Matthews could offer? Everything Buddy had demanded she give up, Quint could return. And on a silver platter. Hooking up with him, rodeo would become her life again. She would have the best horses money could buy. Financial worries would be a thing of the past . . .

So would Salt Lick. And so would he.

Christ! The irony was overwhelming. After he had stayed in Salt Lick all these years on the foolhardy notion that someday, somehow, something would work out between them, what if she was the one who up and left?

He had to talk to her, had to tell her how his thinking had changed. Up to now, it had been easy to blame her for the flaws in their relationship. He'd had fixed ideas what a good marriage should be, but she had refused to give in to them. Had his demands played a part in the breakup? Had his own obstinacy been as damaging as her headstrong ways?

He thought about calling Kathy back and postponing their dinner date, but decided against it. He suddenly didn't want to be left alone with his thoughts. Meanwhile, he began calling the seven released inmates and making nice.

I should have stayed in Dallas.

Debbie Sue sat on her living room sofa thumbing through a new issue of *Horse Illustrated*, listening to Patsy Cline sing her heart out. She couldn't remember when she had been so relaxed.

The last few weeks had certainly given her reason to appreciate the tranquillity of the moment. She couldn't decide if she felt relieved because

Quint had recovered—even to the point of leaving the hospital against medical advice—or because she'd been excused from a Sunday morning round of sex she didn't have her whole heart in.

Well, she wouldn't question fate. She would just enjoy the moment. Sunday morning with nothing to do, nowhere she had to be. What a luxury.

The phone destroyed the peace and quiet. She contemplated not answering, especially when caller ID revealed a number she didn't recognize. But she caved in.

"Hello?" She didn't try to hide the annoyance in her voice.

"Hi, Debbie Sue. Did I catch you at a bad time?"

"C. J., how great to hear from you. I was just sitting here wondering what I should be doing. Talking to you is exactly what I would have picked. Where are you? I didn't recognize the number."

"I'm in Wyoming. Harley and I came up here yesterday."

"Wyoming! Good Lord, C. J., that's like a million miles away. What are you doing up there? Did y'all run off and get married?"

"Heavens, no. I wouldn't do that to you guys, or my parents. Harley had some business here and he asked me to come along. I've never been anywhere, so I just up and said yes. He's already out having breakfast with some stockholders and I'm just sitting here enjoying the view.

"We're in this gorgeous cabin right outside town. The bedroom is a loft that overlooks the downstairs, and one whole wall is glass. And there's the most beautiful scenery. I feel like a country mouse. This doesn't sound like me, does it?"

"No, but that's okay, too. What's the weather like there?"

"I thought of you the second we got off the plane. This may be the most beautiful place on earth. Mountains and trees and snow. Even the smell is incredible. You can't believe how cold it is here. Harley built me a fire this morning before he left. I didn't pack nearly enough warm clothes."

Debbie Sue thought of the temperature nearing the eighty-five-degree mark already and sighed. "How long do you plan on being there?"

"All week. I'll be back to Texas Saturday, but Harley's going to Portland."

"You're not going with him?"

"I have a job to get back to. I may be dating the boss, but I'm not taking anything for granted. It wouldn't be fair to those ladies I work with to leave them shorthanded for so long."

C. J., ever considerate of others.

They spent the rest of the conversation catching each other up on current events. Debbie Sue told about the gift from Quint, the evening at Edwina's, and the trip to the hospital. She mentioned that Vic had received another phone call from his ex-wife, and Ed was more upset than she was letting on.

"I hope things work out for Ed and Vic. I've never seen her so happy. But I don't blame her for being worried. We have no way of knowing about Vic and his ex's true feelings for each other or what they lived through and shared. Those kinds of bonds are hard to break."

"Yeah, I know."

"Just look at you and Buddy. It's been three years and he's still on your mind. Oops, I guess I'd better go. My sweetheart just walked through the door."

"You better get rid of him before Harley comes back." Debbie Sue laughed though her heart felt heavy at C. J.'s comment about Buddy.

"You're terrible," C. J. said, laughing, too. "It's so nice to be able to talk about Harley freely. When I get home, let's all get together. I love you. Tell Ed I said hi."

After hanging up, Debbie Sue sat with the phone in her hand, thinking. She hadn't told C. J. about accepting the job offer from Quint. How could she forget her biggest piece of news? Could it be she wasn't as excited as she ought to be about this new job—if that's what it was? God knew her feelings for Quint didn't rival what C. J. felt for Harley or what Debbie Sue had once felt for Buddy. Or maybe still felt for Buddy. Or whatever.

C. J. and Harley. She still couldn't get used to the idea of them as a couple. God knew C. J. deserved to be treated well and Harley, well, Harley was probably overdue for some caring, too.

*   *   *

By that evening Buddy had given up on reaching Harley or Carol Jean. They could be anywhere. He could reach them both at the office come Monday, so he decided to give it a rest.

Pearl Ann and her tall, handsome Mexican lover. The secret was a well-kept one. Was he married, too? It had to be an association that would seem casual to the average onlooker. The people closest to Pearl Ann should know about him, yet in the dozens of people he had talked to, no one had mentioned a person that fit the description given to him by the bartender.

Buddy had his detective work cut out for him, but this was what he had dreamed of, what he had wanted to do his whole life.

God, don't let me blow it.

Twenty-one

Edwina lay beside Vic watching him twitch and mumble in his sleep. Though she knew a soufflé falling could cause his restlessness, she imagined him dreaming of a mission, saving lives in some exotic land. She gently traced a scar on his shoulder with her long acrylic nails, wondering when and how he had received that particular memento.

It was October 15, three weeks to the day since Brenda had first called. And she had called last night. Edwina had intercepted the message and erased it before Vic heard it. The calls from Brenda usually came once or twice a year. Yesterday's call made two in less than thirty days. Not good.

The message had been neither frantic and guilt-ridden nor an emotional plea for attention. Yesterday's voice had been warm and enticing. Brenda had relocated to San Diego. She talked of mutual friends and invited Vic to come out to the West Coast for a SEAL reunion. The invitation had *not* been extended to Vic *and* Edwina.

Edwina felt guilty for keeping the message from Vic, but as she had reminded Debbie Sue just days before—all was fair in love and war. Coming up against a pining ex-wife was something Edwina was trained for. Beating out a platoon of ex-SEALs was something else. Time for some undercover work, she thought, and slid down, under the sheets.

Over a week had passed since Debbie Sue had seen Quint, but he had called several times. Because they had much in common, they always found topics for discussion. He was so laid back he was practically liquid, which made him easy and fun to talk to. His devil-may-care nature had been what attracted her to him when she was seventeen.

He said he would be in the Salt Lick area in about a week and asked if he could come by. That was the upside to having a suitor who didn't live in town. A local boyfriend or husband saw you not only at your very best, but at your very worst. Someone from out of town, for whom you had to plan in advance, got the best you had to offer all the time—like clean breath, freshly applied makeup, and perfume. And shaved legs.

Her mom had been aghast at the expensive gift Quint had bestowed on Debbie Sue, but like her daughter, once she tried on the jacket, she had been reluctant to remove it. She had even extracted a promise that if she ever won a Country Music Association award, Debbie Sue would allow her to borrow it and wear it in Nashville.

Buddy was requestioning everyone who had associated with Pearl Ann. With her only strong lead out of contention, Debbie Sue had abandoned the mystery solving and left it to Buddy. She didn't have the time or resources to go looking for a killer. She would pay her debts the old fashioned way—by working her ass off.

Besides, her life wasn't *all* work. She had one thing to look forward to. This Thursday Quint would be in town.

It had taken over a week, but Buddy finally tracked Harley down. He ran into him at Hogg's Drive-In, of all places, and asked him if he knew the new suspect in his wife's murder.

Buddy's spirits were dashed when Harley shook his head. "I've got a lot of Mexicans on my payroll, but no one of that description. Some are handsome, but too old or too young. And none of them are tall. Did you talk to the folks at the house? They probably saw more of what went on with my wife than I did."

"I did talk to them. They either don't know or won't say."

"I know you can't see it, but there's irony in the

fact that you believe a Mexican killed Pearl Ann
and that he did it out of love."

"How so?"

"She hated Mexicans. She felt they were beneath her. I don't know where she got the idea."

Buddy knew. In West Texas most Mexicans
were migrant workers who had crossed the Rio
Grande looking for a better life. They were employed mostly as manual laborers, and many
people gave them no credit for being the hard
workers the majority of them were. On the ladder of respect in Salt Lick, only Pearl Ann's family would have occupied a rung lower than a
Mexican migrant worker. Yep, he could see the
irony.

Quint arrived at the Styling Station on Thursday
around three o'clock. The patrons giggled and
feigned horror at being discovered in curlers or
with wet hair by a good-looking man. Being the
dutiful Southern gentleman, he complimented all
and flirted outrageously. Most of the women were
old enough to be his grandmother, but he didn't
seem to notice. He was in his element—women
swooning over him.

"Quint, you're incorrigible," Debbie Sue said. "I
didn't expect you this early. You're gonna have to
wait 'til I finish."

"No problem, darlin'. I'll just run up to the store
and pick up some beer. Can I get you anything?"

"No, thanks. I'm fixin' hamburgers at the house tonight. Beer will be perfect."

"Homemade hamburgers? Great. I get tired of restaurant food."

"Listen," she said, catching him out of earshot of her patrons, "you're not allergic to hamburgers, are you? I mean, it's just plain ground beef and mustard—"

"Thanks for asking. Hamburgers are a safe bet for me."

When Quint left, Debbie Sue moved her last customer, Burma Johnson, from the hair dryer to her station for a comb-out.

"Was that young fellow Quint Matthews?" Burma asked.

"Yes, ma'am." Debbie enjoyed Quint's celebrity status, even though it was limited to country people and rodeo fans.

"My granddaughter gave him a ride to Salt Lick a couple of weeks ago. Ruthie. You know her, don't you?"

An alarm went off in Debbie Sue's brain. She hadn't given any thought to *which* nurses' aide Quint had "sweet-talked" into giving him a ride from Odessa. Oh, yes, she did know Ruthie Gentry, a younger version of Pearl Ann. Everyone in Salt Lick knew Ruthie, as did most of West Texas, Debbie Sue was willing to bet. "Yes, ma'am, I do."

"I'd be leery of him, hon. Ruthie didn't come home that night. She thinks it's a big secret, but her mother told me."

Fuck. Ruthie Gentry counted her conquests in notches on her bedpost. She wouldn't have let Quint Matthews get out of her grasp, oh no. She would view him as her finest trophy.

Debbie Sue had told herself she didn't mind if Quint saw other women. He had said their arrangement wasn't a commitment, and she had agreed. But damned if she was pleased to have him chase after someone on her own doorstep in her hometown. She didn't know how she would learn what happened between him and Ruthie Gentry, but she would. After all, she now had experience as a detective.

Quint returned from the store, and after doing her perfunctory end-of-the-workday duties in the salon, Debbie Sue locked up and they left in separate vehicles for her house.

She assigned the fire-starting task to Quint while she changed into comfortable clothes, all the while stewing over the fact that he might have spent the night with Ruthie.

"I missed seeing Ed today," he said when she put in an appearance on the patio.

She had changed into shorts and a T-shirt and some cute little thong flip-flops adorned with beads. "She left early." Debbie Sue adjusted the patio door, leaving it open a few inches so she could hear the phone.

"What's become of your other friend, that pretty little thing . . . can't think of her name."

"C. J.?"

"Yeah, C. J. I know some cowboys who might like to meet her."

"She wouldn't be interested. She's involved with someone. In fact, she'll most likely be getting married soon."

He chuckled. "That's a waste."

For some reason, the quip rankled her. From out of nowhere, it dawned on her she had never discussed Pearl Ann's murder with Quint. "Do you know Harley Carruthers? Seems like y'all would travel in the same circles."

"Yeah, I know Harley. We go back a ways. Is *that* who she's marrying? That's a little quick, isn't it? I thought Pearl Ann was the only one screwing around in that marriage."

"I didn't say C. J. was marrying Harley. I didn't know you knew Pearl Ann. How come you haven't mentioned her murder once in all this time?"

"I don't know. I guess I didn't think it was a big deal."

Debbie Sue couldn't believe her ears. How could he be so callous? "You didn't think the murder of a man's wife that you go back a ways with is a big deal?"

"Not really. She most likely got what she had coming. That's all."

"That's all? Quint, how could you think someone deserves to be murdered?" A thought evil enough to make her scalp shrink sliced through Debbie

Sue's head. "Unless . . . unless she did something to *you*. Did you fool around with Pearl Ann?"

"Oh, great, here we go. Yeah, I messed around with her a little. So what? It was a couple of years ago and it wasn't in this town. It only lasted a few months."

"A few months?" Debbie Sue couldn't control the strident tone of the question, but she felt proud of herself that she had tamped it down when what she *wanted* to do was clutch her head and shriek.

"Debbie Sue, cut it out. Don't tell me you didn't know what Pearl Ann was. You expect me to break down and cry 'cause she's dead? I'm sorry, I just don't feel that way."

The air around Debbie Sue's head had begun to glow red. "So she screwed around. So what? Are you any better? You didn't even take a breath making sure I knew a roll in the hay was all you wanted from me. That and a little bit of horse talk now and then on the side."

"What is this? Dammit, I—"

"And I suppose you're fixin' to tell me nothing happened between you and Ruthie Gentry?"

"Who?"

"The nurses' aide who gave you a ride to Salt Lick from Odessa hospital."

"Oh. I didn't know what her name was. What about her?"

"You met her grandmother in my shop this afternoon." Debbie Sue restrained herself from adding *asshole*. "She told me Ruthie didn't come home the night she gave you a ride."

"So?"

"So? . . . You're a chickenshit, Quint Matthews."

He stopped fiddling with the charcoal and fixed her with a hard look. "This is heading to a place we shouldn't be going, Debbie Sue."

The phone warbled, but she didn't intend to answer until she gave Mr. World Champion Bullshitter a piece of her mind. She allowed the call to go to her answering machine. Before she could launch a diatribe, her mother's voice came on. "Deb, sweetie, pick up if you're there. I'm at Dr. Miller's with Rocket Man."

Debbie Sue practically stumbled through the patio door opening and grabbed the phone before her mother could say more. "Mom! Mom, I'm here. What's wrong with Rocket Man?"

"Dr. Miller's not sure yet. Can you come? I'd feel better if you were here."

"I'll be there in a minute." Debbie Sue hung up and turned to Quint, momentarily forgetting the knock-down, drag-out fight she was primed to have. "Rocket Man's sick. Do you want to come with me to Dr. Miller's?"

"Yeah, sure. Let's go."

At the veterinarian clinic she found the doctor, her mom, and Rocket Man in one of the treatment barns in back. Dr. Miller was performing an ultrasound on the sick animal's lungs. Her mother told her she had been watching the horse closely since yesterday morning. He had a nasal discharge, difficulty breathing, and showed no interest in eating, even when she offered him a whole box of Twinkies.

"I took his temperature and it was a little over a hundred and two. I decided to load him up and bring him in."

"You should have called me, Mom. It can be dangerous taking a horse's temperature."

"Oh heavens, I've done it a thousand times. I was more worried about him than myself." Her gaze swung to Quint. "Why, my goodness, Quinton, you're all grown up."

"Yes, ma'am. Good to see you again, Mrs. Pratt."

"How're your folks?"

"Just fine. Mom's down in her back a lot and Dad's still mean and ornery." Looking around the treatment area, he let out a low whistle. "This is quite a setup, isn't it? I didn't notice it when I was here a couple of weeks ago. Salt Lick's lucky to have such a sophisticated facility."

"It helps having a rich man depending on it for his own animals. Harley Carruthers built it. I've always thought it a shame an animal has the best of everything in Salt Lick, but a sick person can't get taken care of. But then, you already know that from firsthand experience, don't you?"

Quint laughed. "Yes, ma'am, I sure do."

Debbie Sue could hear they were talking to each other, but she wasn't processing their words. Her attention was absorbed by Dr. Miller and her beautiful horse. Rocket Man must have sensed she was near because he looked at her with big eyes that showed a mixture of illness and fear. Was she near losing him? She couldn't stop the tears that welled in her throat. She moved to his side and began rubbing his neck. *Please don't leave me, Rocket Man. Please.*

A voice she would never stop knowing called from the back of the corrals, just outside the doorway leading from the barn. "Where is everybody? Dr. Miller?" Buddy stepped through the doorway. "I was driving by and saw your pickup and trailer, Virginia. What's going on?"

Debbie Sue wanted to cry out in relief. Buddy's solid stability was what she needed. Only he could understand her attachment to Rocket Man.

"Don't tell me you're in love with this animal, too," Quint said to Buddy.

Debbie Sue was stunned. She thought of grabbing the ultrasound equipment and searching for a heart in Quint's chest cavity.

Buddy shot him a murderous look, then greeted her by touching the brim of his hat. "Debbie Sue." He turned to Quint. "I didn't see your rig, Matthews. You must have parked in front. I thought Virginia might need some help, but since you're here, I'll go on."

"Please don't go," Debbie Sue said, stepping in front of him. "You know almost as much about horses as Dr. Miller. Please be here when he talks to us."

Just then the doctor moved away from his equipment. "You've got a pretty sick animal here. I'll need to do some blood work to check for further infection, but his lungs have fluid in them. He's got pneumonia for sure. His sub-mandibular lymph nodes are swollen." He motioned for Buddy, who walked over and examined Rocket Man's jaws and neck for himself.

"Umm, I see," Buddy said, while Debbie Sue clung to her mother's hand.

"I need to start him on an aggressive broad-spectrum antibiotic that'll kill strep. When the culture and sensitivity results come back, we'll make a change if we need to."

Buddy nodded and rubbed a hand down Rocket Man's neck.

Debbie Sue couldn't quell the panic darting from head to heart and back again. "But he's going to be all right, isn't he, Dr. Miller?"

The vet rested his hand on the horse's flank. "Given his age, he could have a rough go of it, but I think he'll pull through. I'll do everything possible."

Debbie Sue looked at Buddy through eyes blurred with tears. Another heartbreaking scene rushed at her—the day a doctor in Midland had told her and Buddy that their little Luke didn't have much chance of surviving. At four months premature, he was just too tiny. Buddy had been her strength. They had both prayed and fought for Luke, but lost in the end.

Forcing herself back to the present, she found Buddy watching her. Was he thinking the same thing? Was this as painful for him as it was for her?

Quint interrupted her thoughts. "I think you should put him down, Debbie Sue. He's old. He's had a good life, but what's he good for now? He's just an expensive burden."

"No." Debbie Sue shook her head fiercely.

"He's not that ill, Mr. Matthews," Dr. Miller said. "He needs about a week of medication, and if nothing else goes wrong, he should—"

Suddenly Buddy grabbed Quint by the shirt-front and slammed him against the wall with a bang. The smaller man's hat flew off and landed beneath Rocket Man. The horse promptly stepped on it.

"You self-centered sonofabitch. Don't you know how much he means to her? What it would do to her if she lost him?" Buddy shoved his face menacingly close to Quint's. "Do you even care?"

Debbie Sue grabbed Buddy's arm, at the end of which was a cocked fist. "Buddy, stop!"

"Buddy," Debbie Sue's mom cried, her eyes tearing. "Son, you're the sheriff."

Debbie Sue saw her ex-husband shaking with uncharacteristic rage, but he released Quint's shirt and stepped back.

Quint bent down, picked up his hat, and began

reshaping the crown where Rocket Man had stepped on it. He glared up at Buddy. "Stay away from me, you goddamn loser. I *am* thinking of Debbie Sue. She deserves a better life than staying in this shithole town, in that shithole *beauty* shop, baby-sitting a worn-out horse. And waiting for *you* to decide what you want to be when you grow up. *Texas Ranger?*" He huffed. "You wouldn't make a wart on a Texas Ranger's ass."

Suddenly a fist made contact with Quint's chin and he slid down the treatment room wall. Debbie Sue looked up at Buddy, momentarily too stunned to speak. She finally found her voice. "Oh my God. Did I knock him out?"

Without a word Buddy pulled her to him and kissed her as in the old days, when they had been so much in love kissing was all they could think about. A thrill rushed through her. Home. Finally, after the tears she had shed, after the bleak years without him, she was home. She arched to get closer. If she pressed against him hard enough, she would be enveloped by him and wouldn't have to live without him any longer.

Eventually he set her away. "Debbie Sue—"

"Oh, Buddy, I—"

"Buddy? Sweetheart? Are you back here? Bud—ohmygod, what did I step in? . . . Ooohh, yuuuck!" Kathy Bozo came around the corner of the building holding one shoe away from her body and tiptoeing on her bare foot.

Buddy peeled Debbie Sue's arms away and

walked over to Rocket Man. Debbie Sue stared at him dumbfounded, then at Kathy. Had Kathy been here all this time?

"Is everything all right, Buddy? I got cold and you took the keys." Kathy's attention swerved to Quint who was struggling to his feet. Her eyes popped wide. "Is he all right?"

"He's fine," Buddy said, a hint of a tremor in his voice. "You can't hurt a damn bull rider." He dug into his pocket and came up with keys, which he handed to her. "Go on back to the pickup, Kathy. I'll be there in a minute. We've got a sick horse on our hands. I need to finish my talk with Dr. Miller."

"Oh, too bad. Whose horse is it? . . . Oh, Debbie Sue. I didn't see you over there. Buddy, will you be much longer?"

He put a hand on her shoulder and turned her. "Start the engine and let the cab get warm."

Kathy placed both hands on his arm, raised to her tiptoes, and kissed his cheek. Then with a faint little smile, she walked out of the treatment barn.

Debbie Sue flew at Buddy. "You bastard! You call Quint self-centered? And whose best interest did you have in mind when you practically broke my arm shoving me aside so your fiancée wouldn't see you kissing me?"

Buddy's hands opened. "Debbie Sue, I forgot she was even—"

"You forgot? That's supposed to make me feel better? You forgot? Just get out of here, Buddy. *I'll* take care of my horse. Just like I take care of myself."

Quint, now on his feet, brushed straw from his clothing, ran a hand through his blond hair. He glared at Buddy. "That was a lucky punch. You hit like a girl." He clapped his hat on his head. The crown, irreparably crushed, stood taller on one side. "Debbie Sue, let's go. We can talk about this later."

"No. We don't have anything to talk about. All of a sudden I don't like you very much."

"Why? Because I said something you don't want to hear?"

"No. Because you don't care about animals. You don't respect the dead and you don't respect the women you've slept with. And I wouldn't like myself if I kept seeing you or if I went to work for you. As we say in this shithole of a town, don't let the door hit you in the—"

"You're turning me down?" Quint gaped at her. "You can't be serious—"

"Quint, if you don't leave, I swear I'll hit you again."

Quint's gaze shifted between her and Buddy. His jaw muscles worked a few seconds, then he stomped out.

Buddy spoke up. "You did the right thing—"

"You get out, too. I have to take care of Rocket Man."

Buddy hesitated, his hands resting on his belt. "Deb—"

"Go! Now. Your fiancée's waiting, remember?"

His eyes seemed to be pleading, but his mouth

remained closed. Finally he turned and walked out of the barn and left her alone with her beloved horse. It had always been that way, really—just her, her mom, and Rocket Man. No one else.

Before she could tear her hair and wail, her mom and Dr. Miller returned. She hadn't even noticed when they left.

She forced herself to listen as the doctor explained Rocket Man's treatment plan. She thanked him and said she'd be back tomorrow morning. "Mom, can you give me a ride home?"

"Of course. Have you eaten?"

"Please, Mom. I just want to go home. I don't want to make any stops along the way."

As soon as she was in the confines of the little house she had once shared with Buddy, she lost it. Her tears came in great waves, grief mixed with anger. She might never stop crying.

For the next week, each morning, noon, and evening, Debbie Sue drove to the veterinary clinic and checked on Rocket Man. She didn't let herself think about the bill for his stay in the state-of-the-art clinic. Dr. Miller was enthusiastic about his improvement and planned on sending him home by the weekend. Rocket Man seemed to be enjoying all the attention.

Edwina came by and brought an afghan for his hindquarters. "It would be a lot less trouble if you had a dog for a pet." She combed and braided his mane because, she said, "it's important to keep looking *good* when you're feeling *bad*."

Dr. Miller allowed Vic to bring an unfrosted, special Asian ingredient carrot cake to the patient. He was especially interested in the recipe because the horse seemed to have rallied after eating the homemade concoction.

She knew Buddy had stopped by because she could smell peppermint on Rocket Man's breath.

Life moved on.

Twenty-two

Debbie Sue's days returned to the humdrum of pre–Pearl Ann's death. Busy days, money worries. Quiet evenings at home, money worries. Boring.

Rocket Man had been released from the veterinary clinic and, as she had feared, the bill for his treatment left her breathless, even with the employee discount Dr. Miller had given her mom. The upside was that the horse was now as frisky as a colt. Mom had installed him in the barn near the house to keep close watch on him for a few more days.

The gossip about Pearl Ann's death had worn thin. Nothing new had come from the sheriff's office, so Debbie Sue assumed her customers were tired of talking about the same stuff over and over. Since she had given up on collecting the reward, her interest had waned, too.

The atmosphere in the salon was upbeat. Unfortunately, Debbie Sue's attitude wasn't. Her life had sunk into the pits. In the past ten days she'd had to come to terms with the fact that she wouldn't be taking an exciting job offer from Quint, her financial problems were *not* going away, and Buddy hadn't even tried to contact her after the sudden passion they had shared when Rocket Man came down sick.

She was still astonished he would do something so out of character as kiss her when he had Kathy waiting for him outside. She was giving up men. They were too complicated and took too much of the mental energy she should be devoting to saving her ass from bankruptcy.

In a place where no entertainment existed except school sports, citizens had to improvise, so Vic announced a backyard barbecue for the coming weekend. The weather forecast for Saturday was perfect. It was what kept many people enduring the hardships of life in West Texas. While northern neighbors shoveled snow and shivered in frigid temperatures, West Texans basked in seventy-degree days and comfortable low-fifties evenings. A trade-off for the blistering summer heat was only fair.

Debbie Sue couldn't psych herself up for a party. On Saturday she added the last touches to her final cut and curl for the day and made her departure for her mom's house, intending to give her mother a break from caring for Rocket Man. Her mother met her with a firm admonition for even suggesting she would forgo Vic's backyard picnic to stay near the recuperating horse.

"You're only young once," her mother said. "Rocket Man had so much company at the vet's he needs a rest. Go and have fun."

And Debbie Sue, being the dutiful daughter, decided to do just that. She drove home and changed into what she called her high water pants, which other people called capris, banded her hair into a ponytail, and slid her feet into a pair of sandals. She grabbed her contribution to the feast—plastic cups, plastic silverware, paper plates and paper napkins—and she was off. Oh sure, most people put thought and time into preparing what they donated to a big feed. Big deal. If diners didn't have utensils and had to eat with their hands, all the delicious food in the world wouldn't be enjoyable.

Harley was out of town, so she swung by and picked up C. J. In the backyard behind Vic and Edwina's trailer, strands of tiny white lights hung on every protrusion and the smell of smoldering mesquite wood permeated the air.

Meat hadn't even touched the grill and already Debbie Sue's mouth watered. Edwina had gone overboard by making potato salad with her own hands and cooking a pot of pinto beans chock full of tomatoes, chili powder, and jalapeño peppers. A case of cold Budweiser was iced down in a cooler. C. J. had baked a Black Forest cake eight inches tall. Debbie Sue wasn't fond of a beer, barbecue, and chocolate cake combo, but she was game to try anything once, a fact that had often brought regrettable consequences.

Vic was in fine form, wearing a T-shirt with a navy SEAL insignia and a motto that read, "The Only Easy Day Was Yesterday." Edwina told them the saying was the SEALs' motto. Debbie Sue tried to apply it to her own life, but she couldn't because yesterday hadn't been any easier than today.

They piled their plates with more than they could eat and settled down to enjoy.

"Guess where Vic's going next weekend," Edwina said. "I think we should all go with him."

"Okay, I give up. Where?"

"Terlingua."

Terlingua. The world championship chili cook-off. The last good hell-raisin' party left that teenagers hadn't taken over. Of course, hundreds of people competing in a barbecuing and chili-cooking contest probably wouldn't appeal to most kids. "He's cooking in the chili contest?"

"No, but he likes to go. He meets up with some of his friends from the navy. I've never gone with him, but if y'all went, I would. Wouldn't that be a hoot?"

"I've never been, either," C. J. said. "I've lived here all my life and I've never been to Terlingua. Isn't that odd?"

"Not really," Debbie Sue answered. "I've never been, either."

"Well, that settles it." Edwina slapped the table-top with her palm. "We're going."

"When is it?"

"This coming weekend. We'd have to get there Thursday to get a decent camping spot. They're expecting fifteen thousand people this year."

"Ed, I can't afford to close the shop for three days."

"You said yourself, last month was your biggest ever. You need to take some time off. Celebrate a little. This may be the last chance we girls get to go off together and have fun. This time next year C. J. will be married to Harley and you'll probably be back with Buddy."

Debbie Sue sent Edwina a dark look. "I wish I hadn't told you about him kissing me. That does *not* mean we're getting back together. In fact, that kiss may have been the last straw for any chance between us. I haven't heard a word from him since."

C. J.'s eyes rounded. "What? What have y'all not told me?"

Debbie Sue filled her in on the events with Rocket Man, Quint, and Buddy.

"I agree with Edwina, Debbie Sue. You have to get away. If I say I'll go, will you come, too?"

"Whoa, now," Vic said. "My camper only sleeps two."

"Then we'll stay at a motel," C. J. said.

"Won't work. The hotels and motels have been booked for months, maybe even years. I can try to get a larger camper. I'd really love it if y'all came.

I've been wanting Ed to come with me, but she'd get bored when I get with my buddies. Reliving war stories isn't something most women enjoy."

"I know what we could do. I could ask Harley if we can borrow his Winnebago. It's just sitting in one of the barns out at his house."

"How big is it?"

"I don't know. It's bigger than a Greyhound."

"That figures," Vic said.

Edwina followed up. "Well, of course it does, Poodle."

"Ooohh, say you'll go, Debbie Sue," C. J. begged. "It won't feel right without you there."

"You'd better come with us," Edwina chimed in. "We'll make your life miserable with all the funny stories we come back with. You'll always regret not going."

Debbie Sue sighed. "The last thing I need is more to regret. Okay, I'll go."

Later, as she drove C. J. home, her blond friend asked, "Debbie Sue, did you hear about the new lead Buddy has for Pearl Ann's murderer? Harley's real encouraged."

"New lead? No, tell me."

C. J. told about the mystery phone call Buddy had received and his subsequent trip to Dallas. "He's asking everyone close to Pearl Ann if she ever had anything to do with a tall, handsome Mexican man. Buddy said he's supposed to be about thirty-five, well dressed and professional-looking. I told him I didn't know anyone of that description that Pearl Ann might have been with. Hasn't he talked to you about it?"

"No." The new clue struck a familiar chord in Debbie Sue's memory. Her brain strained to make the connection until it came to her. "C. J., do you remember Harley's party when Pearl Ann got so mad because you were dancing with the cook from San Angelo?"

C. J. shrugged and smiled. "Yes, I remember. That's when Harley and I first got acquainted."

"The cook, he was tall and good-looking."

"But he was Italian."

"C. J., he was as Mexican as he could be. His name was a common Spanish name. I can't remember it, but he was well dressed and had a great haircut." The memory grew in Debbie Sue's mind. Pearl Ann could have had only one reason to get so mad over C. J. dancing with the cook. "Oh, shit. Now I know why Pearl Ann lost her cool."

C. J. looked at her, round-eyed. "Really? Why?"

Debbie Sue barreled toward the sheriff's office. She intended only to share the new clue with Buddy, she told herself. She saw no light, hadn't expected to, really.

It was just as well he wasn't there, she thought, creeping home. In a way, she was grateful. If she had seen a light, she might have barged in and made a total fool of herself. Again.

She didn't dare drive by his apartment.

She felt hollow inside and couldn't shake it. As she drove, she made a mental list of how she would fill the hours between now and Monday. She would do constructive tasks she had put off doing, preoccupied as she had been with solving Pearl Ann's murder, followed so closely by Rocket Man's illness.

At home, after putting on a mellow Willie Nelson CD, she stripped off her clothes and stretched out in a warm bath, reading up on pneumonia in horses, knowledge to have in case Rocket Man suffered a relapse.

When the water grew too cool, she climbed out of the tub, dried with a big fluffy towel, and slathered her whole body with scented cream.

Last, she slapped a mudpack on her face and finished the horse pneumonia article while she waited for the mud to dry. Once the mudpack was removed, unable to think of anything else to do to her face and body, she pulled on her oversized nightshirt and brushed her hair a few hundred strokes. She almost didn't hear the faint chime of her ancient doorbell.

Anxiety stabbed her chest. *Mom? Rocket Man?* She shoved her arms into her robe and made her way through the dark house to the front, switched on the porch light, and yanked open the door.

And stood there paralyzed.

"Buddy," she said, deadpan. Instinctively she tugged her robe more tightly about herself.

He stood there, too, grave-faced, hanging on to the brim of his hat. "I thought . . . I'd come by."

"Oh . . ." She blanked out for a full ten seconds. "Well, yes. What's—what's up?" Her voice sounded as if it had climbed an octave. Before she knew it, she had backed up and he had come into the house.

And the next thing she knew she was in his arms.

The tension she had carried inside for three years broke like a great wave and engulfed her and she sobbed against his wide chest. Then he was kissing her, bracketing her face between his large hands as his lips moved over her face, murmuring her name and sipping away her tears. And she was kissing him back, her arms tightly wrapped around his waist.

It seemed perfectly natural and normal to untie her robe, slip her arms out of it, and let it drop to the floor. Her nightshirt followed and she stood before him naked but for her lacy panties.

He set her away and his eyes moved over her. "Oh, God, Debbie Sue. You're so beautiful. I've never forgotten—"

"Don't disappoint me," she whispered, tears close to spilling over.

He pulled her into his arms and kissed her again, his hands touching her everywhere. "I don't have anything," he murmured against her lips.

"I don't care," she sobbed. And she didn't because she knew without a splinter of doubt she was *meant* to be with Buddy. She was *meant* to have his children.

"If you don't, neither do I." He lifted her in his arms and carried her to the bed they had shared the five years of their marriage.

She let him peel away her panties, then he let her help *him* undress. After all, he had on far more clothing than she, and hadn't she always been his helper in all things? Once he was naked, she worshipped him with her hands and mouth, reveling in his soft, deep groans. When he could endure no more, he pulled her up, his mouth finding hers.

There in their wedding bed, the bed she had shared with no man save him, she opened her heart and body and took in his hot, hard flesh. The thing she feared she had forgotten became a profound revival. As he paused above her, breath ragged and desperate, their gazes locked. She could feel his trembling, or was it hers?

"I love you," he murmured. "I've never stopped."

"I love you, too," she whimpered and thought she might rise and float away on a cloud of sheer joy.

Sunlight poured in on them. Debbie Sue awoke and without opening her eyes, snuggled against Buddy's big, muscular body. They had made love all night. And talked. And made love.

He pulled her even closer. "Did we make a baby last night?"

"I don't think so. Did you want to?"

"If that's what's meant to be. Would you be afraid?"

She hesitated, not having thought of being pregnant again. "Maybe. But I'd be more afraid of never trying again."

"You are gonna marry me, aren't you?"

She fought back tears of bliss. "Do we have to adopt Kathy?"

"I figured out the lie she told you. That night when Rocket Man was sick and you said *fiancée*, I finally figured it out. Don't worry. She's not a problem. I settled it."

She squirmed closer to his warm, naked skin. How had she lived without him for three long years? "Oh, Buddy, I'm gonna be so good. I'm gonna learn to cook. I'm gonna do laundry. I wanted to tell you months ago, but—"

"Shh. You're plenty good, just like you are."

"No, I'm not. I'm loud and I cuss and I'm hardheaded."

"I know. And I love all of it."

"Oh, Buddy. I've loved you for so many years, you're part of me, like my arm or my leg. I told myself if you ever came back, I'd be a good wife."

"You were always a good wife, Flash. It was me. I should have been more understanding. I know what losing little Luke did to me, but I didn't think about what it did to you. I should have helped you more. I was just so disappointed in everything, in myself. I lost faith in *us*."

"No, you were right about everything, Buddy. It was me. I know it was me."

He chuckled, a deep, rich male chuckle that surrounded her with warmth and love. "I guess if we're busy blaming ourselves, we won't be blaming each other."

They played in the shower, then dressed, and between the two of them, scrounged together a breakfast from the near-empty cupboards. "I heard about your trip to Dallas," she told him over coffee after they had eaten.

"Little bit of a water haul. Can't find the tall, handsome Mexican."

"Remember last year at Harley's party, when C. J. and Pearl Ann got in a fight?"

"I heard about it. I wasn't there."

"It was a tall, handsome Mexican they were fighting over. Pearl Ann brought him in from San Angelo to cook the Mexican food they served."

"I questioned Carol Jean. Why didn't she tell me?"

Debbie Sue smiled. "She thought he was Italian."

"From San Angelo? Cooking Mexican food?"

"What can I say?" Debbie Sue lifted a shoulder. "You know C. J."

Buddy reached across the table and picked up her hand, placed a kiss on the back, then held it close to his heart. "I thank you, Flash. But I thought your plan was to solve the case yourself. Get the reward. Pay off your debts. Get out of Salt Lick."

"Seems my plans don't work out for one reason or another."

"Yeah." He leaned forward and kissed her. "But you can always make new ones."

She smiled and straightened his mustache. "Yeah, I can, can't I?" This time she leaned forward and kissed him. "Besides, Harley and C. J. can't go on with their lives until this is behind them and I—I was just thinking that . . . I mean, I was hoping the information might help you, too."

He smiled, not a grin but a slow upturn of his lips that brightened the space around them. If she were any happier, her chest would explode.

Twenty-three

Buddy didn't leave until Monday morning. As soon as Debbie Sue had bid him good-bye, she picked up the phone and called Edwina, told her she would be late and why. Her good friend broke into tears and laughter and yelled the news of the reconciliation to Vic.

On the way to the salon, Debbie Sue shoved an old Buck Owens CD into her player and sang along.

By the time Buddy returned to his little apartment and readied for work, he arrived at his office late. His first task was to talk to Harley Carruthers. He soon learned Harley was in Louisiana. After a half-dozen phone calls, Buddy reached him and asked him if he recalled a Mexican cook from last year's homecoming party.

"Only that Pearl Ann threw a hissy fit until I

agreed to hire him," Harley said. "Why are you asking?"

"The cook was tall, dark, and handsome. Mexican."

Harley was silent for a few seconds. "Oh, man, I can't believe it."

"Do you remember his name?"

A few more seconds of silence. "Jesus, I don't, Buddy. Too long ago and I probably didn't pay that much attention in the first place."

"Do you remember how he was paid that evening? Do you have a record of some kind?"

"Pearl Ann said she paid him in cash. All I remember is being pissed off. I never pay anybody cash for anything. But Buddy, that was a year ago. Carrying on with someone for that long wasn't her pattern."

"Did your kitchen help assist him?"

"Gloria did. She was mad that that guy took control of her kitchen."

"I want to go out to your place and talk to Gloria again."

"I think she went to Juarez over the weekend to check on her mother. Won't be back until Wednesday morning. I don't have any way of reaching her, either."

Shit. *Wednesday. He had to stay focused 'til Wednesday.*

He did his chores, looked over the two domestic complaints that had come in, read the dispatches that came in by fax, then set out to interview the local complainants. Until Pearl Ann's murder, drunken disturbances and domestic abuse were the closest thing to crime he encountered.

Later in the day he stopped by the Styling Station. He dragged Debbie Sue outside and told her again how much he loved her, how much he appreciated her help. He added that he was going to San Angelo after he talked to Gloria on Wednesday and would see her when he returned.

"Oh hell! I won't be here," she said, as if the information stunned her as much as him. "I promised Vic and Ed and C. J. I'd go to Terlingua with them early Thursday morning."

Though that piece of news stung a little, he bit his tongue. He had made a promise he would be more open and understanding about what she wanted to do. One of the problems in their marriage had been his attempting to corral her free spirit. "The chili cook-off? You'll never get a room on short notice. Y'all planning on roughing it?"

"Not hardly. C. J. asked Harley to borrow his mansion on wheels. You don't think Edwina would go anywhere she can't plug in her curling iron, do you?"

Damn, damn, damn. He hated thinking of Debbie Sue off partying with ten thousand strangers, but anything he said would come across as mistrust and criticism. "Guess you'll be gone three days, then?"

She must have read his mind because she slid her arms around his middle and kissed him. "I'll behave, Buddy. I promise I won't be out partying behind the horse trailers. I wouldn't even go, but I promised them."

"Hey, I'm not making any demands," he said. "I said I'd change. And I'm trying to."

"I know," she said and kissed him again. "Me, too. I'm cooking something for supper tonight."

"Yeah?"

"Burma Johnson gave me a Mexican casserole recipe. I figured I'd start with something simple. Brave enough to try it?"

"You know damn well I am."

Wednesday morning Buddy was at the Carruthers ranch early. Gloria was uneasy finding the sheriff waiting for her. "I am legal," she told him.

Buddy assured her he wasn't making an illegal immigrant sweep and explained the reason for his visit. She indeed remembered the Mexican cook. "*Bastardo*," she said and spit onto the ground. He had ordered her around in her own *cocina*. His name was Martinez and he worked in a fancy white man's *restaurante* in San Angelo. She apologized for knowing so little, but Buddy assured her the information was very, very helpful.

Buddy drove back into town and informed Billy Don he had to go out of town again, possibly for a day or two. Billy Don, eager to redeem himself, assured Buddy he would make him proud. He wouldn't bother anyone. He would only help. If he became tempted to do otherwise, he would lock himself in the jail.

Sometimes Buddy wondered if Billy Don's family tree was a shrub, but he was so primed for the four-hour drive to San Angelo, he didn't question what the deputy called *helping*.

He arrived in San Angelo shortly after three P.M., thankful the city of San Angelo wasn't like the sprawling Dallas/Fort Worth Metroplex. He reminded himself that a "fancy white man's *restaurante*" was a subjective description that could cover everything from Taco Bell to the country clubs.

By late in the evening he had talked to a dozen cooks and managers, none of whom knew of anyone fitting the description of Pearl Ann's alleged killer. Still, he was so close he could taste it. He checked into a room for the night.

Early Thursday morning Vic, Edwina, Debbie Sue, and C. J. piled into Vic's crew cab pickup and motored to the Carruthers ranch where they picked up Harley's Ultimate Freedom Winnebago. Harley'd had it gassed up and cleaned to perfection just for them. Every surface outside and in shone like a new diamond and it smelled like lemons. When Vic saw it, he let out a low whistle.

Everyone but Vic had overpacked. The only real need in Terlingua, he told them, was a change of underwear.

Edwina had brought clothes for every conceivable occasion and two overnight bags of makeup. She had packed a different pair of shoes for each outfit and an economy-sized bottle of bubble bath.

Debbie looked at the array in awe. "Lanolin-laced, lavender-scented bubble bath? You know, Ed, from what I've heard, most people at Terlingua have to squat behind bushes to pee."

"*Most people* aren't going to be driving up in a three-hundred-thousand-dollar motor home, either."

Edwina told how she had loved calling Earlene and casually asking if her son Curtis could look up this particular Winnebago for her on the Internet. She used the excuse she wanted to plan on what she would need in the way of toiletries. Earlene had choked on her iced tea when Edwina told her it had a split bath with a garden tub. Some things in life are just too sweet not to experience once, she said.

As Vic pulled the luxury motor home onto the highway and pointed it southwest, Edwina sat beside him talking nonstop about what they would do if this vehicle were theirs—the places they would go, the things they would see. Debbie Sue and C.J. explored the interior like children in fairyland. They opened drawers, peered into closets. "Have you stopped to realize," Debbie Sue asked C.J., "that this will be yours someday?"

"Oh, I don't mind. I can put up with anything as long as I have Harley's love."

Debbie Sue gave C. J. a flat look, thinking of her gentleness and the years of laughs her innocent, blond dumbness had fostered. "All I can say, C. J., is Harley Carruthers doesn't have any idea what a lucky man he is."

Her mind shifted to Buddy and she missed him. She hoped he was safe. They hadn't even reached the county line yet and she was already eager to return home and hear how he had fared in San Angelo. For the first time ever, she wished she had a cell phone.

She would just have to force herself to endure what was probably her last party as a single woman. The cook-off had been held for over forty years and was world-famous. People came to it from everywhere. The majority came to party in the spectacular, but ethereal beauty of the Texas Big Bend country. Surely she could find something to enjoy.

Edwina was disappointed to see that their home on wheels was not the only luxury motor home present. Her dreams of being the Queen of Terlingua were dashed. Vic told her not to worry because he was anointing her the Princess of Commandos.

While Vic set up camp, Debbie Sue, Edwina, and C. J. searched for a calendar of events and found one posted nearby. There was no shortage of reasons to party, and from what Vic had told them on the way down, each campsite hosted its own shindig every night. There was opportunity to sign up for every conceivable contest. Clearly an excellent chili recipe wasn't the only thing that was prizeworthy.

Debbie Sue had fun just watching the assortment of people. Doctor, lawyer, rich man, thief. The childhood rhyme played in her head. The roughest bunch was a group of bikers she had seen parked a short distance from their campsite. No doubt they were entered in the "Group Most Likely to Cut Your Throat in Your Sleep" contest. She wished Vic had chosen a different spot to park and wondered if it was too late to mention it to him.

"*Hooyaah!*" The bellow bounced off the mountainous landscape.

Looking around for the source, Debbie Sue saw Vic standing atop the motor home calling out. A chorus of "Hooyaah" echoed from the group of bikers. *Well, great.*

They returned to the motor home to find Vic handing out bottles of cold beer to the bikers. Introductions and salutations were exchanged and Debbie Sue learned the bikers were all retired navy SEALs. She had seen somebody on TV say a U.S. navy SEAL was the deadliest man on earth, and after seeing a flock of them, she believed it.

Edwina announced she had signed up herself, Debbie Sue, and C.J. for the "Margarita Most Likely to Get You Naked" contest to be held the next day.

"I think this calls for a rehearsal," Vic announced and dragged out bottles of tequila.

Debbie Sue had to admit she was having a good time, as was everyone else. Vic was right, the war stories never ended and seemed to get more graphic in detail as time and tequila passed. She longed for Buddy's company, but knowing she would be back in his arms in a few days made the ache bearable.

By late afternoon she, along with C. J. and several others in the group who wanted to still be conscious by the evening's end, stopped drinking and made the trek to look at the natural hot water springs and watch the magnificent sunset.

Strolling back to their campsite, as Debbie Sue and C. J. talked about what they hoped Vic had prepared for supper, Debbie Sue stopped dead in her tracks.

C. J. turned around and faced her. "Ohmygosh, Debbie Sue. You look like you just saw a ghost."

By late Thursday afternoon Buddy felt the hard fist of failure punching at his brain and pride. He had been in and out of every eating joint in San Angelo and knew nothing new except that he might never eat in a restaurant again. How could he be so close and not produce at least another lead if not the suspect?

He had read that detective work, *real* detective work was slow and methodical. He now knew from firsthand experience that was true. Murphy's Law dictated that the last restaurant on his list would be paydirt. Fingers crossed in hope, he walked inside and asked for the manager. An older woman approached him with a friendly smile.

"My name is Sheriff James Russell Overstreet," he told her. "I'm from Salt Lick. I'd like to talk to someone who works here or did work here. His last name is Martinez. He's tall—"

"He's not here tonight. You'll have to come back Monday."

Forcing calm, Buddy reminded himself that Martinez was a common Hispanic name and this didn't necessarily mean he had found his suspect.

"Could you please give me *your* description of Mr. Martinez?" Tall was an unusual description for a Mexican. "I want to be sure I've got the right person."

"Oh, he's the old cliché. Tall, dark, and handsome."

Buddy's pulse quickened "But when you say tall, how tall do you mean?" When he heard tall, he thought of his own six feet and two inches, but other people might have a different perception.

"Tall as you. Is a jealous husband gunning for him? I keep telling Alex somebody'll catch up with him someday."

Deep breaths. Stay calm. "I need to talk to him before Monday. Do you know where I might reach him?"

"Sure. He's in Terlingua. He judges in the chili cook-off every year."

Fireworks shot off in Buddy's head. Terlingua was probably a seven-hour drive from San Angelo. If he left now he could be there by midnight. He thanked the woman and dashed to his vehicle. *Alex Martinez*. He knew where Alex Martinez would be for the next forty-eight hours.

He only hoped it wasn't anywhere near Edwina, Carol Jean, and Debbie Sue.

Twenty-four

"Shit, shit, shit," Debbie Sue said, her heartbeat kicking up.

"What," C. J. asked, "what is it?"

"That cab-over motor home we just walked past. The one with the Texas flag painted across the front. See the guy sitting on the steps drinking a beer?"

C. J. nodded, her blond curls bouncing.

"That's the cook from San Angelo, the one you were dancing with when Pearl Ann picked a fight with you."

"We only saw him the one time, Debbie Sue. How can you be sure?"

"I don't know. I just am. When I saw him, my blood turned to ice. C. J., I think he could be the one who killed Pearl Ann."

C. J.'s big blue eyes blinked. "Wow. Does he know you? Did he look at you?"

"No, he was talking to some other people. Besides, he wouldn't recognize *me*."

"Let's walk past again. This time, *I'll* look."

"Okay, but don't stare. Just look."

The two friends turned and walked toward the camper, strolling as if they hadn't a care in the world. Just as Debbie Sue was about to nudge C. J., the crazy little blond left her side and boldly walked up to the group sitting in a circle.

Yikes, C. J.!

"I was just noticing your Texas flag," C. J. said in her best Scarlett O'Hara drawl. "You've got it wrong. The red goes on top of the white."

The group looked in the direction of C. J.'s pointing finger and broke into laughter.

The Mexican man stood and walked closer to her, staggering just a bit. Oh, he was good-looking all right, a taller version of Antonio Banderas.

"You must not be a Texan," he said to C. J., flashing her a perfect smile, one that was bound to have won him invitations into many bedrooms.

"I am, but I must not be a very good one." She laughed. "I guess I'm wrong. It's supposed to be just like you have it, white on top of red, huh?"

"Have we met before?" He glanced at Debbie Sue for the first time, then turned his attention back to C. J.

"No, I'm sure we haven't." She batted her lashes at him. "I'd remember meeting *you*."

"You and your friend will join us, yes?"

"I'm sorry. We can't just now. But *I* could come back . . . later."

"Ah. Later is perfect. Bring your swimsuit. We'll go down to the springs."

She shrugged, feigning embarrassment. "Okay."

"You are too beautiful to be shy." He lifted her hand. "I'll be waiting."

C. J. returned to where Debbie Sue watched and listened, then turned back, giggled, and wiggled her fingers at him in a wave.

Debbie Sue waited until they had walked a safe distance from the campsite before landing on her. "Are you nuts? What in the hell do you think you're doing?"

"Flirting. That's all I was doing. Flirting."

"Oh, flirting. How about making a date with a killer? Did you forget that part?"

"We don't know he's a killer. Just because he looks familiar doesn't mean he's the one."

"Why are you cheating on Harley? We're in his motor home, for crying out loud."

"I'm not cheating on Harley. I'll just spend a little time with this guy and see if he's the one at the party. I'll find out his name, then I'll tell Buddy."

"We could have sat down with him just now and found out both those things."

"But while I'm at the springs with him, you could search his trailer for proof."

"What? Are you crazy? Proof of what?"

"His involvement, silly."

Debbie Sue's brain churned. C. J. was right. How would Buddy prove this stranger had anything to do with Pearl Ann's death without a tangible piece of evidence? A drunken phone call didn't prove anything. A dance interrupted by the victim didn't exactly spell out a motive for murder.

Motherofgod. She wished Buddy were here.

Just before sundown, she and C. J. eased away from the party Vic had organized, consisting of retired navy SEALs, Arizona rockhounds, and retired Canadian railroad employees who had come south to escape winter. Everyone was having such a good time, no one would even miss the two women.

The plan was a simple one. C. J. and the Mexican man would go to the springs together, leaving Debbie Sue to search his trailer. Afterward Debbie Sue would go down to the springs and tell C. J. she needed help back to their motor home because she was feeling ill. C. J. would leave the man's company and that would be that. *Piece of cake.*

As the two women approached the trailer, they could see the man in front. He was sitting in a chair, and a woman was behind him rubbing his shoulders. She leaned over and whispered in his ear as they walked up. When he saw them, he flung the woman's hands away and stood up. The woman tossed her head and walked off.

"Ladies, I thought you'd forgotten me. I didn't expect to see you both."

"I hope you don't mind," C. J. said. "She's had

an awful lot to drink, and I thought the walk would do her good."

In fact, Debbie Sue had drunk only one beer since spotting the tall Mexican man. She would act tipsy, but she had never been more alert. The only thing disturbing her was the suspect appeared to have stopped drinking also. He was certainly more sober-appearing at any rate.

"Are we going swimming?" Debbie Sue asked. "We've got our suits on."

"Not really swimming." He leaned toward Debbie Sue. "We're going to sit in a big ol' hot tub."

"Uh-oh." Debbie Sue wedged her forearm between herself and the stranger. "If we're gonna sit in water, I gotta pee first. Can I borrow your bathroom? You've got a bathroom in there, don't you?"

"Sure, I have a bathroom. We will wait for you." He helped Debbie Sue up the steps into his RV.

"Nah. Y'all go on without me. I may just go back and go to sleep early. Really, y'all go on."

C. J. tugged on his hand. "She'll be fine."

Debbie Sue could see the temptation of spending time alone with C. J. in the hot tub was too much for the ladies' man. He instructed her to be sure to close his door when she left.

Debbie Sue waited until they walked out of sight. Her heart beat a tattoo as she began her search. She wasn't sure what to look for—old letters or photos, maybe. Something along those lines. She supposed finding a confession would be too much to expect.

In the quiet dimness of the compact motor home, she opened and closed drawers, looked under linens, and went through receipts. She fanned the pages of books, hoping something would fall out. She found several pieces of paper and held them with shaking hands to the light—a Texas map, a proof-of-insurance card—coming through the small windows. She saw the name Alex Martinez several times. Aha! His name.

Completing a thorough search of the back, she moved upfront to the cab. Under the driver's seat, she felt the coolness of a tin box. She pulled it out, carried it into better light in the tiny bathroom and lifted the lid.

Inside she found Alex Martinez's name taped inside the lid, two CDs, and a stained handkerchief folded in half. When she lifted the handkerchief, two articles fell from the folds to the floor. Debbie Sue bent over to scoop them up and stopped, feeling as if she had been stabbed with an icicle. Looking up at her from a photo was the smiling, still beautiful face of Pearl Ann Carruthers. Debbie Sue's heart began to beat so hard, she had to pause and take deep breaths to calm herself.

Lying beside the photo was a gold bracelet that appeared to be broken. A charm in the shape of the state of Texas was attached to its links.

Debbie Sue felt as if she were trapped in the eye of a hurricane. Everything seemed to be whirling and moving around her, yet she was in a silent vacuum. With trembling fingers she picked up the two items and turned sideways for better light. She swallowed a scream when she realized the stain on the handkerchief was dried blood, the same blood, no doubt, that still showed on the gold bracelet and charm. *Ohmygod. Pearl Ann's blood.*

She nearly gagged as nausea swept over her. Tears sprang to her eyes. She hadn't seen Pearl Ann's corpse in the Cadillac, but she had heard tales in the salon. Billy Don's wife had given them a graphic description. Pearl Ann had been shot once in the forehead, almost between her eyebrows. The nickel-sized hole had left her face bruised and discolored, not to mention the marks left by gunpowder. The once-beautiful woman had been almost unrecognizable.

Along with grief and terror, rage began to rise within Debbie Sue. She wanted to put her hands around Alex Martinez's throat and choke the life from him. For sure, she wanted to see the murdering sonofabitch arrested and prosecuted, then poisoned, stabbed, and shot.

She carefully put the photo, the handkerchief, and the charm bracelet back into the small box, then slipped the box into the pocket of her jacket and looked around, preparing to leave the motor home.

Footsteps crunched on the gravel outside and the motor home door opened. "We were worried about you, *senorita*."

She turned toward the sound and found herself staring into the barrel of a gun. And it was in the hand of Alex Martinez, the expression in his Antonio Banderas eyes as grim as death.

"Where—where's C. J.? What have you done with her?"

"Ah, yes, C. J. That is her name? She is back at the springs. I am glad I decided to come back for some wine. You found what you were looking for, yes?"

Debbie Sue faked bravado. "I don't know what you're talking about. I was borrowing the john." Trying to ignore the gun, she made an effort to walk past Alex.

He grabbed her arm and stopped her, pulled her back. "Don't test me, senorita. I *will* shoot you." He released her arm and made a beckoning motion with his fingers. "Give me the box."

Fuck. Fuck. Fuck. With a shaking hand, she took the tin box from her pocket and handed it to him.

"You did not find *this* in the bathroom," he said.

She swallowed hard, but the tight knot in her throat and stomach wouldn't go away.

"Who are you?" he asked. "And how did you find me?"

"The sheriff in Salt Lick's onto you. He's got your description. When I heard it, I knew it was you."

"You and that smart sheriff make quite a couple, don't you?"

She began to sniffle. "Yes."

Gripping her arm again, Alex forced her to the RV door and outside. He pressed the muzzle of the gun into her ribs and pushed her along. "We are going for a walk."

"If you're thinking of killing me, you'll never get away with it. They'll come looking for me. Buddy Overstreet will hunt you down like a dog."

"See that stream of water? That's Mexico on the other side. I will be there before your body gets cold. With *mi familia*. I will be vapor. And you know what you gringos always say—we all look alike."

"Buddy'll still look for you. He won't care *where* you are."

"That may be true, but I get several hours' lead time, he will never find me."

They continued walking. Somehow Debbie Sue's brain continued to function at warp speed. He was forcing her away from the throngs of campers, and to her relief she saw that the campsites stretched out a long way in front of them. To her relief they faced a long walk.

"What did Pearl Ann ever do to you? Please tell me why you killed her."

"I didn't mean to. We were going to live in Fort Worth. She laughed when I told her I had made the plans. She called me a wetback. Told me she was going alone. When I tried to talk to her, she pulled

a gun out of her purse and told me to vamoose. I
wrestled it from her, but it went off and—"

Like I believe that. "Yeah, right. She was shot in
the head. Between the eyes, I think they said." It
came to Debbie Sue it was dumb to confront him.
Better to go along with him. "But look, I believe
what you say. I know how Pearl Ann was. If it was
an accident, you can plead that. You could even
plead self-defense if she pulled the gun . . . But if
you kill me, it's murder."

"Senorita, you think a Mexican that kills the
wife of Harley Carruthers will not get the needle?
No one will believe me."

"You're wrong. Listen to me. In the trial they'll
bring out every little piece of Pearl Ann's life for
public view. And believe you me, she had *quite* a
life to view. The men she slept with—"

"Shut up. Don't say another word about Pearl
Ann. I loved her. I still love her."

Debbie Sue realized they had walked well beyond the campers. The only available light was
provided by stars. Alex pushed her a distance
ahead. Debbie Sue turned and faced him. Why,
she didn't know, because she really didn't relish
seeing a bullet headed straight at her. She just
knew she had to keep talking. "But wait, Alex.
What about the bracelet? Why did you keep the
bracelet?" She slowly inched to the right as she
talked.

"It was a gift because I loved her. I couldn't give
her gold and big diamonds. All I had was my love.

The Texas charm had a little diamond where Fort Worth would be. She threw it in my face."

Alex was following her movement, talking the entire time. He didn't seem to notice that their positions had changed by a full half circle. "Alex, you should let a jury hear your story. It's only fair."

"You should learn to mind your own business. You're a beautiful lady. I am sorry." He raised the gun level with her chest.

Debbie Sue now had the campsites behind her. She remembered seeing on the Discovery channel that someone's chances of hitting a mobile target were significantly lower than hitting an immobile one.

So. She became mobile.

She dashed into the pitch darkness as fast as her legs would carry her. Toward the camp lights. Toward help. Toward safety. She ducked and dodged rocks and brush, zigged, then zagged, then zigged again.

Thirty seconds into her sprint she was blinded by a beam of light coming toward her. She shielded her eyes. Could Alex have gotten in front of her? Should she run from the light? *Shit! Decisions, always decisions.*

Suddenly the light was upon her. An arm grabbed her. She hit the ground with a loud *oomph*. A deep voice ordered her to stay down as a body covered hers. She knew that voice. *Buddy?*

"Stop or I'll shoot!" the voice attached to the flashlight ordered.

Alex Martinez dropped his gun and threw his arms in the air. Seconds later, he practically clung to Buddy as a dozen or more retired navy SEALs and hammer-wielding rockhounds surrounded him.

An hour later, with the killer locked away in the Alpine jail and SEALs and rockhounds high-fiving and toasting one another with tequila shooters, Buddy explained to Debbie Sue how he had come to Terlingua in search of Alex Martinez. He had been talking to Vic and Edwina when Carol Jean had come running into the campsite in a state of panic. C. J. told him she had seen a big Mexican take Debbie Sue into the desert at gun-point, and Buddy had wasted no time.

He questioned campers around Martinez's trailer and followed the direction they pointed out as the last place they saw him walking with a striking young woman. Finding her had been pure luck—or an answered prayer.

Debbie Sue sniffled. "Oh, Buddy."

He pulled her into his embrace, his strong arms wrapped around her, and she finally felt safe.

"I think we need to leave these two alone," Edwina said, grinning. "Buddy may need to interrogate her."

By then Buddy was kissing her, and by the time he stopped they were alone. "I'm glad I already asked you to marry me again. Otherwise you might think I'm after your money."

"I don't have any money," she said in a tiny voice.

"Well, fifty thousand dollars may not be much money to you but it's a heck of a lot to me."

"What do you mean?"

"You deserve the reward. You figured out who murdered Pearl Ann and risked your life confronting the killer. I'm sure Harley will agree."

"But you—"

"Shh." He kissed her again.

Epilogue

A year to the day since the trip to Terlingua had passed. She and Buddy had wasted no time renewing their vows. The nuptials had taken place at her mom's house with Edwina and C.J. serving as bridesmaids and Harley and Rocket Man standing up for Buddy.

She and Buddy had lived for a short time in Austin while he completed DPS training, and afterward he had been assigned to the Midland-Odessa area as a state trooper. His dream of being a Texas Ranger would be a reality soon.

They again lived in the home they had shared throughout their first marriage.

Edwina ran the Styling Station these days. She had taken it on while Debbie Sue and Buddy lived in Austin, and that arrangement hadn't been reversed. Vic hadn't made the trip to California. He spoke to Brenda on the phone and told her she should stop calling him because he had met the most wonderful woman in the world and intended to marry her. Edwina had been eavesdropping and cried for half an hour before Vic could make her understand that *she* was the wonderful woman. Harley had given them the use of the motor home for their honeymoon, and they had toured Vic's beloved U.S.A. for three months.

Billy Don had run for sheriff unopposed and been elected in a landslide victory. Currently Vic was teaching him self-defense. No more idle time for roping the fire hydrant in front of the sheriff's office.

C. J. and Harley had made an announcement of their engagement and a no-expense-spared, cowboy wedding was planned for Christmas.

Alex Martinez pleaded not guilty to the charge of murder. A plea bargain reduced the charge to second degree, and he was given twenty years. He would be eligible for parole in half that time because of no prior history of criminal activity.

Things hadn't worked out too badly for him. He had become a minor celebrity. Throughout the hearings, throngs of woman packed the courthouse to get a glimpse of the handsome man who had killed the woman he loved in an act of passion. He had dozens of marriage proposals, and it was rumored that Benjamin Bratt would be portraying him in a CBS movie version of the story.

The doorbell rang and Edwina and Vic came in carrying platters of food. Tonight was the American Country Music awards. Virginia Pratt was one

of the nominees for Song of the Year. The serious
ballad she had been talked into writing, sung by
Alan Jackson, had been an overnight hit. "Sorry,
You Both Deserve Better" was still riding high on
the country music charts. Now Virginia was one of
the most sought-after composers in Nashville.

"Hurry up, Buddy," Debbie Sue called out.
"They're showing the people arriving. You're
fixin' to miss Mom." Virginia's escort to the
awards ceremony was none other than the vet, Dr.
Miller, her employer of years and her secret lover.

Vic and Ed settled into the loveseat. Buddy
brought in a large glass of Pepsi and handed it to
her before he sat down. All eyes were glued to the
TV set.

To everyone's astonishment, emerging from the
backseat of one of the black stretch limousines was
Quint Matthews.

"Great day in the morning," Edwina exclaimed.

Buddy picked up the remote and made a gesture as if to switch channels.

"Don't you dare," Debbie Sue said. "I want to
see who's the unlucky woman he's with."

Quint reached back into the limo, and a gloved
hand took his. A ravishing redhead made an exit,
giving the crowd a million-dollar smile.

"Wow," Buddy said, "wonder where he found
her."

"I've seen that woman somewhere," Vic said.

Debbie Sue moved closer to the television. "I
don't believe it! . . . Ed, look!"

"My God! Is that Eugene/Janine?"

"I think it is."

Edwina threw her head back and hooted. "Looks like Quint finally got lucky."

This October will be wicked *and* wild, when you're reading the latest from Avon Romance!

HIS EVERY KISS by Laura Lee Guhrke
An Avon Romantic Treasure

Grace Cheval refuses to be one of Dylan Moore's conquests, but to become governess to his new eight-year-old ward seems harmless. And how can she resist the chance to be closer to this alluring man? Yet Dylan has other plans for her, and though she is the teacher, it is he who must teach Grace—about passion, and about love.

A DATE ON CLOUD NINE
by Jenna McKnight
An Avon Contemporary Romance

Lilly's guardian angels are giving her one last chance to finally choose the right man. That man might be Jake Murdoch—a guy who's hot, smart . . . and thinks she committed an insurance scam to the tune of $3 million! But how can he get her to fess up, when he's too busy thinking about how to get her in his bedroom . . . and keeping her there?

THE BEAUTY AND THE SPY by Gayle Callen
An Avon Romance

Nicholas Wright is on the trail of a traitor to the Crown, and would have caught him long ago if he hadn't been found out by Charlotte Sinclair. Now that she is privy to his plan, he has no choice but to kidnap the enchantress and try to steel himself against her charms. But the heat he feels for her may be enough to threaten even a spy's resolve . . .

MASQUERADING THE MARQUESS by Anne Mallory
An Avon Romance

Disguised as a courtesan to get access to the peerage behaving badly, Calliope Minton winds up right in the lap of James Trenton, Marquess of Angelford—and discovers it's a rather nice place to be. But when a mutual friend disappears and they find themselves in danger, will flirtation grow into something much more powerful?

REL 0904

Discover Contemporary Romances
at Their Sizzling Hot Best
from Avon Books

SOMEONE LIKE HIM — by Karen Kendall
0-06-000723-0/$5.99 US/$7.99 Can

A THOROUGHLY MODERN PRINCESS
0-380-82054-4/$5.99 US/$7.99 Can — by Wendy Corsi Staub

A GREEK GOD AT THE LADIES' CLUB — by Jenna McKnight
0-06-054927-0/$5.99 US/$7.99 Can

DO NOT DISTURB — by Christie Ridgway
0-06-009348-X/$5.99 US/$7.99 Can

WANTED: ONE PERFECT MAN — by Judi McCoy
0-06-056079-7/$5.99 US/$7.99 Can

FACING FEAR — by Gennita Low
0-06-052339-5/$5.99 US/$7.99 Can

HOT STUFF — by Elaine Fox
0-06-051724-7/$5.99 US/$7.99 Can

WHAT MEMORIES REMAIN — by Cait London
0-06-055588-2/$5.99 US/$7.99 Can

LOVE: UNDERCOVER — by Hailey North
0-06-058230-8/$5.99 US/$7.99 Can

IN THE MOOD — by Suzanne Macpherson
0-06-051768-9/$5.99 US/$7.99 Can

Have you ever dreamed of writing a romance?

*And have you ever wanted
to get a romance published?*

Perhaps you have always wondered how to
become an Avon romance writer?
We are now seeking the best and brightest undiscovered
voices. We invite you to send us your query letter to
avonromance@harpercollins.com

What do you need to do?

Please send no more than two pages telling us
about your book. We'd like to know its setting—is it
contemporary or historical—and a bit about the hero,
heroine, and what happens to them.

Then, if it is right for Avon we'll ask to see part of the
manuscript. Remember, it's important that you have
material to send, in case we want to see your story quickly.

Of course, there are no guarantees of publication,
but you never know unless you try!

*We know there is new talent just waiting
to be found! Don't hesitate . . . send us
your query letter today.*

*The Editors
Avon Romance*

Avon Romantic Treasures

*Unforgettable, enthralling love stories,
sparkling with passion and adventure
from Romance's bestselling authors*

Avon Romances—
the best in exceptional authors and unforgettable novels!